DEAD IF

Peter James is the international bestselling author of
many award-winning novels. His Detective Superintendent
Roy Grace series, set in Brighton, has been translated into
thirty-seven languages with worldwide sales of over nineteen million copies, and has given him many *Sunday Times*
number ones. In 2015 WHSmith customers publicly voted
him the Greatest Crime Author of All Time and in 2016 he
became the recipient of the coveted CWA Diamond Dagger
lifetime achievement award for sustained excellence. Peter
has also written a short story collection, *A Twist of the Knife*,
and his standalone titles include *Perfect People* and *The
House on Cold Hill*. *The Perfect Murder*, *Dead Simple* and
Not Dead Enough have all been turned into smash-hit stage
plays. All his novels reflect his deep interest in the world of
the police. Three of his novels have been filmed and before
becoming a full-time author he produced numerous films,
including *The Merchant of Venice*, starring Al Pacino and
Jeremy Irons.

Visit his website at www.peterjames.com
Or follow him on Twitter @peterjamesuk
Or facebook.com/peterjames.roygrace
Or Instagram @PeterJamesUK
Or youtube.com/peterjamesPJTV
www.peterjamesbrighton.com

DEAD MAN'S GRIP

A trail of death follows a devastating
traffic accident.

NOT DEAD YET

Terror on the silver screen;
an obsessive stalker on the loose.

DEAD MAN'S TIME

A priceless watch is stolen and the powerful
Daly family will do anything to get it back.

WANT YOU DEAD

Who knew online dating could be so deadly?

YOU ARE DEAD

Brighton falls victim to its first serial killer
in eighty years.

LOVE YOU DEAD

A deadly black widow is on the hunt for
her next husband.

NEED YOU DEAD

Every killer makes a mistake somewhere.
You just have to find it.

DEAD IF YOU DON'T

A kidnapping triggers a parent's worst nightmare and
a race against time for Roy Grace.

DEAD IF YOU DON'T

PETER JAMES

PAN BOOKS

First published 2018 by Macmillan

First published in paperback 2018 by Macmillan

This edition first published 2018 by Pan Books
an imprint of Pan Macmillan
20 New Wharf Road, London N1 9RR
Associated companies throughout the world
www.panmacmillan.com

ISBN 978-1-5098-8341-7

1 3 5 7 9 8 6 4 2

A CIP catalogue record for this book is available from the British Library.

Map artwork by ML Design
Typeset by Palimpsest Book Production Ltd, Falkirk, Stirlingshire
Printed and bound by CPI Group (UK) Ltd, Croydon, CR0 4YY

Visit **www.panmacmillan.com** to read more about all our books
and to buy them. You will also find features, author interviews and
news of any author events, and you can sign up for e-newsletters
so that you're always first to hear about our new releases.

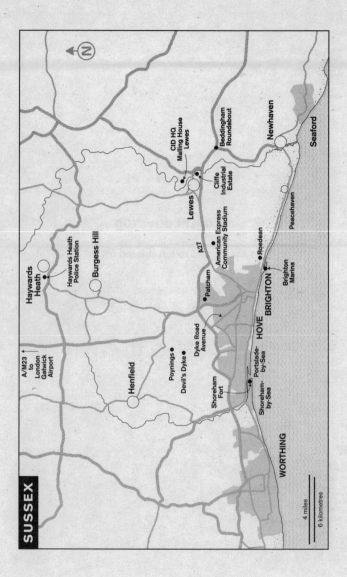

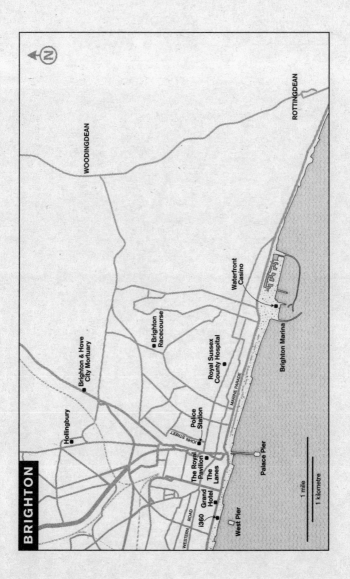

BRIGHTON

N

WOODINGDEAN

ROTTINGDEAN

Hollingbury

Brighton & Hove
City Mortuary

Brighton
Racecourse

WESTERN ROAD

i360

Grand
Hotel

The Royal
Pavilion

The
Lanes

JOHN STREET

Police
Station

Royal Sussex
County Hospital

Waterfront
Casino

MARINE PARADE

West Pier

Palace Pier

Brighton Marina

1 mile

1 kilometre

1

The small white ball skittered over the numbers on the spinning roulette wheel, passing 36, 11, 30. *Tappity-tap.* *Tappity-tap.* It ricocheted off a diamond-shaped bumper. *Tappity-tap.* Danced. Rattling around the rim; hopping over the numbers 12, 35, 3 and catapulting back onto the rim.

Kipp Brown watched it in silent concentration. His nerves were tightropes. This was the moment, as the rotations steadily slowed. The moment when time froze.

'No more bets,' the croupier announced, like a recording on a timed loop. It was pretty pointless; Kipp had no more left to bet. It was all there in those neat towers of chips spread across the baize. Covering his regular numbers, his lucky numbers and a couple of random ones, too.

All there.

The school fees. The mortgage. The hire-purchase payments on his cars.

Tappity-tap.

The dumb ball had no idea just how much was riding on where it landed; no knowledge of just how much money Kipp Brown, the only punter at this table on the high-value floor, had bet on this spin of the wheel. It didn't know just what this particular spin of the roulette wheel meant to Kipp. Nor did the bored-looking female croupier.

So much was riding on just six of the thirty-six black and red numbers. So much.

It was a perfectly formed ceramic ball, less than one inch in diameter. It had no brain. It had no knowledge that the man at the table, watching it the way a buzzard watches a field mouse from two hundred metres high, had bet the ranch on numbers 2, 4, 15 and their neighbours.

No idea at all.

No idea that, until recently, Kipp Brown had been one of the wealthiest men in the city. That on a July night last year he had walked away from this casino with over one million pounds of winnings – the biggest sum anyone had ever won in a single night at Brighton's Waterfront Casino.

Nor did it know that since then he had lost it all again on the very same tables.

That in recent months, with his judgement skewed from the stress of his mounting debts and his train crash of a personal life, he had bet and lost all the equity in his house.

His business assets.

Pretty much everything.

2, 4 or 15. Please.

Tappity-tap. The ball rolled into number 2, then out again.

He sat, anxiously, nursing his drink. It was gone 11 p.m., and he should have left hours ago. He had to drive Mungo to school tomorrow morning and go straight on to an early meeting with a new, potentially large, client. He should be home, getting rest. His eyes were bleary. His brain was tired. Exhausted from chasing losses all evening. But he couldn't help it. The wheel would come good eventually, it always did. Always had.

Hadn't it?

If you stayed at the table for long enough.

Tappity-tap. It danced over 15. Then 4.

Yes!

Four! Fantastic, a home run! He'd done it!

Then as he watched, suddenly and inexplicably, as if pulled by some force, the ball bounced out of 4. Then out of 17, 11, 1, 31.

Come on.

Click.

It settled, nestling between two frets.

The number popped up on the screen above the table.

16.

Unbelievable.

He drained his complimentary Hendricks and tonic, picked out a piece of cucumber and munched it, solemnly and disconsolately, as he watched the croupier scoop away the neat stacks of chips.

A tall, fit man of forty-five, who normally had fine posture, Kipp Brown was stooping badly as he left the table and walked over to the cashier with his wallet full of maxed-out credit cards.

Behind him, he heard the sound that was the music of his life. His secret, second life that few people, other than his wife, Stacey, knew about – and, guiltily, he mostly only told her about his wins, rarely his losses.

Tappity-tap.

Followed by a loud cheer from the group of Chinese who were here, like him, most evenings. It sounded like one of them had a big win. Great. Lucky them.

Every night these Chinese guys were here, adding to their winnings, so it seemed to him.

And every night, just recently, he was here, succumbing to the classic gambler's folly, chasing his losses. Like he had been tonight.

Except there wasn't going to be any more chasing tonight. Not for him.

He was over his account limit with the casino. The cashier tried all six of his credit cards in turn. Then shook her head. She had the decency to look apologetic.

2

The twenty-one-year-old strapped to the steel table, in the windowless basement room, was pleading beneath the blinding white lights. But the sound of the Kinks, 'Mr Pleasant', turned up loud on a constant loop, drowned his voice out – not that anyone could hear beyond this dank, sound-proof room with its rank smell and the open-barred door to the darkened pool area beyond it where, it was rumoured, Mr Dervishi's crocodile lived. Ryan Brent did not believe any of this could actually be happening, could actually be real.

But his tormentor, Gentian Llupa, did. A handsome twenty-three-year-old, with close-cropped, gelled brown hair and a serious, concerned expression, Llupa's one worry was that Ryan might die too soon. Before the one thousand cuts he had been instructed to administer, for the benefit of the camera, could be completed.

'Mr Pleasant is good
Mr Pleasant is kind
Mr Pleasant's okay . . .
Hey, hey
How are you today?'

Echoing the words, Gentian looked down at his victim. 'So how are you today?' Then he added, 'How's your day so far?' It was his boss, Mr Dervishi's, favourite expression and

5

he liked it, too. All of Mr Dervishi's close team used it, as a kind of code. Mr Dervishi instilled good manners and a code of behaviour in all his employees.

His boss was extremely particular. He would want to examine every incision on the naked young man's body. Each one that he was about to make with the Stanley knife's freshly inserted blade, as a lesson to the youth. Each cut would be anatomically correct. One thousand lessons. Starting with the ankle tendons, to make running away impossible. Not that escaping had ever been an option for him.

So many tendons in the human body! That was one of the things he had learned back in his home country of Kosovo as a medical student, before meeting Mr Dervishi and being offered more money than he could dream of to continue his studies in England. Although, currently, Mr Dervishi kept him too busy to resume his studies.

He was going to be working from a colour chart showing the tendons of the human body beneath the skin, which he had Blu-tacked to the wall beside the table. It was really there for Ryan Brent's benefit, to give him an anatomy lesson. Gentian very politely told him in which order he would be proceeding. He had a ball of cloth ready to stuff into Brent's mouth if he screamed too loudly, although Mr Dervishi did not want him doing that, he liked to hear his victim's screams. He liked to show his collection of videos of what had happened to those who crossed him to other employees. It was his way of ensuring loyalty.

Tendon after tendon.

'People say Mr Pleasant is good
Mr Pleasant is kind . . .'

'Please, please!' his victim screamed. 'I will pay the money back. I'll pay it all back. Please!'

'No,' Gentian said. 'You will never be able to. And besides, I do not like people who steal money from the man who gives me a new life. Especially not people who do that and sleep with his mistress as well.'

'I didn't know. Honest! I didn't know. Please don't! I'm a fellow human, like you, mate. Oh God, please let me go. What kind of a monster are you?'

'Probably the worst kind!' Gentian smiled. 'That's not good for you to know that, is it? You see, I am both the worst kind and the best kind. I am honest and I am loyal. I do what I'm told. I could make things very much worse for you, but I don't because I'm just like the guy in this song. I'm *Mr Pleasant*!'

As Gentian picked up the cutter, he announced the count, loud and clear, for his victim's benefit. In order to be pleasant. 'Number one!' he said and peered at the chart. 'Quite a long way to go, eh? *How's your brand-new limousine?*'

'My what?'

'It's just a line in the song, don't worry about it.'

3

Friday 11 August

The call came in on Adrian Morris's private mobile at 11.23 a.m. It was one the Amex Stadium's Head of Safety and Security had been expecting, fearfully, for the past six years. Ever since his beloved football team, Brighton and Hove Albion, had moved to this magnificent new home it had never been, in Morris's mind, a question of *if* – but *when*.

The Amex Stadium was one of the city of Brighton and Hove's great modern landmarks. Designed with majestic, swooping contours to blend in with the rolling hills of the South Downs, it sat on the north-east extremity of the city, a short distance from the Sussex University campus and bordering open countryside.

And, as Morris well knew, it was always going to be a potential target. Security had been at the heart of its design and was state-of-the-art, but he was experienced enough to know that the greatest security systems in the world were only as good as the people who operated them.

A strong male voice with an Eastern European accent spoke slowly, precisely and confidently. 'Mr Morris, I hope this is not an inconvenient time. You need to know there will be a bomb on or under one seat in the stadium tomorrow afternoon. If you wish to prevent this from happening, it is very simple. You just have to arrange for £250,000, in Bitcoins, to be placed in an account you will be given. Very small beer for you, if you consider the potential financial loss of abandoning your first Premier League game. It would be such a shame for your fans and the city. I will call you back later with further instructions. I do apologize if this is not a convenient time. And it would really be better not to involve the police, they will only delay things very dangerously for you.'

Click.

The caller was gone.

The timing was deliberate and impeccable. Tomorrow the stadium would be hosting the team's first home football game in the Premier League – it would be one of the most well-attended and watched games in the club's history. In the city's history.

But Morris still held the phone to his ear. He stared out of the glass observation booth above the North Stand of the stadium at a sea of blue and white plastic seats, each one of which would be occupied tomorrow afternoon, Saturday, for the 5.30 p.m. kick-off. His face felt hot, his body clammy, his mind going into overdrive as he considered what he had just heard.

Real or a hoax?

The display read *Caller ID withheld*. Almost certainly it would be untraceable, made on a burner.

Under the Football Association rules, a club's Head of Safety and Security had seniority over police inside a stadium on match day, from the time the public entered until after they had left. It was a responsibility Morris was happy to accept under normal circumstances, but not now.

He hit the speed-dial button for the mobile phone of PC Darren Balkham. The officer was somewhere on the premises, overseeing the first of the two thorough searches that were routine the day before each match – and repeated again by specialist search officers and sniffer dogs immediately before the public entered on match day.

A veteran of football policing, Balkham had been running the police operations for Brighton and Hove Albion effectively and quietly for twenty years, and under his command there had never been a major incident at a home game. He told Morris he would be right up.

As he waited, Morris considered his options. Calling off the game was not one. Nor was paying the ransom demand. If they caved in this once, they were at risk of being blackmailed for every game here subsequently.

He stared across at the empty seats in the family stand. A pair of them would be occupied by two of the club's biggest fans – his four-year-old son, Finley, and his own father. A photograph of the two of them together sat in a frame in front of him on his work surface, both wearing Seagulls – the nickname for the club – bobble hats.

Moments later, Darren Balkham entered the room, looking grim. The calm, stocky uniformed police officer, who had natural authority, sat down beside Morris, who relayed the call as accurately as he could.

'OK, first thing, Ade, do you have any disgruntled former employees? Anyone you've sacked recently who might want to get back at the club?'

Morris told him he could not think of anyone.

'Have there been any nutters known to your security people recently?'

'No – no one capable of this. But I'll check now with Paul Barber.' He immediately called the club's CEO, apprising him of the situation, and asked him if he thought there was anyone the club might have upset recently, in any way.

Barber replied there was no one he could think of. He

asked, deeply vexed, if this meant the match might be abandoned. Morris assured him not.

The Amex was one of the most modern football stadiums in Europe, if not the world. What few people knew was just how elaborate the security systems were. On the bank of CCTV monitors above him Adrian Morris could, within seconds, zoom in on any one of those 30,750 seats. He could go in tightly enough to read the time on any spectator's wristwatch. The latest technology in CCTV enabled him to see every inch of the building, above and below ground, and the immediate surroundings. No one could enter – or leave – unseen and without being recorded.

Balkham's first action was to contact the Surrey and Sussex Major Crime Team and speak to the duty Senior Investigating Officer, DCI Nick Fitzherbert. He apprised him of the extortion threat and Fitzherbert told him that he would begin an investigation with himself as lead, and inform Ops and the chief officers. He told Balkham that he would also speak to the Force Gold and arrange for an intercept to be placed on Morris's phone. He asked the PC to let Morris know that officers from his Major Crime Team would come and see him.

During this time, with Balkham alongside him, Morris set to work. Firstly, he convened an urgent meeting of his entire security team, and secondly, he put out a request to the 400 stewards who would be attending tomorrow's game to come in two hours earlier than usual. This was followed by a request from Balkham for additional Special Constables to be drafted in for tomorrow, on the advice of the Match Commander.

Next, Morris said he would arrange for the CCTV-monitoring team to check the recorded footage from all cameras around the ground for the past month, for signs of anyone acting suspiciously.

At 6 p.m. that evening Morris's team, along with a number of Expo dogs and their handlers, began the most thorough search of the stadium that had ever been undertaken.

Just as they were finishing, three hours later, his private mobile phone rang again.

'Mr Morris, I hope again this is not an inconvenient moment. You are going to a lot of trouble, most impressive – you are to be commended for your efforts. I will be brief because I'm aware, despite my warning about speaking to the police, that you now have a recording and tracing facility on your phone. But you won't find me, I'm on one of those crappy little phones that doesn't have any geo-mapping facility, OK? So, look, you really are wasting resources. You will not find this bomb, trust me. Just pay the money – to avoid having blood on your hands. This club has come so far, don't you think it would be such a tragedy to see it destroyed for what is petty cash? Please trust me – treat me as your friend, not your enemy. I want to help you. I will call you again later.'

'Who are you?' Adrian Morris asked.

But he was speaking to a dead connection.

4

Three days earlier

A few days after her nineteenth birthday, the hour had almost arrived. These past weeks had seemed an eternity. Florentina Shima was excited, but she was also very nervous.

Perhaps he would not come.

The first thing she did when she woke in her room was to look at his photograph. Her fiancé, Dragan.

Well, he wasn't actually her fiancé, but he soon would be! By the end of today, provided her grandmother agreed the financial negotiations. And not long after, she would be going with him to his home in Serbia, to a new life, to marry a man she would love forever, the way people did in stories, like the way her sister, Eva, had.

Florentina didn't know exactly where Serbia was, but she knew it wasn't far, and she knew she would love it there, because she would love anywhere that she was with Dragan.

She looked at his lean, rugged face and beautiful eyes; at his hair, his rich black curls that gave him the look of a bandit in a cowboy film – but a nice bandit! A few years older than her, but not many, she estimated. She liked the idea that he was older – there was so much he would be able to teach her about life, about the world she craved to know so much more of.

The world she read about in books and saw in films and shows on their television. The whole exciting world beyond their remote mountain smallholding in northern Albania, where she lived with her parents and grandmother with their ten goats, twelve hens, twenty-two sheep, three pigs and one cow, as well as two German Shepherds to protect their animals, which gave them their livelihood, from wolves, bears and foxes.

Dragan also reminded her, just a little, of her older brother, Jak, who she had adored, who had been killed in a motorbike accident five years ago. Her younger brother, Zef, was different: he was quiet, dutiful, resigned – or committed, she never really knew which – to helping out with the animals and to toiling on the sixty dunams of land on which they grew their rotation of crops in the poor soil.

All her friends at the village school she'd attended first, and then the high school in Krujë, had met local guys who they later married. But no one had sparked for her. In her heart, she had always harboured bigger ambitions, to venture out into that wider and much more exciting world. And now, finally, with Dragan it was about to happen.

She looked at the pretty dress her mother had bought her, especially for today, which was draped over the chair. She was excited to put it on. Then she picked up her mobile phone, the one Eva had sent her last year as a birthday present, so the two of them could keep in touch. There was a text message from her.

Paç fat!

Good luck!

Four years ago, Eva, twenty-four, always much worldlier than herself, and scared of ending up a spinster, had heard of a broker who could find potential husbands in neighbouring

Serbia. Leaving her family to go and live in a country where she didn't know anyone, or speak the language, seemed a better option to Eva than living out a lonely life here. Some months later, a pleasant, nice-looking man called Milovan had arrived at their house.

Their grandmother had handled the negotiations, and the old woman decided on *po* – yes!

Milovan paid 20,000 leks to her family and left to buy some gold jewellery and clothes for his fiancée. He returned three weeks later, after Eva had received her passport, to take her away to her new home. Subsequently, she had written regularly to say how happy she was in Serbia, that Milovan had a large farm and was a kind and considerate husband. She now had one baby, with another on the way, and urged her younger sister, Florentina, to try to find a husband the way she had done.

So, she had.

Shortly after midday, Dragan arrived. His name, she had been told, meant *joy*. But when Florentina saw him she was gripped with everything but. Most of all, revulsion and blind panic.

The sheep farmer stepped towards her with a broad grin, revealing just three teeth in an otherwise empty mouth, and wearing the most terrible clothes. He stank. And he looked nearer to fifty than the late twenties of his photograph. He looked older than her father.

Once again, as with her sister, her grandmother took over the negotiations. Dragan was wealthy, the old woman told her, he had over forty sheep. Two hundred hens. Twelve pigs. What was not to love about him? And he was willing to pay a fortune, 400,000 leks. Twenty times the amount Milovan had paid for her sister!

Again, her grandmother decided on *po*. Dragan went off

to make the passport arrangements, and said he would return as soon as they were done to collect his bride-to-be.

That evening, Florentina made a decision. At midnight, when everyone was asleep, after ramming a few belongings and some bread and cheese from the kitchen into a rucksack, she ran. And kept on running. With few clothes, other than those she stood up in, and little money, she slept the first night in a cave, some miles away, with the rank smell of wild animals all around her, awake most of the night, scared. At daybreak she ate her provisions and left, walking for hours down the narrow, twisting mountain road.

Every time she heard a vehicle approaching she scrambled down over the edge of the road and hid in the bushes, scared it might be her father or Zef, coming to look for her. It grew steadily hotter throughout the morning – for the past few days the temperature had been over forty degrees, and it felt that now. After a few hours she was exhausted, frightened, thirsty and hungry. Many kilometres ahead – she did not know how far – was the city of Tirana, her destination. Perhaps there she could find work, maybe in a bar, and the chance of meeting the man of her dreams.

Shortly before midday, traipsing round a bend in the road, she saw over to her left a large bar and restaurant with a pretty garden in front of it. A handful of people, mostly groups of men, sat at tables, drinking coffee. There were fancy cars parked outside. One, she recognized, was a Mercedes. She knew what it was because the rusted shell of a Mercedes had sat, all her life, next to the stall where the pigs lived. Jak used to tell her that one day he would restore this car and they could go driving in it, in a *Mercedes*! Then he had died.

She went inside out of the heat. It was almost empty, apart from a group of men smoking at one table, beneath a

NO SMOKING sign. A young woman behind the bar, about the same age as herself, took pity on her, gave her water and a plate of eggs and a toasted ham and cheese sandwich. When Florentina told her where she was headed, the woman went over to one of the men at the table and spoke to him. He turned and smiled at her.

She returned and told Florentina that he was a nice guy, her cousin, she could trust him and he would give her a lift to Tirana.

Two hours later the man dropped her at a roundabout in the vast city, in the searing afternoon sun, and pointed her in the direction of the city centre. She thanked him, then looked around, bewildered, at all the buildings. Suddenly, she felt both safe and lost at the same time.

She had never before in her life been in a city. Streets rammed with cars and trucks. Shops. Cafés. Restaurants. The roar of motorbikes. The scream of a police siren.

Thousands of people. Strangers, all of them.

She walked past a huge arch with a white statue on top and statues on either side. Ahead was another roundabout, in the middle of which was the national emblem, a black, double-headed eagle mounted on a stone plinth. Nervously, hesitantly, she waited until a group of people crossed, and she went with them. She walked on, past a filling station, shops with awnings, cafés with umbrellas. Past a restaurant with a display of fish on ice just inside the door. A tall, modern skyscraper stood ahead with the name PLAZA HOTEL in red lights along the top. Desperately thirsty again, she came to a park with an ornamental pond with several fountains in it. A group of men sat around, most of them smoking. She walked over, knelt and scooped some water into her mouth.

Where should she go?

She was totally lost and bewildered. No one took any notice of her. Should she go home? Was she crazy to be doing this?

She didn't even know where she would sleep. On the streets? In a park?

Lost in thought, she walked on, her feet sore, and feeling a blister coming on. She reached a busy, confusing junction, with noisy traffic coming from every direction. The Plaza Hotel looked as if it might be the centre of this city. Might someone there be able to tell her if there was bar work anywhere? Or waitressing? Or cleaning?

She stepped out into the road, heard the blare of a horn, heard the scream of brakes. Saw a cement lorry bearing down on her.

She froze.

Then, out of nowhere, a hand grabbed her and jerked her back, hard, just as the lorry thundered past inches in front of her.

Turning, she saw a man, perhaps of her father's age, but smart-looking, with elegant black hair. He was wearing a suit with an open-necked shirt and had all his teeth – nice white teeth.

'Thank you,' she gasped.

'Are you OK?' he asked, pleasantly. 'That was close!'

She nodded.

'Are you sure?' her saviour asked. 'You don't look OK to me.'

'I'm – I'm lost,' she replied.

He told her his name. Frederik. He took her to a beautiful café by a lake. It had white umbrellas and was full of people, many of them young and good-looking.

He bought her a Coke and a sandwich and an ice cream. He seemed gentle and kind and interested in her. He asked her what she would like her life to be. She opened up to him, told him why she had come here, and he listened, sympathetically. Then he excused himself and made a phone call. When he had finished he turned back to her, smiling, and told her his sister was going to join them, and she would help her.

Half an hour later, a glamorous woman came to the table and sat down. She said her name was Elira, and she could help her to start a whole new life, somewhere abroad. Had Florentina ever been abroad, she asked? How about England? Would she like to go there? To a beautiful city called Brighton, where they had a job waiting for her and a nice apartment to live in. But first, she needed a proper meal, and to get cleaned up and have some rest.

Elira and her brother took her to a beautiful house, high on the hills above Tirana – the kind of place she had only ever seen in films. A kind, elderly lady called Irma, the housekeeper, cooked her a meal, led her to a bathroom and helped her afterwards to bathe. Then the woman tucked her into a big, soft bed, where she fell asleep almost instantly.

The next morning, Elira took her into the city. They went to a huge, modern shopping centre called the European Trade Centre, all glass and steel, like nothing Florentina had ever experienced before. Elira bought her fancy new clothes, jeans, a cream blouse, trainers, a light-weight leather jacket and a smart wristwatch, then a new handbag. Next, she took her to a beauty salon, where she had her hair done and make-up, and her nails for the first time in her life.

She felt pampered. Like a millionairess. It felt as if she had landed in paradise and she could scarcely believe her luck.

Elira bought her a small, wheeled suitcase, packed with more clothes and a washbag full of toiletries. They had lunch together, then, in Elira's chauffeured limousine, returned to the mansion in the hills. Florentina spent the afternoon lazing by the swimming pool, truly living a dream.

That evening the housekeeper helped her bathe again, then afterwards Elira dressed her in her new clothes and groomed her long, freshly styled dark hair in front of a mirror.

'You are a very pretty young lady,' she told her. 'You look like a movie star!'

And she did!

Florentina twirled in front of the mirror, feeling like a whole new person. From the desperation of just a couple of days ago, she felt transformed. Strong. Ready for adventure.

The following morning, after she'd enjoyed a huge breakfast, prepared by Irma, of yoghurt, layered spinach pie, salami, eggs and fresh fruits, Frederik came into the kitchen. He stopped and stared at Florentina with a big, warm smile. He told her she was beautiful and that he had spoken to friends in the city of Brighton and Hove who indeed could help her and were looking forward to meeting her. He would give her a passport and documentation, and her parents would never find her there. She would be safe. She would have a great job in a bar, with an apartment of her own, and a chance to make new friends and a new life – and, absolutely, one day she would find the man of her dreams.

To cover her air fare and other expenses, all she had to do for him was one small thing.

5

Adrian Morris's phone began ringing. It didn't rouse him, he was already awake, as he had been for much of the night, lying in the grip of fear, his brain releasing him occasionally into sleep, only to torment him with nightmares.

He was in turmoil. Should he have made the decision to call the game off? Was not doing this something he would come to regret for the rest of his life?

It still wasn't too late.

The room was brightening; from outside came the first tentative sounds of the dawn chorus. Dawn. Dawn breaking on the biggest day in his club's history, and a shadow loomed over it. Question after question churned over and over in his mind. What had he missed? What could he do that he had not already done?

Chirrup-chirrup. Chirrup-chirrup.

For a few seconds, in his hazy mind, he thought it was just another bird joining in the growing orchestra out there in their garden. Then his wife stirred. 'Phone,' she murmured.

The clock showed 5.04 a.m.

Who was phoning at this hour? One of his night-security team?

He reached across his bedside table and grabbed the cordless off its cradle. 'Adrian Morris,' he answered.

The voice chilled him. The same accented English, as polite as before.

'Mr Morris?'

He responded as quietly as he could, walking across the thickly carpeted floor towards the door. 'Yes.'

'I'm sorry for this inconvenient hour, but we don't really have very much time left, do we?'

'Can you hold a moment, please.'

He slipped out onto the landing, closed the door behind him and entered his den, switching on the light and perching on the chair in front of his desk. 'Who am I speaking to?'

'You are speaking to a football fan who is very concerned about your beautiful stadium – and who does not like to hurt people.'

'How did you get this number?' Morris asked. It was his private home landline, and ex-directory.

'By disobeying my instructions and going to the police, you have eliminated my option to call you on your mobile. So I had to make, shall we say, a little more effort. You can get anything if you push the right buttons. Anything, Mr Morris. You can join the football stadium as an ordinary steward and one day rise to become its security boss. Anything at all. And that includes a bomb in your stadium, on or under a seat, this afternoon. Unless you pay the £250,000 I've suggested. This is a small amount. You will today, just in ticket sales alone, take around £1.5 million – and about the same again in drinks and pies, and over £10 million for the television rights. So, for a mere fraction of today's revenue you can sleep in peace and the club will be safe. Would this not be a win-win?'

'In your sick mind, perhaps.'

'Who will come off worse from this tragedy? You, the Amex Stadium or Sussex Police? You would prefer to see fifty – perhaps one hundred – of your loyal fans blown to pieces, Mr Morris? That is all human life means to you? I think you should take a look in your bathroom mirror, and there you'll see the one who has the sick mind. Why don't you sleep on it? I will make contact later to give you one last chance.'

'Look,' Morris said, his brain racing. 'Even if I was to agree, you've left it very late – how could I find a quarter of a million pounds on a Saturday morning?'

'You really should have thought about that yesterday, this is very bad planning by you. I'm glad you don't work for me. Goodbye, Mr Morris.'

The line went dead.

Instantly, Morris dialled 1471 to see if he could get the number. But all he got was the message saying it was withheld. He picked up his wallet, which was lying beside his laptop, and pulled out the number of the Detective Inspector who had come along yesterday with two other officers, after the blackmailer's first call.

Glenn Branson answered on the first ring.

6

At 10 a.m., Kipp Brown's phone vibrated with an incoming text. It was from the racing tipster firm to which he subscribed.

> Good morning, Mr Brown, we have two bets today.
> The first horse is DAAWY and take the 4/1 with
> Paddy. Also back MYSTERY OF WAR and take the
> 4/1 with Betfred. Both horses should be backed this
> morning taking the early price and both are WIN
> bets. Good luck – TONY FORBES

Immediately, Kipp made his daily call to his private bookmaker, recklessly asking him to place £10,000 he did not have on each horse.

7

I'm a bomber! Uh-huh! Boom!

It felt good to be wanted!

Ylli Prek had been told by his mother that his first name meant 'star' in Albanian and his last name came from a freedom fighter.

That's what he was! A freedom fighter with a bomb!

But for the moment, at 3.30 p.m., as he walked away from the train station at the Amex football stadium and across the busy concourse, he was Ylli Prek, football fan. Slung from his shoulder was an elaborate Sony FS7 camera, the kind professionals used.

Although it wasn't a camera at all, of course.

It was a bomb. Filled with nails, bolts and ball bearings. The explosive charge packed inside would be enough, he had been told, to kill at least forty people all around him. And to injure at least one hundred, if not more.

He had in his wallet a ticket for a seat in the South Stand. Quite a lot of adults and children should be killed or maimed, if all went well.

'I'm a bomber, I'm a bomber!' he sang under his breath. A small, thin, bespectacled man of twenty-three, with a beaky nose and a shapeless mop of prematurely thinning dark hair that looked like a bad toupee, squashed beneath

25

a red baseball cap. He strode along in a tracksuit with baggy trousers, with a gait that was a lot more confident than he felt inside.

I'm a star. I'm a freedom fighter!

I've been paid more money than I could ever have dreamed of. My mother will be so happy when she receives it!

This beat the crap out of working in the car wash for the past eighteen months. Wiping, polishing, vacuuming. Damp, cold, constantly numb hands. Shit pay. Shit accommodation, four of them in a single room.

Now I'm a bomber!

Oh yes. Uh-huh!

I have status! I'm a somebody.

8

Saturday 12 August
15.00–16.00

'You wanker!' Kipp Brown muttered under his breath at the security guard manning the entrance to car park A, Bennett's Field. As he drove up to the barrier in his matt-black Porsche 911, he was in a mood because he was late – his own fault, he had been working. It was 3.45 p.m. and he had a bunch of clients whom he and two of his colleagues were meant to be entertaining to a late lunch. And he was angry at himself for trying to be too greedy with his bets today. One of Tony Forbes's tips had paid off handsomely, but he'd had big losses on a series of accumulators he'd bet recklessly large amounts on, online, and was now badly down on the day – although there were still some results to come.

'What's going on here?' he said to the guard.

'We are carrying out extra security checks today, sir. You don't have your car-park pass.' He swung a mirror, on a long stick, under the Porsche.

'Yep, well I couldn't bloody find it. You have my registration on your list.'

'I'll have to make a phone call to check, sir.' The guard peered in, looking at the rear seats. 'Would you mind opening the boot of your car?'

'I have a season ticket and a corporate box. Do I look like a sodding terrorist?'

'Dad,' Mungo cautioned, looking up from his phone, his newly bleached hair, the colour of winter wheat, scraped back into a topknot; his rubbish, cheap Samsung phone that his mean, embarrassing father had bought to replace the iPhone he'd got for his last birthday, and accidentally dropped down a gutter last week. Well, he hadn't dropped it, actually, it fell out of his trouser pocket.

He was trying at this moment to send a Snapchat message to his best friend, Aleksander, who was also going to be here today, but it wouldn't send. This phone was, like, useless.

'What's your problem?' Kipp turned to his son, flipping the catch.

'It's not that man's fault,' Mungo said, as the security guard raised the bonnet at the front of the car.

'Right – so whose fault, exactly, is it?'

The guard lowered the bonnet. 'I've heard back from the office, you're free to go through, sir,' he said politely.

'Is there any point?' He stamped on the accelerator, squealing the tyres as he roared forward, jerking Mungo's head back against the headrest.

'Dad, take a chill pill.'

'What is your problem today?' he said to his son.

'You!' Mungo retorted. 'You're just in a weird mood.'

You would be too, Kipp Brown thought, *if you knew just how much I've been screwed over by that goddamn roulette wheel at the Waterfront Casino. If you were aware that I don't actually know where your next term's school fees are coming from, and that I'm probably going to have to take you out of Brighton College and put you in a state school. That would wipe that smug, sanctimonious, holier-than-thou look from your face.*

Maybe his spread bet on today's football games would

come good, he hoped. A small bet, from his emergency cash stash. If he got it right, he could be back in funds by tonight.

And if he got it wrong?

He didn't want to think about that.

He never wanted to think about those kinds of consequences.

Brighton and Hove Albion had come into the new season on a roll. He needed them to win. Not to draw, not to lose, just to win. And a couple of other clubs as well. Six, actually. They all should. Just like his numbers at the casino should have come up, but didn't.

Today would be different.

Today would put him back in the saddle.

He had a good feeling about today. Despite his son's scowling face.

He had the radio tuned to the specialist football programme *The Albion Roar*. Presenters Alan and Ady were discussing the Albion's chances. He agreed with their prediction that their home team would win, 2–1.

Please God!

He parked in a bay next to a white Bentley GT convertible that he recognized as belonging to one of his clients, property developer Dan Fox. Dan would already be in his box, waiting for him to arrive and no doubt drinking a pint of Harveys.

Mungo pulled down his sun visor and checked his hair in the vanity mirror.

9

On the far side of the Amex Stadium car park, Dritan Nano sat behind the wheel of a stolen, old-model 5 Series BMW, on false plates. He was relieved to see the Porsche arrive; it was an hour later than expected, and he had been beginning to wonder whether something had happened and it was not going to appear at all.

The thirty-two-year-old Albanian had a permanently sad-looking face, which was at odds with his powerful, muscular body mass. Limp, damp-looking hair brushed forward into a widow's peak lay low on his forehead. With large, round eyes, he looked vulnerable in the way a tortoise's head looks out of proportion and exposed when protruding from the safety of its shell.

He watched the Porsche drive past the barrier and pull in to a parking bay. The smartly dressed man and his son, in jeans and a shirt, climbed out and headed off towards the stands. Their body language told him they'd had an argument, the father striding on ahead, the son, hands in pockets, following in his own time.

Dritan had had an argument today, too, and was feeling terrible. Crap. Totally. Crap. He had woken feeling nervous about his task ahead, but full of excitement for what lay beyond. A big day today, in every way.

Until the text from Lindita.

His girlfriend of five years, whom he was due to marry next spring, had gone back, three months ago, to her native Kosovo, because her grandmother had only days to live. Somehow, defying the doctor's predictions, the old bird had struggled on. Then, last week, she had finally succumbed.

Yesterday, he had texted Lindita excitedly, telling her – a little white lie – that he was due a big bonus from his employee, Mr Dervishi, and this would give him enough money to buy the lease of a coffee house. He would quit his job and run the café with her, as they had long dreamed of doing. With luck, he should have the money in a few days, and they could be open for business by October. Lindita would create the snacks and sandwiches – she was a great cook – and he would, by then, have done a barista course.

Last night Lindita had texted him back. She was sorry, she said. She had met someone back home and was not returning to England after all.

He looked at the text again, for the twentieth time or maybe the thirtieth, fighting back tears.

She finished it saying:

> I like u, Dritan, but I don't like some of the things
> you do, u know what I'm talking about. I think it
> would scare me to have a child by u. Somewhere
> inside u is a decent person. Try to find it one day
> and become that person. I am seeing someone
> else and I think he is better for me. I'm sorry.
> Paç fat X

He had tried numerous times to reply but she had blocked him. He couldn't believe it, nor accept it. He loved her so much; they had planned their whole life together. Sure, OK, she knew who he worked for and she had an idea of some of the things that involved; but he had always promised her this was only until he had got enough money together for the coffee house they dreamed of, and she had seemed to believe him.

He pulled her tiny photograph out of his wallet and stared at it. Her short brown hair slanting across her forehead. Her smile. Her green eyes staring at him, filled with warmth and trust.

Now she had found someone else. How, how could she? That hurt so much.

Earlier today he had confided in his friend and colleague, Valbone, with whom he shared the apartment above Mr Dervishi's garages, and who was somewhere in the stadium now. But he didn't get much sympathy. His fellow Albanian told him to man up, and that there were plenty more fish in the sea.

Dritan replied that he didn't want fish. He wanted Lindita.

They'd had a big falling-out.

Now he was aware that he was dangerously distracted, but he didn't care. Nothing mattered any more. Nothing but getting away as quickly as he could, going to Kosovo and finding Lindita. Finding her and convincing her he had changed, totally, completely, utterly. She would believe him, wouldn't she?

He looked at his watch. Less than two hours till kick-off.

Less than two hours to go. He tried to focus on his task, although there wasn't really much to focus on. When the time came, all he had to do was drive.

10

The first fans had already begun arriving at the Amex Stadium an hour ago, some making their way to the private boxes and hospitality suites, most heading to the catering stalls or bars for their pies and pints. All were surprised by a much larger police presence than they could remember. But of course, now they were Premier League, it was bound to be different. Few grumbled, and the security guards carrying out the searches were mostly good-natured.

Ylli Prek, mingling with the crowd, made his way towards the long queue ahead of him at the turnstiles, and saw the security searches in operation. Suddenly the spring in his step was gone and he felt nervous. Nervous of failure. Of what would happen to him if he did fail. What if they checked inside the camera? He'd seen the video, heard the splashing sound. All of them who worked for Mr Dervishi had seen that video and heard that splashing. He didn't know if it was true about the reptile, but he had seen for himself the horrific things Mr Dervishi ordered done to people who failed him.

He'd seen, on another video, Mr Dervishi command his surgeon to slash a man's eyeball open with a razor. He'd watched a man strapped to a table being skinned alive by the surgeon on Mr Dervishi's command. He could easily

33

believe it was indeed true that his boss kept a sixteen-foot-long man-eating Nile crocodile in the basement of his mansion. And regularly fed it bits of people who disappointed him.

But no one asked him to open the camera. One big, tall guy patted him down thoroughly, checked his pockets and made him open his coat.

Then he was through.

Holding his ticket in his hand.

And his instructions in his mind.

Ylli Prek made his way into the South Stand. He found his seat, number 311S, and perched on it, waiting patiently – if anxiously – over the next ninety minutes as the stands filled.

Two small boys sat on their own nearby, both wearing Seagulls baseball caps and the blue-and-white club scarves. He held his camera, with its lens that he could not see through, on his knees. It was safe, he had been assured. It could not detonate accidentally, he could even drop it and nothing would happen, not until he primed it. He glanced a few times at these two boys, feeling a bit bad about them. They'd be blown to pieces, for certain.

But better that than him meeting the crocodile.

Hey-ho.

Boom, boom! I'm the secret bomber! I have no fear!

He might have been just a little less confident had he known that two rows behind him, in the rapidly filling stand, sat Sussex's senior homicide officer, Detective Superintendent Roy Grace, with his ten-year-old son, Bruno.

11

Kipp Brown shot a glance over his shoulder at Mungo, feeling a little bad about his rudeness to his son today. Mungo had been affected, in his own way, just as he and Stacey had been, when his older sister had died tragically. He smiled at him, but Mungo didn't notice. Dressed in skinny jeans, white socks, sneakers and a checked shirt with a Seagulls scarf wrapped round his neck, and that ridiculous topknot, Mungo lagged some distance behind him, engaged in Snapchatting – or Instagramming – or whatever he did on his new phone that he complained didn't do anything.

Kipp waited for him to catch up, then put an arm round him. 'I didn't mean to snap at you, Mungo, I'm just a bit stressed at the moment.'

'At the moment? You and Mum – you're both, like, stressed all the time. It's all about Kayleigh, all the time, like all you care about is her. What about me? Just sometimes.'

'Hey, come on, your mum and I love you very much, you're everything to us.'

'Really?' Mungo broke free of his father's arm and walked silently beside him as they joined the throng of casually dressed people, many wearing team scarves, hurrying through the brilliant sunshine towards the queues for the Amex Stadium entrances.

Mungo suddenly waved a hand at a tall, handsome teenage boy with gelled black wavy hair and called out, 'Hi, Aleksander!'

Almost at the same moment, Kipp saw the figure of one of his clients, accountant Barry Carden, striding past.

'Hey, Barry!'

'Kipp!'

'Good to see you,' Kipp said.

'You too.'

'What do you think of Albion's chances – do you think we'll win?'

'Hey, we've come this far, Kipp. Let's think positively.'

'Totally agree!'

They chatted for a couple of minutes, then Kipp glanced anxiously at his watch. 'I'd better get going.'

'Me too.'

As Carden hurried off, Kipp turned, but could not see his son. He looked all around but there was no sign of him.

For a moment, he hesitated. Shit, the kid was in a foul mood today. He had his ticket, so he'd probably gone on without waiting, up to the box.

He hurried to the South Stand reception, grumpily endured the extra security check, standing patiently as he was wanded, then hurried up the stairs and along the corridor to the hospitality suites. He entered the door marked KIPP BROWN ASSOCIATES and apologized to his invited group of clients for being so late, relieved to see they all had glasses in their hands. He began to work the room. Dan Fox was there with his partner, Liz, and his twin teenage daughters.

'Where's Mungo?' one of the girls asked.

'He'll be here in a minute,' Kipp replied. Then he turned to a very tanned Graham Batchelor and his stunning partner, Sarah Casson. 'You guys look well!' he said.

Graham beamed. 'We've just got married, in Santorini, five days ago, Kipp.'

'Wow, hey! Congratulations! Married life seems like it suits you!' He grabbed a glass of Ridgeview bubbly and toasted the newly-weds, before moving on to another couple, Fraser and Kim Edmonds, also deeply tanned, who told him they were just back from Dubrovnik.

'If you've never been, Kipp, you absolutely must, it's beautiful!' Kim said.

Kipp privately thought that anywhere would look pretty good when you visited it, as they had, on a ten-million-pound yacht.

'How's business, Kipp?' Fraser asked.

'Yep, good.' He forced a smile. 'I thought you guys were always away for the whole of August?'

'Had to get back for this game – today's one of the highlights of my life!' Fraser said.

Kipp glanced around. Still no sign of Mungo.

Where was he?

A waitress served poached salmon salads. Kipp dug into his with a fork, whilst talking animatedly to Dan Fox, before paying special attention to a particularly important guest, the courtly, dapper, wheelchair-bound octogenarian businessman and very public philanthropist Edi Konstandin. He had a large paunch and was dressed every inch the English country gentleman, apart from several vulgar jewelled rings on his fingers.

The Albanian, who was one of the largest employers in the city, owned an empire of businesses that included one of the UK's biggest property development companies, a portfolio of rental flats, car washes, launderettes, coffee bars, cafés and kebab takeaways around the county, and many interests abroad. Kipp suspected that Konstandin used these businesses to launder the much bigger money he made controlling part of the city's drugs and prostitution trade. But he wasn't in the business of making moral judgements about his clients. He'd long ago told Stacey that if he did, he probably wouldn't have any clients at all.

Then music blared out. The fans began singing and waving flags. The atmosphere rapidly became electrifying.

Still no sign of Mungo.

Where are you, kid?

12

Keith Ellis opened the security barrier with his pass card and rode through into the sprawling campus of Sussex Police Headquarters. He dismounted from his Triumph Tiger in the car park of the Contact & Communications Centre, a modern, almost futuristic-looking red-brick building opposite the one that housed the police driving school. It was just gone 4.30 p.m., and the Oscar-1 Inspector – formerly known as Ops-1 – had been on a rest day, but he had agreed to go in to relieve a colleague who wanted to attend his son's seventh birthday party.

Tall and lightly bearded, Ellis cut an imposing figure as he strode across to the side entrance in his Kevlar jeans and lightweight jacket – his last middle-aged throw at being trendy – and pressed his card against the door panel. He felt a twinge of nostalgia, aware he would only be doing this for a few more weeks, after thirty years in varied roles in the force, which included behind-the-scenes at Gatwick Airport, a role in Traffic where he rose to become a Road Death Senior Investigating Officer, followed by a posting as Critical Incident Inspector for East Sussex Division, and now for the past three years serving as an Oscar-1. In this latest role, he had considerable authority and power. Between the hours of 10 p.m. and 7 a.m. the duty Oscar-1 would be one of the very few senior police officers on duty in the county.

He wondered now, as he had done for several months, whether he was doing the right thing in retiring at the end of the year, at just fifty-two. He would collect his handsome pension pot. He'd be able to text jokes to friends without having to worry about being hauled up in front of Professional Standards accused of being racist or homophobic or sexist or animalist or veganist or whatever faction of the Political Correctness Fascists he might have supposedly offended this week.

And yet . . .

As a Chief Superintendent colleague who was also coming up for retirement had recently told him over a pint, once the knowledge was out that you were down to your last year or so, your colleagues put you into the UBB.

It stood, unflatteringly, for *Useless Bastards Box*.

Keith hung up his motorcycle clothing on a couple of pegs in the locker room, put his crash helmet down on a bench, then climbed the concrete staircase, in his black uniform top and trousers, into the open-plan area of the Force Control Room that had been his domain for the past three years. And realized just how much he loved it here. He might be in the UBB these days, but hopefully he could at least show his abilities as a safe, competent pair of hands up to his very last shift.

And this vast room on two floors was where all potential glory – and sometimes sheer horror – for Sussex Police began.

It was where the county's emergency and non-emergency call takers – or contact handlers, as they were called – sat wearing their headsets, in deep concentration. And it was where the rota of highly skilled operators monitored the county's 850 CCTV cameras.

Everything that might involve the police in an emergency call-out began here, in this room. Whether it was a suspicious man posing as a gas meter reader, a road traffic accident, a mugging, a bank robbery, a rape, a suspected terrorist, a firearms incident or an air disaster, any 999 call would be answered and assessed in this room. And he would have the responsibility for handling the first stages of any major incident resulting.

UBB.

Huh.

No way! If he could have just one juicy job sometime between now and retirement, he'd show them just how damned good he was!

He wasn't going to have to wait very long.

13

Although Roy Grace was enjoying a precious day out with his son, and a day away from work, he was, like all police officers, rarely fully off duty – and today he was the on-call SIO. As Bruno studied the programme, commenting knowledgeably on the team squad and wondering who would be selected for today's game against tough opposition, Manchester City, his father was preoccupied, staring around the terraces.

Grace was looking for the faces of local villains he had encountered during his two decades of policing the city of Brighton and Hove, always interested to see, in particular, who was sitting with whom and what new criminal alliances might have formed or be under discussion. In addition today, having been briefed by DCI Fitzherbert, he was being extra-vigilant as a result of the threats that had been made to the stadium.

He had already clocked something of interest, as people filed in and took their seats: a low-life drug dealer and car thief, Alan Letts. Letts was sitting beside one of Brighton's oldest and nastiest villains, Jimmy Bardolph. Bardolph, a scabby, scarred creep, had once been a henchman for one of Brighton's biggest crime families, but these days had long been a busted flush. The pair were engaged in earnest conversation and Grace would have loved to have been able to eavesdrop. What were they discussing? Not donations to a charity, that was for sure. He made a mental note to inform a colleague at Specialist Crime Command Intel.

'Hello, Roy!' a voice said right behind him.

He turned to see a retired police officer, Mike Hird, and his son, Paul. He greeted them briefly then noticed two people seated next to them, smiling at him. He recognized Cliff and Linda Faires, who ran the Brighton Shellfish & Oyster Bar on the seafront.

'Enjoyed those oysters last week did you and the missus, Roy?'

'We did, very much! We tried to get my son, Bruno, to try them, but he preferred his prawn sandwich.' Grace resumed scanning the crowd.

'So, Papa, who will win, what will be the score?' Bruno said.

'What's your prediction?' Grace asked his son. 'Are you looking forward to seeing the Albion's German midfielder, Gross?'

'From Ingolstadt,' Bruno said, solemnly. 'He is good. But I think Manchester City will win, two–nil.'

'We're meant to be supporting Brighton, aren't we?'

Bruno nodded, looking as ever his serious self. 'But I don't think they will win today, not with their formation. They have it wrong.'

The players were coming out onto the pitch. The roar of the crowd began as a ripple, then rose in a crescendo as everyone got to their feet, clutching the blue-and-white flags that had been placed on their seats, singing, heartily, the club anthem, 'Sussex by the Sea', interspersed with chants of, 'ALBION!'

Grace noticed the man in the baseball cap, with the big

camera, two rows in front of him. Something about his body language seemed odd. The man was looking around him, nervously, edgy, then fiddling with a dial on the top of his camera. A professional-looking job of the kind favoured by paparazzi or perhaps bird-watchers – *twitchers*. Or, he thought with his ever-suspicious mind, peeping Toms. Because of yesterday's threat, Roy continued to watch him, not liking the look of him. If he was press, he would have been with the others in the middle of the stadium's West Stand, behind the dugouts, or at the far end, behind the goalposts. Probably just a fan, like a lot of others, with a passion for photography.

Ylli Prek raised his camera and pressed his eye to the viewfinder, pretending to take pictures in case anyone was watching. Then he laid it down on his lap again and peered at the dial on the top. Ordinarily, it would have been for setting the shutter speed. But on this camera, it was the timer. Twisting it would prime the bomb. The options were one minute, five minutes, ten minutes and upwards in further increments of five minutes. He had been instructed to wait until the game had started, just in case of any delay, then to allow himself enough margin to get well clear of the stadium; but not to let it run to half-time, when the stands wouldn't be so full. And not to leave the camera on its own for so long that people would get suspicious.

Fifteen minutes, Ylli Prek decided. Or would ten be better?

Roy Grace kept a steady, uneasy eye on the man.

14

Adrian Morris, seated at his command centre in the back row of the Amex Control Room, was studying the crowds in the stands. Casting a vigilant eye across all of them, row by row. Despite his near-sleepless night, he was more wide awake and alert than ever before in his life.

The caller had not rung again.

Why don't you sleep on it? I will make contact later to give you one last chance.

The Head of Safety and Security's regular complement of sixteen were at their seats in the Control Room now, concentrating on their computer screens or on the bank of CCTV monitors, rather than watching the match itself. Seated alongside him were the Police Match Commander, Chief Inspector Andy Kundert, as well as the Safety Officer, and a radio operator. In the middle row were two police radio operators, three CCTV operators, the External Controller and loggist. In the front row were the SECAMB Ambulance Service Manager, the St John Ambulance Commander, the medical radio operator and a British Transport Police officer.

Today, in addition, also peering intently at the row of CCTV screens, was Detective Inspector Glenn Branson, here in his own time – with Roy Grace's encouragement –

using the game as a developmental opportunity to broaden his range of skills for his hoped-for next step up the police career ladder – to become a Chief Inspector.

Both inside and outside the stadium was the largest police presence ever for an Albion game. There was effectively a ring of steel around the place.

The Chief Constable had been informed. A high-level strategic command meeting, with the Gold Commander, Superintendent Jason Tingley, had taken place at midday to review the situation. In the six years since the Amex had opened, this exact scenario had been rehearsed several times. The Gold Commander's decision had been to go ahead with the game, but be ready to evacuate if there was any cause for concern.

Armed police marksmen stood in the wings in full public view to give added assurance to the fans, covering all four stands; two Armed Response Units were in place outside. Adding to the police presence, NPAS-15, the police helicopter, had been overhead several times and was on standby.

Morris was relieved they were going ahead with the game, but the caller's words still rang fear in his heart.

Mr Morris, there will be a bomb on or under one seat in the stadium tomorrow afternoon . . . Who will come off worse from this tragedy? You, the Amex Stadium or Sussex Police?

He had toyed with whether to let his young son come to the game with his grandfather. He had not told his wife all the details, knowing exactly how alarmed she would have been and what she would have said: that they shouldn't go. He'd fretted about them all night, feeling stuck between a rock and a hard place.

His concern was that if anything did happen in the

stadium, and word got out that he'd known of the danger and had prevented his son and his granddad from attending but let the game continue all the same, there would be hell to pay.

In the end, he'd convinced himself that the stadium was safe.

But why hadn't the caller rung again as he had said he would?

Suddenly the door opened and one of the stewards, Keith Waring, a stout man in his sixties who had been part of the Albion security team for as long as Morris had been there himself, came in and hurried up to him, holding out his mobile phone. 'Ade,' he said, looking puzzled. 'I've got a call for you – come through on my private phone. I asked if I could take a message but the bloke says he has to speak to you in person and it's very urgent.'

Shit, he thought, taking the phone. 'Adrian Morris,' he said. And immediately heard the unpleasantly familiar, polite, accented English voice. He felt a mixture of relief and deep apprehension.

'Mr Morris, I thought I would give you a little time to consider what we discussed.'

'I thought you were going to call me earlier? It's five minutes till kick-off.'

'You are the Head of Safety and Security. It is within your remit to postpone the game and evacuate the stadium. Really I would advise you to do this.'

The display showed again that the caller ID was withheld.

'How did you get this number?'

'I can get any number I have to, in order to reach you on a line that is not tapped by the police, whom I advised you not to contact. I can see them all with you up in the

Control Box. You will never see me. Postpone, Mr Morris, really, I am saying this in your best interests. Evacuate. Then pay the money as I will direct you. Understand that I am not a greedy person. You now have just under four minutes.'

The call ended.

Morris immediately turned to the Match Commander, telling him what had happened, including Glenn Branson in the discussion.

Kundert called the Force Gold, Jason Tingley, and updated him.

The players were on the pitch and the roar from the crowd rose in a crescendo. Thirty thousand fans were on their feet, clapping, chanting, waving flags and banners.

'Gold says it's your call, Ade,' Andy Kundert said. 'He'll support your decision either way.'

Morris then spoke with Jason Tingley himself, and together they reviewed the current threat assessment. He made the decision to continue with the match.

As he put the phone down, he shook his head, then raised his arms in a helpless gesture. The biggest day in the club's recent history. Their first home Premier League game. Could he really screw it all up for the Seagulls and the legion of fans here?

'We know there's been nothing planted under the stands,' Morris said. 'If anything is in here, it's been brought in – and everyone's been checked.' He looked over at the South Stand, trying to pick out his father and his son.

What to do?

What the hell to do?

The whistle blew. Brighton and Hove Albion had won the toss and chosen ends, and Manchester City kicked off. But Adrian Morris wasn't watching his home team in their blue-and-white strip, nor was he watching the opposition in their maroon kit. His eyes were fixed to the bank of monitors, studying every single person in the stadium.

He checked on his son, Finley, sitting with his granddad, and in the same row noticed a young man wearing a red baseball cap who suddenly stood up and seemed to be making his way out. So soon after kick-off?

He zoomed in with the CCTV on the seat the man had vacated, and saw a camera lying on it. Thousands of pounds' worth of kit. Got to be pretty trusting to leave that behind, he thought.

Then an icy chill swept through him.

From the conception to the construction of this stadium – which had been to the most robust specification of any football stadium in the nation – they'd liaised closely with the Anti-Terrorist Squad, and all his security team had had intensive training from them in what was now known as the 'HOT Principle'. This had originally been devised in consultation with British Transport Police, to minimize the inconvenience to rail passengers any time an unidentified package was spotted at a station. There had been a time when the discovery of a bag or rucksack lying anywhere in a railway station, without an apparent owner, would result in immediate evacuation, causing hours of delay, missed flights and all the other knock-on consequences.

The HOT Principle stood for *Hidden*, *Obvious* or *Typical of the environment but left unattended for some time*, and set down a series of assessment protocols for a suspicious item based on these.

The camera looked serious and very expensive, more like something a professional press photographer might use. But, equally, he knew there were plenty of keen amateur photographers among the fans. Right now, he decided, he had cause for concern but not immediate alarm. No one genuine would leave a valuable item like this unattended for more than a couple of minutes.

He radioed the Stand Manager, Annette Day, asking her to take a quick look at the camera on seat 311S. She replied that she would.

He spoke to his CCTV chief operator, giving him a description of the man in the red cap, then anxiously concentrated on the bank of monitors above him. He saw the man, who was short and dressed in casual sports clothing, hurrying through the stadium complex, looking nervously around him. Morris punched buttons on his control panel to bring up different cameras, trying to track him as he ran along the empty corridor and approached the double doors signed SOUTH STAND WASTE MANAGEMENT – NO UN-AUTHORIZED ACCESS.

He switched to the next camera, covering the doors and the turnstile just beyond. But all he got was a blank screen – it wasn't working.

Shit, shit, shit.

Instantly, he alerted security, gave them a description of the man and told them to find and apprehend him, and to summon a police officer to question and search him. He alerted the Match Commander, and called out to the match officer, PC Darren Balkham, who was up here also monitoring the game, and apprised him of the situation.

Should he text his father and tell him to take Finley and leave the stadium? He desperately wanted to but he knew that if he was that concerned, he should order a full-scale evacuation of everyone.

Balkham hurried up to the control desk and studied the close-up of the camera. Yes, he agreed with Morris and the Match Commander, it might be innocent, but could they take the risk? They would give it a couple more minutes, time for the man – if genuine – to have a pee or get a drink and return to his seat.

To his relief, Annette Day, in her tabard, came hurrying down the stand steps towards the seat.

Roy Grace watched the steward, a middle-aged woman, excuse her way past the fans directly in front of him, to the seat on which the camera lay.

Good, he thought, that security here was so vigilant.

Annette Day looked at the camera, which had its lens cap off and attached by a cord. Then she stepped back into the aisle and spoke into her radio.

15

The steward's body language worried Roy Grace. He watched her talk to the man in the next seat along, who shrugged his shoulders. She turned to the people in the row behind, asking them questions.

Telling Bruno to stay where he was, Grace slipped out into the aisle and hurried down to her.

There was a sudden surge of energy from the crowd. A massive roar.

'ALBION . . . ALBION . . . ALBION!'

But any thoughts of the game were far from Grace's mind: he was in full professional mode. 'Hi,' he said, holding up his warrant card. 'I'm a police officer. Are you worried about that camera?'

She joined him in the aisle. 'I've been asked to check it out, sir, yes. Did you see the man who was sitting there?'

'Yes, and I wasn't happy about him. He was looking very nervous.'

Annette Day spoke into her radio to Morris. 'Sir, I'm with a police officer, Detective Superintendent Grace, who was sitting a couple of rows behind and has concerns about the man who left his seat and the camera.'

Adrian Morris straight away sent out an instruction to all stewards to go to Priority Messages on their radios. It was code for a potential major incident. He updated Andy Kundert, who immediately ordered all police officers in the ground to switch their radios to TX Inhibit, which would block any transmission – a standard procedure for a suspected bomb, as many explosive devices used by terrorists could be set off by transmission from a mobile phone.

Next, Kundert updated Oscar-1 on the developing incident, giving him brief details, then asked Morris to arrange for the Expo dog handler, Anna Riis, who was at the stadium on standby, to check the camera out urgently.

The dog handler appeared with her springer spaniel, Brayley, wearing a fluorescent green harness labelled EXPLOSIVES SEARCH.

A fresh chant broke out. 'WE ARE BRIGHTON, SUPER BRIGHTON, WE ARE BRIGHTON FROM THE SOUTH!'

Several people stood up to avoid their view being blocked by the handler, which had a ripple effect, and in seconds the whole stand was on its feet. The steward directed the handler to the suspect device. The excited dog stood, placing both paws on the edge of the seat, pointing at the camera with its nose. Then, as it had been trained, it tapped its right paw, several times.

Now for Adrian Morris the nightmare had become real.

16

Saturday 12 August
Earlier that day

Passengers at Tenerife Airport were buckling themselves into their seats on the BA flight bound for London's Gatwick Airport, four hours away.

Among them were retired Brighton solicitor Martin Diplock and his wife, Jane, a former legal executive. They were both a little apprehensive, as were many of the passengers of a similar vintage to themselves who were old enough to remember that Tenerife's other airport to the north, on 27 March 1977, was the scene of the deadliest accident in aviation history. In thick fog, the pilot of a KLM Boeing 747 misheard the instructions of the control tower and began taxiing, straight into the path of a Pan Am Boeing 747. Five hundred and eighty-three people were killed.

But the elegant young woman seated beside them, in designer jeans and trainers, an expensive-looking leather jacket, a bling watch and sharply styled brown hair, who told them she was in transit from Albania, seemed even more anxious than themselves, trembling and perspiring, and constantly looking at her watch as if fixated by it. And each time she looked, her lips moved, as if she was doing some kind of mental arithmetic.

The unspoken thought went through both their minds, however irrational they knew it was, that she might be a terrorist, anxious about the timer on a bomb. To make conversation, Jane asked her if she was OK. The young woman assured her in limited, broken English that she was fine, this was only the second flight in her life and she was a little nervous, that was all. She was fine, thank you, really!

Jane Diplock felt better, too; she seemed a sweet little thing, not sinister at all – although how could you really tell?

The cabin crew closed the doors, but there was no sign of the engines starting. Then the pilot's voice came through the intercom, calm and steady and very apologetic. He said there was a technical problem and they were waiting for an engineer. There was likely to be a delay of thirty minutes, maybe a little longer. Meanwhile, passengers could continue to use their electronic devices.

Martin Diplock checked the time. 12.10 p.m. It was a four-hour flight and they were due to attend his son's birthday dinner in Brighton this evening – it would be tight as the plane wasn't scheduled to land until 16.40.

The young woman produced a mobile phone with a gaudy cover from her new-looking handbag and started to play a game on it. After a couple of minutes, she looked at her watch yet again and began, feverishly, doing more mental arithmetic.

After almost an hour the pilot came back on the intercom. He was very sorry he told them, the engineer was delayed. He would give them a further update shortly.

The woman looked increasingly anxious. She was perspiring more heavily now.

'Are you OK?' Jane Diplock asked her.

She nodded, her complexion pale, then began counting again on her manicured fingers, her lips moving as she did so.

17

There wasn't much anyone could teach Stephen Suckling about mechanical diggers, grabbers and Jaw Crushers. He was fifty-two, and he'd held an operator's licence since he was twenty-seven. After ten years of back-breaking manual labour on building sites – much of it in shite weather – he figured out there had to be an easier way for someone with few academic qualifications to make a living.

Such as the guys on the sites driving the bulldozers and cranes, for a start. They were inside their cabs, cosy and dry, and, he subsequently discovered, took home a far fatter pay packet than most of the manual labourers. So he'd got himself some qualifications by attending night school.

Since then he'd driven pretty much every make and model of construction-site vehicle that was out there. Then he spotted a job advert that really appealed – and was the successful applicant. For the past eight years he'd been contentedly employed at the four-acre Shoreham Harbour depot of the Recycled Aggregates Supplies division of Carter Contracting, driving a yellow caterpillar-track excavator and operating the fifty-ton Premiertrak R 400 Powerscreen Jaw Crusher. That monster machine reduced the piles of rubble brought in daily by the company's endless chain of lorries into different grades. Some would provide footings for the construction industry, some for highways or foot-paths, car parks or drains.

There wasn't much, after this length of time, that anyone could tell him about crushing concrete, nor demolition rubble, nor asphalt – although asphalt was his least favourite stuff because on hot days, like today, it stuck in the grabber's jaws, and had to be laboriously scraped away by hand. *His* hands, as he was the sole operator on this site.

That was one of the things he liked most about this job. His bosses, working out of a Portakabin at one end of the site, pretty much left him to it, and so long as he kept up with the constant deliveries, working away at the different piles, his hours were his own, and there was no asshole of a site foreman to shout at him.

The county was currently going through a building boom, which meant demand for aggregates was at a premium. For Stephen Suckling, this meant lots of overtime and a nice, fat wage packet every Thursday.

He also had a very secret, very nice little earner on the side.

Right now, Suckling, with his muscular body and shaven head, dressed in a high-viz vest over a grubby singlet and jeans, was sitting in the cabin of his JCB, operating the levers to dig the bucket deep into the side of a pyramid of rubble. He raised it in the air, swung it round and emptied the load into the hopper of the Jaw Crusher, which made a grinding roar. Tiny pieces rode up the Crusher's conveyor and tumbled to the ground, forming a new pyramid.

He could set the level of the Jaw Crusher into different gradings. Type 1 would be recycled rubble for the construction industry. Type 6F2 would be a smaller grading, mostly for drains or for the footings of a new road.

That was what this particular pile was for – the road in a new housing development near Horsham.

He had chosen to work on this Saturday for two reasons. Firstly, because his bosses had asked him, and it was all on overtime pay. Secondly, because no one was around. They were all at the Amex Stadium, watching the Albion's first league game of the season, against Manchester City. He would have liked to have been there too, to support his home team, but the money was too good today. He wasn't just getting overtime from his Carter Contracting bosses, he was getting a very big bung from a certain Mr Jorgji Dervishi – an Albanian paymaster who regularly gave him five grand in cash to not notice human body parts inside a particular pyramid of rubble. Limbs, torso and a head which he would crush beyond all recognition, and in a week or so would be safely buried beneath hundreds of tons of tarmac. Forever.

And tonight, after he had finished here, he was looking forward to going to a barbecue at some friends' with his wife, Aileen – and most of all he was looking forward to a cold beer. He could murder one now.

As the rubble dropped off the end of the conveyor he saw what looked like a human hand. Almost instantly, it was covered by more finely ground rubble. Then he noticed, dispassionately, what might have been part of a human head. Some hair and an ear?

He swung the machine round, dug back into the pyramid and raised another bucket-load in the air.

Then there was a sound from the JCB he had never heard before. A *chunk-chunk-chunk* grinding sound. The whole cab vibrated, alarmingly.

Then silence.

A red warning light flashed on the dashboard.

Shit, fuck.

He peered out of the cab window, alarmed, at the bucket, which was halted high in the air.

Especially at the object hanging over the side.

Unmistakably, a severed human arm. It was wearing a shiny wristwatch.

Shaking, he turned the ignition off, then back on again, and pressed the starter button.

Nothing happened.

'No, no, no!'

He tried again. Then again.

Nothing.

The arm dangled. Too high for him to reach.

In desperation, he climbed out of the cab and, monkey-style, tried to climb along the extended, articulated boom of the machine, holding on to the hydraulic cylinder that would raise the second boom, to which the bucket was attached. He reached the linkage, hauled himself over, then tried to slide down the next section, to the bucket.

He lost his grip.

Plunging, his head struck the side of the bucket six feet below, then he fell another fifteen feet to the hard ground, landing upright with a sickening crunch, a snapping sound and searing pain from his legs as he crashed face down.

He cried out in pain, desperately tried to move and screamed again in agony.

Then he lay rigid with panic.

Oh Jesus, no.

The lower bone of his right leg was sticking out through his jeans. His shattered left leg lay at an impossible angle, partly beneath his body.

He tried to raise himself with his arms, but the pain was too excruciating.

Above him, he heard the cry of gulls. And above him he also saw the bucket. The human arm. The wristwatch glinting in the afternoon sun.

Thoughts spun through his pain-addled mind. He tried to haul himself along the ground towards the JCB. Stared around the site, at the piles of grey and brown rubble. At two parked blue lorries' signs – written in the red lettering of his employers. CARTER. A skip filled with junk wood, plaster and cartons that he had removed from some of the building-site rubble that had come in recently. At the green roof of a warehouse on the wharf across the water, on the far side of Shoreham Harbour.

It was dawning on him that going to that barbecue tonight was not going to happen. It was also dawning on him that this was the least of his problems. He crawled again, a few inches nearer the caterpillar tracks of the JCB, then stopped, crying out in pain.

What the hell to do?

He felt in his jeans pocket. The hard lump of his mobile phone was there. Thank God! He eased it out, every movement shooting further pain through his body, dialled 999 and asked for an ambulance.

In his blurred and confused mind he wondered, perhaps, if the paramedic crew might not look up and notice anything amiss.

18

The coded message the dog handler relayed to Adrian Morris via the police radio operator told him the sniffer dog had detected possible explosives in the suspect item.

Morris informed the Match Commander, who updated Oscar-1. He in turn alerted the duty officer at the Explosives Ordnance Division, based in Folkestone – and emailed him a photograph of the camera, lifted from the stadium's CCTV. The EOD, who were normally one hour and ten minutes away, on blue lights, would make an instant assessment from the image, using guidelines set out by NaCTSO, the National Counter-Terrorism Security Office, for the area of evacuation required in the event of a suspected bomb.

Less than one minute later Kundert's phone rang. It was the EOD duty officer. 'Sir, it looks a relatively small object. We have a unit at Gatwick Airport on a training exercise and we've dispatched them – they'll be with you in thirty minutes. We'd like you to immediately clear a minimum area of fifty metres around the object. One hundred would be preferable, but given your situation, we'd be OK with fifty.'

He relayed the information to Morris and everyone present in the Control Room. One hundred metres would mean a total evacuation of the stadium, and a crowd-control nightmare. One potential danger they needed to be mindful of was that of secondary explosive devices, a classic terrorist tactic, where explosives would be placed in the Rendezvous Points to where the evacuated crowds would be directed. For this reason, the club kept these RV points a secret, regularly changing them. If they just evacuated the South Stand, where the suspect camera was, and part of the East and West Stands, they could put the people in safe RV points in the concourse and immediately outside. But more than that and they would have to send them home. Which would mean the match was abandoned and would have to be rearranged.

They all agreed to an immediate partial evacuation. With luck, if the device turned out to be a false alarm, there was a possibility, albeit slim, of recommencing the game.

Kundert called Oscar-1 and informed him of the decision.

Keith Ellis immediately ordered a Roads Policing Unit escort to meet the EOD vehicle at the junction of the Gatwick slip road and the A23, and help speed its journey to the stadium.

As he put down his radio, his phone beeped.

It was Roy Grace.

The two of them went back a long way. Ellis had been Roy's sergeant at John Street police station, when Grace had been a uniformed probationer, nearly twenty years ago.

'What's the update at the Amex, Keith? I'm here with my son.'

'They're not happy with the camera. EOD are on their way.'

Roy turned and looked at Bruno and thought, *I need to get you out, now.*

19

In simulations, it had proven possible to evacuate every stand within eight minutes. Could that be achieved now, Adrian Morris wondered? He prepared to hit the panic button and order the total evacuation of the South Stand and the partial evacuation of the neighbouring West and East Stands – the seating blocks immediately adjacent – and called up on his screen the announcement he was about to read out over the public address. He glanced at his watch, every second feeling like an hour, his throat tight and his mouth dry, then read the words over to himself:

'We regret that due to a security incident, play has been suspended. We are carrying out a partial evacuation in the stadium. Supporters in blocks A–E in the East and West Stands and all supporters in the South Stand are asked to leave in an orderly manner, and follow the instructions of the stewards and the police outside. A decision whether the match will restart will be made as soon as possible.'

The protocol was that he would order all concessions and toilets to be closed, immediately.

Oh God, he thought, staring again at the camera, then at the message, his guts twisting. *Am I doing the right thing?*

But is there any other option?

20

'What is happening, Papa?' Bruno asked his father, seeing him end the call.

Grace looked back anxiously at the camera on the empty seat. 'I don't know, Bruno.'

He was desperate to get his son – and himself – away from that camera. Ellis had confirmed his worst suspicions, that something was wrong about it, about the man who had left it there. Very wrong. And now he had all the information he needed.

But he was in a quandary. If he did rush Bruno out, and a few minutes later the bomb detonated, there would be questions asked. He was a police officer, aware there was a bomb, and he simply fled with his son?

All around him fans were on their feet, roaring, totally focused on the game. They wouldn't take any notice of him if he did try to warn them. But the longer they stayed, the greater the risk that the bomb, if real, would detonate. Any second now, the game would be halted and there would be a public address announcement to evacuate. Surely?

'I think there's a suspect item in the stadium, Bruno,' he said, trying not to look obviously at the camera, but unable to keep his eyes off it.

'Is this a terrorist attack?' Bruno asked.

He squeezed his son's arm. 'Hopefully a false alarm.'

'Will they stop the game for a false alarm?'

'Let's hope it's just that.' Again, he looked anxiously at the camera. Thinking it through. If they evacuated the stadium, could the game be restarted later today? They would have to wait for the Army Explosive Ordnance Division to arrive, and from experience that could be a couple of hours. Once here, the EOD would send a robot to examine the camera and assess it. Then they would either try to disrupt it or, more likely, carry out a controlled detonation of it.

There was no way the match would resume today. And the public relations damage to the city, on its most important match ever, would be immense.

'Don't you think mathematics is important, Papa?' Bruno said, turning to him.

'Mathematics?'

'All these terrorist bombs.' Bruno nodded solemnly. 'They kill sometimes twenty people, sometimes one hundred and twenty. There are twenty-four thousand people killed every week on the roads of the world, in traffic accidents. But no one stops people from driving. There are thirty thousand people in this stadium today. So, if a bomb exploded, maybe one hundred would die. That's a pretty small percentage, don't you think?'

Roy Grace looked down at his son, curious that he knew all this data, and concerned by the matter-of-fact nature of his voice. 'Bruno, I don't consider one unlawful death to be acceptable and nor should you.'

He shrugged, saying nothing.

What exactly was Bruno trying to tell him? Was it his way of dealing with his fear of this new paradigm, the terrorist threat that blighted everyone's lives these days?

Or was something else going on inside his head? A reluctance – or inability – to grasp reality?

'How would you feel if your best friend was blown up, Bruno?'

'Erik?'

Erik was his best friend back in Munich. The two of them played competitive online battle games against each other, most days.

'Yes, Erik.'

'Then I'd be the winner!'

21

No one took any notice of the two men, wearing high-viz jackets over dungarees, pushing a wheelie bin across car park A. Out of immediate sight of the entrance gate, they halted beside a dark-green BMW and opened the rear door. Tipping the bin on its side, the lid opened and they pulled out a young man, roughly, bashing his head on the edge of the door.

He cried out in pain.

They clambered in either side of him, and the waiting driver accelerated away as fast as he dared without drawing attention.

One of them grabbed the boy's phone and tossed it out of the window.

'Hey!' he yelled.

'We don't want to be tracked, asshole!'

'What's going on?'

'Shut the fuck up,' the other man in the rear growled, putting his hand on Mungo's head and pushing him down, roughly, out of sight.

Scared of these aggressive strangers, Mungo did what he was told. He shut the fuck up.

22

Roy Grace looked at Bruno, trying to fathom out his son's thought process.

He glanced back at the camera, then at the glass-fronted Control Room at the far end of the pitch. *Come on, come on, guys, when are you announcing the evacuation, for God's sake?*

Then the words of his training came back to him.

Think the unthinkable.

The *unthinkable* was a bomb detonating at the city's first Premier League game.

He was thinking hard about the guy in the red baseball cap, who had been looking around nervously, then had hurried from the stand, leaving his camera behind.

Thinking about all he knew of terrorist bombs from his training and from the International Homicide Investigators Association conferences he had attended in the USA over the years, many of them covering in detail terrorist bombing atrocities, one thing that had stuck in his memory was that every bomb needed a detonator. It could be a timer that fired a spark that detonated the device. Or a text sent to a receiver that would detonate it. Or impact. Or a motion sensor.

He did a fast assessment. Looked at his watch. It was

less than five minutes or so since the man had left his seat. That ruled out a motion sensor that would set the device off – if it was indeed a bomb. More likely a timer or a text detonator. But the perp would want to be well clear of the stadium grounds before it went off. At five minutes, he would not be, yet.

He made a snap decision.

One he knew might cost him dear. Maybe his career. Perhaps his life.

The words of the former Chief Constable rang in his ears.

Whilst everyone else is running away from danger, we're the people who run towards it.

'Stay here,' he commanded Bruno.

He left his seat, clambered past the rest of the fans in their row, and down the aisle. For a second, he studied the camera on the seat along from the older man and the small boy.

And saw the timer where the shutter-speed setting should have been.

Ticking down as he watched.

1.23

1.22

1.21

23

Ylli Prek hurried in through the doors marked SOUTH STAND WASTE MANAGEMENT – NO UNAUTHORIZED ACCESS. He had to trust his boss's word that the camera outside had been disabled. He entered a foul-smelling room, with a grimy concrete floor and stark tiled walls.

It was filled with green and red bins, mostly with their lids open and overflowing with bagged waste. Labels above them read GLASS, FOOD WASTE, DRY MIXED RECYCLING, GENERAL WASTE.

The last bin on the right, under GENERAL WASTE, had a grey lid that was shut. Ylli opened it, glancing nervously at the door. From the pockets of his tracksuit he removed a bobble hat and scarf. Then he hurriedly stripped off his tracksuit to reveal a blue-and-white Seagulls shirt and blue jeans beneath. He dumped the tracksuit top and bottoms into the bin, along with his cap, and pulled on the bobble hat. Then he walked back to the doors. His boss assured him there would be an evacuation of the stadium, if the bomb did not go off first. All he had to do was to slip out and he would be unnoticed in the panicking crowd all trying to get as far away from the stadium as they could.

But at this moment there was no sound of any panic.

He opened one door a few inches and peered out. He heard the roar of the crowd. The game was still in progress.

He closed the door again, shaking with nerves. Something felt wrong.

24

Roy Grace, holding the heavy camera, frightened it would explode at any moment, turned and raced up the stairs towards the stand exit.

.57

.56

Had to get the device away from the players, from the crowds. He looked around. Where?

Where?

Where was safe?

.52

His brain was racing.

Some years ago, shortly after the stadium construction had been completed, he'd been given a tour of the building, along with several other police officers, by the Head of Safety and Security. There was a tunnel on the far side, through which the players came out to the pitch. It ran past the changing rooms, and out to the players' secure car park at the rear. But that would mean running round the pitch.

Was there a better way?

Then he remembered.

A short distance away was another tunnel. It would probably be deserted now – no members of the public would be there, although there would be plenty above.

Yelling, 'Police!' at two startled stewards in the doorway, he sprinted past them and along past the stark, cream columns of the deserted concourse, narrowly missing colliding with a man who came out of the toilets. He reached the tunnel and turned into it, racing past machinery, utterly terrified the camera would detonate at any moment. Then to his dismay he saw steel security shutters, down, at the far end.

No!

.39

Just as he reached them they began to rise, clattering upwards. Agonizingly slowly.

Come on, come on!

.34

The instant there was enough clearance, he ducked under and through into the wide, deserted area outside the ground.

Should he dump the camera here and run?

The wall of the stadium was a hundred metres or so behind him. Too close.

Had to get it further away. At this distance, the EOD might still want a full evacuation.

.27

He sprinted on towards the station, running down the incline, beneath the railway bridge and towards the deserted university rugby pitch. As he reached the barrier fence, the timer showed nine seconds left. He hurled the camera as hard as he could at the playing fields and watched it tumble through the air, then as it fell towards the grass he threw himself to the ground and waited, breathless, gulping down air.

He heard only the faintest thud.

Nothing more.

A whole minute passed.

Nothing.

He continued waiting, then cautiously stood up and peered across at the camera lying in the grass some distance away. His shirt stuck to his back; he was drenched in sweat.

'Good throw, sir!'

He turned to see a steward in a high-viz jacket.

'Thank you,' he gasped, tugging out his handkerchief to mop away the perspiration running down his forehead.

'You're blooming nuts, if you don't mind my saying, sir!'

Grace grinned. 'I'm OK with that.'

'I was in the army, out in Afghanistan. I once had to lob a grenade that had been tossed into our foxhole. Never managed to throw it as far as that.'

'Yep, well, I just closed my eyes and imagined it was a rugby ball.'

The steward shook his head. 'Tut-tut. Saying that at a football game, sir, that's heresy, that is.'

Several more stewards and police officers rushed out towards them.

25

Mungo, Kipp Brown wondered, watching the game but very distracted by his son's absence.

Where on earth are you, Mungo?

No way would he be missing the game, he had talked of little else for the past three months.

Suddenly he cursed himself. Previously, when Mungo had an iPhone, he and Stacey could always check where he was on the Find My Friends app. Now, with the cheap phone he had bought him to replace it, to teach him a lesson for losing his iPhone, there was no app on which Mungo could be tracked. He hit *Mungo Mob* on his Favourites list. Held it tight to his ear. It was hard to hear the ringing above the roar of the crowd all around him. He heard it ringing once, twice, three times, four times, five times. Then his son's voicemail.

'Yeah, this is the right number for Mungo Brown. Leave a message unless your name's Hugo, in which case go stick your head in a microwave and refry your already fried brains.'

He ended the call and was about to put the phone into his pocket when, through the din, he heard the ping of an incoming text.

Mungo, no doubt, he thought with relief surging through him. Mungo asking him where he was.

He looked at the display.

And froze.

26

In the Amex Control Room, Adrian Morris, on his feet, switching from CCTV monitor to monitor had, to his disbelief, watched Roy Grace run out with the suspect device and throw it into the deserted university playing field.

It was at least three hundred metres from the fortress-like outer wall of the stadium.

The EOD commander had requested only fifty, although with a preference for one hundred. He turned to the Match Commander. 'What do you think, sir?'

'I think Detective Superintendent Grace needs his head examined,' Andy Kundert said.

Morris updated the EOD commander and sent him a new image, with the distance estimation, asking if he would be happy for the game to continue uninterrupted.

He replied in under a minute that he was.

27

Kipp Brown stared at the text, from a number he did not recognize, that had pinged in on his phone. He read it a second time, then a third.

> Mr Brown, we have your son. We have also connected to the Amex Stadium CCTV network. If you call the police, or attempt to speak to any officer in the stadium, you will never see Mungo alive again. We will always know exactly where you are and who you talk to. We will see everything you do and hear everything you say. In the meantime, leave the stadium now, go home and we will contact you soon with our requirements for saving Mungo's life.

28

It felt like a giant, unseen hand had reached out of nowhere and pinched tight all the air around him. Kipp Brown's vision momentarily blurred, as if he had put on someone else's glasses.

Images cascaded through his mind. Newspaper stories of abducted children, television appeals by distraught parents, televised *Crimewatch* reconstructions. Detectives standing in front of microphones, flashlights strobing across their grim expressions, reading out prepared statements.

This could not be happening to him.

Could not.

How could anyone have kidnapped the boy in full view of 30,000 people?

Completely oblivious now to anything that was happening in the game, he excused himself to the clients sitting beside him, told his two colleagues to look after everyone and hurried through the box and out of the door. Shaking and clammy, trying to think clearly what to do, he closed the door behind him and stood in the deserted, carpeted corridor.

How was he going to tell Stacey? She was still hurting and, like himself, probably would always be hurting from the death of their daughter, Kayleigh, four years ago. Ever since, they had both been overprotective of Mungo.

Shit, this could not be happening to them. Please God, no.

Only a few weeks ago he'd watched a documentary about a family whose daughter had been abducted, raped and murdered. The film had shown the distraught parents identifying her body in a mortuary.

Mungo might be irritating at times but he was, at heart, a good kid. Even if he didn't show it all the time, Kipp loved his son to bits.

As did Stacey.

He loved her to bits, too, but she'd had a wall round her, since Kayleigh died, that most of the time he was just not able to penetrate. He tried, and they'd both been in therapy, but the grief had not gone away for either of them. He had thrown himself even harder into his work – and into gambling, in part, for sure, as an escape.

Although born in New Zealand, he had moved with his parents to England when he was eight. Growing up in a modest house in a Brighton suburb, Kipp had always cycled everywhere, to meet friends, to play football and tennis. His bike – and the freedom it gave him – had been a major part of his childhood and he'd tried to encourage his children to do the same. But all that had changed four years ago, on Kayleigh's twelfth birthday. They had bought her a hoverboard. Excitedly testing it in a park near their home, she had shot out of control into the road and under the wheels of a lorry.

Perhaps it was because he'd been affected by the death of his older sister, or perhaps it was just the growing culture of today's kids, but Mungo didn't actually go out that often any more, preferring to stay at home in his room,

Snapchatting and Instagramming and online gaming with his friends, just occasionally meeting up with them to make videos for his YouTube channel.

Kipp worried about the way Mungo seemed at times to be almost a recluse, and his lack of interest in playing any sports, other than at school. He'd had many discussions with Stacey about this. Yes, it was good to know Mungo was home, safe, but wasn't overprotecting him just as dangerous? Stacey disagreed. Kipp had come across statistics that more children were abducted and murdered by strangers in 1936 than in 2016 and that it was the media that spread worry among parents. He had repeatedly tried to impress these figures on Stacey, who wasn't having any of it. So far as she was concerned, ever since Kayleigh's death, beyond the gates of their home was a sewer teeming with all kinds of predators, just waiting for their son to emerge, unescorted.

What was he going to say to her now?

Could he have brought Mungo to a more secure place in the world than this stadium?

Scenes from television dramas, documentaries and news footage all blended together in his mind. The body of a small boy found in reeds beside a river. The body of a boy lying in sand below cliffs, shielded by a crime scene tent. The body of a boy discovered by a dog in remote woods.

He went down the two flights of the staircase and out into the near-deserted South concourse.

Through tear-blurred eyes, he looked at two police officers standing a few yards from him, desperate to speak to them but wary of the grim warning in the text.

He stared back down at his phone, his hands shaking, and tapped a reply. It took several goes before he hit the right letters and symbol.

Who are you?

It wouldn't send. It was blocked.

Mungo taken from here in broad daylight? How? With all these people here?

He looked up and around the deserted area. Heard the sudden, ecstatic roar of the crowd. Had someone scored? It didn't matter. Nothing mattered.

Nothing but Mungo.

Who was watching him and where? He glanced up at the stadium wall. At the row of dark windows, high beneath the finely curved roof. Was it someone behind one of them who had their son?

Thoughts were spinning through his mind like a roulette wheel that, instead of numbers, had options written in each slot between the frets. What would he say to his wife? What were his choices?

Tappity-tap. Phone Stacey.

Tappity-tap. Say nothing and wait for further instructions.

Tappity-tap. Go to a steward and say his son was missing.

Tappity-tap. Ignore the text instructions and inform the police.

He glanced at his watch and did a calculation. It was over two hours since he had seen him. So, where was he? Here in the grounds, still? Or taken away?

How scared was Mungo? Were they hurting him?

Never, in all his life, had Brown kowtowed to bullies or threats. He needed to think this through, fast, take some kind of decisive action.

How?

What?

They were going to send a ransom demand for money.

How much? Everyone in this city thought he was as rich as Croesus, and with good reason – he had always given that impression, as PR for his business. One evening some years ago, at the Snowman Ball, after a particularly good financial year and far too much of a particularly good red wine, he'd stood up during the auction and pledged £100,000 to Chestnut Tree House, the children's hospice that the event was in aid of. It made headlines in the *Argus* newspaper, and from that moment onwards, viewed as a golden couple, he and Stacey were approached for help by an endless succession of charities, as well as people with hard-luck stories – some chancers, some genuine. And, in truth, he found many requests hard to resist.

So many good, small local charities desperately in need of funds. Too many people whose lives were blighted because they were unable to afford the cost of medical treatment or hearing aids or travel to take their dying child to America to Disneyworld. He and Stacey had set up their own foundation and had since given away many hundreds of thousands of pounds. But during the past year, with his finances in meltdown, the donations had ceased. Only temporarily, he sincerely hoped. All the money he'd put into that fund he had taken back to keep the business solvent.

And a huge chunk of that had gone to the casino's bank on Thursday night, he thought ruefully. As it had, it seemed, every time he'd been there just recently.

He looked around and back up at the dark windows. Somewhere close by, someone was looking at him. Smiling perhaps, laughing. Savouring his distress.

Already counting the money they were planning to extort from him.

> We will see everything you do, and hear everything
> you say.

No, actually, you won't, he thought. *You're not quite as clever as you think. No one ever is.*

He hurried towards the toilets, entered a cubicle and locked the door. From his inside jacket pocket, he removed the secure encrypted phone he used for all his confidential transactions with banks and clients, and with it, took a photograph of the text message on his normal phone. Then he switched that phone off, detached the back case and, for good measure, removed the SIM card and battery, placing all the parts on the lavatory seat.

He opened the door a fraction and peeped out to make sure no one had followed him in, and quickly checked that all the other cubicles were empty. Then he dialled.

The call was answered by a female.

29

Inside the Sussex Police Force Control Room, Keith Ellis was relieved that the immediate crisis was over and the match was continuing. Although he wondered about Roy Grace's actions, and the inevitable bollocking he would be facing. Whilst the police brass might publicly laud heroes, privately a reckless action by an officer could be a disciplinary offence – though surely they would realize that Roy could have saved a huge number of lives.

He settled into the tall chair at his screened-off and raised command centre, from which he could oversee the whole of his domain. The ground floor and open mezzanine housed a team of eighty people. Some were serving police officers, dressed in black polo shirts, the rest were civilians, identified by their royal-blue polo shirts with the words POLICE SUPPORT STAFF embroidered in white on their sleeves. Directly in front of him was a bank of CCTV monitors. Using the toggle on his control panel he could instantly view and move any of the cameras in the county.

To his left was the CCTV area, where all of Sussex's cameras were monitored around the clock by a rota of four people. The rest of the two floors was filled with rows of desks and computer terminals, each manned by either a radio controller, who would speak directly to any police unit, or an operator handling the emergency calls. It was the operator's role to grade any of 2,000 emergency calls that came in on an average day into one of four options: *Immediate response*; *Respond within thirty minutes*; *Respond when possible*; *Deal with by phone*.

Keith was feeling the buzz of excitement he always got during a major incident, as he liaised between the pilot of the helicopter, the Match Commander, PC Balkham and the Explosive Ordnance Division Unit which was under police escort to the stadium.

What could ever possibly replace this adrenaline rush after he retired? He thought about one of his predecessors and good mate, Andy Kille, telling him over a pint how much he missed the buzz, and that attending local council meetings in a Scottish village and growing olives in Spain might have their moments, but none that matched situations like this.

Suddenly a FLUM – a flash unsolicited message – appeared on his core screen. Then he saw contact handler Grace Holkham signalling urgently to him, and calling out, 'Sir! Sir!'

'Yes, Grace?' He jumped down and hurried over to her.

'I think we have a kidnap.'

'What details have you got?'

She filled him in quickly.

'Kipp Brown?' he queried.

'Yes.'

'Is that the guy in the radio ads, you know the ones, "Trust Kipp"?'

'I don't know, sir.'

He sat down beside her, pulled on the spare headset and spoke into the microphone. 'Hello, Mr Brown, this is Inspector Ellis. I understand your fourteen-year-old son has gone missing at the Amex Stadium. You've had a text from someone purporting to have abducted or kidnapped him advising you a ransom demand will follow, and you are currently calling from a secure encrypted phone in a toilet in the grounds? Is this correct?'

'Yes, but listen, they've threatened to kill him if I contact the police. Can you keep this completely under wraps?'

A ransom demand indicated to Ellis that this was a kidnap, rather than an abduction, which was at least a positive. Abductions of minors were often for child sexual exploitation purposes and frequently did not end well. But kidnappers had a motive, blackmail. Financial gain with a threat. With kidnappers, there was the ability to negotiate, as kidnappers wanted something.

There were two ways to handle a kidnap: overt, with uniform officers involved, or covert, undercover. With a covert operation, it was crucial not to tip-off the kidnappers that the police were involved. Everything was restricted. Guidelines for any kidnap victim under the age of eighteen were that the operation should be overt, unless circumstances dictated otherwise. But they were just guidelines. Using his judgement from the information available to him at this moment, Ellis opted for covert. Which meant everything was to be restricted to himself and his deputy, otherwise known as Oscar-2. And the report would not, for the time being, be put on the police national computer, because that could mean a zealous uniform police crew in the area turning up at Kipp Brown's house – which was very likely under surveillance now by the kidnappers, if they were well organized.

'Mr Brown, for the moment we will run this as a covert operation. I need some details from you, but first, in case we lose contact for any reason, I want to give you a code word for you to use when you call in or we call you, to ensure it's you, and that you know it's us.'

'A code word?'

'We just need something simple, sir. Shall we say *apple*?'

'*Apple*?'

'Or anything else that would be easy for you to remember.'

'*Apple* is fine.'

'Right, when did you last see your son?'

'About two hours ago, when we arrived here at the Amex.' Brown went on hastily to explain the circumstances. Then as requested by Ellis he read out the text he had received and added, 'Please get him back. Look, the text is very clear about my not contacting the police – if I want to see my son alive again. Perhaps I shouldn't have contacted you, do you think?'

'Sir, you have done exactly the right thing.'

'Have I?'

30

Followed by two stewards and two uniformed police officers, Roy Grace limped across the concourse. He'd pulled a muscle in his right thigh and it was really painful, but that was the least of his concerns at this moment. He was anxious to get back to Bruno, and he wanted to see what the EOD found when they arrived and examined the camera.

As he reached the top of the aisle in the stand, again mopping his face, he could see Bruno, absorbed in the game. His job phone began vibrating in his pocket.

He pulled it out and glanced at the display. No caller ID.

'Roy Grace,' he answered.

A thunderous roar from the crowd drowned out the voice at the other end, as everyone rose to their feet.

'Hang on!' he said, and retreated down the steps into the exit tunnel, where it was quieter. 'OK,' he said, 'I can hear you now.'

'Guv, it's Keith Ellis. Gather you are quite the man. Glad to know you are a live hero and not a dead one.'

'Yup, well I'm quite glad, too. I've spoken to the Match Commander and he's taking control of dealing with the suspect device.'

'Which hasn't yet detonated, despite all your best efforts.'

'Haha.'

In a change of tone to one more serious, Ellis said, 'We have another situation. I have you down as the on-call SIO, is that correct?'

'Yes, tell me?'

'Looks like we've got a kidnap, guv. A man at the Amex arrived with his fourteen-year-old son before the start of the game, and his boy went missing shortly after. He's now received a text warning him not to speak to the police if he wants to see the boy alive again, and that he'll be getting a ransom demand. The boy's under eighteen, so guidelines say this should be run as overt, but my view is we should start covert, though it's up to you and Gold.'

Kidnap. Grace thought fast. He'd done the kidnap negotiator course some years back, and handled a number since. Most reported kidnaps turned out to be scuzzy low-life on low-life jobs over small drugs debts. The last one he'd handled, just a few weeks ago, had been someone kidnapped and beaten for a fifty-pound debt. It had been over within four hours.

Another recent one, that turned out not to be a kidnap at all, was a 999 phone call from a woman in the nearby town of Burgess Hill, who had reported seeing a man bundled into a car and driven off. They were four drug dealers who had gone to the house of a fellow dealer who had ripped them off for a couple of thousand pounds, intending to give him a beating. But he'd set on them with a baseball bat, knocking one of them senseless and badly hurting two of the others. They'd pulled their unconscious accomplice into the car and raced off.

However, something about this felt more serious.

Grace's immediate thought processes were, firstly, what kind of kidnap was this? And, secondly, what were the pros and cons of handling this covertly or overtly? Thirdly, and critically, was to ask himself the question: *What is my job here?*

A question to which he already knew the answer.

To recover the boy safely.

Fourthly, he mentally fast-forwarded to a potential inquest in the Coroner's Court in eighteen months' time. And the grilling that could face him in the dock.

Detective Superintendent, you knew a child's life was at risk if the police were involved. Yet you ignored the request to make this a covert operation?

Policy was a generalization, just that. Policy stated that police officers should not put their lives in danger. But as earlier with the camera, sometimes tough, spur-of-the-moment decisions had to be made. The only thing ultimately that mattered, regarding breaking policy, was that you could justify your actions.

The guidelines were clearly spelled out. If the person taken was below the age of eighteen, the operation needed to be overt, rather than covert – but depending on overall circumstances. In addition, there was an established Child Rescue Alert procedure. If that button was pressed, the media would instantly begin to report it. Did he have enough resources in place to cope with the information, much of it from the public, that would flood in? The appeal would go out on local newsflashes, radio stations, advertising hoardings. Once the button was pushed, it was near impossible to stop the chain of events that would be set in motion.

But if he did that, for sure the kidnappers would know the victim's father had gone against their explicit instruction – and in any event, he didn't have enough information on the boy and his disappearance to instigate the process.

This had to be – for now at least – a covert operation, and he would explain his actions later if he got hauled over the coals – as was likely, knowing his boss, ACC Cassian Pewe.

One of his first priorities was to eliminate any possibility of a hoax. And his immediate thought was whether there was a connection between the bomb threat that was happening here, now, and the missing boy.

He thought it through, rapidly. What were good reasons to link the bomb threat to the kidnap?

One, the Amex had never before had a bomb threat.

Two, there had never before been a kidnap here at the Amex.

Now there was both a bomb scare and a kidnap on the same day.

They had to be connected, surely? Was the bomb scare intended to create a smokescreen for the kidnap? But something about that did not make sense to him.

'Where's the father now, Keith?' he asked.

'Currently in a toilet in the South Stand, nervous of being seen with the police. He's called us on a second, encrypted phone, that he says he has for business purposes.'

'We need an urgent trace on the phone number the text came from, Keith.'

A loud voice right beside him startled Grace.

'What up, Roy – what's going on?'

He turned to see the tall, burly figure of police Crime Scene Photographer Peter Allen standing in the tunnel entrance.

'Hold on one sec, Keith,' he said, then turned to the CSI. 'Peter, I've got an urgent situation. My son, Bruno, is five rows down. Can you tell him I've been called away – and run him home after the game?'

'Sure, Roy. I was just going out for a pee. I'm sitting only a few rows behind with my boys, I know where he is.'

Grace thanked him, then turned his focus back to the Oscar-1 Inspector. 'OK, Keith, what information do you have on the father – who is he?'

'His name's Kipp Brown.'

'Kipp Brown?' Grace frowned. 'As in "Trust Kipp"?'

'Dunno, but it's an unusual name.'

'And this kidnap sounds real to you?'

'Very real.'

'I've met Brown before, he's a piece of work. This could be embarrassing.'

'Oh?'

'Don't worry about it.'

'Guv, we're using the code word *apple* for identification.'

Grace hurried to the South Stand toilets. Entering the gents, he wrinkled his nose at the strong stench of urine and disinfectant. All the cubicle doors except for one were open. He walked up to it, hoping he wasn't in the wrong place, and called out, 'Hello? Mr Brown?'

'Who is that?' said a deep, suspicious voice with the faintest trace of a Kiwi accent.

'Apple,' Grace said first. Then, 'Detective Superintendent Grace, Surrey and Sussex Major Crime Team, sir.'

'You've come fast.'

'I was already in the grounds, watching the game.'

The door opened a crack. A tall, good-looking man, with black hair swept back, greeted him. He reminded Grace, he realized, of the actor Alec Baldwin.

'We've met before,' Brown said, tersely. He looked deeply worried and on edge.

'Yes, we have, back in April.'

There was an awkward moment of silence between them. In April, Brown had briefly been arrested on suspicion of murder, after being incorrectly identified as a suspect, and then released. Brown had been rude and arrogant, Grace remembered.

'Just so you know,' Brown said, coldly, 'I haven't murdered my son.'

'Shall we put the past behind us and focus on now?' Grace suggested.

Brown nodded.

'So, can you give me a recap of what's happened?' He pulled out his Dictaphone and began recording.

The Independent Financial Advisor quickly summarized, and showed him the text on his phone. Grace took a photograph of it. 'You've tried texting back?'

'Yes. It's blocked. The thing is, Detective Superintendent, I don't know what to do – I can't risk Mungo's life by involving you openly.'

'Without looking into all the facts, sir, there seems to be a pretty clear kidnap motive here. You are very high profile in this city, known to be wealthy, and whoever sent this has stated there'll be a ransom. The absolute priority is to get your son back safe. Don't try to deal with this alone, whatever your views on the police. We will deal with this covertly for as long as we can.'

'What if these people kill him?'

'The text you've been sent is unambiguous: whoever has taken Mungo is after your money, that's what this appears to be about, not harming your son. Would you be prepared to pay a ransom? We would do our best to protect your money and recover it, but it could need an initial outlay.'

'Ordinarily, yes. But a ransom could be a problem at the moment.'

'In what way, sir?'

'I have a bit of a cash-flow issue.'

'How much could you raise in a hurry, if you had to?'

'Not a lot. Look, this is confidential, right?'

'Absolutely.'

'I've been going through a bad time – bit of a run of bad luck. My marriage is rocky, I've not been focused on work and I've lost some big clients. I'm mortgaged up to the hilt, I'm on my overdraft limit and my cards are all maxed out.'

'And whoever has taken Mungo is not going to believe that, sir, right?'

'Nope.'

'Are you able to lay your hands on any cash?'

Brown blushed. 'Not legally, quickly, no.'

'Legally?'

'I have a client account containing substantial funds, but I can't touch that.'

'Understood. OK, we have a team of kidnap negotiators and set procedures that work very effectively, and confidentially, but you're going to have to trust us.' Grace looked him in the eye.

'Doesn't seem I have much option,' Brown said.

'The text warns you not to contact the police. But your son was missing for some time before you got this text. It is perfectly reasonable to assume that before receiving it you would have asked stewards and the police here if anyone had seen your son.'

'I guess,' Brown said, reluctantly.

'When exactly did you last see Mungo?'

'About five minutes after we arrived – we were late

because of the traffic. Just as we were heading towards the reception he saw a friend and started chatting.'

'Which reception area?'

'The one for the South Stand.'

'Do you know this friend?'

'Not very well – I've heard him mention his name, Aleksander, he's one of his online gaming pals at Brighton College with him.'

'Alexander?'

'Yes, but spelled with a "k-s".'

'Do you know his last name?'

'No.'

'We'll ask the college. Go on.'

'Then I bumped into a client and got distracted.'

'What's his name?'

'Barry Carden, he's the managing partner of a substantial firm of accountants and business advisors in Brighton.'

Grace checked the spelling of Carden's name with Brown.

'I was chatting to him briefly, then I had to get to my box – where I had a number of clients as guests. I looked around and Mungo had vanished. I wasn't that bothered – he had his ticket and he'd been a bit pissed off with me, so I figured he'd probably made his own way in, and I went on. But he didn't appear. Then I got the text.'

'And you haven't seen him since?'

'No.'

'Your son was angry with you?'

'He lost an iPhone I'd bought him, and to teach him a lesson I got him a cheap replacement. He was angry because he thought I was being mean.'

'Have you tried phoning him?'

'Of course, several times. It rings and goes to voicemail.'

Grace jotted down some notes on his pad, including Brown's address and phone numbers, and the boy's number. 'How would you describe your relationship with your son?'

'He's an antsy teenager. I try to instil some values into him, but his mother dotes on him, spoiling him, telling me I'm being too harsh.' He hesitated. 'We lost our daughter in a road accident four years ago. I guess we both want to keep Mungo wrapped in cotton wool and struggle to accept that he's nearly fifteen and growing into a young man – one of us always drops him at school and picks him up. It's hard –' he shrugged – 'I guess – when you've lost a child.'

'So, your relationship is – how would you describe it?'

'Most of the time like being in a war zone. On occasions like today an uneasy truce. The truth is I love him to bits – but I'm trying to toughen him up, to face the real world.'

Grace noted that down, then looked up. 'Where did you leave your car?'

'In car park A.'

'Can you give me a description of your son?'

'He's fourteen, about to be fifteen. Five foot seven, fair hair with a topknot.' He thought for a moment. 'He's wearing a checked shirt, jeans and trainers – and a Seagulls scarf.' Brown showed him a few photographs on his phone and Grace took them immediately onto his own, via Air-Drop.

'Do you have any other children?'

'No.'

'Have you informed your wife? Are you still living together – you said things were rocky?'

'Yes, we're together. It's been tough since our daughter died. Hopefully we'll eventually get through it.'

Grace smiled, sympathetically. 'Wasn't it Aristotle who

said that the gods have no greater torment than for a mother to outlive her child?'

'If he did, he was right. He could have added the father, too.'

'I'm sorry.'

Kipp nodded, distractedly. 'Thank you.'

'Mungo uses social media?'

'Instagram and Snapchat.'

'With what usernames?'

Brown gave them to him.

'Any others?'

'Not that I'm aware of.'

'He has a computer, presumably?'

'Yes, lives on it. He actually doesn't go out or socialize much, physically, with any of his friends, which my wife encourages. He spends most of his time in his bedroom, gaming with them online.'

Thinking about Bruno, Grace nodded. 'I know what you mean. I've a son a few years younger, and he's the same. We'll need that computer, quickly.'

'Please get him back safely,' Brown pleaded.

'We will, I'm sure, sir. But I'm going to need you to do exactly what I tell you. What I want you to do is go back out now, and act nonchalantly. Do what you've been instructed in the text and go home. I'll contact you in a short while and I'll get a trained kidnap negotiator to guide you.'

'Please keep it under wraps.'

'I'm not going to give you any information about our tactics, Mr Brown. You've asked the police for help, and if you want us to help you, then you'll have to accept that we do know what we are doing and we have a lot of experience in this field. The text message about not speaking to the police is loud and clear. I see and hear it. But if you want us involved, you'll have to trust us. Do we understand each other?'

Brown held up his encrypted phone. 'You'll only use this number, won't you?'

'Doesn't look like the other's much use at the moment,' Grace said, glancing down at the iPhone on the toilet seat with its SIM card and battery next to it.

Brown gave him a thin, tearful smile. 'You'll get him back, you will, won't you? You'll find him and bring him back? I love him. He can be a right little sod sometimes, but I love him so much.'

'We'll do everything we possibly can to ensure he comes back to you safely and quickly. We'll be getting an undercover team into your house to help you as soon as possible. If the kidnappers contact you again before that's happened, stall them as best you can.'

'How?'

'You're a successful businessman. I'm sure you've stalled people before. Think of something plausible. Tell them you have a client with you and ask them to call you back in an hour. Anything. OK?'

'I'll do my best.'

31

Grace waited in the toilets for some minutes after Kipp Brown had reassembled his phone and left. A number of thoughts raced through his mind, the first being if someone was going to kidnap a teenage boy, why on earth do it here, where there were more security officers and CCTV cameras than anywhere else in the city. But if, as Brown said, his mother kept him wrapped up in cotton wool, and they always took him to school and picked him up themselves, perhaps there weren't many opportunities for the kidnappers. And there was an old police maxim, that if you wanted to hide something, the best place was in plain sight. This stadium could not be more in plain sight.

He dictated some notes to himself, then made a series of phone calls to the small, tight number of his team members he would need.

This was the so-called 'Golden Hour' – the immediate period following a crime, and particularly a crime-in-action, when the trail of evidence would still be fresh. Mungo Brown disappeared possibly up to two hours ago. How far away could he be now?

Oscar-1 had informed the Force Gold, Superintendent Jason Tingley. The Superintendent, like Grace, had considerable previous kidnap and abduction experience, the

100

highest profile of which was a school teacher who had run off to France with an under-age pupil. In response to Tingley's questions, Grace assured the Superintendent that in his view this was not a hoax. As Gold, it was Tingley's role to set the strategy. Crucially, he supported Grace's decision to stay covert.

In conjunction with Gold, Grace decided against sealing off an area with road blocks, because not only could that alert the kidnappers that the police were involved, but in two hours they could be many miles away in any direction – even, God forbid, out of the country by now. The photographs of Mungo Brown Grace had taken from his father's phone were immediately circulated to Sussex Police and the neighbouring counties of Surrey, Hampshire, Kent as well as British Transport Police, and to all officers and border control staff at airports and harbours, on an all-ports alert. It was on a sightings-only basis and no media were to be told.

Roy Grace left the toilets and hurried round the deserted concourse. *Clear the ground under your feet,* was one of the first rules for any major crime investigation. Flashing his warrant card at stewards, he made his way up to the Security Control Room.

Morris, Kundert, Balkham and Branson were all in the command centre. At this moment, they were looking at one of the CCTV monitors, at the close-up of the camera in the long grass. As soon as they saw Grace, they gave him a round of applause.

'You are fucking nuts, boss!' Glenn Branson said.

'Thank you for what you did, Roy.' Adrian Morris smiled at him.

'I had my son with me,' Grace said. 'I didn't see any option.'

'My son's here, too, with my father,' Morris replied. 'The other supporters will never know how close to disaster they were. Thank you, again. You'll be a bloody hero in the *Argus* on Monday!'

'You are, like, going to get such a bollocking from ACC Pewe,' Branson said.

'Bring it on!' Grace replied, feistily. 'We have another major problem on our hands right now.' He nodded to the police officers and to Morris. 'Let's go next door and I'll update you.'

He led the way into the small private room adjoining the Control Room, then informed the team, and explained it was critical that the enquiry into Mungo Brown's kidnap remain covert at this stage.

The game on the pitch below them was on a knife edge but none of the team in the Control Room was watching.

'Boss,' DI Branson said, 'if someone was planning to kidnap Mungo Brown, why here? It doesn't make sense to have taken him here – to have gone to such an elaborate plan right under the noses of all the security guards and cameras.'

'I don't completely agree with you,' Grace said. 'There are reasons why it might make sense. And I'm not making any assumptions, but one hypothesis is that the bomb scare and the kidnap are related.'

He knew from long experience that the simplest and most obvious was usually the right answer.

Was it the case here?

The simplest and most obvious explanation was that the bomb scare was a smokescreen for the kidnap of Mungo Brown. But Glenn Branson's point that it didn't make sense to kidnap someone in a place where there were more CCTV cameras than anywhere else in the city, or the whole county, was well made – except he wouldn't have known how protected the boy was by his parents.

The DI shook his head, repeating himself. 'Boss, there must be plenty of opportunities for someone planning to kidnap the kid that are better than this.'

'Maybe, and I'm going to task someone with finding that out, Glenn. I'm going to set some parameters and policy. Ade, I need all CCTV footage in the thirty minutes before kick-off, and since, checked. If Mungo Brown did enter the stadium, you'll have it logged somewhere?'

'Every turnstile has a barcode scanner, Roy, and all the season tickets are barcoded. Juveniles flash a different colour. If the lad went into the stadium, we'll be able to find out which entrance.'

'If you can do that quickly. And if it showed he entered the stadium, I want it searched top to bottom in case he's being held here, somewhere.'

'Right.'

Grace looked at Branson. 'Glenn, I know this is a day off for you, but not any more, I'm going to need you as my principal negotiator – you've done the course, haven't you?'

'I have, boss.'

'I'm setting up my team in the Silver Command Intel suite at HQ and you'll keep in contact with me there.'

'Understood.'

'We know that Mungo Brown and his father arrived here just under two hours before kick-off. Both of them must be captured on CCTV. The immediate priority is to locate the images, and then see what we get from there. If he has been taken from the grounds, it has to show up on a camera,' Grace said. Then he turned to Morris.

'Ade, take control from the club's standpoint. All the time we've got people here, we have potential witnesses –

and maybe the perpetrators. At the end of the game can we make an announcement saying if Mungo Brown is in the stadium, can he go to Reception to meet his father.'

He toyed with having the exits managed, but realized that with the number of people here that would be an impossible task.

The Control Room door opened and a tubby steward in a hi-viz tabard came in, puffing with exertion, holding up a mobile phone. He went straight across to Morris.

'Sir, we just found this lying near the entrance to the car park.'

32

Adrian Morris took the phone, then immediately passed it to Grace.

'One of my colleagues spotted it being thrown out of the window of a green BMW that left the car park at high speed about fifty minutes ago,' the steward said to Morris.

'Did he get a description of the car or its index number?' Roy Grace asked him.

'Yes, sir!' the attendant said, proudly fishing out a scrap of paper from his pocket and handing it to him. 'It was a 2013 BMW 5 Series. And he got part of the plate.'

'E 13 DU,' the Detective Superintendent read out. Fishing a pair of gloves from his pocket, he tugged them on and took the phone. It was a basic Samsung. He was aware of the correct procedure that a mobile phone should be handed immediately to the Digital Forensics Unit, but there was no time for that. Later, he would write up his decisions in his Policy Book.

He pressed the button to pull up the address book. Scrolling through the few names, he came to 'Aleksander', and remembered his conversation with Kipp Brown.

He scrolled down through the address list and came to another name, 'Dad'. There were two numbers. He recognized the second as the number for Kipp Brown's encrypted phone, and pressed to dial it.

Moments later he heard Kipp Brown's voice, sounding overjoyed with relief.

'Mungo! Where are you? Are you OK? I've been worried out of my wits. Where are you? Are you safe?'

'Apple,' Grace said. Then went on, 'Mr Brown, I'm afraid this is not your son, this is Detective Superintendent Grace.'

Kipp Brown's voice sounded like he had fallen off a cliff. 'Oh God. Don't, please don't say—'

'Sir, I'm calling from a Samsung mobile phone that was found in the car park at the Amex a short while ago.'

'What? How did it get there?'

'Could your son have dropped it?' Grace said, tactfully, remembering Brown had told him Mungo had lost his previous phone.

'Knowing him, very possibly.'

'Right, sir. As I said, go straight home and we'll be back in touch.'

'I'm in my car, on my way there now. Don't you have any CCTV?'

'That's being checked now, sir.'

'Shit,' Brown said. 'Shit, shit, shit.'

Grace waited for his outburst to finish. Then he said, 'We're going to find your son.'

'You know what?' Kipp Brown said. 'It would be nice if I had some confidence in you people – but the way I've been treated by you in the past doesn't give me much.'

A bit rich, Grace thought privately, considering that on their previous encounter Brown had lied to him and his team. 'I'm going to do all I can to restore your confidence, sir.'

'Yeah, right.'

Immediately he ended the call, Grace phoned through to Keith Ellis, asking him to have checks done on all ANPR – Automatic Number Plate Recognition Cameras – that the BMW might have pinged, giving him the part of the registration number he had: Echo One-Three Delta Uniform.

Then he began to study the phone more carefully.

Being careful not to delete or change anything, first he looked for text messages. But there were none. Strange, he thought, but remembered that his own son, Bruno, only really used Instagram and Snapchat to communicate. There wasn't much functionality on the phone at all. Certainly, Kipp Brown was teaching his son an effective lesson about losing his expensive iPhone. Except that this cheap device, with apparently little data on it, was not helpful to them now.

He checked for voice messages. There was one.

'*Where are you, tosspot?*'

It was from a well-spoken boy. Roy guessed him to be around Mungo Brown's age. The phone's voice announcement timed it at 3.32 p.m. today. The caller's number was withheld.

Was it Aleksander – the youngster his father had seen him talking to before he vanished? He remembered Kipp Brown's words, a short while ago:

About five minutes after we arrived – we were late because of the traffic . . . he saw a friend and started chatting.

Except that didn't chime with the message.

'*Where are you, tosspot?*' That indicated this boy was waiting for him, expecting him. Then again, maybe Mungo hadn't bothered telling his father his friend was going to be there – it didn't sound as if son and father were getting on too well at the moment.

A few minutes later, Keith Ellis called Grace back. 'Guv, vehicle index Echo One-Three Delta Uniform?' the Oscar-1 repeated back to him.

'Yes, yes.'

'The information I have is that a 2013-registered BMW, identical green colour and model, was reported stolen in Crawley sometime between 2.30 a.m. and 11 a.m. this morning. And this is interesting, Roy, another identical BMW with the index Echo X-ray One-Three Bravo Delta Uniform – which is a match – was written off last month following an accident.'

'Sounds like this stolen BMW might have the false plates that match the totalled one,' Grace said. It was a frequent trick when cars were stolen.

'It does, guv.'

'Nice work, Keith, let me know when you have any updates.'

As Grace ended the call, the CCTV operator turned to him and said, 'I've just pulled off the full number plate of that BMW you had a partial for, from a camera in car park A.' He read it out to him.

33

BA flight 2731 had finally taken off nearly two hours late from Tenerife. It now touched down at London Gatwick Airport just after 6.30 p.m. local time. Martin and Jane Diplock were upset that, even allowing for a speedy passage through passport control and baggage reclaim, after going home to freshen up and change, they were unlikely to arrive at Christopher's birthday dinner much before 8.30 p.m.

But at this moment, Jane Diplock was more worried about the young Albanian woman seated beside her. The woman was sweating profusely and her pupils were dilated. Just a few minutes earlier she had vomited into a sick bag.

'Would you like me to ask one of the cabin crew to get you a wheelchair?' Jane asked her, kindly.

Florentina Shima looked at her, vacantly. 'No, thank you, I fine. I fine.'

All the same, the retired couple insisted on staying close to her as they navigated the seemingly endless airport corridors. Martin and Jane each took one of her arms, as her walk became increasingly unsteady.

The couple were very seriously concerned about her as they approached the passport control. Reaching the point where they were due to be separated, the Diplocks going into the E-Passport line and the young Albanian woman into the long, snaking queue for non-EU passport holders, Jane Diplock again asked her if they should find someone to assist her.

But the young woman vehemently rejected the suggestion.

'I'm fine, I'm good. OK? Thank you! Nice to meet you!'

Wishing her well, they parted and said they would see her down in baggage reclaim.

Florentina joined the queue.

She was feeling terrible. Her vision blurring. She looked at her watch, calculating.

Her head swam. She was feeling increasingly giddy, remembering something Frederik had told her. *Watch the time. Watch the time. Sixteen hours, the absolute maximum.*

The clock had started ticking early this morning, Albanian time.

Two hours of delay.

She was fast approaching sixteen hours.

But she was nearly there. Nearly. Nearly. Just one person in front of her and she would be at the passport desk, where there was a nice-looking Border Control Officer, wearing a hijab.

The officer's name was Shakira Yamin. As with all Border Control Officers on passport duty, she had been trained to look up and look ahead. To keep a constant, vigilant eye on everyone in their queue, to spot anyone loitering, hesitant, or whose body language was nervous.

Five minutes earlier, she had already clocked the elegant, attractive young woman with a pallid complexion, unsteady on her feet and looking at her watch anxiously.

The floor seemed to be moving beneath Florentina, as if she was standing on a conveyor belt.

The Border Control Officer in the hijab turned into two people. Then four. Then back to two again.

To her horror, Yamin saw the young woman, now one back in the line, fall sideways. She lay on the floor, her face sheet white and clammy, like a heart-attack victim.

Yamin hit the panic button beneath her desk, summoning the airport emergency medical team and her own security team.

34

Kipp Brown drove home from the Amex almost on auto-pilot, immersed in thought. He hit the clicker for the gates and drove in, round the wide driveway, his tyres crunching on the gravel. He circled in front of the lawn, which was dominated by a mature monkey-puzzle tree, and pulled up in front of the house. Stacey's Volvo wasn't there; a small relief in one way as she would become distraught the moment she knew. That was one thing less to face right at this moment, while he tried to keep his thoughts focused.

But just to check, he pressed another clicker to open the garage double doors. Her convertible Mercedes SL was in there, but not her Volvo. Then he remembered – she was playing in a tennis tournament at her club in Hove, the Grasshoppers. Several deep barks came from inside the house, from their German Shepherd, Otto.

Despite the evening sunshine, Wingate House had a dark and foreboding feel. When they'd come to view it, ten years ago, Kipp had instantly fallen for its imposing, baronial look. The 1920s seven-bedroom Edwardian mansion made a statement. One of the grander houses in the city, with its snooker room, basement cinema, swimming pool and hard tennis court, it would be a showcase for his success, as well as a great place to entertain clients. And a far cry from the tiny house where he had grown up.

Back then, when Stacey had cautiously asked him whether they could really afford to buy this place, he had assured her yes, they could comfortably afford it. His business was growing rapidly, profits piling up; he couldn't put a foot wrong. He really believed he had the Midas touch, and so did his clients. Word of mouth spread and spread. He became the go-to man in Brighton if you needed a mortgage, wanted the best return on investment funds or a good deal on the numerous other services he offered. Anything you required in the world of finance, you could 'Trust Kipp' to get it for you.

Back in his schooldays at Dorothy Stringer, his best friend was Charlie Lang. Charlie's dad, Neil, was a well-known bookmaker. They lived in a fancy house, with sea views, in Brighton's ritzy Tongdean Avenue, and his father drove a two-tone beige and brown Rolls. Whenever Kipp went there for tea, Charlie's dad would regale him with racing stories about big winnings.

When Kipp was nine, his father had died suddenly from a heart attack. Kipp liked to boast he got his taste for gambling, whether on the stock market, the horses or the gaming tables, from his mother. His earliest childhood memories were of her forever sat in front of the television, fag dangling from her lower lip, the racing pages of the *Mirror* open on her knees, shouting at the horses on the screen. Or of her coming back from bingo after a big win and throwing an armful of notes into his bedroom. He didn't know then that she was gambling away the life insurance money she had received after his father's death.

His early childhood was constant feast or famine. Days when there was nothing to eat in the house except mouldy bread and the scrapings from an already scraped-out Marmite jar. And other, rarer days, when his mother had a big win and they'd trundle a trolley around a supermarket, his mother telling him to grab anything he wanted and put it in.

At some stage of his childhood, he could not pinpoint exactly when – perhaps around the age of fifteen – he'd begun to realize he had a talent for mathematics. He started taking an interest in the way his mother bet on the horses. And on bingo. From tips he gleaned from Charlie Lang's dad, he found himself giving her advice on odds, and her winnings became more frequent and bigger.

He left school early, having talked himself into a job as a bookie's runner with Neil Lang. He did this for a couple of years, making what he thought was good money at the time. Then, at a race meeting at Brighton Racecourse, he got chatting to a big punter, called Steve Crouch, who seemed to take a shine to him and offered him a job.

Crouch was boss of a successful Brighton Independent Financial Advisor and Wealth Management company. Over the next few years, Kipp rose from the bottom rung of the ladder to become one of their top advisors, before deciding at the age of twenty-eight to go it alone. Now, seventeen years on, he was one of Crouch's most formidable competitors. Or had been.

It seemed sometimes as if for years he'd been blessed with almost magical powers of prophecy, that any investment he made for his clients came good, way above the annual average for fund managers; then, suddenly, after Kayleigh's death, the wheels fell off.

He knew the reasons. He had begun drinking heavily, and gambling heavily, too, as a way of taking his mind off his grief. Stacey had retreated into a shell, not letting him touch her for over a year. Then, stupidly, he'd had a fling with an old flame he had bumped into by chance. Sadly, a short while after, the woman had been found murdered, and he was briefly a suspect. Although he'd tried to keep it under wraps, Stacey had found out. He'd been trying to repair the damage by regularly coming home with flowers or a surprise gift of a piece of jewellery or tickets to see a favourite band of hers, but with little effect, so far.

His wealth management performance – once an impressive 14 per cent year-on-year growth for his clients' money – had diminished to just 2 per cent last year, barely above bank interest rates. In his view, part of the business of wealth management was pure gambling. You bet your clients' money for them at different levels of risk, which they dictated. From the high risk, gambling on something like coffee bean crops being abundant or failing, down to the more mundane areas, such as fixed-interest government bonds. In this currently turbulent world there were huge gains to be made – or lost – on commodities, and on metals like gold. He'd managed throughout this past year to get most things badly wrong. On some occasions, spectacularly wrong.

As Stacey had become increasingly distanced and withdrawn, he'd found solace in gambling. Online poker and blackjack, and sometimes online roulette, too. Gambling had always been his way of relaxing. And always remembering the grand lifestyle of Neil Lang's family.

These days his favourite places, locally, were the Premier Bar at Brighton Racecourse on race days – doing the maths, placing accumulator forecasts with the Tote on race meetings around the country – or playing the tables at Brighton's Waterfront Casino. Just as in his early days in financial management he'd had that golden touch, it had always been the same with the casino. Stacey used to love coming with him back then, agog at how he always seemed to walk away from a roulette wheel thousands of pounds up, and on more than one occasion, hundreds of thousands.

Not any more. His magic touch, if it was ever that and not simply a long winning streak, had deserted him. Online, in the casino, at Brighton Racecourse and, even more crucially, at work. He blamed it on his marital problems distracting him.

But his clients, many of whom had entrusted their entire life savings to him, weren't interested in his marital problems.

And when the ransom demand came in, as surely it would, the people who had taken Mungo wouldn't be interested in his marital problems either.

35

Just when Keith Ellis thought his shift couldn't get any more hectic, it did.

It began with another FLUM, flashing in red on his screen. An emergency that one of the call-takers here would handle. Many of these 999s turned out to be time-wasters – drunks or children misdialling or some idiot whose pet parrot had gone AWOL. But, equally, often the emergency was real. He would never forget one that had been given to him to handle, a distraught young woman telling him her boyfriend owed money for drugs and that he would have his kneecaps done if he didn't pay.

Followed by the screams of both of them as the threat had been carried out.

'Sir!'

He turned to his deputy for the shift, Matt Johns, a former Chief Petty Officer who had been a civilian call-handler for the past twenty-one years, and one of the most experienced members of staff here.

'Yes?'

'Got a paramedic from the ambulance service attending an accident at Shoreham Harbour. He's just called in to say that he's seen a suspected human body part in the bucket of a JCB digger.'

'Oh yes?' Ellis said, a tad cynical. He'd dispatched a unit two weeks ago to a construction site where a suspected human arm bone – a humerus – had been discovered. Subsequently, on examination, forensic archaeologist Lucy Sibun had informed him it was the leg bone – tibia – of a sheep.

'It looks like a human arm, sir.'

'Never did anyone any 'arm, did he?' Ellis replied.

His gallows humour fell on deaf ears.

'Armless, eh?' he tried again.

To be greeted by more silence.

'Before I send an on-call SIO, can you give me a good reason for the paramedic's suspicion? That it's not just the bone of a cow or a pig or a sheep?'

'Yes, sir. None of those animals wear wristwatches. Not as a general rule.'

36

A white lorry, with the logo and name PORTSLADE DOMES-
TIC APPLIANCES, drove slowly down Dyke Road Avenue, the
exclusive residential street that ran along the spine of
the city, dividing Brighton from Hove.

The driver, Mike Roberts, was known affectionately to
his colleagues, on account of his muscle mass, as Gorilla.
His colleague in the cab with him, Iain Scotland, was short,
with no neck and the build of a bulldog. Scotland had
begun his working life as a removals man, before a major
change of career. Both men had been selected as suitable
for this job for their physical strength – which they were
about to need.

Dressed in the company uniform of green T-shirts with
logos front and back, and blue dungarees, they were travelling slowly, peering at the house numbers and names as
they cruised past gated mansion after mansion.

'This is where I'd live if I won the lottery,' said Roberts.

'Yeah?' said his colleague. 'Well I won it three weeks ago,
but I still can't afford a pad like one of these.'

'You won the lottery, Iain?'

'Yup.'

'You never told me! How much?'

'Thirty-seven quid.'

The driver laughed. 'And how much did that cost you?'

'A fiver a week for the last six years, if you want to know, Mike.'

He did some quick mental arithmetic. 'Fifteen hundred quid. Not a great return on your investment. I read you've more chance of being hit by lightning than winning the jackpot.'

'You did? I read you've more chance of being killed by a goat.'

'Goats kill people? How?'

'With their horns, I suppose.'

'I'd better beware of the missus in future.'

Iain grinned, then peering across through the driver's window, he suddenly called out, 'That's it, there, Wingate House, on the right!'

The driver braked, switched on the hazard lights and pulled sharply over to the left, blocking the cycle lane. Opposite them was a substantial residence, set well back from the road, with an in-and-out circular gravel driveway and tall wrought-iron gates. An ostentatious matt-black Porsche was parked close to the front entrance.

Opening his door, Iain Scotland said, 'I'll run across and get him to open the gate.'

He jumped down, then looked up and down the road, taking in everything with his trained eye. There was a small blue van some distance up the road, but no parked vehicles close, and no one obviously lurking anywhere on the ground or up in any of the trees. He crossed over, up to the left-hand gate, and pressed a button on the entry panel, which had a camera lens above it. After a short delay, a wary-sounding voice said, 'Hello?'

'Apple,' Iain said. Then immediately added, 'Delivery for Mr Brown.'

After a brief pause the gates began, jerkily, to open.

He stepped out into the middle of the road, with his hands raised to stop the traffic, and the lorry began to swing across it. He walked backwards through the gates, waving the vehicle in. The driveway was wide enough for the lorry to pull up alongside the Porsche.

There was the sound of barking from inside the house. As the hydraulic hoist at the rear of the vehicle began lowering a massive cardboard box, seven feet high by four feet wide, to the ground, the front door opened and a tall man emerged, restraining a large German Shepherd by its collar. 'It's OK, Otto, it's OK!'

'Mr Kipp Brown?' Iain Scotland enquired.

'Do you have any news?' Brown asked anxiously.

'I'm afraid not, sir. May we bring this in?'

'Yes – you OK with dogs?'

'Fine, sir,' he said, presenting him with an electronic pen for signature. 'The fridge-freezer you ordered.'

Brown took it, giving him the faintest smile of acknowledgement, and scrawled his name between the two black electronic lines.

Then he stood in the doorway, still holding the dog, as the two men manhandled the vast package onto a porter's trolley.

'Shit!' one said.

'Fuck!' said the other.

They trundled it to the bottom step, then swearing and cursing more, they manhandled it up all three steps to the front door, inside and into the hallway, where they stopped and levered the box off.

The hall was elegantly lined with framed black-and-white photographs, some portraits of Kipp Brown, his wife and their children, one of a pretty young girl in a riding hat, astride a horse, one of a much younger Mungo, standing with a fishing rod in one hand and a large fish, and several atmospheric ones of the skeletal remains of the West Pier.

Kipp Brown shut the door behind them, but continued to keep a restraining hand on the dog's collar.

'Shit, you are heavy bastards!' said Mike Roberts, addressing the package. Then both he and his colleague produced their warrant cards and showed them to Brown.

'Detective Constable Roberts and Detective Constable Scotland of Surrey and Sussex Major Crime Team, sir.'

'Nice of you to bring me a fridge I didn't order. Just what I need,' Brown replied sourly.

Scotland produced a Stanley knife from his dungaree pocket and proceeded to work the blade carefully down one side of the package to create an opening.

Brown was astonished to see a huge black man-mountain with a shaven head step out, immaculately attired in a sharp suit. He was followed by a slim, tall man in his twenties, also suited. Otto, startled, barked at both of them.

The man-mountain looked warily at the dog, then grinned at the creature. 'I reckon you're just a big wuss, aren't you?' He knelt and stroked him. 'What's your name, boy?'

'Otto,' Brown replied.

'Otto, you and me are going to be fine,' he said and stood up. He pulled a warrant card out and held it up. 'Detective Inspector Glenn Branson, Surrey and Sussex Major Crime Team, sir, and this is my colleague, Acting Detective Sergeant Jack Alexander. We're your covert negotiation team – and I'm desperate for a pee.'

Brown pointed towards the end of the hall. 'Last door on the left.'

Branson hurried off.

Brown looked quizzically at the three remaining police officers. 'So, where's my fridge?' he asked sarcastically.

'Couldn't fit it in the box, sir,' Scotland said, apologetically. He pointed a finger towards the disappearing figure of Branson. 'That big bugger took up most of the space.'

37

Twenty minutes after Scotland and Roberts departed, taking Mungo's laptop with them, as well as a clone of Kipp Brown's phone, the two detectives installed themselves safely out of sight in the windowless basement cinema room of the Browns' house. They were setting up what, they assured Kipp Brown, was a secure encrypted comms system and intercept on all his phones.

In the kitchen, fighting tears and wondering what he would say to Stacey when she arrived home any moment now, Kipp boiled the kettle to make the two detectives the coffees he'd offered. As he was about to pour, Otto barked.

'What is it, boy?'

He heard the front door open.

For an instant, his heart jumped and he ran into the hall, desperately hoping it might be Mungo.

It was Stacey.

He followed the dog along the hallway to her.

Her blonde hair, which she used to wear long and flowing, framing her pretty face, had recently been chopped into a severe, razored style, with a sweeping fringe lying to one side. It made her look quite butch, despite the very feminine tennis whites she was wearing.

'Hi,' she said robotically. He leaned forward to kiss her

on the lips, but as she always did now, she turned her face, offering him only a cheek.

'How was the tournament?'

'Fine. Nicky and I won.'

'Great! Well done.'

There was no reaction back.

He smiled, awkwardly. 'Remind me who Nicky is?'

'You've met her several times – Nicky Felix – she runs a company called Box2. That green dress I wore to Ladies Day at Ascot came from her.'

'Ah, right. That was lovely.'

'She's doing really well – selling around the globe. Might be a possible client for you.'

'Yep, good thought.'

'So, it's just you and me and Mungo tonight,' she said. 'A nice romantic evening on our own,' she added, with a hint of sarcasm. 'How was the football – who won?'

He stared at her dumbly.

'Hello? The football – the big game?'

He didn't know who had won, he realized. He'd been so preoccupied since leaving the stadium, he hadn't thought to check.

She waved her hand in front of his face. 'Hello? Are you OK?'

'I – I—' he faltered.

'Did Brighton win – the Seagulls?'

He stared back in a daze, helpless.

She peered at him more closely. 'Your eyes are red – have you been crying?'

He looked down at the floor, lost for words. His brain was racing but couldn't get traction. He didn't know what to say to her.

The colour began draining from her face. 'What is it?'

she said. 'What's the matter? What's wrong?' Then, suspiciously, 'Is it Mungo? Has something happened to him? Where is he?'

It took him a while before he could look her in the eye. 'I don't know, Stace,' he said.

'What? What do you mean?' She stared at him, bewildered. 'What do you mean you don't know where your son is? Where is he, Kipp, where the hell is he?'

'When I last saw him, he was at the stadium, talking to a school friend, I think.'

'You *think*? Which school friend was he talking to?'

'Aleksander.'

'So where is he now?'

'I—'

'Where is he?' She was trembling, her voice quavering. 'Where is he? He's all right, please, he's all right, isn't he?'

He wasn't sure what to say. What could he say? 'I – don't know, babe.'

'You don't *know*?'

He nodded, lamely.

'What do you mean? You took him to the football – you've lost him?' She looked totally panic-stricken, her eyes darting around wildly as if she didn't know which way to look or turn.

'I bumped into Barry Carden and was chatting to him. I thought Mungo was right by me with his friend. Remember Barry?'

'That's just so typical of you. All our time together, whenever you've seen someone you might do business with, you forget me, ignore your family, and home in on them. Am I right? So you've just left him there – left him at the stadium somewhere and come home?'

Then suddenly Stacey looked past him, startled, as if

she had seen a ghost, and he heard Detective Inspector Glenn Branson's voice.

'Could you show me where the fuse box is, sir?'

'Excuse me, who are you?' Stacey rounded on him, confused. 'You're not our normal electrician.'

Kipp Brown took a deep breath, then told her everything.

38

On the A23, two miles north of Brighton, Mike Roberts, driving the PORTSLADE DOMESTIC APPLIANCES lorry as fast as he dared safely, saw strobing blue lights in his mirror and heard a siren. He pulled into a lay-by a short distance ahead, putting on his hazard flashers. A police motorcycle pulled up in front of him.

The rider dismounted and hurried up to the passenger door. Iain Scotland passed Mungo Brown's laptop out of the window. The rider ran back to his machine, put the computer in his pannier and raced off into the distance.

Fifteen minutes later, ignoring the building's slow lift, the police motorcyclist, holding the boy's laptop and the clone of his father's phone, ran up to the second floor of Haywards Heath police station. He passed the hall of fame – or notoriety – of convicted villains, on the wall, and rang the buzzer at the entrance to Digital Forensics – as the High Tech Crime Unit was now named.

Aiden Gilbert, a stocky, energetic civilian with short dark hair turning to grey, and dressed in a blue T-shirt, jeans and trainers, greeted him. He led him in and through to the large, open-plan office, to his desk where he signed a receipt, for chain-of-evidence purposes, for the laptop and the clone. With him were three colleagues, similarly casually dressed, Daniel Salter, Jason Quigley and Shaun Robbins, a retired police officer who had returned as a civilian to this unit.

Quigley immediately plugged a USB into a port on Mungo's Mac, while Salter set to work on the phone, to identify the source of the text. The motorcyclist left and the unit members waited patiently for the ten minutes that it took for the contents of the computer to upload. They had been instructed to look, urgently, for all communications Mungo Brown had had in the past four weeks, on email and on social media.

When the download was complete, Quigley plugged the USB into his own system and immediately, with the others peering over his shoulder, began studying his large Apple Mac screen.

This unit was one of the very few in Sussex Police to have escaped the current round of budget cuts, and had recently benefitted from extra funding. They had also benefitted from the Proceeds of Crime Act, under which any computer seized from someone convicted of a drugs or pornography offence was ordered by the courts to be confiscated and destroyed – or used for crime-fighting purposes. Digital Forensics had gained several high-powered Macs and large screens from this, including the one he was now using.

Mungo Brown's mail began to appear. Seconds later they were up to date.

The most recent of them, sent at 2.40 p.m. this afternoon, was addressed to Aleksander Dervishi.

See u at the game. It's gonna be lit!

39

In Roy and Cleo's isolated cottage close to the village of Henfield, a few miles north of Brighton, Bruno, home from the match having been dropped off by Peter Allen, was upstairs in his room, pounding away on his drums. To Cleo's relief he had the acoustic pads on and the sound was tolerable.

Noah, now thirteen months old, was sleeping in his cot in his room. Cleo, who ran the Brighton and Hove City Mortuary, was on-call this weekend. She was sitting on the sofa with their nanny, Kaitlynn Defilice, watching an episode of *Celebrity Pointless*, both of them munching their way through a gigantic bag of popcorn. Roy had called, sounding stressed, telling her he didn't know when he would be home and not to expect him back until very late, if at all tonight. She knew the score when there was any major crime investigation, and even more so when it was the kidnap of a youngster.

She felt for the family of the teenager who had been taken, and one of the many things she admired about Roy was just how much he cared for all the victims and their families. In all probability, he would be working through the night and crash out for a few hours in his office. She was in for a long night, too, as she had been notified by a

Coroner's Officer that body parts had been found at a re-cycling depot at Shoreham Harbour and a Home Office pathologist was in attendance at the site. At some point during the evening she would be getting a phone call requesting her to attend to recover the parts to the mortu-ary. But with luck that would be much later, and she'd get to the end of the show, at least.

But just a few minutes later her work mobile phone rang.

'Cleo Morey,' she answered, doing a good job of mask-ing her reluctance.

Although married to Roy Grace for nearly a year now, she had retained her maiden name, to avoid confusion at work.

'Hi, Cleo.' It was another Coroner's Officer she had worked with on a number of occasions, Michelle Websdale, in mid-Sussex. 'I wonder if you could help us out? They're in the middle of a refurb at Crawley Mortuary, with half the fridges out of action and workmen in tomorrow, and we've a suspicious sudden death on our hands – a young woman who collapsed in the passport queue at Gatwick – both Coroners have agreed for the body to come to Brighton. The police have requested a Home Office pathologist to do the PM. Dr Theobald is the on-call one and he's available tomorrow morning.'

Shit – actually, double-shit, Cleo thought. Ordinarily the victim of a sudden death at a weekend would be recovered to the mortuary and placed in a fridge to await a routine postmortem on Monday morning. But when it was suspi-cious, a Home Office PM would have to be carried out as soon as possible – as was the case now. A Home Office postmortem was a lengthy and more detailed process than a basic one, and Dr Frazer Theobald was the slowest and most pedantic of all of the pathologists – although to be fair to the man, the most thorough. It meant that she would be at the mortuary from 8 a.m. tomorrow and would be lucky to get home by mid-afternoon.

With Roy at work all tomorrow on the kidnap case, Noah and Bruno would be at home on their own with the nanny, when Cleo had planned to spend precious time with both of them. Because they were currently short-staffed at the mortuary, there was no one else she could call in. And she had no option but to agree, because Websdale had always been helpful to her.

'Where is she, Michelle – in the medical centre?'

'Yes – as she was brought there before she died, Dr Theobald doesn't think there's any forensic evidence to be taken from the scene, so he's happy for her to be moved.'

Neither ambulance crews nor police officers would normally transport a dead body – their hands were full, round the clock, with the living. The onus of collecting the dead fell to the mortuary teams. Cleo, as the Senior Anatomical Pathology Technician for Brighton and Hove City Mortuary, was responsible for recovering bodies within the Brighton and Hove area – and occasionally beyond.

Sometimes, she found it a sad task. Entering a flat or a house where an elderly person had lived alone and lain dead for days – or even weeks – before the neighbours noticed something wrong. The post piling up. A horrible smell. Sometimes, the job could be gross and stomach-churning. Bodies washed up on the beach that had been partially eaten by fish and crustaceans. And on occasions, especially when it was young victims of road traffic collisions, it was heartbreaking. The one thing she always tried to do was to give every corpse some dignity. She treated all of them with respect, and when there was to be a viewing, took pride in doing their hair, applying make-up and trying to make them look as presentable as she could.

At least a sudden death at passport control would not be too stinky or visceral, she thought. Picking up the phone, she pressed the speed-dial button for her on-call colleague, Darren Wallace.

Despite the grim environment of the Brighton and Hove Mortuary, processing up to eight postmortems a day, Wallace, who had begun his working life as a butcher's assistant, had retained an infectious enthusiasm for his job. 'Hi, Cleo!' he answered eagerly, as if he had been looking forward to her call. 'What have we got?'

She told him and they arranged to meet at the mortuary in thirty minutes' time, to drive the Coroner's van to Gatwick for the recovery.

Cleo asked Kaitlynn to prepare a salad and take a lasagne from the freezer for Bruno, then got ready and hurried out to her car.

40

With tears streaming down her face, her hands shaking, Stacey cut open a packet of digestive biscuits and tipped them onto a plate. Kipp checked through the freezer drawers to see what they had. The two detectives had told them they would remain in the house with them until Mungo had been safely returned, and they would appreciate some food.

Stacey, who knew the contents of the freezer better than her husband, who could never find anything either in there or the fridge, told him to move out of the way and unearthed a stack of pizzas, several fish pies and frozen vegetables, and four loaves of bread, dropping most of them on the floor in her distress. Along with the eggs they had in the kitchen, there was at least enough for a couple of days, although the tall guy looked like he needed to eat twice as much as anyone else.

Kipp carried a tray with two mugs of coffee and the plate of biscuits down to the basement, feeling even more gloomy than before. On top of everything else, he'd lost his large bet at the football, and Sandown Park had been a catastrophe, also. He'd got the first five winners, but the sixth had been soundly beaten, and the seventh had refused to leave the starting gate. He was down over twenty thousand pounds on the day. Twenty thousand he did not have.

He needed to win that, and much more, back urgently. A dark thought had been occurring to him for some time now, and it was becoming more tempting. All gamblers went through streaks. Just as surely as you knew a winning streak would turn into a losing one sooner or later, you also knew that a losing streak, so long as you could stay in the game, would turn back into a winning streak. He had sole control of his clients' money. Currently, because of uncertainty in the stock markets, he kept several million pounds liquid, waiting for signs of an upturn or good opportunities. That's what his highly paid team of analysts were there to do. Advise him when and where to place funds.

But only he could give the instructions to the bank to move those funds.

If he put any into his own account he would be breaking the law. But so long as he paid the money back and quickly, no one would ever have reason to notice. He could do it, he argued with himself, if he really had to. But the thought made him very nervous.

Back upstairs, Stacey had a large wine glass in her hand, already half empty. 'I just can't believe you let Mungo out of your sight. Talking to a bloody client. Do your clients mean more to you than your family?'

'Stace, the Amex Stadium is one of the safest places on earth. Police everywhere, a million CCTV cameras. And no, my clients don't mean more to me than my family. All through our marriage I've worked my butt off to give us a good lifestyle. Where do you think this house came from? Where did the Mercedes you always wanted come from?'

'One of your rare gambling wins,' she retorted, the barb striking home, painfully. And a bit too truthfully.

So much that she said these days stung him. He stared at the photograph of the two of them, next to the one of Mungo and Kayleigh, on the antique dresser behind her. They were leaning back against the terrace railing of a mountain café in Zermatt, Switzerland, with the Matterhorn rising out of a crystal-blue sky behind them. Both had their fancy ski jackets unzipped and were wearing dark glasses. Stacey, with her wild blonde curls, was grinning at the camera, her hand behind his neck, teasing his hair as she loved to do. No woman he'd ever met had turned him on like she did. And until Kayleigh's death, he'd never had such a close mate as Stacey.

God, they had been so happy. Back then.

While Kayleigh was alive.

Until that dreadful morning of her birthday. She'd been so pleased with that hoverboard. He remembered the moment of panic on his daughter's face as she had suddenly shot forward out of the park. Out into the road. The screech of brakes. The scream.

The silence.

Stacey had sought solace in booze ever since. She was high-maintenance. She'd told him her secret one day, soon after they'd married, that she'd been sexually abused by her father. The monster had abused not only her but all three of her sisters – and her brother. And her weak mother had been in denial throughout their childhood, desperately trying to cover everything up in an attempt to hold her train crash of a family together.

It had left Stacey deeply insecure. In need of proving something to herself – a sense of self-worth. At nineteen, she'd been a *Mayfair Magazine* nude centrefold, in an attempt at shocking her family and getting attention. She went from that to horses, taking up eventing; then to starting an escort business; and then she'd designed a range of handbags.

Kipp first met her soon after he had started to make serious money as an Independent Financial Advisor, when she'd set herself up in yet another business venture, this one finding homes in the Brighton area for the upwardly mobile. He'd registered as a client. She found him a house on the smart Barrowfield Estate – and by the time he'd exchanged contracts, they'd fallen in love and she'd agreed to move in with him.

But after their kids were born he realized, too late, where he had gone wrong. He'd thrown himself into expanding his business, at first failing to recognize Stacey's postnatal depression after Kayleigh's birth, and her need for attention. And boozing.

And then Kayleigh had died.

'Stace,' he said. 'He'll be OK, we'll get him back.'

'And if we don't?'

'We will.'

'Oh, sure we will, just like that, eh? Just like your winning horses, right? Just like your killer poker hands, yes? Just like you have all those can't-fail roulette systems. Mungo will be back. Just like your numbers will turn up, right? Just like they always don't. You're such a loser. I can't believe you let him go.'

41

At this time of year, on a balmy Saturday evening, many people in the city of Brighton and Hove were on their big night out. Filling the restaurants and bars, some getting ready to start clubbing. Tonight many would be commiserating over their home team's 2–0 defeat by Manchester City, but at the same time they would be celebrating their team's first ever Premier League game. The police would be out in force, too. Every Thursday, Friday and Saturday night, all year round, Operation Marble did its best to prevent downtown Brighton from becoming a booze- and drug-fuelled war zone. There would be fights, spitting, swearing and arrests. Scantily clad chavs, Hens in daft outfits and vomiting Stags in stupid hats.

Far removed from all this were the patients in the wards inside the large building that was currently masked by hoardings, cranes and bulldozers. The Royal Sussex County Hospital, some distance away from the action, was going through a much-needed renovation, with temporary entrances everywhere and makeshift signs.

The helmeted medical student on the Kawasaki motorcycle, whose name was Gentian Llupa, cruised slowly past, along Eastern Road, and then up the side of the vast, sprawling site, taking mental notes of opportunities, checking for

CCTV cameras. He didn't need to take that risk. It was almost fully dark, but why rush? And hey, the guy he had come to see wasn't going anywhere tonight.

If his plan worked out, the man wasn't going anywhere ever again.

Other than to the mortuary.

42

Major Crime was housed at the Sussex Police Headquarters, in one of a group of featureless brick buildings that were originally dormitories for police recruits. The Intel suite was housed on the first floor, a modern, airy conference room with a long white table, black and chrome chairs and a charcoal carpet. There were large wall-mounted monitors and it was wired with all comms systems, prepared 24/7 for any Major Enquiry or Incident team to move in within minutes and be instantly operational.

Seated around the long rectangular table were Roy Grace and his rapidly assembled team of detectives, analysts and researchers.

On the wall behind Grace were mounted three whiteboards. One contained a family and association chart of all Mungo Brown's known family and friends. On another was a series of photographs, taken from the Amex's CCTV cameras, showing Mungo Brown and his father arriving at the stadium, Mungo talking to another boy, then both of them disappearing into the throng of people heading to the entrances. On the third whiteboard was a sequence of photographs of a man in a red baseball cap. The first showed him leaving his seat shortly after the start of the game. Subsequent pictures tracked him through the stadium until he

disappeared, shortly after a sign reading SOUTH STAND
WASTE MANAGEMENT – NO UNAUTHORIZED ACCESS, where
a camera was not working.

'The time is 8.45 p.m.' Grace turned to DS Exton. 'Before
we get started, welcome, Jon, we're delighted to have you
back – you're looking well, your break has obviously done
you good.' Then, glancing down at his notes, he addressed
the rest of the team. 'Right, this is the first of what will be
regular briefings around the clock for Operation Replay. I'd
like to remind everyone this is a crime in action, currently
being run as a covert operation owing to threats made to
the father of the kidnap victim about not contacting the
police.'

'Operation Replay?' Norman Potting commented.
'Would have been a match replay and all if it hadn't been
for our hero Roy Grace here saving the day.' The old Detective Sergeant pointed a finger at him. 'Instead he helped our
team to a two–nil defeat!'

Kevin Hall, a burly, genial detective constable in his
mid-forties, chuckled and turned to Grace. 'You are bonk-
ers, guv. I'm just glad we're sitting around this table and not
on our hands and knees at the Amex doing a fingertip
search for your – er—'

'Fingertips?' Potting suggested.

'And the rest of you,' Hall added.

'I'm quite glad about that,' chipped in Crime Scene
Manager Alex Call. 'It's really not a nice job.'

'Yep, well I'm pretty glad about that too,' Grace said. He
was less glad about the flak he knew, almost certainly, he
would be getting from his boss, ACC Cassian Pewe, over his
actions. He had already had a near-apoplectic voicemail
from him – to which he had not yet responded. That was a
joy to come.

'What's the latest from the EOD on the device, sir?' asked DC Velvet Wilde, another recent recruit to his team.

'I've had an update from Oscar-1,' Grace said. 'In the absence of anyone claiming the camera, the EOD carried out a controlled explosion. The fragments have been retrieved by the EOD team and taken away for analysis. We won't know for some time what sort of device it actually was. But we're not concerned with that – our task is to one hundred per cent focus on returning Mungo Brown safely to his parents.'

'But, boss,' DS Exton said, 'don't you think there's a likely link between the bomb threat and the kidnap?'

'There may well be, and there's another SIO working on that with the Amex team and Nick Fitzherbert. I'll be liaising closely with him. He'll keep our team constantly updated with their intelligence, and that's why there's a picture of the suspect bomber on display in this room.' He turned to the Principal Analyst, Annalise Vineer. 'That will be one of your actions, to coordinate the intelligence around the Amex operation and any links.'

'Yes, sir.'

Grace glanced down at the notes prepared by his assistant and went on. 'OK, this investigation is into the suspected kidnap of a fourteen-year-old boy, Mungo Brown, son of the well-known Brighton businessman Kipp Brown.'

'That arrogant tosser!' Jon Exton exclaimed.

'Thank you, Jon,' Grace retorted sharply.

'Trust Kipp?' Norman Potting interjected.

'Correct, Norman, that's him,' Grace replied. 'Mungo went missing sometime before the start of the Albion game today at the Amex.' He read out the text Kipp Brown had received. Then he went on to summarize the information he had to date.

'The last email communication from Mungo Brown, which the High Tech Crime Unit sent to me, was at 2.40 p.m. this afternoon. It was addressed to an Aleksander Dervishi and said: "See u at the game. It's gonna be lit!" Now the significance of this is that shortly after arriving at the ground, Mungo's father, Kipp, saw him talking to this boy. I've also heard back from the Amex that Mungo Brown's season ticket was not logged at any entrance, which makes it unlikely he ever entered the stadium at any point, unless he used – or was coerced into using – someone else's. The fact that so far he has not been identified on any exterior CCTV footage indicates to me that he may at some point have entered the stadium and may still be there – or was secreted away, disguised, somehow. The kidnappers must have had a plan.'

He took a sip of coffee. 'A full search of the grounds is in progress – there are a lot of places someone could be concealed. All CCTV footage is being scanned. With the network of cameras they have at the Amex, he will have been picked up on several. I've also requested all police body-worn camera footage. We know the boy's mobile phone was seen being thrown from an older model BMW 5-Series car leaving the Amex car park at high speed. We have the index number, and an ANPR plot of the car's possible movements is being carried out by Oscar-1. Digital Forensics have Mungo's phone and computer. They are doing a backwards plot on his movements for the past week to see if there are any unusual patterns, and to see who he's been communicating with.'

He looked at his notes. 'One person of interest to us is this man in the red baseball cap.' He pointed at a photograph on the whiteboard. 'We have secreted two officers, DI Branson and Acting DS Jack Alexander, into Kipp Brown's house to monitor all calls he receives, to guide him and his wife and provide reassurance, and assist with any negotiations. At this time, the only lead we have is that when last seen, well before kick-off, Mungo was talking to the boy whom we believe to be Aleksander Dervishi.'

Annalise Vineer raised her hand. 'Sir, we have some information on this boy.'

'Go ahead,' Grace said.

'If he is Aleksander Dervishi, he's a pupil at Brighton College, same year as Mungo Brown, and according to his headmaster who was spoken to a short while ago, they are close friends. Now this might be of significance. His father, Jorgji Dervishi, is a person of interest to us. He was a former kind of consigliere to the boss of a London-based Albanian crime family who went rogue some years ago. We believe he came down here in a similar role for a branch of his family in Brighton, and that he has links to several Eastern European criminal networks. A few interesting facts about Mr Dervishi. He has a glass eye and people say it's easy to spot – it's the friendlier of the two.'

There was a titter of laughter.

'He also has an artificial right hand. He tells people he lost it – and his eye – fighting in the Kosovo conflict. But we understand he actually lost his hand working on a piece of farm machinery as a child, and he lost his eye in a fight in a bar. He is not considered good news by anyone.'

Grace stared at her, feeling a deep chill. During the 1998–9 Kosovo conflict, when ethnic Albanians opposed ethnic Serbs and the then-government of Yugoslavia, Albanians were given asylum in a number of European countries from the ethnic cleansing that followed. One of the places declared an official relocation centre was the city of Brighton and Hove, which took an influx of two thousand of them.

The majority of Albanians who had come here were decent, hard-working and law-abiding. But along with those came a brutal organized criminal element. Some of these, structured around ethnic groups and family or friendship ties, using Kanun laws, modelled themselves loosely on the Sicilian Mafia with similar lines of command and ranks, but without their rigid discipline. And like many modern crime organizations, they dealt in drugs, arms, human trafficking, modern slavery, human organs and counterfeit goods, their reach stretching from Israel to South America. This criminal element liked to show off its brutality both to insiders and to the public at large, and frequently committed acts of violence in public as a lesson to others. Yet at the same time, internally, this fraternity maintained strict codes of honour, one of them being scrupulous punctuality.

'There's another factor that may be significant, sir,' Vineer said.

'Tell me?'

'The Albanians have a social code of honour known as blood feuds. Their word is *hakmarrja* – I got this from PC Denero who is working closely with the Brighton Albanian community. It's all about the salvaging of honour, avenging a murder or humiliation. She has intel from the Met that the crime family that Jorgji Dervishi screwed over is planning revenge.'

'Could this kidnapping be connected in some way – is that what you're thinking, Annalise?'

'I think it's worth throwing into the mix, sir.'

'OK, we need to find out fast if Kipp Brown's ever had financial dealings with any of the Albanian community.'

Mindful of the texted threat to Kipp Brown he had seen,

and which he had already told his team about, he made a note to contact the Force Gold, Superintendent Tingley, with this update straight after the briefing.

'Good work, Annalise,' he said.

His mobile phone rang. Excusing himself, he answered it.

'Roy Grace,' he said.

It was Glenn Branson.

'Boss, we've got a second text from the kidnappers.'

43

Kipp Brown stood in his son's bedroom, his heart heaving. The room smelled of a mix of fresh paint, the sour odour of rodents and pond weed. The walls had recently been redecorated from the bright yellow that had been there for years to the very specific mushroom colour Mungo had requested, reflecting his growing adult tastes. Kipp thought about this with a tinge of sadness. About how his son spent ages on his hair in the mirror every day.

The teenager was already taking an interest in girls. Soon, he would be dating, and in just a few years he would be gone to university or out into the big wide world, to whatever the future held, and independent of his family.

Kipp worked his way along the rodent cages, firstly feeding the mice, putting in a small chunk of cucumber, which Stacey told him Mungo always gave them, and replenished their water. Next, he topped up the hamsters' food bowl, followed by the gerbils', and finally tapped what he hoped was the right amount of feed into the tropical fish tank.

The tidy room was like a shrine to his son's passions, Kipp thought, looking around carefully – something he never had the chance to do when Mungo was here. Against the headboard was a cushion printed with a bison's head and a row of cuddly soft toys. On the bed's black, grey and white check counterpane lay an open *Reservoir Dogs* boxed souvenir set, comprising a video of the film, a silver comb made to look like a cut-throat razor, a handcuff lapel pin and key fob, a Zippo lighter and a jar of hair gel, labelled DRESS GROOVIER.

A row of *Star Wars* helmets sat on a black shelf, high up. On another stack of shelves were lined up a film clapper-board, a video camera, a baseball glove, a fake snake, a *Detective Deadpool* DVD sleeve, two large speakers, a boxed set of the *Stanley Kubrick Archives* and a neat row of every kind of Coca-Cola can – red, black, silver, green, orange and pink – as well as, randomly, a Rubik's cube.

Ranked along one wall was a row of kayaking medals. Mungo had been passionate about the sport until a year or so ago, when he seemed to have lost interest – perhaps coinciding with the occasional smell of cigarettes or alcohol or hash on him, one more sign, along with his deepening voice and facial hair, that he was moving on from childhood.

When he finished with the pets, Kipp sat on the bed. God, how much he loved this wilful and bright kid. Sure, they fought at times, and Mungo could really piss him off when he was in the mood to do so. But he loved him with all his heart.

Where are you? What has happened? Who has taken you?

Please be all right.

He looked at the small desk, above which, on the wall, was mounted Mungo's large monitor. The laptop had been taken by the police and hopefully they might find clues on that.

In need of some air, he went downstairs, through the

kitchen, opened the patio doors and walked out into the garden in the falling dusk, past the swimming pool with its cover on and down the terrace of lawns, each with a neat bed of flowers either side, towards the tennis court at the far end. The ground was damp with dew, the moisture seeping into his loafers, but he barely noticed.

He looked up at the basketball net fixed to the side of an oak tree. Mungo used to spend hours throwing a ball, aiming for that net. He was fighting back tears as he stared at it, then heard a voice behind him.

'Sir? Mr Brown?'

He turned and saw the big detective. 'Mr Brown, you've got another text.' He handed him the phone.

Kipp stared at the message on the display.

> Drive to the Devil's Dyke, alone. Three hundred
> yards south of the Devil's Dyke Hotel is a derelick
> Second World War pillbox. Instructions await you
> there. Go alone if you want to see your son again.
> We will be watching.

He noticed the misspelling of 'derelict'. It was like a knife twisting inside his guts, reminding him of Mungo's spelling. He was slightly dyslexic, which was why there were few books in his room. He looked at Branson. 'I know that place well, Mungo used to love flying a kite up there.'

He and Mungo used to love doing all kinds of stuff together. Flying model aircraft. Fishing. Not any more.

It was a popular spot, with commanding views across the Downs and across Brighton towards the English Channel. And a dead end. A narrow country road led up to it. A road which could be observed, easily, from any number of concealed points.

'What do you suggest?' he asked the detective.

'That you go there, sir, and take your encrypted phone as well as this one. We've installed a tracking device on it. Seems like your son's kidnappers have planned carefully and chosen smartly. Go there and call us when you can. Let's see what they have in mind.'

Kipp hurried indoors and told Stacey.

'I'm coming with you,' she replied.

'No,' he said, adamantly. 'It says to go alone.'

'What if it's a trap?'

'It's not going to be a trap. Whoever has taken Mungo wants money. Let me find out how much they want.'

Very reluctantly, she agreed.

44

Saturday night at Tosca Ristorante in Shoreham was in full swing, with every table taken by locals or residents of Brighton and Hove, just a few miles to the east, who had made the short journey here.

The entrance to the place, which served some of the best Italian food in the county, was on the buzzing Shoreham High Street and the long, narrow room stretched back to an open terrace overlooking the River Adur. Its proprietor, Enver Godanci, an energetic, bespectacled man of forty-five, sporting designer stubble and wearing a blue-and-white polka-dot shirt loose over black chinos, ran between his kitchen and his customers, anxiously supervising everything, ensuring, as he did every night, that his growing legion of regulars was happy.

Business was booming, so much so that he had bought the next-door building and knocked through, creating a second dining area, which was tonight filled with Albanians, celebrating at a party he regularly hosted for his fellow countrymen who lived locally. Their national double-eagle flag hung above a banner sporting the emblem and the words ALBANIANS IN SUSSEX.

Godanci had come a long way since entering the UK twenty years earlier, fleeing the Kosovan war. After a spell working for the prison service and then the social services in the late 1990s, he spent three years in the kitchen of one of Brighton's Italian restaurants, before having the courage to strike out on his own. Now, through his understanding of what people liked to eat – and the environment in which they felt comfortable and pampered – he had not only expanded this restaurant, but had recently acquired a second premises in nearby Southwick, where business was also booming. As he emerged from the kitchen carrying a massive pizza for a group of youngsters celebrating a birthday, he noticed a familiar figure striding purposefully into the restaurant.

In her late forties, with cropped and gelled fair hair, she was dressed in a short-sleeve black T-shirt and dungarees and had a tattoo on her left arm of an elderly lady's face ringed with flowers. A round metal badge, on which was the double-headed eagle symbol and the legend ALBANIANS IN SUSSEX, was pinned to her T-shirt.

Godanci delivered the dish then hurried over to the woman, Constable Nikki Denero, who was the liaison officer between the force and the Sussex Albanian community. For many years this community had shunned the police. Coming from a corrupt dictatorship with brutal, equally corrupt police, many Albanians found it impossible to believe that police in any other country could be decent, caring people. Accordingly, they never turned to the local police to handle any issues, preferring to handle disputes directly themselves.

The eye-opener for PC Denero had come five years ago, at 2 a.m. one morning, when an Albanian had been found impaled on railings, having fallen – or more likely been pushed – from his bedsit window five storeys above. First on the scene, she had stayed with the man, who was miraculously still just alive, all the way to hospital, where he was pronounced dead on arrival. She had then been confronted by a wall of silence over his death.

That had been the start of her personal mission to break down the mistrust of the police and the bad name this gave Albanians in the local community, and she had made huge strides with many of them – much of it due to the support and help of Enver Godanci.

'*Përshëndetje!*' she said.

'Nikki, good to see you! You've come for the Albanian evening?'

'Actually, no, Enver. Could we talk in private?' the officer said.

'Sure.'

He led her through the kitchen into the tiny rest room behind it, where there was a table and four chairs, with a wall-mounted television. 'Drink?'

'I'm good,' she said.

'So?'

Looking worried, the Constable said, 'We have a very serious situation. A fourteen-year-old boy has been kidnapped today – taken from the Amex during the match. His best friend, apparently, is called Aleksander Dervishi. He's the son of Jorgji Dervishi.'

Godanci's cheerful countenance fell away, and she saw the flash of concern.

'Jorgji Dervishi?'

'You know him, Enver?'

'Of course. Everyone in the Albanian community knows him.'

'A bad man, right?'

He looked around nervously, as if scared they might be overheard. 'Very.'

'What do you know about him?'

He shrugged. 'My friends – we keep well away. He deals in everything – girls, drugs, you name it. He screws around with people's heads. You arrive to see him early, he tells you that you are late. If you arrive late he tells you you're too early. He offers money-lending at crazy interest rates. He is not the kind of guy I want to do business with – nor my friends.'

'I need your help urgently, Enver. Is there any way you could find out very discreetly if any of the Albanians you have here tonight, for the party, have had any dealings – or know anyone who has – with a Brighton IFA called Kipp Brown? But it's really important this is kept low-key.'

He looked at her. '*Trust Kipp*? That guy from the ads who promises he can get you a cheap mortgage or car finance?'

'That's him.'

'I'll ask around.'

'Thanks, Enver. Tell them they're not going to be in any kind of trouble, I just need to know.'

He looked hard at her. 'Yeah, OK, I trust you.'

'Tell any of them they can trust me, too.'

'What exactly is your interest in Jorgji Dervishi?' he asked.

'I can't tell you exactly – take a guess.'

He shook his head and looked at her quizzically. 'You want me to tell all my Albanian friends to trust you? But you don't trust me? How is that right?'

45

Adrian Morris was doing a check of the stadium, as the crowds slowly dispersed from the bars. His mobile phone rang. It was the same male voice with the Eastern European accent as before.

'Mr Morris, you will have learned by now that there was no detonator in the camera device. Please do not think this was an oversight, it was deliberate. I have no intention of killing and maiming hundreds of innocent people – that is a decision I leave to you.'

'Who the hell are you?' Morris said, calmly but angrily.

'Just listen to me very carefully. Now you understand we are capable of making and delivering a viable device to your stadium, perhaps next time you will take me more seriously. I will be back in touch – you have many home games this season. Goodbye, Mr Morris.'

The call ended.

46

Kipp Brown liked quoting to his friends something the head of design at Porsche, back in the 1960s, had once said: 'The essence of a great car is that each time you get in and sit behind the wheel, it must make you feel it is your birthday.' And, normally, that was just how Kipp Brown felt. Normally. Normally, he loved this car. The driver's seat that hugged him. The smell of leather. The cockpit, with the red needles on the speedometer and rev counter. The blatter of the expensive, finely tuned engine and the feeling of the precision of its engineering. The adrenaline rush when he pressed the accelerator and felt the surge of the car in the small of his back and the pit of his stomach.

But not now. Not tonight as he drove fast along the narrow, twisting road, the lights of oncoming cars momentarily blinding him, then flashing past. He was feeling numb, enveloped in an aura of evil darkness. His soul was heavy.

Please be OK, Mungo.

Oh God, please.

Tall grass and hedgerows sped past either side of him in the beam of the headlights, the needle of his speedometer jigging between 60 and 90 mph, the engine whining behind him. He braked and slowed as he took the final right turn and accelerated up the hill, cresting it and entering the almost-deserted car park. Several cars were parked outside the red-brick structure of the Devil's Dyke Hotel.

He pulled into a bay, switched off the ignition and sat, looking around in the darkness, feeling nervous as hell. The door of the hotel opened and a tarty-looking blonde came out, unsteady on her high heels, holding the hand of a thuggish man with a shaven head, wearing cut-off jeans and a wife-beater sleeveless vest. They made their way over to a pickup truck and got in. After a few seconds the engine started and the vehicle drove off.

He opened his door and got out, then stood, listening to the fading roar of the engine. The night air was chilly and dewy. He looked carefully around but could see no sign of anyone else. Slowly, and nervously, he made his way across the wet grass towards the crumbling brick structure he knew so well from his school days. As did almost every kid who grew up in Brighton.

During the Second World War the British military built a series of strategic machine-gun posts along elevated positions across the whole of the south of England. If they failed to down the German fighter planes and bombers on their way in, they would try again with their ack-ack guns to get them on the way back.

Decades later, with the guns long removed, these brick pillboxes were great places for kids to explore – and for playing Cowboys and Indians or any other kind of game. This one up here on the Dyke, with its dark, dank interior, often littered with cowpats, had always held a sense of excitement and mystery for him – and history.

As he reached it, he looked around again. There was a tinkle of laughter behind him. Four more people had emerged from the hotel, holding glasses and sparking up cigarettes. He heard a shrill cackle of laughter.

Laughing at him?

He watched them. There was another shrill laugh. Then, as he entered through the hole in the wall which passed for a door, he smelled the familiar rank stench of dung, urine and lichen. He pulled out his phone, about to switch on the torch app, when a sharp *ping-ping* right behind him made him jump.

He spun round in shock, expecting to see someone. Instead, he saw a ghostly green light, at eye-level. The light was emitted by a small mobile phone taped to the wall. On the display was a poorly lit close-up photograph of Mungo. Grey duct tape was wound round his face, below his nostrils. His eyes were wide open in fear. Darkness surrounded him, but Kipp could just make out a shape of what looked like his topknot. He could have been in a cave, a cellar, a closet.

A sudden ping from the phone startled him.

A text.

> **Good man. You are being sensible coming alone. Take this phone home. We will use it for the next instruxxion on how to save Mungo's life. Do not text back. Do not speak to the police, unless you want directions to Mungo's corpse.**

With shaking hands, Kipp removed the phone and the tape and, ignoring what he was told, tapped out a text back.

> **I will pay whatever money you want, I promise. Just tell me how and where to send it. Please do not hurt my son.**

He tried to send it, but nothing happened. It was blocked.

He tried again. Then again.

It would not send.

He waited for several minutes, then pocketed the tape and the phone, and stepped back out of the structure, looking around fearfully into the darkness. Was someone out there, watching him?

Where?

He studied the few vehicles in the car park. No sign of a figure or movement in any of them. Was someone out in the darkness with night-vision binoculars?

He walked slowly back to the car park, his shoes sodden from the long, wet grass, then stood beside his Porsche, looking around before unlocking it. When he finally climbed in, he sat and waited. Five minutes. Ten. He tried sending the text again, without success.

He drove home slowly, thinking. Thinking. Again, a spelling error. *The next instruxxion.*

Who had sent it? Who had taken his son?

Had he made a big mistake contacting the police? Were they watching his house, not fooled by the fridge delivery? He put the phone down on the passenger seat, glancing at it repeatedly as he drove home, waiting for it to light up and ping with another text. But it stayed dark and silent.

Stacey opened the front door before he had even reached it. Her eyes were red and hollow, her face gaunt, as if she had lost several stone in weight in the past hour. Her breath reeked of booze. 'What? What news?'

He showed her the phone, with the text and the photograph of Mungo. When she saw that she collapsed, sobbing, into his arms.

'We'll get him back safely, babes, I promise you.'

She continued sobbing uncontrollably.

He steered her through into the living room. The television was on, showing a recording of *The Crown* from earlier that evening. On the coffee table in front of the sofa was a wine glass, and a nearly empty bottle of white wine. He sat her down and put the glass in her hand, then went off in search of the two detectives, down in the basement.

Branson studied the photograph of Mungo. His younger colleague, Jack, produced an elaborate scanner, which he placed right against the phone. Then he tapped some keys on the device. 'Sending the image for enhancement to Digital Forensics,' he said. 'Let's see if we get any clues from it.'

Within half an hour, another text came in.

47

It was almost dark now outside the windows of the Digital Forensics suite. But neither Jason Quigley, Dan Salter, Shaun Robbins nor Aiden Gilbert noticed. They were all focused on the image that the Acting Detective Sergeant had just sent through.

The image of a teenage boy with terror in his eyes and grey duct tape across his mouth. Surrounded by darkness.

The team dressed casually in here. Despite the endless shocks from the frequently grim and often brutal images of child pornography that they all had to look at regularly in this job, they did their best to keep the atmosphere as cheerful as they could. Quigley, in a polo shirt, jeans and sneakers, tapped his keyboard, starting the process of enhancing the image, whilst trying to stop it turning grainy. He was using a development of software created originally by NASA for the first moon landing in 1969.

The four men watched as the background slowly lightened. Mungo Brown was seated on the floor, leaning against a bare, flint wall. Quigley tapped more keys and suddenly the image zoomed in. First on the boy's frightened eyes. Then the duct tape across his mouth. Down his torso, his hands out of sight behind his back. Restrained by something.

Then there was a close-up of a wall socket.

'This could be of interest,' Quigley said. 'Anyone spot it?'

They all shook their heads.

He went in closer, and now the socket became very clearly visible. It looked old-fashioned, yellowed, with three round pinholes, one smaller than the other two. 'Who's the eldest here?'

'Probably me,' Aiden Gilbert said. 'I'm fifty-two.'

'When did you last plug anything into a round-pin socket, Aiden?'

'Never.'

Jason Quigley nodded, with a self-satisfied grin. 'My point exactly! You aren't going to see one in any house in the UK that's been modernized in the last forty years.'

'So, this socket predates that, Jason?' Dan Salter quizzed.

'It sodding predates Noah's Ark! There's got to be a clue here.'

'That we're looking for a derelict property?' Gilbert said.

'Smack on the money, boss!'

Daniel Salter's phone rang. It was his contact at the phone company EE.

'Hi, Joe,' he said. 'You have? Brilliant!' He wrote down the details. 'Well done, mate!'

48

Shortly before 10 p.m. Roy Grace, shirtsleeves rolled up and a mug of coffee beside him, was sitting at his workstation in the Intel suite, updating his Policy Book and looking once more at the latest information that had come in from Digital Forensics. He had already given the action to two analysts, following the information, to search for derelict properties within a twenty-mile radius, although he felt that was a slender hope.

The mood in the room was purposeful but sombre. Everyone was concerned for the missing boy, and on top of this was the sense of disappointment that Brighton and Hove Albion had lost, 2–0, in the football. Not that there would have been any noticeable jubilation in this room had they won. The intensity of concentration was so strong that the outside world, unless it materially affected their investigation, was for now irrelevant.

A key person they needed to speak to was Mungo Brown's school friend, Aleksander Dervishi, the friend his father had seen him talking to shortly before he had disappeared. They had spoken to Aleksander's mother, Mirlinda, a couple of times. The first time she told them he hadn't returned from the football yet, but she wasn't worried. He'd told her he was going to another school friend's house in

163

Brighton after the game, to work on a video for a YouTube project for school, and their chauffeur would collect him when he was ready. The second time she was spoken to, by DC Boutwood, she was sounding anxious, saying he wasn't answering his phone.

As he made notes, Grace went through a mental check-list, trying to ensure he was not missing anything, as well as checking online through the National Crime Agency's kidnap protocols. He repeatedly looked down at his phone, at the two texts Glenn Branson had forwarded to him, the first an hour ago, the second just moments ago.

> Drive to the Devil's Dyke, alone. Three hundred yards south of the Devil's Dyke Hotel is a derelick Second World War pillbox. Instructions await you there. Go alone if you want to see your son again. We will be watching.

> Good man. You are being sensible coming alone. Take this phone home. We will use it for the next instruxxion on how to save Mungo's life. Do not text back. Do not speak to the police, unless you want directions to Mungo's corpse.

Roy Grace stared also at the photograph of Mungo, in the darkness, with grey duct tape over his mouth. He could see the terror in his eyes. Poor kid. One of the worst night-mares for a child. Something from which the boy would never fully recover, because kidnap victims rarely did. After they – hopefully – found him, Mungo would be haunted by nightmares for the rest of his life and very possibly end up dependent on medication and in therapy. Let alone the traumatic impact on his family. That was one of the conse-quences of this ugly act that the perpetrators probably did not think or, more likely, care about. With most major crimes, it was rarely just the victim who suffered a life sentence of fear and instability.

He read through the texts again, once more clocking the two spelling errors, 'instruxxion' and 'derelick', and thinking about them. Someone dyslexic? He turned to DC Kevin Hall, sitting close to him. 'Any word from Digital Forensics?'

'Not so far, guv. But they're looped in and on it with all the phone companies, and they're carrying out cell-site analysis to try to locate the device that sent this, as well as checking if it had geo-mapping, which would give us the location where it was taken.'

There was a sudden appetizing smell of French fries in the room.

'Nice to think whoever's taken Mungo would be dumb enough to leave their geo-mapping on,' Grace said.

'Indeed.'

He was about to say something else when he was interrupted by DC Alec Davies. 'Sir, what was it you ordered?'

'Ordered?'

'To eat. From the Big Mouth Burger Bar. John Palmer's just made the delivery.'

'Great, I'm ravenous. A cheeseburger and fries with onion rings, thanks, Alec.'

His phone rang.

'Roy Grace,' he said.

He heard a hubbub at the other end; it sounded like the din of a rammed pub or bar. Then, above it, he heard a precise, clear voice.

'Detective Superintendent, it's PC Denero. I have some information you requested.'

'Great, Nikki, what have you got?'

'Well, sir, from what I've been able to find so far, this

Kipp Brown character has been cultivating clients from the Albanian business community in the city. He appears to be the go-to man for them for unsecured – or poorly secured – cash loans and mortgages. I'm with twenty or so Albanians at the moment and almost all of them have had dealings with him – pretty happily, they assured me. You might be interested to know that Edi Konstandin is one of his major clients.'

'When you've finished, could you come to the Intel suite at HQ CID? I'd like you on my team until we find the boy.'

'Yes, sir – I could be there in an hour.'

'Thank you.' Ending the call, he looked down at the texts again. The spelling errors.

> instruxxion
> derelick

The kind of mistakes that might be made by someone for whom English was their second language?

He looked behind him at the whiteboards, stood up and went over to the one on which there was now an association chart for the dominant Brighton Albanian crime family. At the top was the name Edi Konstandin, who Intel put as the local Godfather – the equivalent to a Mafia Don or Capo. Directly beneath him was the consigliere, Jorgji Dervishi, Aleksander's father, and beneath him the underboss, Valdete Gjon. He turned to another whiteboard, on which was the photograph of the man in the red cap.

'This is a person of extreme interest to us. He vanishes just after the sign for the South Stand Waste Management. OK, we know from all the CCTV at the Amex that people cannot just disappear there, so what happened? My hypothesis is that this camera was deliberately disabled at this point. It was done so that Man-in-Red-Baseball-Cap could change his clothes and perhaps so that Mungo Brown could be concealed somewhere at the same time. The contradictory evidence regarding Mungo is that his phone was recovered after being thrown from a BMW car leaving the car park at high speed. How did he get from the stadium to the car park without being seen?'

He looked around at a sea of blank faces.

'Is his middle name *Houdini*, guv?' Norman Potting asked.

'Thank you, Norman,' Grace retorted. 'His middle name is actually Eric.'

'Houdini's real name was Erik Weisz,' Potting retorted.

'Is that helpful to our enquiry, Norman?' Kevin Hall interjected.

Potting mumbled that it probably wasn't. Hall, answering a call on his phone, did not hear him.

Grace, ignoring the banter, said, 'I've contacted Forensic Podiatrist Haydn Kelly, who is, fortunately, available and is on his way down from London now. I've also contacted the Met Police Super Recognizer Unit, and they are sending down one of their team. I'm going to have both Haydn and the Super Recognizer look at all footage of the crowd leaving the Amex after the game, to see if they can spot Red Cap, either from his gait or a facial feature.'

Ending his phone call, Kevin Hall said animatedly, 'Guv, I may have something.'

Grace looked at him. 'Yes?'

'DI Branson got the IMEI code off the phone Kipp Brown brought back from the Dyke – I sent it straight to Digital Forensics and we have a result from it!'

Criminals used pay-as-you-go phones – so-called *burners* – under the impression these could not be traced. That was true to an extent, but every phone had a unique IMEI code that could be accessed by entering a series of digits and numbers: *#06#. This would reveal the identity of the phone, from which Digital Forensics could find out its provenance and history.

Excitedly, Grace asked, 'Tell me?'

'Well, guv, this is interesting. It's a phone that's been used before by a character called Fatjon Sava – who was linked to this burner two years ago. At the time, we had him on file as one of Dervishi's henchmen. Do you remember the case of an Albanian left in the middle of Churchill Square with both his eyes burned out with a cigarette lighter? The charmer who did this, who was never identi-fied, sent a text on behalf of Mr Jorgji Dervishi to the victim, politely warning him not to tread on Mr Dervishi's toes again.'

'Nice work, Kevin,' Grace said. 'What happened – was Dervishi arrested?'

'No, the Albanian wall of silence came down. No one would say a word, not even the victim's wife, she was too frightened. But we knew Fatjon Sava was probably the offender, although we didn't have sufficient grounds to arrest him.'

'The eyes have it,' Potting announced, looking around, pleased with himself.

No one smiled.

Grace's thoughts immediately returned to the spelling mistakes. Someone not quite a hundred per cent fluent in the English language, or someone trying to misdirect him? He looked down at his notes, thinking, before looking up again at his team. 'OK, we understand that Mungo Brown's best friend at Brighton College is Aleksander Dervishi, son of Jorgji Dervishi, and Dervishi might well have had business dealings with Kipp Brown. I want Dervishi interviewed tonight.'

'It's late, guv,' Hall said. '10.15 p.m.'

'This is a kidnap, Kevin, where every second counts. I don't care if it's 3 a.m. Call him and tell him we need to speak to him tonight, urgently. Hopefully his son will be home and you can talk to him, too. If Dervishi is difficult you can tell him he can do it the pleasant, informal way or we can arrest him in connection with the blinding of one of his countrymen – and the phone.' He looked around at his team, considering who might be appropriate to interview him. Detective Sergeant Norman Potting was a blunt straight-talker who could stand up to anyone. To offset him, DC Velvet Wilde, who had a more subtle approach to people, might make a good foil. He gave them the action.

Moments later his phone rang again. It was Oscar-1, Inspector Keith Ellis.

'Guv, we've just had in an ANPR track on BMW index Echo X-ray One-Three Bravo Delta Uniform's movements. It pinged three cameras after leaving the Amex Stadium.'

'Which direction, Keith?'

'It headed east on the A27, past Lewes. The last camera to pick it up was at the Beddingham roundabout, where the vehicle either carried on eastwards towards Polegate and Eastbourne or could have turned right on the A26 and down towards Newhaven and the cross-Channel ferry port. But it didn't get picked up by the next camera along the A27, nor the next one on the A26, just north of Newhaven. And I've got some significant further information on the vehicle. The East Sussex Fire and Rescue team are currently tackling a car on fire on a farm track just off the A26 south of Beddingham. It's the suspect vehicle, index Echo X-ray One-Three Bravo Delta Uniform.'

'Shit!' Grace said. 'So, it might have put Mungo Brown down somewhere in that area.'

'Sounds very likely, guv.'

Sensing a possible breakthrough, Grace jumped up from the table and walked over to a large-scale map of Sussex on the wall in front of him, still holding his phone to his ear. He picked up a red marker pen from a holder beneath it and drew a circle round the area that Ellis had given him, which covered several square miles.

'This is mostly rural, farming community all around here, Keith,' he said. 'Any number of barns. Sounds very possible Mungo might have been taken to a hiding place in this area.'

'It does,' Ellis said.

Grace thought hard. Both the A27, which was the main route connecting East and West Sussex, and the A26, which had ferry traffic to and from Newhaven Harbour, were busy roads. Whoever had taken Mungo, and had then dumped and torched the BMW, must have left in another vehicle either parked down that farm track or which had been driven there to pick them up. But with the numbers of vehicles travelling on both roads, it would be a near-impossible task to check up on them all. Mungo might have been transferred to another vehicle and taken to the Newhaven–Dieppe ferry, and spirited away to France – although the plug in the photograph indicated otherwise. However, all that meant was that the photograph had probably been taken in England. He could then have been taken on to France. Or the kidnappers could be holding him somewhere inside the red circle.

The police helicopter was equipped with a heat-seeking camera, which could detect living – or recently dead – bodies out in the open or inside buildings. 'Keith,' he said.

'Can you see if NPAS-15 is available to do a fly-over of the area, looking at barns, outbuildings, anywhere Mungo might be?'

'Right away, guv.'

Ending the call, Grace turned to DC Hall. 'Kevin, get on to the Newhaven ferry company and find out the times of any sailings to France after 6 p.m. today. It's a three-and-a-half-hour crossing, so if Mungo Brown is on a ferry, perhaps locked in the boot of a car, it's possible he's not yet in France. Then arrange with the port authorities in France to be vigilant and to look out for a teenage boy, possibly with a topknot, in any vehicle leaving the ferry – and get a photograph of him pinged to them.'

Hall nodded. 'Yes, guv.'

Keith Ellis rang back. 'NPAS-15's attending an RTC in Kent, guv. Won't be available for at least ninety minutes.'

'God love our budget cuts!' Grace said, frustrated. Until a few years ago, when the then Home Secretary, Theresa May, had started to decimate police budgets around the country, Sussex Police had had their own helicopter. Now they not only had to share one with Kent and Surrey but, because it doubled as an air ambulance, it was only occasionally available when it was actually needed.

'Cheer up, boss,' Norman Potting said. 'The good news is that the money saved on our helicopter is helping people in need. Such as al-Qaeda and ISIS terrorists getting legal aid of a quarter of a million pounds a pop to fight their deportation orders. There's always a silver lining, eh?'

Grace's phone rang again. It was Glenn Branson.

'Boss, we've just had a ransom demand come in. And it's a strange one in a couple of ways.'

49

The receiving bay of the Brighton and Hove City Mortuary was on the far side of the building, out of sight of the general public. Whoever originally designed the building was clearly on a mission not to make it look grim – and had fallen victim to the old adage that 'No good deed goes unpunished'.

From the outside, the building looked like the kind of provincial, pebbledash-rendered bungalow with a steeply pitched roof and an attached garage that would, in estate agency parlance, have ideally suited an elderly retired couple. But the very innocent cuteness made it all the more grim when anyone realized what this building actually housed: a large postmortem suite, fridges capable of holding up to eighty bodies, a chapel and viewing room, and an office.

Cleo loved driving, and Darren Wallace, her deputy, was always happy to ride shotgun beside her. Their very silent passenger was zipped up in a black plastic body bag in the rear.

On the busy M23 motorway south from Gatwick Airport towards Brighton, in the dark van with the Coroner's emblem on each side, Cleo and Darren had been chatting about the new lady in Darren's life, called Natasha, whom

Cleo had met and really liked. This was a tough job of many parts. You had the grim task of recovering bodies – sometimes badly mangled in accidents, charred or decomposed or partially eaten by insects or crustaceans – and helping to prepare them for postmortems; you tried, where it was possible, to make them look presentable for their loved ones to view; and you had the constant emotional challenge of receiving the loved ones who had come to identify their wives, husbands, partners; often it was someone who had kissed them goodbye just hours before.

You needed to have some normality you could escape to at the end of your day – or night. Cleo counted her blessings constantly that she had finally found love with such a decent and caring human being as Roy. Although she never stopped worrying about him. In the relatively short time they had known each other, and even shorter time they had been together, he had put his life on the line in the course of his job on too many occasions for her liking. And she knew that for as long as he remained in the police service, he always would. His commitment to what he did was an essential part of the man she had fallen in love with and married, the father of their child, the man with whom she wanted to spend the rest of her life.

Each day that he was at work, she tried not to think about the knock on her door that might one day come from two police officers. But for now, as they arrived at their destination, Cleo's mind was focused on the pretty young woman she and Darren had zipped into the bag. All she knew about her at this stage was her name on her passport, Florentina Shima, which the Border Agency said was a bad forgery. Her possessions had consisted of a small amount of clothes and toiletries, and a mobile phone, all of which had been taken for analysis.

Cleo drove behind the mortuary, which was well out of sight of the public, reversed up to the doors, clicked the button to raise them, then reversed further into the receiving bay.

Mindful of her bad back, injured from lifting the body of a 350-pound woman a few months ago, she helped Darren move the young woman out of the rear of the van and wheel her through into the chilly interior of the mortuary.

Before doing this job, Cleo had worked in a number of hospitals as part of her nursing degree. Mostly, the workplaces she previously knew had a quieter, slacker feel at the weekends. But ever since she had started here, every day, whether a weekday or weekend, felt the same – it was always quiet and still. Although tonight it was particularly silent and cold. The only sound was the tick of fridges, the hum of their motors and fans.

The hospitals had mostly smelled sterile. This mortuary smelled of decaying flesh and clinical disinfectants, an odour that seemed ingrained into the walls – and the very soul of this place. If asked to explain why she had ever applied for this job, she probably couldn't. She found it grim, but fascinating. A kind of twilight world where life met death. A place where she could help and comfort the living in a time of deep distress. A place where she could make a difference in some small way. And she found it, constantly and morbidly, engaging.

The mortuary was clinical in the extreme. The harsh, cold lighting. The grey tiled walls and tiled floor. Everything designed to be sterile and minimize the risk of infection. Hoses and drain gullies to wash away blood. The scales for weighing every cadaver's internal organs. The trophy cabinet where bits of metal recovered from bodies had been placed. Pacemakers that would explode during a crema-tion. Shrapnel from historic war wounds of veterans.

The place gave her a buzz every time she entered. Sometimes she wondered, irreverently, what she would do if a fridge door opened and someone climbed out. That had not yet happened here, but some years ago her predeces-sor, Elsie, had told her that a woman certified dead by paramedics on the beach had once sat up, asking where she was. And, sometimes, genuinely dead corpses did move or make sounds from the gases building up inside them.

Those gave Cleo the real heebie-jeebies. There was little dignity in death, but one of her tasks was, always, to try to find it.

Although she was a suspected drugs mule, because of the nature of her death Florentina was classified as High Risk – someone who might have died of a contagious trop-ical disease – and was to be placed straight into the mortuary's isolation room, where the postmortem would be conducted under sterile conditions tomorrow.

As they laid the young woman on a gurney, Cleo unzipped the bag enough to look at her face, so like a por-celain doll.

You're just a teenager, she thought. *What happened?*

Hopefully, Dr Frazer Theobald would find out tomor-row.

Knowing that until then she must not touch anything, she zipped up the bag again and pushed Florentina Shima into the room, where the two of them lifted her onto the postmortem table.

They carefully disinfected and sterilized the mortuary van, then returned to the office to fill in the requisite forms, before washing diligently, locking up and heading home.

50

Open a Bitcoin account. If you wish to see Mungo
alive again, you will send the sum of £250,000 as
directed shortly. We will contact you again. By the
way, how is your new fridge?

Roy Grace stared at the latest text purportedly from the
kidnappers, which Glenn Branson had forwarded. The
ransom demand. And he understood Glenn's comment, *it's*
a strange one.

The mention of the fridge was, he presumed, to
underline that they were watching Kipp Brown. Fine. But
what bothered him was the amount of the ransom
demand and the vehicle through which the kidnappers
wanted it paid.

He called the DI. 'Glenn, what's going on? Who kidnaps
someone for this amount? Who in God's name would go to
all this trouble for a relatively poxy £250k? More likely to be
a million – or even five million – wouldn't you think?'

'But we've dealt recently with a kidnap ransom of just a
hundred quid,' Branson reminded him.

'You're right,' Grace said. 'But those small demands –
from fifty quid to a few hundred – are usually just scuzzy
little squabbles over drug debts. Something doesn't feel

right about this. They've made spelling mistakes, maybe they missed off a zero. What's Brown saying?'

'He wants to pay.'

According to the law, although blackmail was a criminal offence, paying a ransom was not. If someone wanted to pay a ransom demand, they were free to do so, and there was nothing the police could do to stop them.

'Tell him he's crazy if he does. They're not going to stop at £250k, they're just testing the water.'

'Why would they do that?' Branson asked.

'Because no one's going to go to this amount of trouble for peanuts, matey. Risk fifteen years in jail for pocket money?'

'It's all relative,' Branson replied. 'To someone who's chopping up his door frames to keep warm in winter, £250k is a fortune, right?'

'Maybe, but it worries me. There's something very ama-teurish about the amount. Explain to Brown and his wife that if they pay this ransom money, it may not be the end. There's likely to be another demand. Then another. His kidnappers believe Mungo's father is a rich man with deep pockets.'

'And how do I explain that if he doesn't pay, his son might die, boss?'

'Very simply. They've done all this, risking a decade or longer in jail for the money. They're going to be after bigger bucks than 250 grand. Just tell him to play the long game. If Mungo dies, what do the kidnappers have? Nothing but a murder investigation, with the odds against them. We catch around ninety per cent of all killers in the UK, year on year. Tell Kipp Brown to keep them sweet, to say he's going to download the Bitcoin app. Play for time. Meanwhile, let's see what our good friend – not – Mr Dervishi has to say.'

He looked at Norman Potting and Velvet Wilde.

Then he was interrupted as his phone rang. It was his boss, ACC Cassian Pewe. And he was incandescent with rage.

'Roy,' he said. 'Just what is going on? A bomb scare at the Amex, a kidnapped boy and now a dismembered body at a crushing plant. Meantime you are watching footy and playing lunatic heroics while you're supposed to be the on-call SIO. I want to see you first thing tomorrow, in my office, 9 a.m., and you'd better have some bloody good answers for me.'

Grace was well aware his actions at the Amex had given Pewe the excuse to discipline him that he had long looked for. But right now, he did not care.

'Yes, sir,' he replied.

Fuck you, he thought.

51

'So what made you join the police?' Norman Potting asked his colleague, seated beside him, as he drove the unmarked Ford up the hill, heading towards the east of the city.

'My dad was a police officer in Belfast,' Velvet Wilde said in her Northern Irish accent, the smell of pipe smoke on Potting's clothes reminding her of him. 'He was killed by a car bomb during the Troubles. I made the decision that as soon as I was old enough, I would do something to stand up against any kind of tyranny or intimidation.'

'I like feisty women,' Potting said. 'Good on you.'

She said nothing.

Potting was silent for a beat. Street lights flashed by, overhead, briefly illuminating their faces. 'Like I said,' he repeated, 'I like feisty women.'

'I'm sure Brighton is full of them, gagging to get laid by you.'

He smiled. 'Are you allowed to say that these days with all the political correctness about workplace harassment?'

'You know what, Norman, so far as I'm concerned most of it is absolute bollocks.'

'I agree with you, Velvet. So would you permit me to tell you that you're a very attractive lady?'

'Well, that's what my partner tells me,' she said.

'Ah.' Potting nodded. 'He's a lucky man. What's his name?'

'Julia.'

There was a long silence. 'Right,' Potting said, clumsily.

'I understand your fiancée was a police officer who died in a fire,' she said.

He nodded, gloomily. 'Bella. She was the love of my life.'

'I'm sorry.'

'Thank you.' He shrugged. 'You're happy with Julia?'

'She's the love of *my* life. Very happy.'

'You're lucky.'

'I am.'

The satnav indicated half a mile to their destination. They were high up above the cliffs of East Brighton and in daytime they would have had commanding views, to their right, across the English Channel. Now it was a vast, inky blackness.

'I heard that Detective Superintendent Grace lost the love of his life, too,' DC Wilde suddenly said.

'Well, he's very happily married now,' Potting replied, guardedly. 'He lost his first wife but I couldn't say whether she was the love of his life.'

'How did he lose her – what was her name – Sandy?'

'He doesn't talk about her much. As I understand, they married when he was quite young. Then he came home, on the evening of his thirtieth birthday, after they'd been married ten years, to find she had vanished.'

'Vanished?'

'Into thin air. No note or message. He came home to take her out for a birthday dinner and she wasn't there. I think they found her car at Gatwick Airport, but there were no transactions on her credit cards, nothing. He spent ten years looking for her – I heard he even consulted mediums.' He shrugged. 'Eventually he had her declared legally dead and married a lovely lady, Cleo, who runs the Brighton and Hove Mortuary. They have a baby son, Noah.'

'She is so nice – I've met her. And did he ever find out what happened to his wife?'

'Only very recently. Sandy was in a coma after being hit by a taxi in Munich and then died – leaving behind a ten-year-old son he never knew existed.'

'His son?'

'As I understand.'

'God,' she said. 'How does he cope with that – how does his new wife?'

'He doesn't talk about his personal life much. Not at work, anyhow. But I've known him a long time – he's pretty resourceful.'

She shook her head. 'None of us ever knows what's around the corner, do we?'

'That's why we do this job,' Norman Potting said.

'Because we don't know what's around the corner?' She looked puzzled.

'Exactly.'

'In what sense?'

He pulled out his warrant card. 'One day, when you're as old as I am, you'll understand. This card, this job, it lets us see around blind corners. Whether we like the view or not.'

'We're not about to like the view ahead, right?'

Norman Potting shook his head. 'That's never an option. We don't *like* or *dislike*. We just do what we do. Roy Grace says all we can do as police officers is to try to lock up the villains and make the world a slightly better place.'

'And do we?'

'Lock the villains up? Or make the world a better place?' he asked.

'Make the world a better place.'

'I think we help stop it getting worse.'

52

Gentian Llupa passed an hour, inconspicuously, at the rear of a crowded pub close to the Royal Sussex County Hospital. He sipped a Diet Coke, whilst watching a darts match that was in progress between a local team and one from Ipswich, the Thrasher Vipers, who all wore smart black-and-orange shirts. One member of this visiting team, heavily tattooed and sporting a Lincoln beard, was punishingly accurate. The Thrasher Vipers were indeed *thrashing* the local team, Llupa thought with a smile.

He left the pub and slipped out into the darkness. One thing he had learned as a medical student was that hospitals tended to be pretty chaotic places. Anyone could walk around the corridors and wards unchallenged. But even so, just to be safe, beneath his motorcycling leathers which were now folded and locked inside the motorbike's pannier, he had put on blue surgical scrubs, a stethoscope round his neck and an ID tag bearing the name Dr Tojo Melville, which his boss, Mr Dervishi, had given him.

He strode down a long corridor that smelled of disinfectant and mashed potato, passing a hand sanitizer, a caged trolley, an empty wheelchair, a lift, toilets and a multi-coloured sign naming the various wards on this floor. He passed a stack of empty blue and green plastic crates, two filled pink garbage bags, a row of noticeboards pinned with information leaflets, a yellow warning triangle stating CLEANING IN PROGRESS. A young, grief-stricken couple stood, hugging each other. An orderly walked past, from the opposite direction, giving him a cursory, respectful nod.

He reached the sign for Albourne Ward, Orthopaedic Unit, and stopped, peering in. Then, pulling his surgical hat low over his forehead, he approached the nursing station.

It was an open ward, comprising twenty-six beds, but to his right there were doors to four private rooms. Still no one took any notice of him. The nursing station was staffed by a pleasant-looking Asian man engaged on a phone call and two female nurses studying some paperwork. On the third door was the label STEPHEN SUCKLING.

As he hesitated outside, the door suddenly opened. A middle-aged woman, in jeans and a baggy blouse, blew the occupant a kiss and told him she would be back in the morning.

He turned his face away as she walked past him and waited until she had left the ward, then opened the door, walked in and closed it behind him.

The mechanical digger and crusher operator lay in the bed, both his legs held up by traction pulleys. He had been brought in earlier today, Llupa had been informed, with multiple fractures to the tibia and fibula in both legs, as well as fractures to his sacrum and coccyx. Much of his lower half was currently encased in plaster.

Llupa knew, from these injuries, he would not be walking again for many months and then for the rest of his life he was likely to have a severe limp. Well, he thought, that was one blessing. Stephen should be grateful to him for sparing him that suffering, no?

It was a small room, with pale-green walls and a wash

basin with a soap dispenser. Above the bed was an Anglepoise lamp; there was a drip stand with two lines cannulated into the back of Suckling's hand, two plastic chairs, a freestanding tray on which sat a glass, a jug of water and a box of tissues, and monitoring equipment with a display showing his blood pressure, 180 over 70 – *High*, thought Gentian – and his heart rate, 87 – *Also high*, he thought.

'Hello!' he said, breezily, to the patient. 'How's your day so far?'

Suckling looked at him groggily, heavily sedated. 'Not that great, actually.'

'Too bad. Mr Dervishi said to say hello, and how sorry he is about your accident.'

Suckling peered at the man in blue scrubs with the stethoscope dangling from his neck.

'Mr Dervishi asked me to explain to you that this is not personal. It is simply that shit happens.'

'Shlit shappens,' Stephen Suckling echoed. He watched the doctor replacing one bag of fluid attached to a drip line, grateful for the care, grateful for the constant numbing of the agonizing pain he had been in before they brought him here.

Within seconds of the doctor leaving his room, he started feeling happy. Incredibly happy. Life was great.

He felt full of love. All his cares were drifting away. Everything was wonderful. Boy, would he and his wife have a celebration when he got out of here!

He was only dimly aware of a steady *beep-beep-beep* sound.

The monitor's display was turned away from him so he could not see it.

The blood pressure reading began to drop, steadily and rapidly. Along with his heart rate: 62; 51; 47; 35; 22.

Somewhere out in the night, hazily, he heard the roar of a powerful motorcycle. And somewhere nearer he heard a steady beeping. It sounded like the warning from a lorry reversing.

A few minutes later, the heart rate on the monitor flat-lined.

53

Velvet Wilde looked at her watch. It was just after 11 p.m. 'Does Mr Dervishi know we're coming?'

'Yes,' Norman Potting replied. The Detective Sergeant's driving made her nervous – he barely looked at the road, seemingly treating it as a distraction from their conversation and from looking at her.

He drove them up a steep hill at the far eastern extremity of the city of Brighton and Hove, the posh Roedean area, with clifftop views across the English Channel. High above them, to their left and lit up like a Christmas tree, was a white, colonial-style mansion with a columned portico, surrounded by large grounds. He pulled the car up in front of tall metal gates, put down his window and pressed the button on the elaborate panel. Instantly a light shone on them.

'Who is this?' a guttural male voice asked.

'Detective Sergeant Potting and Detective Constable Wilde,' he replied.

'You are thirty minutes late,' the voice replied, curtly.

Potting glanced at his watch. 'We said we'd be here at about 11 p.m. It's now 10.55 p.m.'

'You are thirty minutes late.'

'No, we are not late, we are actually five minutes early,' he said firmly in his West Country accent.

'Mr Dervishi has gone to bed.'

Potting turned, puzzled, to DC Wilde, who frowned, then again spoke into the panel. 'I was told Mr Dervishi would see us at 11 p.m.'

'You wait, please.'

'No,' Potting said, loudly. 'You wait and you listen. Tell Mr Dervishi that if you don't let us in, he will be arrested. So he has the choice of seeing us now in the comfort of his home or being taken into custody and spending the night in a cell.'

'I will speak to my boss.'

'You do that, sonny Jim.'

Potting and Wilde sat in the car, in the darkness. 'Can we do that?' she asked. 'Arrest him?'

'We're in a fast-time kidnap situation. Dervishi is linked to a mobile phone that's been used by the kidnappers. You bet we bloody can.'

She smiled.

Suddenly the gates began opening.

They drove through and up the steep driveway. Four large men, almost as motionless as statues, and dressed in black, lined the drive, watching them suspiciously. As they neared the house, which had a quadruple garage to one side, two rottweilers appeared out of the shadows, barking savagely. Potting slowed the vehicle, not wanting to hit either of them, and pulled up in front of the porch. The dogs jumped up at the sides of the car. There was the piercing, high-pitched screech of a whistle and the dogs turned their heads, suddenly calming down, and padded away. Two men, sporting coiled earpieces and dressed in black suits and shirts, appeared seemingly from nowhere. One was enormous, with hair reduced to stubble and wearing dark glasses, striding with an arrogant swagger towards them. His colleague had almost ridiculously broad shoulders from working out, that seemed out of proportion to his small head, as if he had been the victim of an erroneous transplant. He had short, dark hair that finished in a widow's peak some way down his forehead, and dense eyebrows, giving him a permanent, worried frown. In contrast to the bully-boy appearance of his colleague, he seemed less threatening.

Potting and Wilde opened their doors and got out of the car.

Dark Glasses said, 'You are thirty minutes late.'

'No,' Potting said. 'I'm telling you we are not.'

'You are thirty minutes late. Mr Dervishi is a very punctual man, he does not like people being late. You have upset him.'

'Really?' Potting said. 'Well let me tell you, he has upset a lot of people also.' He looked at the silent man with the widow's peak. 'You and baldy-pops work for him, do you?'

'He is our boss,' he said, unsmiling.

'Fine.' Potting looked at each of them in turn. 'You have a choice. Either you take us to him this minute, or you are both nicked. Under arrest for obstructing justice. Understand?'

In reluctant silence, they ushered the two detectives through the front door into an imposing hallway that, Potting thought, could have been the entrance to a stately home. It was lined with classical oil paintings, busts on plinths and fine antique furniture, with a grand staircase at the far end. A distinct aroma of cigar smoke hung in the air.

From above they heard a cultured female voice with a trace of an Eastern European accent. 'What's going on, Valbone, Dritan? Is it Aleksander? Is he home?'

'Two detectives wish to talk to Mr Dervishi, madam,' one of the henchmen said.

'Oh God.'

A handsome, immaculately coiffed woman in her late thirties hurried down the stairs. She wore a velour tracksuit and suede Gucci-monogrammed slippers; her hands sparkled with ornate but classy rings and she held an equally sparkly mobile phone in one. Looking at Potting and Wilde, she asked, anxiously, 'Is this to do with Aleksander? Has he had an accident? Is he all right? Please say he's all right, yes? I'm his mother.'

'Mrs Mirlinda Dervishi?' Potting quizzed.

'Yes.'

He showed her his warrant card and explained who they were. 'We'd like to speak with both your husband and your son very urgently, madam.'

'Aleksander is not home. I was worried something has happened – I don't know where he is. He was going after the football to a friend, to work on a school video project. I phoned the friend's house a little while ago and his mother told me he never went there – unless I got it wrong and he is with other friends. I keep trying his phone and he is not answering.' She held up her hands with a gesture of despair. 'It's after 11 p.m. and he is only fourteen. He was going to phone Valbone to collect him when he was ready – I—'

She was interrupted by one of the bodyguards who had greeted Potting and Wilde. He spoke to her in a harsh-sounding foreign language and immediately she looked relieved. Turning back to the detectives, she said, 'Aleksander has just texted him, saying he will be sleeping over with his friends at a house in Hove – a different friend, I had it wrong. Everything's fine.' She smiled. 'My husband is in his office. I take you.'

Mirlinda Dervishi turned and spoke briefly and sharply to both bodyguards, again in the harsh language. The shaven-headed one answered her back and she raised her voice in reply, clearly angry at him. Gesturing the detectives to follow her, she strode down the hallway and stopped in front of a door. She knocked, then opened without waiting for a reply and ushered Potting and Wilde through into a large, masculine study, which smelled strongly of cigar smoke.

High up, all around, above the wall-to-wall bookshelves filled with antique, leather-bound tomes, were mounted stuffed animal heads on wooden plaques. A stag with massive antlers, a wildebeest, a giraffe and a zebra, plus the so-called 'Big Five' – a lion, elephant, buffalo, leopard and rhinoceros. Velvet Wilde looked at them in both revulsion and anger; she didn't like anyone who could be proud of killing such beautiful creatures. There was a studded black leather sofa and two matching armchairs arranged around a glass-topped coffee table and at the far end of the room a vast, vulgar walnut desk with ornate gold inlays.

It was occupied by a man who immediately got to his feet. He was short and wiry, with a cocksure, arrogant demeanour that was barely masked by his welcoming smile. His hair was razored to a hard-looking dark stubble and much of his face was covered similarly. He was dressed in a thin, black polo-neck jumper and jeans with a flashy belt buckle. The fingers of his left hand were adorned with jewelled rings and on his right hand was a black leather glove holding a torpedo cigar.

Potting recognized him from his photograph and stared at him, trying to figure out which was his glass eye.

Dervishi pointed at the two chairs in front of the coffee table, and joined them. Speaking in a genial voice with a much stronger accent than his wife's, he said, 'Detective Sergeant Potting and Detective Constable Wilde?' His gaze lingered approvingly on the female detective.

Potting held up his warrant card, but Jorgji Dervishi dismissed it with a wave of his hand. 'It is good of you to come, my wife is getting very anxious about our son – you see, this is just not like him, not typical at all. Aleksander, he normally always tells us his plans.'

'Mr Dervishi,' Potting cut him short. 'We would like to talk to your son urgently, but we also need to speak to you.'

'Of course!' he said. 'Please sit down. May I offer you a drink? I have good whisky – you like thirty-year-old Craigel-lachie?' He raised a cut-glass tumbler to display its amber content. 'Or Napoleon brandy, a glass of wine, coffee?'

'No, thank you,' Potting said.

Wilde shook her head.

'So, to what do I owe the pleasure of two detectives visiting me at this late hour?' His eyes lingered on Wilde as he drew on his cigar and blew out a perfect smoke ring, as if trying to tease approval from her.

'Does the name Fatjon Sava mean anything to you?' Potting asked, watching the man's eyes carefully – still trying to decide which was the glass one. But all he saw was a flicker of uncertainty as Dervishi stared fixedly back at him.

'A man by this name worked for me once, yes. But he was an idiot. I dismissed him a long time ago. So, how else may I help you?'

Potting still could not spot the prosthetic. 'A fourteen-year-old boy was kidnapped today at the Amex Stadium,' he said. 'His name is Mungo Brown and we understand he and your son are good friends at school.'

'Yes, this boy has been here a few times – I think they play computer games. He has been kidnapped? When?'

'He was last seen talking to your son an hour and a half before the start of the match this afternoon – around 4.00

p.m. Later, a ransom demand was made by text from a mobile phone that we have linked to a former employee of yours, Mr Fatjon Sava. What can you tell us about him?'

After a moment's hesitation, Dervishi said, 'I told you, Sava was an idiot. A psycho. The moment I realized this, I fired him. I'm trying to be a good citizen, you know?' He smiled, unconvincingly.

'Very laudable,' Potting said, a tad more cynically than he had intended to sound.

'Are you still in contact with Mr Sava?' Velvet Wilde asked.

'No.'

'Are you able to give us an address for him?' she persisted. 'Or anyone who could?'

Suddenly, without any warning, Dervishi's gloved right hand began to rotate.

Both detectives stared at it.

It went through 180 degrees. Then another 90 degrees. Then a complete 360 degrees. 'The war in Bosnia,' Dervishi said. 'A grenade with a faulty timer. I was lucky, it could have been worse. As a result, I have a hand that is better than the one God made.' He smiled at them. And now, clearly, Potting could see the glass eye, the right eye. Glinting. The one that, he had been told, looked warmer.

That was true, he realized.

Dervishi drew on his cigar again. 'I would of course connect you to Mr Sava, if I could. I have the greatest respect for your police force in Brighton. But I have had no contact with this gentleman for over a year. I don't know even if he is in this country or back in Albania or Kosovo. Is there anything else I can help you with? I am here, at your service.'

'We need to speak to your son, urgently,' Potting said.

'I would very much like to speak to him, also. He went to the football today and has not come home yet.' He shrugged. 'But you know how kids are today.'

Potting stared hard back at him. 'Actually, no, I don't.'

The glass eye glinted. 'They are very independent, Detective Sergeant Pothole.'

'Potting,' he corrected.

'Forgive me. Sometimes my English is a little – how you say – erratic.'

'Like your memory?'

Dervishi smiled. 'Indeed. Now, if you have no more questions, I would like to wish you both goodnight.' He stared at Velvet. 'Such a shame not to get to know you better, Detective Constable Wilde. Perhaps another occasion?'

She stared back at him, facing him off. 'Maybe in court, one day?'

Dervishi laughed. The confident laugh of an untouchable.

She asked, 'We'd like the address of where your son is at his sleepover, please.'

'He will be home tomorrow, perhaps it is better to talk to him then?'

'This is a kidnap situation,' Potting said. 'Every minute that passes is important. We need to talk to him tonight, as soon as possible. He may have seen something of vital importance to our enquiry. We'll need to pick him up and bring him here for interview.'

Dervishi pressed an intercom button on his desk and spoke in a foreign language. A gruff voice replied on the speaker. Dervishi picked up an ornate fountain pen and scrawled on a notepad. Then he tore the sheet off and handed it to Wilde. 'This is the address where Aleksander is staying. I don't think they will be pleased to see you so late.'

'I don't think Mungo Brown's parents would be pleased to know we let a vital witness get his beauty sleep while their son is being held bound and gagged, Mr Dervishi,' Wilde retorted coldly. 'How would you feel if it was your son?'

'If it was my son, I can tell you I would not be putting my faith in the police to get him back.' He picked up his cigar, drew on it and blew out another perfect smoke ring. It coiled slowly upwards, expanding and dispersing towards the ceiling as the two officers left.

Dervishi waited, seething in silent fury, until he heard the sound of their car starting. Then he stabbed his intercom again and barked out an instruction. His two bodyguards hurried in. The consiglieri did not look a happy man.

54

As Norman Potting waited for the gates at the bottom of Dervishi's drive to open, Velvet Wilde was entering the address the man had given them into the car's satnav.

'What a sweetie,' she said, sourly.

'It's what we're up against with some of the Albanian community,' Potting said, tapping the steering wheel. 'There's your problem with Johnny Foreigner.'

'I don't think that's very politically correct,' she chided, as he drove out onto the road.

Potting grunted. 'The Albanians don't trust us, they see us as the enemy.'

'Let me guess which way you voted in the Brexit referendum,' she said. 'Out, right?'

'Too right. And you, bleeding heart liberal, voted Remain?'

'Yes, I voted for the future and you voted for the past. You know why? Because you're a grumpy old dinosaur.'

He gave a sardonic smile. 'I voted for Brexit to keep the likes of Jorgji Dervishi from polluting our country.'

As they drove west in the darkness, street lights strobing across their faces, she turned to him. 'It seems to me, since joining the force, Sarge, there are two kinds of coppers. Those who went into the job because they wanted to make a difference and those who joined up because they liked the idea of putting on a uniform and being in authority. Which category do you fall into?'

'It may surprise you that it's the first. I wanted to try to make a difference. Once, long ago, I believed in human decency.'

'Not now?'

'If you dig deep enough you can still find some. My lovely Bella was the most decent person you could ever find.'

'She sounds it. I am truly sorry for your loss.'

'Thank you.'

'Do you think maybe you've not dug deep enough into the Albanian community in this city? That you're making judgements based on prejudice, not on the reality of their situation?'

'You heard Dervishi. He said that if his son was kidnapped, he wouldn't be turning to the police. That's the problem we're up against with them, they settle their scores violently and sometimes publicly. They don't trust us.'

'I don't think it's Sussex Police that they don't trust. It's the whole notion of authority. They've had a very different upbringing in their country from us here. Years of living in a brutal police state, of communist suppression under a monster dictator – Enver Hoxha. I seem to remember he once proudly declared Albania to be the world's first atheist state. For generations, they've lived in fear of authority, terrorized by corrupt officials. I don't think that culturally they can accept the idea that police officers could be decent people, because never, in all their history, have they been able to trust their own police. That's the hard task in front of us, to change that.'

'Admirable sentiments, young lady.'

'Norman,' she said, good-humoured, but forcibly, 'do not attempt to patronize me, ever. Understood?'

He raised his hands in surrender. They drove in silence for some minutes. A marked police car, lights flashing and siren wailing, shot past them. An ambulance, also on blues and twos, wailed past in the opposite direction. They passed trolleyed girls and equally drunk males, some staggering from bars and clubs, others standing in long lines to get in. Street fights. Police being chatted up or spat at, or in the thick of brawls. Saturday night in Brighton. Normal.

Entering the maze of streets in the quieter backwater of Hove, Potting kept an eye on the arrow on the satellite navigation screen, following it as they drove alongside Hove Park. He stifled his third yawn.

'Past your bedtime?' Velvet Wilde said with a grin, as he turned right and up a steep gradient. 'Need an old-people's nap?'

'Let me tell you, madam –' he began, then stopped as she read out a house number to their left.

'Thirty-seven.'

Then another, as he slowed the car right down. 'Thirty-five.' Then, 'Thirty-three,' she said. As he stopped the car, she unhooked a torch from its bracket in the footwell, switched it on and shone the powerful beam at the smart but considerably more modest house than Dervishi's. It was detached, 1930s, in the mock-Tudor style popular throughout the city. A dark-coloured Kia was parked outside. It was now shortly before midnight and the house seemed to be in total darkness.

They got out and walked up the short driveway towards the front door, Wilde holding the torch. As they approached, two security lights clicked on, almost dazzling them. A tiny creature, too fast and too small to identify, shot off in front of them and into the undergrowth.

The door had two bullseye windows and a spyhole. Norman Potting looked for the bell. He found it and pressed it, but they heard nothing. He pressed it again for longer. There was still no reaction. The officers glanced at each other and then he gave a true policeman's knock. *Ratta-tat-tat-tat-ratta-tat.* He followed up with another.

A light came on behind a curtained window above them. Another light came on behind the door. There was the click of a lock, followed by a short rattle as the door opened a few inches, restrained by a safety chain. A cautious male voice. 'Hello?'

'Detective Sergeant Potting and Detective Constable Wilde, from Surrey and Sussex Major Crime Team,' Potting announced. 'We're very sorry to disturb you at this hour but we need to speak urgently with Aleksander Dervishi, whom we understand is on a sleepover tonight at your house.'

'Aleksander who?'

'Dervishi, sir.'

The door closed, they heard the rattle of the safety chain, then it opened again, wider. A man in his sixties, with silvery hair, some sticking up, stood blinking at them, sleepily. He was dressed in striped pyjamas and slippers. '*Delvichy* did you say?' he asked, frowning.

'Aleksander Dervishi. We were told he was staying over at your house tonight, sir. Could I ask your name and who lives here?'

'My name's Andrew Griffin and I live here with my wife, Gill. I'm sorry, I think you must have the wrong address. I don't know anyone of that name. We don't have sleepovers here – my daughter, Rebecca, who's in her twenties, is away for the weekend.'

The man was clearly telling the truth. Potting apologized, saying they must indeed have the address wrong. As they walked back down the drive he turned to Wilde. 'Either Dervishi gave us the wrong address or his son gave him the wrong one. The question is, accidentally or deliberately?'

In the car, Potting held the scrap of paper with the address up to the interior light. There was no mistaking, it was correct.

He dialled Dervishi's number. It went to voicemail. He left a message that the address was wrong, and asked Dervishi to call him back, urgently. Ending the call, he turned to his colleague. 'Plan B?'

'Yep, well so far Plan A hasn't worked out too well. Any thoughts on what Plan B might be, Sarge?'

'I do, and I know a man who might agree.'

He dialled Roy Grace's number.

55

'Plan B!' Aleksander Dervishi said. He giggled.

The two boys were in the cellar of the isolated, derelict Victorian farmhouse, one of many properties Aleksander's father owned awaiting planning permission for redevelopment.

Mungo reached over, removed the joint from his hand and took a deep toke. 'Plan B – what do you mean? Plan A is still good, right?'

'You don't know my father.'

'You don't know mine,' Mungo said. 'The mean bastard.'

The two boys sat on the stone floor of the musty cellar, in the dim light of two thick, flickering candles. Discarded McDonald's cartons from their dinner lay beside them, the cardboard of one cannibalized to make the joints Aleksander had rolled. Mungo took another toke and passed it back to Aleksander. Above them, faintly, in the darkness of the night sky, they heard the *wokka-wokka-wokka* of a helicopter that was doing a steady sweep search, using a powerful searchlight shining down from its underside.

'I'm serious,' Aleksander said. 'Plan A is dead. There's been a fuck-up of some kind.'

Mungo took back the joint and toked again. 'So, un-fuck it up.'

'I will – but it means going home.'

'Shit, you're not leaving me here, alone?'

'Hey, stay cool, dude! You've got plenty of rats and spiders down here to keep you company!'

'That's not funny. And it's not our plan. And I'm cold and I'm still hungry. I've got the munchies. Do you have any chocolate?'

'You ate it. I'll bring some tomorrow.'

'Alek, you are not serious, you are not leaving me alone here. No way. No which way. You're not losing your fucking nerve, are you? Come on, we're in this together.' There was panic in Mungo's voice. He picked up the roll of duct tape they'd used earlier for the photograph, stared at it, then put it back on the floor. 'Look, we – we send them another text. Give my father one hour to send the money or I die.'

'Dude, you are not thinking straight. First your dad has to set up a Bitcoin account. Then you have to have an account that can't be traced for the Bitcoins to be deposited in.'

Mungo stared at him. 'Your guys – your dad's bodyguards, right? – Valbone and Dritan – I thought they had it sorted – like, we're giving them a generous cut. I thought they had an account that couldn't be traced, right?'

'Don't worry, they're good dudes, I've known them since I was just a little kid. They hate my dad, they think he's a brutal asshole. They're with us, one thousand per cent. It's happening – might just take a bit longer than we planned.'

'How much longer?'

'I'll find out.'

'I need something more to eat. I can't believe you didn't bring anything else.'

'One spliff and you turn into, like, a Dyson, dude!'

Aleksander said. 'You've eaten six chocolate bars. On top of a Big Mac and fries and two doughnuts.' His watch suddenly lit up with a message and he looked at it. 'I gotta go, Valbone's here.'

'You are so not going, Alek.'

'Trust me, I'll be back in the morning. And I've got to charge my phone, I'm almost out of juice.'

'What about my phone? Why did the morons take it from me?'

'So you couldn't be tracked, dumbo!'

'Don't leave me, Alek, I'm scared. I can't stay here alone.'

'Just remember why you're doing this, OK? You wanted to piss your dad off, get back at him, get some money from him. Right?'

'Not really, it's not about the money.'

'What do you mean? This is *all* about the money, that's why we're doing it!'

Mungo shrugged. 'Yep, well I know it is for you, Alek.'

'And it's not for you? What is it for you?'

Mungo was silent, close to tears. 'I just wanted to see how much they really love me.'

'You're not talking any sense.'

'They always, like, worshipped my sister.'

'Kayleigh – who died, right?'

'She was – whatever you call it – the apple of my dad's eye. I never really felt I mattered. Since she died it's been a shitload worse. Kayleigh, Kayleigh, Kayleigh. Sometimes I feel like they don't even see me, that I don't even exist. No one was bothered about me when she died, whether I missed her or not. I'm the brother that got forgotten. They never ask me how I feel about it. You know what I really feel? That they're upset she died and I'm the one who lived, and that maybe they'd have liked it the other way round. That's why I'm doing this, to test them, to see if they really do care – you know – like, enough to pay the ransom.'

'So, hang loose.'

'Easy for you to say. You're going home in a warm car to food and your bed. What am I meant to do?'

'Be a brave soldier!' Aleksander stood up. 'I'll be back as soon as I can in the morning. Meantime, I'll send Valbone back with a stash of food for you, OK?'

'And a torch and some toilet paper.'

'What brand would your precious, tender bum like?'

'Screw you.'

Mungo sat miserably as his friend, guided by the light of his phone, headed up the staircase.

Halfway, Aleksander stopped and turned round. 'Dude, stay cool. Valbone will be back in an hour.'

'Did you even listen to what I just said, Alek?'

His friend grinned. 'I did – you're having a funny five minutes, it's the weed, you'll get over it.'

'It's not a *funny five minutes*. It's why I've bloody done this.'

'Cool, understood, see you in the morning, dude.'

'Do you have another joint you could leave me?'

'I did, but we just smoked it.'

As his friend vanished upstairs, the dope having little effect, Mungo stared around. At the guttering candles. The bare walls. The spiders' webs. He was really scared. This wasn't working out – how had he ever thought it possibly could? But now they were too deep in.

Shit.

Shit.

Maybe he should just go home. But what would that

achieve, apart from dumping Alek in the shit for helping him? What a mess.

What a bloody mess.

He shivered.

Then he began to cry.

56

Ylli Prek began to cry. He shivered with cold. He didn't know what the time was or how long he had been down here in the dimly lit basement room below Mr Dervishi's house, naked, handcuffed to a hard chair fixed to the floor.

In front of him was a steel gurney, with a tray of surgical knives and other instruments on a stand beside it. And only inches to his right was a barred door, like in a prison, to the darkened, rank-smelling pool area where Mr Dervishi's Nile crocodile, Thatcher, lived. Earlier, when the two men had brought him down here, Mr Dervishi had followed, telling him that he would be back later with a doctor who would be cutting limbs off him to feed to Thatcher. He asked Prek to consider what it would be like to watch a crocodile eating his body parts while he was still alive and conscious. Parts that had been surgically removed without an anaesthetic.

Ylli Prek was petrified. He had crapped himself and wet himself. He sat in the stench of his own excrement and the sour, damp reek of the reptile and its lair. Suddenly he heard footsteps behind him and turned his head.

'How's your day so far?' Mr Dervishi asked, approaching him with a half-smoked torpedo in his gloved hand.

'Not great.'

'No? Such a shame.' Dervishi sounded genuinely sorry.

On the wristwatch on his boss's other arm, Prek saw the time. It was just coming up to 1 a.m. Dervishi gave him a look of distaste and wrinkled his nose. 'What a disgusting smell – were you never potty-trained?' He puffed on his cigar, exhaled and waved the smoke around with his hand. He glanced at the barred door and the darkness, tinged with a faint green glow, beyond.

'Don't worry, Thatcher,' he called out. 'I will get you a nice piece of meat very soon. Would you like this man's right or left leg first? Or perhaps all of him at once?'

He looked down at Prek. 'Do you know how a crocodile likes to prepare his meal?'

The man looked petrified.

'He likes to take his meat underwater and keep it there for a while, to tenderize it.' He smiled. 'How would you feel as you were dragged beneath the surface by a crocodile? By your leg or arm? And your last thought, as you could no longer hold your breath and began to drown, would be to think about that creature eating you, bit by bit, over the coming weeks. Do you like that thought?'

'Please, Mr Dervishi, please understand that I did what you told me,' Prek pleaded.

'No, Ylli. I was expecting the stadium to be evacuated and the match abandoned, that was your mission. It didn't happen. You failed me.'

'No!' He shook his head in terror. 'Please, I did what you instructed me. I did. I left the camera there, on the seat. I did. I primed it, I followed your instructions, I don't understand why it did not explode.'

Dervishi stared at him. 'So, it didn't work out. But I'm a very fair man, Ylli, I've come to offer you a deal.'

'Yes? Please. Please, I will do anything.'

'I know that,' Dervishi replied. Then he smiled. 'I'm going to turn you from a loser into a hero. Do you like the sound of that?'

'Yes, yes I do, thank you!'

'Oh, I'm not so sure you will be thanking me. But I will be thanking you, I promise you. Does it sound good?'

'Yes!'

'Ylli, there was a great Hollywood film producer called Darryl Zanuck. He won three Academy Awards – Oscars – pretty impressive, right?'

'Oh yes, very.'

'He made *The Sound of Music*, *Jaws* and *Driving Miss Daisy*. Not bad, eh?'

'No, I liked *Jaws* very much. Very scary.'

'Very scary indeed. You know, I still don't like to swim in the sea. Do you like to swim in the sea, Ylli? Does it worry you that a shark might eat you when you do?'

'I can't swim.'

'No?' Dervishi said. 'OK, so you've never had to worry about being eaten by a shark?'

'No, no, sir.'

'Lucky. Do you consider yourself lucky?'

'No, Mr Dervishi sir, not lucky, not really.'

'Well let me correct you. Ylli, this is your lucky day. Does it make you happy to hear that?'

'Yes.'

Dervishi went out of the room and returned holding a large, raw chicken. He opened the barred door and called out into the darkness, 'Sorry, Thatcher, it is only chicken tonight, not human meat – but who knows what tomorrow will bring, eh?'

Prek, still shaking with fear, saw the man lay the chicken down at the tiled edge of the pool, retreat and close the door again. Almost instantly, he heard a sudden deep thrashing of water. He saw two reptilian claws appear on the tiles, followed by another whoosh of water as the creature lifted itself up and Prek stared into the gaping mouth with its rows of massive, uneven teeth. They clamped over the chicken and, seconds later, with another deep splash, the crocodile was gone.

'I have a proposition to put to you, Ylli. To save your life. How do you feel about that?'

'Yes! Yes please.' Prek was staring, mesmerized, at the darkness beyond the barred door.

Dervishi took another drag on the shrinking stub of his cigar and tapped some ash off the end. It fell to the floor. 'Mr Darryl Zanuck was famous for one thing he used to tell people. He used to tell them, *Don't say yes until I stop talking.*'

Ylli Prek said nothing, watching him.

'Do you understand that, Ylli?'

'Yes.'

'I'm going to give you a second chance. Are you happy about this?'

'Yes, yes please, I am.'

'Good, so now wait until I have finished talking before you say *yes* again.'

57

Shortly after 1 a.m., Roy Grace made himself a fresh cup of coffee and went back into the Intel suite, tired but running on adrenaline and caffeine – and pure cussed determination to find Mungo Brown. So far, the helicopter search of the suspect area had produced nothing and it had returned to its base to refuel. There had been no reported sightings of the teenager at Newhaven, where every vehicle had been checked, nor from the French port of Dieppe where the last ferry had docked and a similar check had been carried out.

He had, with some misgivings, sanctioned Norman Potting's request to arrest Jorgji Dervishi if necessary. Under normal circumstances it would have been pushing the envelope too far to arrest him simply for being linked to the phone, and passing on a wrong address, but these were not normal circumstances. A boy's life was at risk and that upped the ante considerably.

He wrote his reasons down in his Policy Book to cover his back against the inevitable grilling he would get from Cassian Pewe, after Dervishi had got some of his powerful city contacts to throw their weight around. But that was for later. He instructed one of his team, burly DS Kevin Taylor, to liaise with the Duty Inspector at John Street police station on accompanying Grace's team to Dervishi's address.

Not knowing what they would face at Dervishi's fortified home, Taylor might need a group of Local Support Team officers to accompany DS Potting and DC Wilde to effect entry. The LST were the specially trained crowd and riot control police, who were also equally specialized at putting in doors and forcing entry. Little fazed them.

Hall, seated opposite him, holding his phone to his ear and stifling a yawn, suddenly perked up. He put the phone down and called across to him. 'Boss! That was Dan Salter at Digital Forensics. He's just heard from the phone company. A phone signal from the texter's phone was identified by triangulation in our target area made at 12.55 a.m.!'

'Brilliant!' Grace said.

'It puts it within a three-mile radius of where we are looking – somewhere between the Beddingham round-about and Newhaven.'

Immediately, Grace called Oscar-1 and was glad to hear the voice of Inspector Keith Ellis, who had remained on duty. He updated him, and Ellis said he would get the heli-copter back over the area as quickly as possible.

Moments later his phone rang. It was Norman Potting.

'I've got the troops ready, chief.'

'Nice work, Norman!' Grace said, elated. He jumped up and turned to Kevin Hall, opposite him. 'You in a party mood?'

'Always. Especially on a Saturday night.'

'It's Sunday morning now – in case you hadn't noticed. But hey, let's not split hairs.'

'Never, boss.'

'Rock 'n' roll!'

58

'Boss?'

Dervishi held his phone to his ear and looked at his clock radio: 2.52 a.m. 'This had better be good,' he said, angrily and sleepily.

Beside him, Mirlinda stirred. 'All OK?'

'Hold on,' he said into the phone. He gave his wife a reassuring caress with his good hand, slid out of bed and walked out of the room, naked, holding the phone to his ear. 'Yes, Dritan?'

'There are police outside the gates, boss. They say if we don't open the gates they will force entry. We see several police cars and a van. What should I do?'

'Is downstairs to the basement sealed?'

'It is.'

The basement was soundproofed, and the entrance concealed by a bookshelf that moved across it when the security switch was activated.

'Let them in, and I will go out to greet them.'

'Yes, boss. Is this a good idea?'

'You have a better one?'

There was silence down the phone.

He went back into the bedroom, put on his dressing gown and slippers, then closed the door behind him, went downstairs and along the hallway to the front door. As he reached it he heard loud knocking and a shout of 'POLICE!'

He opened the door. In front of him he saw the male detective who had been at the house earlier, with the pretty female one standing next to him, and several others behind them.

'Jorgji Dervishi,' Potting said. 'I am arresting you on suspicion of conspiracy to kidnap and obstructing the police . . . You do not need to say anything but it may harm your defence if you do not mention when questioned something which you later rely on in court. Anything you do say may be given in evidence.'

Dervishi frowned and gave him a puzzled smile. 'Detective—?'

'Potting.'

'Detective Potting, I am not in any way trying to obstruct the police. On the contrary, I really wish to help the police in this distressing enquiry.'

'Is that right?' Potting asked. 'If I may say so, you've been doing a great job so far, giving us a false address for your son.'

'Look, Officer – Detective Potting – I'm as angry as you about this. But my son is now home.'

'He is?'

'Yes, an hour ago. I was going to call you in the morning.'

'We need to speak to him urgently.'

A worried-looking Mirlinda Dervishi, in a dressing gown, came hurrying down the stairs. 'What's happening, what's going on?'

'The officers just wish to speak to Aleksander, my love,' he replied, and turned back to the policemen. 'Of course, if it's important.' Then he looked at Roy Grace, who was now standing next to DC Wilde. 'And you are?' he questioned.

Grace showed his warrant card. 'Detective Superintendent Grace, Surrey and Sussex Major Crime Team.'

'Nice to meet you,' Dervishi said.

Grace said nothing.

'Would you like me to accompany my son or would you
prefer to talk to him alone?'

'He's fourteen?' Potting said.

'Yes.'

Potting turned to Mrs Dervishi. 'Are you willing to act in
the role of Appropriate Adult, Mrs Dervishi?' he asked.

'He's my son! What do you think? No?'

'Bring him down to us,' Potting said, and signalled to
two of the Local Support Team to accompany Mrs Dervishi
up the stairs.

A few minutes later a tall teenager, barefoot, in jeans
and a creased T-shirt, came down the stairs and sat,
morosely, at the huge white marble kitchen table. Opposite
him were his father, mother, Norman Potting, Velvet Wilde
and Roy Grace. Both the patio doors out onto the garden
and the entrance to the hall were blocked by police officers.

Grace turned to Jorgji Dervishi. 'Two of my officers will
accompany you to another room and I'll speak to you again
after I've spoken to your son.'

'I want to be there while you speak to him.'

'I'm afraid that's not possible, sir. Is there a room you
can wait in?'

'My office,' he grumbled.

Grace turned to two members of the LST and addressed
them. 'Mr Dervishi is under arrest. He's not to use any
phones or communicate with anyone.'

They led him out of the kitchen, swearing loudly in
Albanian. Grace turned to the boy.

'Aleksander,' he said. 'We are sorry to wake you up in the

middle of the night.' He seemed agitated and Grace noticed his pupils were dilated. He detected a whiff of cannabis.

'I'm cool with that.'

'Where do you go to school, Aleksander?' Roy Grace asked, watching his eyes closely. They went to the right as he replied.

'Brighton College.'

'And Mungo Brown is there with you?'

'Yes.'

Again, his eyes went to the right. From this, Grace knew they would mostly go to the right when he told the truth – and to the left when he lied.

'The reason we are here and need to talk to you so urgently, Aleksander, is that your friend, Mungo, has been kidnapped. You were the last person he was seen with, shortly before the start of the match at the Amex yesterday. According to his father, you were chatting to him, then a few minutes later you had both disappeared. Where did you and Mungo Brown go?'

His eyes flicked to the left. To construct mode. Constructing a lie, Grace wondered?

'Umm – we – we went to a food stand to get a burger because he was hungry.'

'Wouldn't he have had lunch in his father's box?'

'He wanted a burger. He said all the people in the box would be boring.'

'You went through the turnstile together to get into the stadium?'

Again, Aleksander's eyes flicked to the left. 'Yes.'

'Are you sure?'

Mrs Dervishi interrupted. 'Don't say anything, we need a lawyer.'

'It's true, Mum, he wanted a burger!'

'Aleksander,' Grace said. 'Your friend Mungo had a season ticket like you. When you go through any entrance to the ground, the ticket is logged. There is no log that Mungo or you went through the turnstiles yesterday. It doesn't look like he entered the grounds. Are you certain he did?'

'Aleksander!' his mother cautioned again, more forcibly.

The boy was quiet for a moment, thinking. 'I'm trying to remember, no. I – I – maybe we went to a place that was outside the stadium.'

'What did you eat there, Aleksander?' Grace said calmly and quietly, as if he was talking to his best friend, rather than to a teenager.

Again, his eyes moved left. 'Burgers,' he replied.

'Burgers?'

He nodded.

'Aleksander, you don't have to answer me if you're not happy, but I need to ask if you are remembering clearly. There are no burger stalls outside the stadium. If you want a burger, you have to enter the ground. Do you want to think again back to yesterday, about where you and Mungo went?'

His eyes were now all over the place, shooting from left to right, wildly. 'Well.' His eyes veered left. 'Yes. Mungo said he'd be in trouble if he didn't go to his dad's box, to talk to a bunch of his dad's dull clients. So we parted, and I went to the game.'

'And did you see Mungo afterwards?'

'No.'

'Are you absolutely sure, Aleksander?'

More hesitation. His eyes flicked to the left. To construct mode.

'Yes.'

Grace looked hard at him. Something was very wrong. Why was the lad lying? Was he scared of his monster of a father or was something else going on? He'd probably been smoking weed. With his friend Mungo or with other friends? Was the wrong address that Dervishi had for him tonight a mistake caused by the drugs he had taken? Or was the boy being disingenuous?

If so, what was he hiding?

'Aleksander,' he said, leaning in closer to him. 'When did you last see Mungo?'

A big flick of his eyes to the left. 'Like I said, before the game started. Before kick-off.'

'Are you telling me the truth?'

'Yes.'

'Are you sure?'

He shot a look at his mother. 'I am, yes, absolutely.'

'I don't believe you, Aleksander,' Grace said. 'You've lied to me about entering the stadium. You've lied to me about having a burger outside. What else have you lied about?'

'Aleksander!' his mother interjected, forcibly.

He said, defiantly, 'I do not tell lies.'

'I would beg to differ,' Potting interjected suddenly, to Roy Grace's irritation. Just as he felt he might be getting somewhere.

'Where were you this evening, Aleksander?' Grace asked, gently but firmly.

'With friends.'

'What were you doing with them?'

He hesitated. 'Working on – you know – on a YouTube video project that we have.'

'Was Mungo with you?'

'He didn't show up.'

'Aleksander,' Grace said. 'You gave your parents an

address where you were tonight, but it was incorrect. Did you make a mistake?'

'I must have.'

'Or was it because you were all taking drugs and didn't want to get caught, perhaps?'

His mother, looking shocked, said, 'Is this true?'

He shrugged. 'Somebody had a joint – it was no big deal.'

Grace raised an eyebrow at the boy's mother.

'Never! Aleksander's a good boy, he never takes drugs,' his mother said in an angry burst.

'Except tonight, Mrs Dervishi, perhaps?' Grace turned to him. 'Is that right, Aleksander?'

He looked miserable, his face screwing up, fighting tears.

'Would you let me have the correct address for where you were tonight, please?' Grace asked.

Suddenly, the boy buried his face in his hands and began sobbing.

His mother went over to him and put an arm round him. 'It's OK, darling, it's OK.'

He shook his head. 'I only did it to help him,' he blurted. 'To get even with his father.'

'You only did what, exactly?' Grace asked.

Aleksander, sobbing uncontrollably, told him – but not quite everything.

59

Ting!

Kipp Brown sat alone, early morning, playing a one-armed bandit in the deserted high-rollers' room of the Waterfront Casino in Brighton Marina, aware the staff were waiting patiently for him to leave so they could close up for the night. He raised a hand in acknowledgement as someone brought him a fresh Hendricks and tonic with a slice of cucumber.

The stake on this machine was a £25 token, and the jackpot – four bars lined up – would pay out £50,000. He was close. Close!

The reels were spinning now and he could feel that jackpot coming closer. With each spin for the last hour, in between the cherries, lemons and apples, a jackpot bar would appear and stop on the winning line.

Ting!

Now two had lined up.

He inserted another token and pressed the button.

The reels span again.

Ting!

One bar stopped.

Ting!

Another!

Ting!

Another!

Ting!

The fourth! Yes, he felt a burst of happiness. Yes, yes, yes!

But no tokens poured out. He waited. Come on, come on!

Ting.

Suddenly, the light changed. Darkened. Slowly, a sense of dread enveloped him. He wasn't in the casino at all, he realized, he was in bed, at home. He had been dreaming. It wasn't the slot machine, after all, it was his phone. He lay still, not wanting to disturb Stacey. Until he remembered they were in different rooms. He was alone, in a spare room where he had been sleeping for several months.

He'd lain awake for hours tonight, lapsing into intermittent dozes. Waiting. Waiting for a further text. Instructions on where to pay the ransom. Anything.

Ping.

He grabbed the handset and peered at the screen.

60

Blue light pulsed eerily across the central reservation barrier to their right and the grass verge to their left, as Roy Grace drove at high speed along the A27. They were heading east along the Lewes bypass. Kevin Hall, beside him in the front, kept watch on the satnav screen. Aleksander Dervishi sat in silence in the rear of the car with his mother. In his mirrors Grace could see the headlights and blue flashing lights of the car with Potting and Wilde in, following behind.

They crossed a roundabout and went down a long, sweeping hill. Another roundabout sign appeared on the screen, with options to turn right to Newhaven or go straight on to Eastbourne and Polegate.

'Aleksander,' Grace said. 'One thing you've not told us is how you got home tonight?'

'I texted Valbone and told him to pick me up from this roundabout, right ahead.' He was still crying.

Kevin Hall turned and looked at the boy in the darkness. 'Can you direct us from here?'

He sniffed and nodded. 'You go straight over the roundabout and carry on for a few hundred yards. When you see a traffic island, turn right.'

The island loomed ahead in the beam of the headlights.

Grace indicated right, leaned forward and switched off the blue lights, slowing rapidly. In his mirrors, he saw the car behind him also indicating, and its blue lights shut off, too.

'You go up the hill a little way,' Aleksander directed.

Grace drove up a steep, narrow lane, with cottages and houses to the right, for several hundred yards. Suddenly, in front of him, he saw two tiny lights, sparkling like gemstones. Then a fox shot across their path, into the undergrowth to their left.

'Coming up, turn right,' Aleksander said.

There was a sign, saying PRIVATE ROAD. Grace turned into it and drove as fast as he dared along a deeply rutted cart track. The suspension bottomed out several times, jolting all of them. They passed a derelict barn, then Grace saw the shape of a house ahead, to their left. As they drew closer he could see a sizeable stone cottage.

'This is it – I think,' Aleksander said.

'You think?' Grace asked.

'Well, I'm pretty sure.'

Grace's watch showed it was approaching 4 a.m. He saw an overgrown driveway and turned into it. To his left were several rusting bits of agricultural equipment and ahead was a short, steep incline. The wheels spun on the wet grass, the car twitching until they got traction. He crested the hillock and stopped by the front door. Potting pulled up behind them.

Grabbing a torch and stifling a yawn, Grace climbed out and stood in the damp night air. The others in the car joined him, along with Potting and Wilde. 'This is the place?' he asked the boy.

He gave a forlorn nod. Above him a full moon burned intensely in the sky, casting a glow almost bright enough to read by across the entire countryside.

They approached the oak front door, Aleksander Dervishi and his mother hanging back. Grace could see it was ajar, and went straight in, shining the beam around a small, musty and bare hallway. He hesitated, then turned to Aleksander. 'If you call out to him, it won't frighten him. OK?'

He nodded. Then in a small voice said, 'Mungo! Hi, I'm back!'

There was no response.

Louder, this time, he called out, 'Hey – er – Mungo – dude, I'm back!'

Still nothing.

'Mungo!' he called out. 'Mungo!' He looked at Grace. 'Maybe he's sleeping – down below.'

Grace handed him his torch. 'Why don't you lead the way?'

The five of them followed the teenager down a steep wooden staircase, Grace walking slowly and warily, the treads feeling rotten, as if they were barely taking his weight. A cobweb touched his face and he brushed it away with his hand. The musty smell was much stronger down here, combined with damp and the sickly-sweet stink of dry rot. But there was also a faint, lingering aroma of French fries.

The torch beam swept over some remains of McDonald's cartons and two partially burned-down candles. Close to them, Roy Grace noticed a couple of what looked like stubbed-out joints on the floor.

'Mungo!' Aleksander called out. 'Mungo!'

There was no response.

'This is where I left him,' he said to Grace.

'Are you completely sure?'

'Shit, yes, of course I'm sure. This is where we were!' he said, in a sudden burst of anger and frustration. He shouted out, much louder now: 'Mungo! Where the fuck *are* you?'

Silence.

'Could he have gone somewhere, Aleksander?' Grace asked him.

'No, he was waiting for me to come back with some food.'

'And he was OK that you left him alone?'

'He wasn't happy, but yes, he was OK with it. You know, I –' he hesitated.

'What?'

'Nothing. Well, we had a bit of weed.'

'And now he's gone. Where do you think he could be?'

'He must be here, somewhere.'

'You're sure you are not mistaken?' Potting asked.

'No, I am not mistaken.'

As Grace shone his torch around he glimpsed something blue-and-white on the far side of the room and hurried over to it. A Seagulls scarf.

Aleksander ran to it and picked it up. 'This is Mungo's!' He called out again, 'Mungo! Mungo!'

There was still no response.

Tugging a couple of evidence bags from his pocket, Grace knelt down by the two joints. He picked up each in turn with his handkerchief and popped them into individual evidence bags, which he sealed and put in his pocket. For the next five minutes, guided by Aleksander who appeared to know the property well, they searched every room, every closet, and up in the loft. Finally, they assembled in the hallway.

'Mungo's not here, Aleksander,' Grace said. 'So where is he? I'm not crazy about going on wild-goose chases at four in the morning. Do you have something else you'd like to tell us?'

'Please tell them anything you know, darling,' his mother implored.

'Look,' Grace went on. 'You've been very silly and irresponsible, and I think you know that. But if you can take us to him, now, that will count a lot in your favour. OK?'

'He was here,' he said, wretchedly. 'I promised him I would send him food and I would be back with more food in the morning. I don't know where he is, I really don't.'

Grace believed him. The kid was broken, way beyond telling lies any more.

Where had Mungo Brown gone?

'Are there any outbuildings?' Kevin Hall asked.

'Just a collapsed shed,' Aleksander said.

'What time did your father's employee, Mr Valbone Kadare, pick you up?' Grace asked.

'About 1 a.m.'

'He came home half past one,' his mother confirmed.

'Mungo was hungry?' Grace asked him.

Aleksander nodded. 'He had the munchies. We both did.'

'Do you think he might have gone off to try to get some food?'

'There's nowhere for miles around here,' Norman Potting said. 'Brighton's the only place he could get anything at this hour – and how would he get there?'

'Hitch a lift?' Velvet Wilde ventured.

'I told him I would send Valbone back with some for him.'

'Where's Valbone now?' Grace asked.

'We don't know,' Mirlinda Dervishi replied. 'My husband's trying to get hold of him.'

'Could Mungo have gone home?' Kevin Hall asked.

'How?' Aleksander replied.

'I'll phone his father and check,' Grace said. But as he pulled his phone out, it rang.

It was Glenn Branson.

'Boss,' he said. 'There's been a development. Kipp Brown's had another text – from a different phone. And it's not good. I'm sending it to you now.'

61

Seconds later, Grace received it.

> The price for your son has just gone up. We will
> now require £2.5 million value in Bitcoins. We will
> be in touch with details where to pay this. Don't be
> stupid and go looking for Mungo. If you succeed in
> finding him without having paid, all you will have is
> a corpse. Sorry to text so late. You will soon receive
> payment instrucions. Have a nice rest of night!

He showed it to everyone. 'Do you know anything about this, Aleksander?' he asked.

'Two and a half million?' the boy said, looking totally confused. 'This was not our plan. No. No, I—' He began to cry again.

'Can you get cell-site analysis on this, Glenn?' Grace asked.

'We're on it.'

He stared at the text.

> payment instrucions

Yet another spelling error, he observed.

'Aleksander, tell them what you know, for God's sake, tell them!' his mother implored.

The teenager stared blankly at her. 'I don't know,' he said, lamely. 'I don't know. This is – this is not – I – this is not our plan.'

'Tell them the truth!'

'I am. I am telling the truth.'

Grace stepped out of earshot and updated Branson on the latest development at his end. 'What does Kipp Brown say? If absolutely needed, could he stump up this ransom – even just for a few hours?'

'He's just told me he's close to bankruptcy,' Branson replied. 'He's had a disastrous gambling run in the past few months and is virtually broke. He was going to be hard pushed to come up with the original 250 grand. Let alone this.'

'Yes, he implied that to me.'

'Everyone thinks Kipp Brown is richer than God,' Branson said. 'He flies clients around in private jets, lives in a fuck-off house, child in private education. And he dotes on his son. I believed him when he told me he doesn't have that kind of money. What are we going to do? Don't the National Crime Agency have funds for these kinds of situations?'

'Two and a half million? You are joking – they used to have a small amount but I don't even know if they have that any more.' Grace thought quickly. 'OK, we know from Aleksander Dervishi the kidnap was a set-up by a very devious couple of lads, to screw some money from Kipp Brown. I don't know what this new demand is about. The kid's vanished. Is it real this time or another part of their dumb plan? What the hell are we dealing with here?'

'I don't know, boss. Any ideas? Hypotheses?'

'I'm all out of them. And I'm just about to have our one suspect, Jorgji Dervishi, de-arrested.'

slowed and they'd driven for a long while at a much steadier speed.

At one point he heard a siren and his hopes rose. But it howled on past them and away into the distance.

After what seemed an eternity, they stopped again and he was lifted out, clumsily, then carried a short distance. He could hear the sound of the sea and smelled salty air. Nothing else. Dead silence. No other clues as to where he might be. Then the footsteps of his captors. Their voices. They entered some kind of chamber and descended steps. Then he was dumped roughly on his back onto a hard, cold surface, with the sound of lapping water only inches away.

A moment later, he cried out in pain as the tape across his eyes was ripped off, and he lay blinking against the bright light of a torch. He cried out again as the tape over his mouth was also ripped off, forcefully.

'Aleksander!' he shouted. 'Where is Aleksander?'

There was no response.

'I'm desperate for a pee! Please! I have to pee!'

Again, no response.

'I'm going to piss my pants. Please.'

'So, piss in them,' a voice said in heavily accented English.

A bottle of water was jammed between his lips.

He took a sip and spluttered as he choked. One of the men helped him sit up a little. The bottle was replaced by a chocolate bar and crammed into his mouth. He chewed and swallowed. As soon as he had finished he was pushed, roughly, back down, a hand pinning him by the neck.

He shook in fear. Were they going to kill him? But they wouldn't have given him a drink and food if they were going to do that, would they?

Was this Aleksander's idea of a joke?

Fresh tape was pressed in place over his mouth and pulled tight against his cheeks. He saw the glint of a knife blade. Something tugged hard on his right ear and he let out a muffled scream as he felt a sudden searing pain in it. He saw a bandage raised in the air, then felt it taped over his burning ear. He felt something warm trickle down his neck.

Then he was lifted up again. Each of his captors taking an arm, he was carried down steps and into water that came up to his waist. The two men cursed as they splashed through it and down into what seemed like an underground chamber. Ahead was an ancient, partly submerged cannon, water slopping over its wooden plinth. They carried on, continuing through the water for some yards, towards it, the roar of the sea growing louder. Then he was hoisted up, his legs were grabbed and pushed backwards, and as he was lowered again his feet touched something solid and rested on it.

'Look up,' a voice said, shining the torch beam.

Mungo looked. And saw a metal hoop in the arched brick ceiling, high above him. From it was suspended a length of wire, ending in a noose.

'Now look down,' he was commanded.

He did what he was told, his terror increasing as he realized what was happening. His feet were on a block of concrete about two feet high and a little over one foot wide, that was under water. Then his arms, already bound with cord behind his back, were tugged further backwards, as he heard the clanking of a chain.

'You be OK,' one man said. 'Tide going out. Is good. When tide come back in, is not so good.' He laughed and so did his companion.

Strong hands on Mungo's shoulders suddenly forced

him down, and he sat on the narrow plinth of the cannon, water lapping over his waist. Then, despite his feeble attempt to resist, the noose was pulled down over his head and tightened round his neck. As he moved his head, he felt it sharp against his skin.

'Like razor wire. You move, you die,' one of the men said.

The other held up a phone and took a flash photograph. Then they began walking, splashing, away.

'Don't leave me, please don't leave me,' Mungo tried pleading. But it just came out as a series of muffled grunts. 'I can't move my arms. Please.'

He heard more laughter.

Footsteps receding, the bobbing beam of the torch fading away.

Mungo realized if he slipped off the plinth he would either hang or garrotte himself.

He sobbed in terror. He wanted his mother. His father. Aleksander.

Please help me.

63

At a few minutes before 8.30 a.m., Roy Grace stood in the shower adjoining the Intel suite, then shaved and put on the fresh boxers and shirt he always kept in the office for such situations, swallowed a tepid coffee and grabbed a muffin from a tray someone had brought in.

He ate it while he strode across the Police HQ campus, in a strong, warm breeze. After a long night and just two hours of sleep he was feeling fractious and in a combative mood, ready for whatever crap Cassian Pewe might throw at him.

As he walked down the steep hill, towards the rear of the Queen Anne house where the brass had their offices, he saw a van emblazoned with the name VALETPRO. A man was busy polishing an immaculate, old-model convertible Jaguar XJS.

'Nice shine!' Grace said.

'Thanks, black's a difficult one.' The man fished out a card and a product sampler. 'If you need your car doing anytime, mate, we're in the area.'

'Whose car is this, by the way?'

'Mr Pewe's.'

'Ah, right. That figures.' He went into the building.

The Assistant Chief Constable's assistant showed him in

to the almost absurdly grand office, with its magnificent view out across Lewes and the South Downs. The one thing that put a smile on Grace's face was the knowledge that with space on the HQ campus getting tighter and tighter, partly thanks to the rehousing of the East Sussex Fire and Rescue team here, soon Pewe might be having to share this with the other top brass.

As usual, the ACC sat behind his huge, neat desk in his crisp white shirt bearing the epaulettes with the gold ACC crescent, his fair hair, like the rest of him, immaculate. Without rising, he said in his voice that sounded snide even on the rare occasions when he was being pleasant, 'Good morning, Roy, tea or coffee?'

'Coffee, please, as strong as possible.'

Pewe barked a command into his intercom, then looked at him, leaving him standing. 'Long night?'

'You could say that.'

'You are the Head of Major Crime for this county, Roy. In the last twenty-four hours, we've had a bomb threat at the Amex – which you responded to like a total madman, breaking every police regulation we have for dealing with such situations. A teenager kidnapped. Dismembered human remains found at Shoreham Harbour – which are still in the process of being recovered – and now the sudden death in hospital of the digger operator who found them. And on top of that a young woman dead at Gatwick Airport. What on earth is happening? Has the Surrey and Sussex Major Crime Team totally lost the plot?'

'Hang on a minute, you can hardly hold me and my team personally responsible for all these incidents.' Grace continued, facetiously, 'I haven't killed or dismembered anyone, to the best of my knowledge,' although he thought at this very moment he would like to. More calmly than he felt, and still uninvited to sit, he gave an account of all that he was aware of.

Pewe listened pensively, making the occasional note with a fountain pen. When he had finished, the ACC looked down at his notes, then back up at him.

'You are aware, are you not, of the current delicate situation with the Albanian community in our city? Of all the hard work that Inspector Boniface and PC Denero are putting in, trying to build bridges with them?'

'Very aware, sir.'

'The optics aren't good. So, who's driving the bus?'

'Bus, sir?'

Pewe shook his head, looking angry. 'What you need to understand, Roy, is that we need to integrate multiple initiatives into a systems-level approach, OK?'

Grace stared at him blankly. He had no idea what his boss was talking about. The ACC had recently attended a management course at the police training college. He seemed to have taken away from it a load of gobbledygook, in Grace's view, and not much else. With each recent meeting with him, Pewe seemed to be growing increasingly incoherent.

'Have you considered a thought shower, Roy?'

'A *thought shower*?'

Pewe banged his fist on his desk. 'Do I need to spell everything out? Are you in the twenty-first century or the Middle Ages? A thought shower. Getting your whole team together and inviting their blue-sky views.'

'I do that at every briefing, actually, and always have. I just don't call it that name.'

'Oh, so what do you call it?'

'Just a *briefing*, sir,' Grace replied, calmly.

'Just a *briefing*?' Pewe echoed. 'Are you sure it's not all getting lost in the shuffle? I'm worried that you're not using your resources to the full, that you're trying to solve all this on your own. You do understand the aggregation of marginal gains, don't you, Roy?'

Pewe's PA brought in his coffee. Grace took the cup, gratefully, blew on it and sipped. 'I'm not entirely sure I do.'

'It's simple, Roy. There is no "I" in the word "team".'

But there is one in obnoxious bastard, thought Grace, privately.

'You think I'm a bit of a shit, don't you, Roy?'

Grace stayed silent.

'I just like to know where you and I stand. You see, a friend will always ultimately betray you, but an enemy stays the same.'

'Meaning exactly what, sir?'

'No pretence between us. You and I are both in the same war against criminals. I don't like you and you don't like me. I'm fine with that, it cuts out the bullshit and saves time. Two years ago, you got me transferred, and I've never forgotten that. You did something incredibly stupid yesterday, with that bomb. You broke all the rules about procedure and you know it. I'm considering having you suspended for risking your life, needlessly, and endangering the lives of others.'

'I took a calculated risk, sir, and I'd be happy to go through my reasons. At least on this occasion I did have valid reasons.'

'And there are other occasions when you didn't?' Pewe asked.

'Perhaps you've forgotten, sir, eighteen months ago you were in a car that went over the edge of Beachy Head, with a sheer 500-foot drop beneath you. The car was hanging by a thread. I put my life in danger by climbing over the edge and helping to pull you out. If I hadn't, you would be dead. So, it was OK to put my life on the line to save you, but not OK to put it on the line to save, potentially, hundreds of lives in the Amex? Is that going to look good – sir?'

For once, Pewe had no response.

64

Kipp Brown had no response, either. He sat at the breakfast bar in the kitchen, in a loose shirt, jeans and loafers, unshaven, cradling a mug of coffee and staring at the wall. Stacey was still in her dressing gown, her face pale, with no make-up.

'You are not serious?' Stacey said.

He shrugged, set down the mug and dug, gloomily and with no appetite, into a bowl of muesli, aware he needed to eat something to keep up his strength after a near-sleepless night.

'Kipp, you are not, seriously, going to play hardball with whoever's taken him, over our son's life? Please don't say you are going to do that – you're not, are you?' Her eyes were red from crying.

He stood up and put an arm tenderly round her. She didn't shrug it off. 'I'm not playing hardball, Stace, honestly. I will do anything I can to get Mungo back safely, but I just don't have that kind of money – not at the moment – I don't have it.'

'What do you mean? It's all gone on the gaming tables and horses?'

'I'm just in a bad cash-flow situation – temporarily – negative equity.'

'Negative equity – what's that in plain English? What do you mean, *negative equity*?'

He took a deep breath. 'I'm flat broke, Stace. Skint. I've barely enough money to cover next month's mortgage on this house. And Mungo's school fees. I haven't got the sort of money they're asking for.'

'You are not serious?'

'I wish to hell I wasn't, but I am.'

'But you've got millions in your discretionary client account, you always have, you told me you keep a percentage of all your clients' portfolios liquid, waiting for investment opportunities.'

'I can't touch that money.'

'Why not?'

'Because it's not mine, it belongs to my clients.'

'How much do you have there?'

'Around fifteen million at the moment.'

'Fifteen *million*?'

'About that.'

'Bloody hell! Kipp, two and a half million is peanuts, they wouldn't notice it missing. You just tell them you invested it and the market moved the wrong way, or whatever bullshit speak you use.'

'Sure, Stace. You'll come and visit me in prison, will you?'

'You know how to move money around, for God's sake, you do it all the time for your clients!'

'Yes, but I don't steal it.'

'It's not stealing, it would just be borrowing, surely?'

'Stace, I cannot take money from my client account. You want me to risk being banged away for a decade for embezzlement and my career over?'

'So, you'd rather Mungo died?'

He stared at the wall again. At the antique Welsh dresser. At the framed picture of Mungo with his sister. Mungo was seven then, wearing a red school cap, a neat grey blazer and shorts, pulling an impish face at the camera.

Stacey said, tenderly, 'Darling, do you remember soon after he was born? You came to the ward and held him in your arms, and looked down at him, and you said how much you loved him. That you would take a bullet for him?'

He nodded, bleakly.

'But not any more? You wouldn't take a bullet now? What's changed?'

'Nothing.'

'You love him as much as you did that day?'

'More.'

'But not enough to take a bullet for him now?'

He stared down at his fingers. At his nails, which he normally kept immaculate, noticing several of them were bitten down to the quick. 'Shit, Stace. Oh shit. Yes. Yes, of course I would.'

She kissed him. 'I love you.'

It was the first time in a very long time he had heard those words.

'I love you, too,' he replied.

And meant it.

65

Ordinarily on a Sunday, the Brighton and Hove City Mortuary would be as silent as – the grave, Cleo Morey thought. But at 9.30 a.m. today it was a hive of activity. Since its expansion, the postmortem room consisted of two separate spaces divided by an arch, with a separate isolation room, where Florentina Shima had lain overnight.

Inside the isolation room now, Cleo stood with her assistant, Darren Wallace, dressed like everyone present in white boots, green scrubs, gloves, a surgical cloth hat and gauze mask. Crime Scene Photographer James Gartrell was in the room as well, meticulously videoing every stage of the postmortem being carried out by the Home Office pathologist. Outside the door stood Coroner's Officer Michelle Websdale and DI Nigel 'Joey' Roissetter, from Surrey, who had been appointed the SIO on this suspicious death.

When this PM was finished, another Home Office postmortem, on the human remains recovered from the crusher site, would be carried out. But at the moment, Cleo had been told, a search was continuing there for further body parts, especially for the head and other limbs which were currently absent.

On a metal tray above Florentina Shima's body, Theobald was carefully dissecting her brain. Her sternum had been removed and placed across her pubis. Her breasts and stomach, either side of the incision down her midriff, were clamped back, exposing her ribcage and intestines coiled beneath. On the wall in front was a chart for listing the weights of the brain, lungs, heart, liver, kidneys and spleen of each cadaver examined here.

Over the course of the next hour her brain was weighed, then placed in a white plastic bag, ready to be put inside her ribcage when Theobald was finished, so that when her body was finally released to an undertaker, she would be buried or cremated with all her organs.

Some while later, after dissecting her heart, lungs, liver and kidneys, occasionally bagging tiny samples for laboratory analysis, and taking blood, urine and vitreous samples for toxicology testing, he moved on to her intestines. After the first incision, Theobald made a rare comment.

'Oh dear!'

Cleo moved closer, and watched him pull out, to her horror, something with the size and appearance of a chipolata sausage. He made a wider incision, which revealed more of the same. One was split open, spilling out a white powder, much of which had evidently been absorbed into the dead young woman's body.

Condoms. Each containing a package of a drug. By the time Theobald had finished, Cleo had counted forty-nine. The Exhibits Officer present logged and secured them.

It appeared the initial suspicions had been correct, and that poor Florentina Shima was a drugs mule. Duped by someone totally unscrupulous into swallowing what was probably hundreds of thousands of pounds' worth, street value, of a drug – heroin or some variety of cocaine, Cleo judged from the colour. The one that had burst had, it would appear, given her a massive and fatal overdose.

Cleo had seen a similar thing, a couple of times before. Doing this job, she saw so much. She had to comfort so many people whose loved ones had been brought in here. Husbands, mothers, fathers, sons, daughters, partners who had gone out to work in the morning and died in a car crash. Or had suddenly dropped dead from an aneurysm. Or who had been stabbed to death in a pub fight. The last time a body had affected her so much was the Christmas before last. A sixteen-year-old had gone out on his moped to get a pizza for himself and his girlfriend, four days before Christmas. A van had made a sudden U-turn in front of him. She kept looking at him and thinking about what a terrible time this Christmas would be for his girlfriend and family. How crap death so often was for people.

She felt that now, staring down at this beautiful teenager who just the day before had had her whole life in front of her. The victim of some unscrupulous shitbag who had somehow conned her into this, with assurances of a large reward, perhaps a new life.

Who are you? What made you do this? How desperate were you to take this risk? What is your story?

She turned away and hurried back to her office to get a tissue.

66

A burning pain in his neck startled Mungo, his eyes heavy and feeling desperate for sleep, and he cried out, but made only a muffled noise.

He heard the sound of waves.

Blinking, he stared around. Shivering with cold, his wrists and his neck hurting, badly. Trying to gather his thoughts. For a moment, he thought he was having a night-mare, but then realized he was awake.

Remembering now.

Help. Help. Help me.

He was shivering from the damp chill and his sodden jeans and shoes, and was perched, precariously, on the concrete ledge. The water had receded and he was no longer immersed from the waist down.

He felt exhausted. He desperately wanted to shift his position, but remembered the wire noose, and was scared to risk moving too much and hanging himself.

Shivering, he wished he had on something warmer than his thin hoodie.

Water was trickling beneath him.

He looked around, ahead, upwards. Above him was a domed brick ceiling. Like a tomb. A shaft of light came through a slit in the wall, reminding him of ones in medieval castles he had seen in *Game of Thrones*, where archers would stand and fire arrows through. He heard the roar of what sounded like the sea.

Aleksander. Where are you?

He tried to call out his friend's name, but again his voice stayed trapped in his gullet. He could not open his lips.

What was his friend's game? He felt totally bewildered. Had Aleksander double-crossed him in some way? Why? What—?

He was remembering the men in black, in balaclavas, entering the room in silence. One of them taping his mouth. The other restraining his hands behind him. The two of them carrying him out. Putting him in the boot of a car. The journey. Rolling around. The stink of petrol. He had lost track of time. Then they hauled him out. He could hear the sound of the sea. Breathed in fresh, salty air. He was carried a short distance. Into a partly submerged chamber or tunnel. Down steps. The dank smell of weed and rotting fish.

The smell in his nostrils now.

Looking around, he noticed slime covering the walls either side of him. And the ceiling. Tendrils of weed on the walls, all the way up almost to the roof. At high tide, this chamber would be completely flooded, he realized. He looked down at the ground below him, one moment covered in water, then just puddles remaining as it retreated. Saw a small, white, dead crab. Another roar of the sea and a small amount of water sluiced in, then retreated. The crab was moved a few inches.

Tide going out. Is good. When tide come back in, is not so good.

Panic-stricken, he wondered what the time was. Daylight. Was the tide going in or out? He tried turning his head to read the time on his watch, but the wire stopped him. He looked up at the ancient-looking brass hoop set into the ceiling above him, and the wire coming down from it, taut, to the noose round his neck. Behind him was the barnacle-encrusted cannon.

'Gmmmh. Hlllpwwwwww!' he shouted in frustration through the restraint over his mouth.

Aleksander, you bastard, just what are you bloody doing?

Thoughts strobed through his mind. Where was he? What was the time? Who had brought him here? Why? What was going on?

He heard another sluicing sound of water. Heard it running along the floor beneath him. Saw the little dead crab shoot past him and then get beached as the water retreated. The tide must still be going out. *Please*. Was it low tide now? His mind went into overdrive, thinking about the geography classes at school which never interested him. Tides. There had been a whole class on tides just recently. The pull of the moon. Spring tides, neap tides, the planets' effect on the tides. New moons and full moons gave the most extreme tides – the highest and lowest.

The high-water mark was about three feet above him.

It had been a full moon last night.

Which meant the tide would be both at its lowest and highest.

He stared up again at the high-water mark, shaking in terror.

Then he heard the sound of a metal door opening and closing. Footsteps. Thank God! Aleksander finally coming back!

A sudden bright beam of light dazzled him. A camera torch.

The tape was torn from his mouth. But before he could

speak a man in a balaclava pushed a water bottle between his lips. He drank greedily. It was jerked away and immediately replaced by a spoonful of muesli. He ate it, hungrily, then another, and another. Then drank more water.

But as he said, 'Pleesh – shwat shi—?' fresh gaffer tape was stretched across his mouth.

He yammered, desperate to get some response from the men. Pleading with his eyes. But there was nothing.

He heard the footsteps fading away. The sound of a metal door opening then closing.

Clang.

A brief silence.

Then the sound of a breaking wave.

67

Kipp Brown sat in his den at his computer. He entered the codes for his client account and checked the balance. It was over £15 million. £15,758,002, precisely.

The consequences of moving any of this to his own personal account were dire. Regardless of the moral justification, this was money entrusted to him by clients for investment purposes. Taking even one penny of it would be fraud. If discovered, he would be stripped of his licence and face a prison sentence. The idea of taking two and a half million was unthinkable.

As was the idea of doing nothing to save his son.

So long as he concealed the transactions, making it look like he was placing the money in securities of some kind, and then replaced it before anyone asked any questions, it would be OK, he'd get away with it. If any of his colleagues questioned the transactions he'd be able to explain them away. Just so long as he replaced the money quickly.

And he could! He could replace that money easily, of course he could. All he would need would be a good week on the casino tables, on the horses and online. He could replace it and no one would be any the wiser.

He logged out, feeling a bit more hopeful.

68

At 10.15 a.m., Grace was back in the Intel suite and in a fractious mood after his face-off with Cassian Pewe. He dutifully checked on his terminal everything else that was going on in Surrey and Sussex, the counties for which he was responsible. Two other Major Crime investigations were in progress. One was the bomb at the Amex, being run by DCI Fitzherbert; the other was the death of a young woman who had died in the passport queue at Gatwick Airport, which was being run by DI Roissetter.

Wanting an update on the Amex, he rang the incident room. Fitzherbert wasn't available and he was put through to the deputy SIO running the bomb enquiry, Detective Inspector Jim Waldock. 'What's the latest, Jim?' he asked.

Waldock, who was in his early fifties, had recently surprised everyone in Major Crime by having a gastric band operation, dropping from a whopping twenty-four stone to just fourteen stone, seemingly overnight. Perhaps in panic over failing his annual 'beep' fitness test. With it, his energy levels had increased massively.

'I've just had a call from the Explosive Ordnance Division, Roy,' he said enthusiastically. 'The camera – a Sony FS7 – was a viable bomb in every aspect except one.'

'Oh?'

'How technical do you want to get?'

'Try me.'

'The innards of the camera had been scooped out and replaced with a plastic explosive known as PETN – pentaerythritol tetranitrate – structurally very similar to nitroglycerin. Along with RDX, it's apparently the main ingredient of Semtex. There was a kilo of the stuff inside the camera, packed with nails and ball bearings. It's one of the most powerful explosives known. It detonates at 8,000 metres a second. If it had gone off it would have killed two or three hundred people in the immediate surrounding area, and wounded countless more.'

'Shit,' Grace said.

'And you were heroic enough to run out with it!'

'I might not have done if I'd known what was in it! So why didn't it go off?'

'Because, they say, there was a timer on it but no detonator to set it off.'

'No detonator?'

'None. A totally viable device, made by someone who clearly knew what they were doing, but no detonator.'

'What's that about?'

'Good question, Roy,' Waldock said.

'They made an extortion demand, then planted a bomb that would not explode. Why?'

'Perhaps to show they could, if they wanted, plant a viable device?'

'Meaning we could expect another bomb threat in the future – and this one for real?'

'Very possibly.'

'What clues do we have about the caller's ID, Jim?'

'Other than speaking in heavily accented English and

using different burners for each call, nothing so far, Roy. We've sent voice samples for analysis.'

Grace thanked him, then focused back on the latest briefing he was holding for his exhausted team, several of whom, like him, had been there all night. They had been joined by Forensic Podiatrist Haydn Kelly and by a PC from the Scotland Yard Super Recognizer Unit, Jonathan Jackson. On the monitor behind him was the ransom demand text.

> The price for your son has just gone up. We will now require £2.5 million value in Bitcoins. We will be in touch with details where to pay this. Don't be stupid and go looking for Mungo. If you succeed in finding him without having paid, all you will have is a corpse. Sorry to text so late. You will soon receive payment instrucions. Have a nice rest of night!

'Someone ought to give whoever sent that a spelling lesson,' Norman Potting said, then mimicked a lisp. '*Instrucions?* Hello?'

There were a few grins.

'Maybe there's a clue in that, Norman,' Grace said, in no mood for humour.

'A dyslexic?' ventured DS Kevin Taylor.

'Or someone for whom English is not their first language?' countered Kevin Hall.

'Perhaps Albanian?' DS Exton suggested.

'Perhaps,' Grace replied. Then he said, 'OK, I have two hypotheses.' He pointed at the screen behind him. 'The first is that this is a pile of shit. The second is that it's real.'

DS Scarlett Riley, his replacement for Tanja Cale who had transferred to Professional Standards, said, 'Boss, do you really think it's a hoax – something about the Albanian community, from our past experience, makes me think not.'

Despite his tiredness, Grace was thinking very clearly. Events had taken a turn that made him believe that whilst they had established earlier it had been some kind of a stupid prank between kids, the kidnap had suddenly become real. His first task now was to motivate his team, get them out of the hoax mindset and get them refocused.

'I'm with you, Scarlett,' he replied. 'I think this is now real and we are going to treat it as such. I don't know what's going on, nor who is behind this, whether Dervishi or someone else completely, but my further hypothesis is that at some point during the night the situation changed dramatically – perhaps someone seeing an opportunity here. Possibly Jorgji Dervishi himself. Or a former employee of his.' He turned to DC Hall. 'Kevin, I'm giving you the action of ring-fencing Dervishi's house – I want round-the-clock surveillance on him and I've put in a request for a tap on his phones.'

He next addressed DCs Emma-Jane Boutwood and Velvet Wilde. 'EJ and Velvet, I want you to revisit all the CCTV footage from the Amex and see if you can pick out Mungo Brown. He has to be on it somewhere. Haydn and Jonathan will join you. Make sure you include the footage from the body-worn cameras of all police officers at the match.'

Then he addressed his two analysts, Giles Powell and Louise Soper. 'Because of Dervishi and the IMEI code on the phone Kipp Brown picked up being linked to an Albanian, I'm making a further hypothesis that this demand has come from someone, or some group, within the Albanian community. We know the Albanian criminal gangs are highly organized and professional – in addition to being ruthless. This is a massive ransom demand. From what I've been able to ascertain so far – and from Surrey and Sussex's past experience in professional kidnaps – the gangs would never use just one vehicle, but use a second as back-up. They wouldn't want to risk blowing everything with a puncture or a breakdown. I want you to do convoy analysis. We have a good starting point, the house between Beddingham and Newhaven where Aleksander took us. I'm giving you the action of checking all ANPR cameras in that vicinity, then using the onion-ring principle, starting from the middle and working out, spreading your search. See if you can identify a pair of cars moving together through different locations.'

The recent direct-entry recruit DI Donald Dull – who had already gained the nickname of Spreadsheet Man – raised a hand. 'Sir, I could perhaps help with the analysis and preparation of a spreadsheet.'

'That would be very helpful, Donald,' Grace said. He stared up at the enlarged photograph of the boy that Mungo's father had given him. A cheerful, good-looking young man with a mop of fair hair and a cheeky grin.

I don't know what mess you've got yourself into, Mungo, but I'll get you out of it, somehow, he promised.

Somehow.

What worried him was dealing with the Albanian criminals, who used brutality to send messages to the community. In recent years there had been plenty of very public displays of violence by Albanian gangsters. Killing a teenage boy, if they did not get what they wanted, would be their way of sending just such a message about being taken seriously.

He looked up again at Mungo Brown's photograph.

We will now require £2.5 million.

He looked back down at his notes. Checking he was missing nothing.

Most kidnaps were resolved within hours. But the longer they went on, he knew from grim experience, although he shared this with no one, the less chance they would have of finding the victim still alive.

69

Shortly after 10 a.m., Sharon Sampson shouted goodbye to her husband, who was somewhere upstairs, and stepped out of the front door of their house on Shoreham Beach to take two of their dogs, working cocker spaniels Cider and Becks, for a walk – or, more accurately, for the dogs to take her. The boisterous Becks, still a puppy, yanked hard on the lead, ignoring his owner's shrill commands – 'Heel! Heel, Becks, heel!' – while Cider was better behaved, and proud of it.

Struggling to keep upright in the blustery wind, and to hang on to Becks until she reached the place where it was safe to let them free without any risk of them running out onto a road, she hung on to the leads, yanking Becks's and shouting, futilely. They traversed the grass verge above the pebble beach until they reached the end of the street at the parking area for the Shoreham Redoubt, more colloquially known to locals as Shoreham Fort.

Constructed in the 1850s to defend the harbour against an anticipated invasion by Napoleon III, it had been capable of housing a garrison of thirty-eight soldiers. The intention was to provide a rota manning the six massive cannon and the rifle stations sited behind a long, low brick wall behind a ditch. There was a network of tunnels beneath, along which soldiers could move, unseen and protected from enemy fire, giving a clear line of sight across the pebbles to the sea and to any vessel attempting to enter the port.

The invasion never happened, the fort was abandoned and for nearly a century and a half Mother Nature steadily reclaimed the remote, windswept and desolate site, until 2003, when it became the passion of local historian Gary Baines to restore it, with a grant from English Heritage, and the support of volunteers.

Sharon Sampson knelt to unclip the leads. To her left beyond a row of picnic benches was the River Adur, and the picturesque shore-front of Shoreham Village on the far side. To her right was a long, crumbling, buttressed flint and brick wall, with dunes and a shingle beach beyond running down to the English Channel. A green, corrugated-iron structure, erected during the Second World War, housed a small museum of the fort's history, which was manned sporadically, when funds allowed. And equally, when time allowed, the volunteers attempted to shore up the fort walls against the constant battering from the salty winds fresh off the English Channel only yards away, and from regular vandalism by local youths well aware that the police rarely came along here on their patrols.

As she walked on, the dogs racing happily ahead now, Becks bouncing around, Sharon's pulse suddenly began to race, also. Ahead of her was the café, an attractive white clapboard hut with the sign FOOD FOR FORT and a mural that always made her smile of two seated Victorian police constables. When it was open it sold ice creams, sandwiches and soft drinks.

But today something was different about it. Something wrong. She quickened her pace and as she grew closer she could see spray-paint graffiti above the mural. In large writing were the words *Pigs = Filth* and *Mick Likes Big Tits*.

Sharon considered it her civic duty to phone in every fresh incident of vandalism she encountered here. It angered her that such an important part of Sussex's history was so poorly protected. Glancing around to see if there was any other graffiti that had appeared since yesterday, something quite different caught her eagle eye.

She frowned at the steel door at the entrance to one of the six brick chambers that housed the cannon. She had been taken down there once, by Gary Baines, but you could only go at low tide as much of the chamber was now below sea level. It was on the schedule of restoration projects, but this particular gun emplacement was a very long way down the list of priorities.

Something was odd about the door. Different. Definitely. She took a step towards it. Before retiring to spend more time showing her dogs, she had worked as a continuity expert on film and television sets. Her brain was programmed – she had no idea how or why – to register anomalies, and it was definitely registering one now. But what?

Then she realized. There was a padlock and chain, both of them shiny new. The old rusty one she was certain had been there yesterday had been replaced. But there was only one person who could possibly have replaced it: that was Gary Baines. And at this moment Gary was away on holiday in Cornwall where he had been for over a week, though he was due back later today.

She pulled her phone out of her anorak pocket and dialled 999. When it was answered she requested the police.

It was almost a minute later that a female voice said, 'Police, emergency, how may I help you?'

'Do you realize how long you've taken to answer?' Sharon Sampson said, indignantly.

'I'm sorry, madam, we are very busy. What is your emergency, please?'

'I would like to report new vandalism at Shoreham Fort, please, and something suspicious.'

'Suspicious?'

'A new padlock, and I don't know why it's there. It might be pikeys, stealing metal from the cannon – they steal it from everywhere, don't they?'

'The location is Shoreham Fort? May I have your name and phone number?' Although she made the request, Grace Holkham in the Force Control Room already knew who the caller was. Sharon Sampson was one of their regulars. All the same, she still dutifully noted it in the CAD log to go up on the system as a reported crime.

The woman went on to describe the graffiti, to mention again the suspicious new padlock and to explain that the man in charge of the restoration was away. When she had finished, the call handler said, 'Madam, with respect, you have called the emergency number, 999, and this is not an emergency situation. Really you should be reporting this on the police force's non-emergency number, 101.'

'Look,' Sharon said, indignantly. 'You may not consider the destruction of our heritage an emergency, but I do, and I expect you to do something about it. Kindly get a police officer here right away.'

'I'll see what I can do about getting someone along to investigate, madam,' Grace Holkham assured her.

'I won't hold my breath,' Sharon Sampson replied.

'We are very busy at the moment, I'm afraid, madam. A lot of it because of calls like yours,' she added, unable to resist the dig.

The sound of barking distracted Sharon. She looked, in alarm, as Becks, barking furiously, raced towards a tiny Yorkshire terrier.

'Becks! Becks!' she yelled and broke into a run. 'Becks!'

The spaniel grabbed the tiny dog by the scruff of its neck and began shaking it.

'BECKS! BECKS! BECKS!'

In the Force Control Room, Grace Holkham terminated the call, fuming at the woman's insensitivity. She stared at the screen, at the serial she had created for this call.

> Vandalism at Shoreham Port. Suspicious new padlock. S. Sampson.

The truth was that twenty years ago when she had first started in this job, she would have sent a response or local officer to take a look, albeit on a non-urgent basis. But now with police resources stretched so thin, she was constantly having to make judgement calls that might seem, to the general public, callous. Tapping the keyboard again, she added the words No further action.

70

'You little shit!'

His father's steel claw clamped his left shoulder and his good hand the right one, jerking him out of bed and sending him crashing to the carpeted floor of his bedroom.

Aleksander looked up in terror. He had never seen his father so angry.

He was shaken, then shaken again so hard, he felt dizzy. Then shaken again.

'You little piece of scum.'

'Dad – I—'

He stared into his father's cold glass eye. Then into his good eye that was equally cold.

His father shook him again. 'You little shit!'

'Dad—'

He smelled rancid cigar smoke on his father's breath. And his dense cologne.

'You fucking little shit.'

The boy trembled.

'Just what are you trying to do to our family? You've brought the police on us. Are you happy about that?'

'Dad, please.'

'Please? Please? Please what?'

Aleksander began crying.

'You want to sob? You don't have balls? I have son who has no balls? Shall I cut them off so you'll know what it really feels like to have no balls?'

'Dad!'

Dervishi pushed his hand down between his son's legs, found his testicles and crushed them hard in his hand.

Aleksander screamed, his stomach constricting in pain. He vomited, then lay on the ground, hands over his balls and sobbing.

Dervishi stood up, brushing vomit from his tracksuit in disdain. 'I was proud of you once. Not any more. You use-less piece of shit. Who helped you?'

His son stared up at his father in terror. 'I can't tell you.'

'No?'

'Dad, they'll kill me.'

He gave his son a bemused smile. 'Really? *They* will kill you?'

Aleksander nodded, frantically.

'And I'll kill you if you don't, OK? Believe me, you don't want me to kill you, you really don't.'

'Dad, *please.*'

'Jorgji!' Mirlinda called from downstairs.

'Don't move,' he said to his son. 'Not one inch.' He stepped away, opened the bedroom door and shouted back, 'Yes, what?'

'There are police officers outside who want to speak to Aleksander.'

'Tell them they have to wait. He's not speaking to them without a lawyer.'

Mirlinda shouted back, anxiously, 'Jorgji, if I don't open the door they will break it down.'

'Let them in,' he shouted back. Then, looking at his son

in fury, 'I don't care what you've done, you say nothing, OK, nothing until we have a lawyer here. OK?'

Cowering, the boy nodded.

His father kicked him, hard, in his backside.

71

Miri Nela kicked the ball hard. The goalie made a desperate dive as it shot between him and the folded sweater which served as the left goalpost and bounced off the grassy mound behind him.

Watching from a bench at the side of the disused bowling green in Hove's St Ann's Well Gardens was PC Nikki Denero, wearing jeans, trainers and a yellow T-shirt printed with the slogan ALBANIANS ROCK! Her partner, Ellie Yarrow, was similarly attired and their lurcher, Horris, sat between them. Spread around them on other benches and on the grass, drinking, eating sandwiches, chatting and laughing while the seven-a-side game progressed, were about thirty Albanians, sitting in small groups, two with babies in buggies.

Nikki felt a deep sense of pride. This picnic had been her initiative, a further step forward in building bridges between Brighton's Albanian community and Sussex Police. Immediately to her left, Lana, rocking her baby, cheered. She was married to Miri, who was developing his business here, Balcony Tea, specializing in a range of Mediterranean-inspired teas. Good, decent people, totally integrated into the city and much liked by both the Albanian and local community. As was everyone else who had come along, enjoying a rare sunny day in what had, otherwise, been a bit of a rubbish summer.

On a bench to Nikki's left sat Valmira Bislimi, watching her husband playing whilst trying to keep their two-year-old daughter occupied on the grass in front of her. The whistle blew for half-time and Valmira's husband, Rinor, tall and perspiring heavily, came over, kissed his wife, then knelt beside his daughter.

'Well played, Rinor!' Nikki Denero said. 'Two goals! Amazing!'

He turned towards her, panting, his face alight with joy. 'Thank you!'

To her surprise and delight, Nikki suddenly spotted the suited figure of Detective Superintendent Roy Grace striding towards her, clutching two bottles of rosé wine in his hand. She had invited him, but never expected him to actually join them.

'Donation for the picnic!' he said.

She thanked him, and introduced him to Rinor.

The two men shook hands. 'Very well played,' Grace said. 'A great setup for that goal!'

'Thank you.'

Rinor Bislimi was the reason he had come. Intelligence on the man had associated him with some of the Albanian criminal fraternity, although Grace knew that in recent years he had left that behind and concentrated on building a string of dry-cleaners. 'Would it be possible to have a quick word?' Grace asked him.

The Albanian shrugged, then said, 'Sure, how can I help you?'

'Does the name Fatjon Sava mean anything?' Grace asked.

All the energy seemed to drain from the Albanian, suddenly. 'Fatjon Sava? Why are you asking me this?'

'You know the name?'

He was silent, reflecting. 'Fatjon Sava?' he said again. 'Yes – but—'

'But what, Rinor?' Denero interjected.

Grace watched the exchange, curious about where this was going.

'I can't talk about this man, please,' he said to Grace. 'Please do not ask me.'

'Why not?' Denero persisted.

Rinor looked frightened. His eyes darted to his wife, to Roy Grace and finally back to PC Denero. 'Because I have young family. OK. I go now?'

'Yes, you can go!' Roy Grace said.

As he watched the young man run across the pitch towards his teammates, he turned to his colleague. 'What's that all about, Nikki?'

The PC stood up, indicating for Grace to follow. They walked some distance away from the group, stopping in front of the bowling green café. 'Fear,' she said and shrugged. 'The problem we always have. Fear of the police and fear of retribution.'

'What do you know about this man, Fatjon Sava, Nikki?'

'Sava used to be one of Jorgji Dervishi's lieutenants. I understand they had a big falling-out around two years ago and Sava set up a gang of his own. They've been involved in a turf war subsequently. He's linked with another Albanian on my radar, Kushtim Kona. Both are known to have a particularly nasty MO – they have gang members back in Albania who torture and kill the families of anyone here in Brighton who crosses them. That's probably why Rinor doesn't want to talk to you, sir.'

'A good enough reason.'

'What's your interest in Sava, sir?'

'He's linked to a mobile phone used in the kidnap. We need to find him very urgently. Can you help locate him or this Kushtim Kona?'

'Leave it with me, sir.'

'Time is critical.'

'I understand, sir, I'll do everything I can.'

72

'Long night, officers?' Jorgji Dervishi asked, politely, from behind his desk, seated as he was when Norman Potting and Velvet Wilde had first been here yesterday, the stub of a cigar in the ashtray. The room smelled of stale cigar smoke.

'You could say that,' Wilde replied.

Peering at Potting, Dervishi said, 'No time to shave, eh?' He grinned. 'I could be a detective, right – your Sherlock Holmes might have noticed a detail like this!'

'Mr Dervishi,' Potting said, without responding to the remark, 'we wish to talk to your son, Aleksander, again.'

'You may,' he said, 'as soon as my lawyer is here.'

Potting shook his head, holding up a clutch of documents. 'As I told you last night, we can either do this the easy way for you or the hard way.'

Dervishi playfully rotated his artificial hand again. 'Is that right? Would you be threatening me?'

Potting leaned forward into Dervishi's face and placed the document he was holding on his desk. 'I have here a search warrant for this house. I can also call up the Local Support Team, who you saw last night, and we can take your house apart, and arrest you and your son. Your choice.'

'And exactly what grounds do you have for arresting Aleksander and me?'

'For your son, conspiracy to kidnap. For you, Mr Dervishi, a young woman, travelling on a false passport, with her intestines packed with cocaine with a street value of over £300,000, who died at Gatwick Airport yesterday evening. In her possession was a mobile phone with just one number programmed into the SIM card. It is of an ex-directory landline at a kebab house in Brighton that you own. Now, giving you the benefit of the doubt as a fine, upstanding local businessman, I'd like to think you would know nothing about this.'

'You would be correct.'

'Good, I am very pleased to hear that – although my governor might beg to differ. But let's park that, shall we – and just have a chat with your son?'

After a moment's reluctant hesitation, Dervishi pressed his intercom button, picked up his phone and said, 'Mirlinda, bring Aleksander in here.'

A few minutes later, Dervishi's wife, dressed in a purple tracksuit and slippers, her face pasty white without make-up, brought in a tearful Aleksander. He was wearing a Star Wars top and tracksuit bottoms. The pair sat on a studded leather sofa to the right of the two detectives. The woman looked scared.

As the two detectives had prearranged, Velvet Wilde spoke gently to the young lad.

'Aleksander, your friend Mungo is in big trouble. The little joke that you and he plotted to play on Mungo's dad has backfired and now we believe his life is in very serious danger. Are you willing to help us find him?'

The boy nodded, desolate.

'OK,' she said. 'We know you had help getting him away from the Amex Stadium and driving you to that derelict farmhouse at Beddingham – Valbone and two men you say you didn't know. Can you tell us where they are now? But first, I need to caution you, and as we're carrying out an urgent interview to save life, I intend to continue here, rather than taking you to the police station.'

Aleksander sat twisting his hands together and staring down at them as if his life depended on doing this.

She prodded, still gentle. 'Aleksander?'

He continued twisting his hands.

'You're not in trouble, Aleksander. We know you just did something silly and you probably thought it was a laugh, but now we believe Mungo's life is in real danger, we need you to help us save him.'

His voice came out as a whisper. 'Yes.'

She smiled at him. 'Was there anyone else who was involved with you?'

He looked at her, then his father, then his mother. 'I – I can't – can't get them into trouble.'

'Tell her,' his father commanded.

His face reddened, and he began crying.

'Tell her!' his father said again, more harshly.

'Jorgji!' Mirlinda tried to calm him. 'He's very upset.'

'Yes? I'm upset, too. Tell her!' he said again to Aleksander. 'Tell the police officer otherwise you are going to be arrested and go to prison.'

'No!' his wife cried out.

'It was just Valbone,' the tearful boy whispered. 'As I told you already, just Valbone and the two men I didn't know.'

Valbone and Dritan had always been good to Aleksander, whereas his father's other security guards treated him contemptuously. He hadn't been able to help telling them about Valbone, but he was still determined to protect Dritan's identity – and he genuinely did not know who the other man was.

Fuming, Dervishi stabbed the intercom then shouted into it, 'Dritan! Come in here right away!' Then he picked up his phone and hit a speed-dial button. He left an angry message. 'Valbone, I've left five messages for you, where are you? Call me right away.'

The smaller of the two men who had let Potting and Wilde in last night came into the office. He was dressed all in black, as he had been before, with the coiled earpiece.

'This is Dritan Nano,' Dervishi said, by way of intro-duction, and turned to the man. 'Dritan, these are two detectives from Sussex Police. Can you please tell them where Valbone is?'

He shrugged. 'I don't know, boss. Valbone bring Alek-sander home about half one this morning, then later he say to me he need cigarettes and is going out to buy some from a garage. When I wake this morning he no here.'

'What vehicle would he have been driving?' Norman Potting asked him.

'One of the Range Rovers.'

'You have the registration number?'

As soon as he was given it, Potting texted it through to the Intel suite, asking for an urgent ANPR trace on it.

'Is there anything else you can tell me, Aleksander?' Wilde asked the very scared-looking boy.

Before replying, he looked at his father, then his mother. 'No,' he whispered.

73

Mungo didn't know what time it was. He kept drifting towards sleep, only to be instantly jerked out of it by the noose digging into his neck or by cramp. Listening to the lapping of water made his thirst worse.

He struggled repeatedly with his arms behind his back. So far as he could work out, his wrists were tied with cord of some kind and attached to a length of chain. He kept trying to rub the cord against the chain, over and over.

Were they coming back, ever? Or just going to leave him to drown as the tide rose further?

Suddenly he heard voices.

Outside.

Through the slit in the wall.

Kids playing, messing around.

'Hey, Mick!'

The tinkle of breaking glass. A burst of laughter.

'Get in there!'

It sounded like two boys. Right the other side of the wall. He tried to call out to them, tried for all he was worth. But all he could make was a feeble yammer: 'Mnnn-nmmmm. Mwhrrrrrrr.'

The voices faded. Silence again.

He wanted to be home, in his room, on his computer. It

was his birthday in a fortnight and he'd asked for a new Xbox like the one Aleksander had. He'd been excited for the past month about it. Was he going to die without ever getting it?

A faint metallic clang.

Had he imagined it?

A scraping sound. Another clang, louder. Voices. Footsteps. The splashing of feet through water. Was it Aleksander, finally come to rescue him?

His hopes were instantly dashed as two figures in balaclavas, black windcheaters, jeans and gumboots appeared. One holding a carrier bag, the other a camera.

'Mrrrrrrhlmmmmmm!' he tried to call out to them.

One leaned down, and with a leather-gloved finger picked at something on his face. He shrieked in pain as tape was ripped away from his mouth and cheeks, leaving them stinging. A plastic bottle was held up to his mouth and he drank greedily, gulping the cold water, not daring to stop in case they took the bottle away, gulping the contents until the bottle was empty.

Next, he saw the man dig a hand in the bag and produce a sandwich. He removed it from the packaging, held it out to Mungo's mouth. It was too dark to see what it was but he bit into it, ravenously. It was egg. He chewed and devoured both halves in just a few bites, followed by another – ham. After he had swallowed that, another bottle of water was shoved in his mouth.

Mungo drank until it was pulled away. 'Who are you?' he asked. 'What do you want? What do you want?'

The man crammed the plastic bag into a pocket, without speaking, and his colleague held up a sheet of paper with some kind of graph on it, close to Mungo's face. The other man raised a camera and took a series of flash photographs.

'Please, who are you?' Mungo begged again. 'Who are you? Please – please let me go. Please let me—'

The man holding the sheet of paper stepped away. The one with the camera remained in place. The other one reappeared with a roll of grey duct tape. He pulled a length tight across Mungo's mouth, slashing the end with a knife and wrinkling his nose. 'You've messed yourself,' he said in a coarse voice, with a foreign accent.

'Less than six hours to high tide,' his colleague with the camera said, in a similar accent. 'Hope you are good at holding your breath, little boy.'

The other laughed. 'Let's hope your daddy's pockets are deeper than the water, eh?'

The men splashed away.

'Grmmmmmmm! Grmmmmmmmmmm!' Mungo cried out desperately.

He heard a distant metallic clang.

Then just the lapping of the sea.

The dead crab washed past his line of vision.

74

Roy Grace entered the Intel suite, which was a hive of concentration and quiet activity. At the far end, Forensic Podiatrist Haydn Kelly and Super Recognizer Jonathan Jackson were studying CCTV footage from the Amex, on separate monitors.

The two analysts, Giles Powell and Louise Soper, were focused on ANPR camera information that was being fed through to them live, via the Force Control Room. Powell, a grey-haired, sixty-four-year-old former Roads Policing Unit sergeant, had worked for Sussex Police as a civilian in the decade since his retirement. He was tracking the Range Rover index, KK04 YXB, registered to Jorgji Dervishi, which had apparently been driven from the Dervishis' home by his chauffeur, Valbone Kadare, at around 3 a.m. this morning.

Powell had picked up the vehicle on a series of Automatic Number Plate Recognition cameras along the coast road, heading east, through Rottingdean, Saltdean and Peacehaven and then on the road leading to Newhaven, which had clocked it at 3.48 a.m. He'd checked the next ANPR towards Seaford, and the one on the A26 at Beddingham, but it had not appeared on either of them. He widened his search, in case the Range Rover had taken one of the country roads on which there were no cameras, calculating all of its possible routes. But if it had diverted off the main roads, it would have been picked up, eventually, on the main A27 arterial road.

It left him with three alternatives. Either the vehicle had parked up somewhere in the countryside, the driver had changed the licence plates, as was a distinct possibility, or it had headed down into Newhaven Port itself.

Powell reported his findings to DS Riley.

The red-headed Detective Sergeant looked at her watch. It was now 11.20 a.m. 'Get on to Newhaven Port,' she instructed him, 'and see if any of their CCTV picks it up. Check the ferry.'

Newhaven, the DS knew well, was both a ferry port to France and also a major container hub. Vehicles – as well as antiques – stolen within the south east, would disappear inside containers at Newhaven Port and be shipped out within hours. Recent-model right-hand-drive Range Rovers fetched a black-market premium in countries that drove on the left, such as Malta and Cyprus, and further afield, in India and parts of Asia, Australia and New Zealand.

'Nice work, Giles,' Grace said. 'But the chances are we may have already lost it – if you can now help Louise, that would be good.'

Louise Soper, in her forties, with long brown hair and a calm demeanour, was concentrating on trying to identify pairs of index numbers. She was searching, initially, in the area where the torched BMW had been found. It was a daunting task, as this was just off the main road, the A26, carrying constant traffic between Newhaven Port and the Beddingham roundabout from where vehicles either routed east, towards Polegate, Eastbourne and, potentially, Folkestone and the Eurotunnel, or the car ferries of Dover, or on the A27 to Brighton and all points west, or branching off north towards London on the A23.

It helped that at that time of night the traffic was relatively light. But it was still a huge challenge. She briefed Powell, who was seated next to her. What she was looking for were the same two vehicles, in close proximity, pinging a series of ANPR cameras, which would indicate they might be travelling in convoy. She had narrowed her search down to twelve pairs of numbers, which she sent over to him.

Fighting tiredness, after just a few hours of sleep, Giles Powell made himself a strong coffee and set to work on the laborious task of logging vehicle movements in the Beddingham area and comparing them to vehicle movements in the wider areas of Sussex and its bordering counties of Kent, Surrey and Hampshire.

Kevin Hall suddenly called out, urgently. 'Boss! This just in!'

Grace stepped over to the DC's workstation and peered at the screen. On it he saw video footage of a frightened-looking boy he recognized instantly as Mungo Brown. From the quality of the footage he knew, immediately, this was taken on a different camera to the one that had sent the earlier images of him.

Mungo was slumped, his mouth taped, and with what looked like a bloodstained bandage over his right ear. A wire ligature was round his neck. A woollen-gloved hand held a crumpled sheet of printout by his face. It was a tide table. It showed the low and high tide times for today for the Shoreham area.

Low tide was 11.32.

High tide was 17.40.

The hand withdrew the document from the frame.

The camera pulled back to a wider angle and panned

down. It showed water a couple of feet below where Mungo was perched on a slab or ledge of some sort, his arms restrained behind him. A dead crab floated into shot, moving backwards and forwards in the tide, now just a foot or so deep.

Then a close-up of a photograph showing the high-water mark, several feet above the boy.

Followed by another image of the tide chart, as if as a reminder.

An instant later it was replaced by a typed, large-print sign which read:

BY 17.40 TODAY WATER LEVEL IS
ABOVE MUNGO HEAD

Grace stared at it. 'Shit. Send it to me. Have you got any geo-mapping or triangulation on the location?'

'We're working on it, guv, but it looks like these villains are tech-savvy and have disabled geo-mapping.'

Grace's phone rang.

It was Glenn Branson. 'Boss, we've just had another communication from the kidnappers – it's come in on Stacey's phone.'

'Texted?'

'Yes, same as before. They're now requesting £250k in Bitcoins, as a down-payment on the £2.5 million. They want it paid by 2 p.m. or they let Mungo Brown drown.'

'A down-payment?' Grace said, raising his voice, angry and frustrated. 'What are these jokers playing at? You put a down-payment on a sofa or a car or on a house, you don't put a down-payment on a child's life, for God's sake!'

'I agree, boss,' Branson said calmly. 'I'm wondering if they've got wind of Brown's finances.'

'Bitcoins?' Grace had only a vague idea about the

internet currency and how it worked. But one thing he did know was that crypto currencies were increasingly the currency of choice for criminals around the world, because these transactions were hard, if not impossible, to trace. 'What's the next move?'

'They're going to issue further instructions on confirmation that Kipp Brown has the money. He needs to buy them online – and there's a problem with that.'

'Yes?'

'He doesn't have that sort of cash readily available.'

'What?'

'Seriously.'

'He's well connected – he can't drum up £250k to save his son's life?' Grace said angrily. 'Come on!'

'It's real, boss, from what he says. The mortgage lender is about to repossess his house. He's behind on the finance payments for his and his wife's cars. He's maxed out – gambling debts, apparently. All his credit cards and debit cards.'

'Glenn, if these kidnappers are serious, they're not going to let this boy die – he's their golden goose.'

'So how should Brown reply?'

'Well, it's looking to me like he's going to have to make some payment. The problem with Bitcoins is we've no way of recovering it for him – with cash we'd always have a chance.' He thought, briefly. 'It's Sunday morning. UK banks are shut. Tell him to stall, play for time, that he can't do anything until tomorrow.'

'I've tried, boss. He says the whole point about Bitcoins is they're nothing to do with banks. All you have to do if you want them fast is to download an app – you can look for them on a certain website. So, ideally, he'd simply buy Bitcoins and then send them as instructed by the kidnappers – where they would be untraceable.'

'How many people have that kind of money lying around their homes?' Grace replied.

'You're missing the point. He could do it all from his online banking account.'

'Money he says he doesn't have in his account. Or any account.'

'Exactly. And he's in panic mode.'

'Get him to calm down. With all his resources, not to mention wealthy clients, he's going to be able to lay his hands on £250k somewhere – maybe his bank will help him out tomorrow. Explain to him they're not going to harm his son so long as they can see money on its way. He's a smart guy, he must know how to handle people.'

'I'll keep trying, boss.'

Ending the call, Grace sat down at his workstation, wishing he could believe what he had just told Glenn Branson. But from what he had learned about the criminal fraternity within the Albanian community, violence, rather than negotiation, tended to be their response to situations. They could choose to make an example of Kipp Brown by cynically and callously killing Mungo, as a warning to other businessmen in the city to stump up ransom demands if one of their children was ever taken.

Throughout his career, people had constantly surprised Roy Grace, to the point where little shocked him any more. There was the facade they showed the world and there was the reality behind, lurking in the shadows. The police were strongly against paying ransoms, but the current circumstances, as they were no closer to finding Mungo Brown, meant that some payment was becoming inevitable, to buy time.

The next briefing was due for 11.30 a.m., twelve minutes' time; he turned his focus back to the video and the message:

DEAD IF YOU DON'T

BY 17.40 TODAY WATER LEVEL IS
ABOVE MUNGO HEAD

He looked at the map on the wall. On it was the county of Sussex broken down into police divisions. Beyond, to the east and west, the counties of Kent and Hampshire. Miles of coastline, inlets and rivers. Rye to the east; Chichester to the west. A coastal search just of Shoreham alone would take many hours, if not days. And they had just over six hours.

Alec Davies came up to him. 'Sir, in case it's of interest, I've just heard from Forensics at Guildford. They've obtained something from the fingerprints of a severed hand found at the crusher site of Carter Contracting, at Shoreham.'

'Yes?'

Eagerly, the young Detective Constable said, 'He's iden-tified as Ryan Brent – he's got form for small-time drug dealing. For the past two years this man has been employed by Jorgji Dervishi to collect the cash, daily, from his car wash and kebab empire. Several other body parts have been recovered from the site so far, all bearing evidence of torture – what appear to be razor cuts to his skin.'

'He's been employed by Dervishi?' Grace repeated.

'Yes, sir!'

'Nice work, Alec,' Grace said.

Just over six hours.

A £250,000 ransom demand.

Sent from where? Hopefully Digital Forensics would find that out, quickly.

Mungo Brown's father claiming to be unable to drum up that amount of money.

They had to stall the kidnappers and locate the boy, somehow.

Somehow.

How?

What the hell was Jorgji Dervishi's involvement? He could arrest him again, based on what Alec Davies had just told him. But would that serve any purpose? Perhaps it was better to cut the Albanian gangster some slack and keep watch on him.

'Sir?' An excited voice brought him out of his thoughts and he looked up.

The analyst, Giles Powell, was standing in front of him, holding a sheet of paper. 'Sir, we may have found something!'

75

Stacey came into Kipp's den, crying. 'I can't bear this,' she said. 'I can't bear this, I can't bear this, I can't bear this. Get him back, please, please get my baby back. Please get him back.'

'I'm going to, I promise.' He stared through the open window, feeling a warm breeze on his face. Looked at the covered barbecue beside the swimming pool. A glorious summer Sunday. Ordinarily he'd have had a swim. Perhaps played some tennis with Mungo, then a late barbecue lunch. Mungo loved his special burger recipe.

Stacey walked across and put her arms around Kipp, clinging to him like a drowning person clinging to driftwood. 'Please. Please. Please.'

His heart felt like it was twisting, tearing at the sinews that held it in place. 'Stace, I love him as much as you do.'

'You don't know how much I love him. He's all we have in the world. I couldn't bear it – if – if anything happened to him – I just couldn't.'

He felt her tears on his hair, on the back of his neck. He found her fingers and squeezed them. 'It won't, trust me,' he said. 'Trust me, Stace.'

'Trust Kipp?' she said, disentangling herself and standing back, staring at a photograph of Mungo grinning, looking unsteady on a paddleboard. 'Really? I should *trust Kipp*?'

'Stace.'

She laughed, a hollow, mocking laugh. The laugh of a total stranger. 'Trust Kipp! Of course! I'd trust you anytime. Why wouldn't I trust a man who would put his business in front of his son's life?'

'Because I won't,' he said.

'Then prove it, prove it now.'

A text came in on Stacey's phone. She looked.

> Tell your husband to go his office now. Await
> instructions and a package. Tell the police again
> and this time your boy does die.

'Oh God no.' She handed the phone to Kipp and sobbed while he read it.

A package.

What could that mean? he wondered.

An icy gust of fear swept through him.

What did *a package* mean?

Mungo parcelled?

Dead?

He sat still, struggling not to throw up. Then he stood, abruptly, grabbed his phone and headed for the door.

'Where are you going?' she asked.

'To the office.'

'To the office? Now?'

'I'm going to do it, OK? I'll pay the ransom, I'll move some funds around, cover my tracks. I can check the client discretionary fund from here, but I can't make any transactions – a security thing – it can only be done from a computer in the office, where the code changes daily.'

'Be careful.'

He looked back at her. 'You want me to be careful or you want me to get Mungo back?'

'Both.'

'It's going to be one or the other.'

76

'How long have you worked for me, Dritan?' Jorgji Dervishi asked with a kindly smile, soon after the police officers had left.

'Ten years, sir, Mr Dervishi.'

Despite being a foot taller and weighing one hundred pounds more than his boss, Dritan was afraid of the man.

'And in these ten years, have I ever given you any reason to be unhappy with me?'

'No, Mr Dervishi.'

'None at all?'

'None at all.'

Dervishi lit a cigar. 'Yet you wish to leave me and go home to Albania? You don't like to work for me any more?'

'It isn't that. My girl – Lindita.'

'She's very pretty but she doesn't like that you work for me, does she?'

'Why you say that?'

Dervishi pointed at his own eyes. 'I see it in how she looks at me. She thinks I am a bad influence on her sweet little man, yes? You want to go back home, where she is going to convert you into a good little citizen, eh? Run a little shop together – no – a coffee house, right?'

'I don't know.'

'But you have to go.'

'Yes.'

'But now you find out today that the cut you were going to get from my son's plan with his friend is no longer going to happen, right?' He blew a smoke ring. 'Gone, yes, like a puff of smoke? You had plans for this money? Enough to start your own business with your sweetheart, Lindita?'

Again, Dritan said nothing.

'This money would go a long way in Albania – much further than here, I think. It would buy you a very nice coffee house in Tirana, perhaps?'

'Maybe.'

Dervishi smiled. 'I think the timing could all be very perfect! Perhaps we come to an arrangement, a deal in which I forgive you, in return for a little favour. How would you like it if I fly you home tonight on my private plane, out of Brighton City Airport, with the £60,000 or whatever it is your friend Valbone has screwed you out of – would this be of interest to you?'

'What would this favour be?'

'Your colleague – friend – Valbone, did he ever say he was unhappy with me?' he asked.

'Never, Mr Dervishi.'

'Never?'

'Never.'

Dervishi drew pensively on his cigar. 'You are very well acquainted with Thatcher, are you not?'

Dritan nodded. Thinking about Lindita's text. He knew Thatcher was one of the things she had been referring to.

I don't like some of the things you do, u know what I'm talking about.

'You have seen, my trusted Dritan, how Thatcher likes human body parts, especially arms and legs?'

Dritan nodded, feeling a little sick with fear, wondering what was coming.

'You would not like me to inflict one thousand cuts on you and then feed your right arm to Thatcher, would you? And watch him eat it? As punishment for what you and Valbone had planned?'

'No, Mr Dervishi.' He was trembling.

'Of course you would not.' Dervishi looked at his computer screen, momentarily distracted by something on it. Then he tapped deftly on the keyboard, before returning his attention to his employee. 'How is your mother, Dritan?' he asked, suddenly changing the subject.

'My mother?' Dritan frowned. In ten years his boss had never asked him any questions about his family, so why now? 'My mother is good, thank you. She is well.'

'She and your father in that village, they still work their little farm, don't they?'

He hesitated. 'Yes.'

Dervishi nodded. 'Your *gjyshe*, too, she lives there and helps them. You are fond of her, are you not?'

'I love my grandmother very much,' he replied, curious that Mr Dervishi suddenly seemed so interested in his family. 'Very much. She was always so good to me – and she looks after my kid brother.'

'Your kid brother – he's just eighteen now?'

'Nineteen.'

'Nineteen.' Dervishi nodded. 'Nineteen, in a wheelchair, with the mind of a two-year-old.'

'My mother had a difficult birth with him, he did not breathe for too long – he got brain damage.'

'That's too bad. So, for your grandmother he will always be her little baby grandson?'

The bodyguard pursed his lips and nodded.

'So, Dritan, all I ask you to do is to find Valbone. Find his associates also, the ones who arranged, behind your back, to take Mungo Brown. Find them and explain to them all I am not happy – am I clear?'

'Explain to them?'

'Explain. You understand what will happen if you do not, Dritan?'

'I understand.'

'You understand or you *think* you understand? You look a little confused to me.'

'I understand, Mr Dervishi.'

Dritan's phone beeped with an incoming text.

'Please,' Dervishi said. 'Check your phone. I believe you have a new text.'

Dritan did as he was told. He saw a photograph of a small rustic dwelling taken with a telephoto lens. A pig was visible in the foreground and a farm dog in the distance.

'You recognize this house, Dritan?'

'Of course. My family's home.'

'Where you grew up?'

'Yes.'

'Take a look at the details on the photograph. Check the time and date,' Dervishi said, calmly.

Along the top of the image, Dritan saw the date, yesterday; and the time, 4 p.m. 'Who took this?' he asked.

'Someone who is there to protect them.'

Dritan gave his boss a quizzical stare, part frightened, part angry. 'To protect them? Really?' He clenched a fist. 'If anyone hurts them—'

Dervishi placed his cigar in the ashtray and raised his hands. 'No one will hurt them. Not if you do what I tell you when you find Valbone. *If* you can find him.'

'I will find him.'

'Of course you will.'

Dritan said nothing.

'Use your motorbike, their number plates are harder for cameras to recognize. Attach a fresh plate.'

'Yes.'

'Very good. When you have finished, go straight to the Lewes warehouse. I will meet you there to make the payment and arrange your safe transport to the airport, if you are able to confirm to me the job is done. Yes?'

Dritan nodded, dubiously.

Jorgji Dervishi reached down to the floor, lifted up a Waitrose carrier bag and handed it to him.

Dritan took it. Whatever was inside was heavy.

'Please explain to Valbone this is a little gift from me to him. To show no hard feelings. To thank him for his years of working, loyally, for me.'

Dritan looked at his boss uncomfortably, then peered inside the bag. Immediately, his mouth went dry and his heart felt heavy.

'You have any questions, Dritan?'

'I can trust you? I do this and you fly me in your private plane, yes? I can trust you?'

Dervishi shook his hand. 'I give you my *besa*.'

Besa was a word of honour. No Albanian who gave *besa* would ever break it. Dritan left on his mission, reassured.

77

They drove their two vehicles carefully, making sure they would attract no attention. They had staked out the long-term car park at Gatwick Airport two nights ago and selected an Audi A4 and a Volkswagen Golf half an hour after their owners had parked them and taken a bus, with their luggage, to start their holidays – wherever they were destined. So long as the cars were properly taxed, insured and MOT-tested, there should be no problem with the police, and the owners would not know their cars were missing until they returned from their travels. Long before then the vehicles would have been torched, somewhere remote.

Now, at midday, headed away from Shoreham Fort, Fatjon Sava drove the Audi, followed by Kushtim Kona in the Golf, through the entrance to the Hove apartment complex. Along with their partner in this plan, Valbone Kadare, they had rented a fourth-floor apartment as their temporary safe house.

As they climbed out in the underground car park, Kushtim, a bundle of nerves since leaving their victim in the gun emplacement, said, 'Are we sure we trust this guy, Fatjon?'

'With my life. Valbone is my brother!'

They rode the lift up, walked a short distance along the corridor and stopped outside flat number 112. There was a spy hole in the door.

Kona rang the bell.

It was opened a short distance, accompanied by the rattle of a safety chain. A shaven-headed face peered out, nervously, then smiled.

'One moment!'

The door closed. There was another rattle of the chain, then it opened again. The two men entered, each in turn kissing Kadare. Within minutes they were seated round the kitchen table toasting each other with shot glasses of rakia. They were careful not to drink too much of the clear liquid and, after two glasses each, they switched to strong Skenderbeu coffee.

The room grew thick with the fug of cigarette smoke. The three of them exchanged stories, laughing. Periodically Valbone stepped away to check his phone and his computer, and all the time keeping an eye on the time – and tide. They did not want Mungo Brown to drown – not until they had all the money. At some point they would have to go and move him, but all was fine for now, there were still a good three hours to go before the danger point was reached.

And on his phone, a pulsing blue dot, the signal from the tracker they'd placed under Kipp Brown's Porsche up at the Dyke last night, showed he was on the move. He had left his house and was heading in the direction of his office. Sensible man.

Valbone's phone rang.

He answered it, good-humoured. 'Yes? Hey, Dritan! My friend! Come and join us – we have good mulberry rakia here!'

He gave him the address. Then he turned back to his colleagues. 'It is all going to plan! Hey! By tonight we will be wealthy men. In twenty-four hours, we will all be very rich men. One more glass, heh?' He charged all the glasses, then picked his up. 'A toast?'

They all clinked together and downed the contents.

Then his mobile phone rang again.

78

In the suite, Roy Grace stood over Giles Powell's shoulder as the analyst pointed excitedly at figures on the monitor.

'Sir, this pairing is interesting.'

Grace saw two car registration numbers on the screen. RW15 AVU and TR57 GPN. 'Yes?'

'These both pinged an ANPR camera at the Beddingham roundabout at 3.21 this morning. At 3.41 they pinged another just outside Newhaven Port. At 3.57 one at Peacehaven. At 4.07 one at Saltdean. At 4.16 they were both picked up on another ANPR camera on Marine Parade, Kemp Town. At 4.22 a.m. they were picked up by another on Kingsway, in Hove, both cars heading towards Shoreham. They were next picked up by an ANPR in Shoreham. Then nothing for some while.'

'Are you sure, Giles?'

'From their last recorded position, they could have headed north, through Southwick, in which case they would have been picked up by an ANPR on the A27, or continued west, and been located on the one towards Steyning. Or they could have driven into the harbour.'

'Any other options?' Grace asked.

'They could have headed into Shoreham Beach, sir.'

Shoreham Beach was a vast warren of upmarket houses

and apartment blocks, located between the harbour mouth and the beachfront to the west.

'Have you done a check on these vehicles?'

'Yes, sir,' Powell said. 'RW15 AVU is an Audi A4, registered to a Mr Richard Sanderson of Harewoods Lane, Haywards Heath, and TR57 GPN is a Volkswagen Golf registered to a Mr Iain Maclean of Adelaide Crescent, Hove.'

'What do we know about either of them?'

'No criminal records. I've given the details to DS Exton's Outside Enquiry Team, sir, to see if they can locate these people or relatives urgently. But one possibility is they're away on overseas trips, which is why their cars were selected.'

'Quite possibly,' Grace agreed.

'Now this is where it gets interesting, sir: an hour after disappearing, bingo! We see the pair again apparently retracing their steps, pinging the same ANPR in Shoreham and on Kingsway in Hove heading east. Then disappearing.'

'Heading somewhere into Hove – or Brighton?' Grace asked.

'In my opinion, yes.'

Grace thought for some moments. 'Having deposited Mungo Brown somewhere in the Shoreham or Shoreham Beach area?'

'Yes,' Powell said. 'Or Southwick – or somewhere to the west.'

'I think it's significant they went to Newhaven at the same time that Valbone Kadare went there in Dervishi's Range Rover, which has subsequently disappeared. Could they have gone to pick him up after he dumped the car somewhere? Perhaps in a container?'

'That would fit, sir.'

Grace called Oscar-1. An inspector who had taken over

from Keith Ellis was on duty. He asked her to put out alerts for sightings of either the Audi or Golf, but with a strict instruction that the cars were not to be followed or stopped. Next, he asked her to put in place an immediate search of Newhaven Port for the Range Rover, index KK04 YXB. When he had done that he turned to the map on the wall. Shoreham Beach was an area that he and Cleo had once considered moving to, but the property prices had been prohibitive. The video and the tide chart made sense. Somewhere close to the water, for there to have been a crab present. A cave or a cavern? The whole Sussex coast was riddled with caves and had once been a smugglers' paradise. It was fishing and smuggling that had, back in the seventeenth century, been the start of Brighton's rise to prosperity.

Grace turned back to the map, studying the Shoreham area, trying to put himself into the mindset of a kidnapper. *Where would I hide someone in this complex?*

The waterfront of Shoreham Harbour was a good seven miles long. It would take days to search it properly. They now had, according to the demand sent to Mungo's father, little over five hours.

79

Valbone looked at the display on his phone. It showed the caller's number was withheld. After hesitating, he answered. 'Yes?'

A hushed, frightened voice, barely above a whisper, said, 'Valbone?'

'Yes, Aleksander?' he said, recognizing the voice instantly.

'My father knows about you – your involvement – and he's very angry. You are now in danger, I just wanted to warn you.'

'What does he know?'

'About our plan. He made me tell him.'

'We're cool, Aleksander. But good of you to call.'

'You know my dad's a very dangerous man. I think you should abort, Valbone.'

'Don't worry, Aleksander,' he replied. 'I can be very dangerous, too.'

80

Kipp Brown used to joke to clients that his company had police protection. His new offices were almost next door to the former headquarters of Sussex CID on the Hollingbury industrial estate at the northern extremity of the city. But he wasn't in a joking mood now as he parked his Porsche in front of the modern three-storey building. He felt a bit like a naughty schoolboy, having given the two officers in his house the slip by telling them he was going out for a walk for some air. Climbing out, he looked all around, feeling nervous as hell.

Fretting about the word 'package'.

To his relief, he couldn't see anything.

Punching in the passcode on the keypad, he pushed open the main entrance door and looked on the floor for any delivery company's card – ordinary mail was not delivered here at weekends – but there was nothing. He entered the silent premises, checking that the door clicked shut behind him. The reception area had been carefully designed to impress, to make clients feel they were somewhere special, but to be welcoming and not intimidating. It was modern, with glass furniture and tan leather sofas, large plants and smiling photographic portraits on the walls of himself and his colleagues.

The office had that silent, Sunday feeling. The receptionist's empty desk. The smell of floor polish. The water dispenser in the far corner made a brief gurgling sound, then stopped.

He was going against the original advice of the Detective Inspector. Branson and his colleague had cautioned him and Stacey about paying any ransom. In the old days, the DI said, when banknotes would be handed over in a bag, there was a good chance of recovering some or all of the money. But in the modern, murky world of cryptocurrencies, where transactions could be untraceable, there were no safeguards.

Nor, Branson informed Kipp and Stacey, was there any guarantee the kidnappers wouldn't simply take the money and vanish. It was vital, he urged them, that before making any payment, they had evidence Mungo was alive and unharmed, and that a plan was agreed for his safe return.

It was easy for Branson, Kipp thought, it wasn't his son. Their lives had been a nightmare for the past four years since Kayleigh had died. Now they were in another nightmare. Nothing mattered, nothing at all, except getting Mungo back. If he had to go to prison for taking clients' money and lose everything he had to get their son back, so be it.

Ignoring the lift, he sprinted up the open-tread glass stairs, walked past the rows of empty desks in the huge open-plan area, lights coming on automatically as the sensors picked him up, and entered his own private office at the far end.

It was functional rather than swanky. There was a six-seater table, with a conference phone, and several pictures of clients' businesses – past and present – on the walls, along with ones of a charter helicopter, a high-rise development and a warehousing complex. On his large, tidy desk, and on the wall, were framed photographs of Kayleigh, Mungo and Stacey.

He sat down and after checking there were no emails from the kidnappers, he heard another text ping in. It was detailed and specific, and in the space at the bottom was a black-and-white square QR code.

> Go to https://www.coinbase.com/dashboard. Open an account. Buy Bitcoins to the value of £250,000 and place them in your wallet. When you have done that, download the QR reader app on your phone and scan the QR code below. It will take you to our wallet. If you then enter the 33-digit code, the money will transfer instantly. Be warned of the consequences of any delay.

Mindful of DI Branson's instructions, he composed a text back.

> I will do this on receipt of proof that Mungo is safe and unharmed. I need to know your plan for releasing him to my wife and me.

It would not send. He was blocked from replying.

Shit.

He opened his browser and entered https://www.coin-base.com/dashboard.

A sign-in request appeared for his name, email and a password. He entered them and instantly received a message that an email had been sent to him for verification. He checked his inbox, saw the one at the top and clicked on it. He was then asked to tick a box confirming he was not a robot.

A new page appeared, headed in blue letters: Welcome KB – Let's get started.

There was a row of headings beneath: email; phone; upload to; payment; buy.

Under that was the message: Welcome to Coinbase! This guide will help you buy your first digital currency! Please start by choosing your account type.

There were two boxes, one marked INDIVIDUAL, the other BUSINESS, which was followed by: Submit an application to sign up as an institution.

He clicked on that and saw, to his dismay, the message: To open a business account, you'll need to submit additional proof of your business records. Verification with Coinbase may take up to three business days.

Shit.

Three days he did not have.

He was totally out of his depth with this new kind of currency. Sure, he'd had a few clients asking about the investment potentials, but from what he'd read there seemed too much danger. He had built his business on sound advice and caution, but now he regretted not having done further research into what was undoubtedly a growing – if potentially nefarious – new financial paradigm.

What if this was just a scam? Or he did something wrong and the money simply disappeared into the ether? He needed advice from someone, but who? There was one person he could think of, his former boss from some years back, Steve Crouch. Although their companies were now rivals, since he had left to start out on his own, there had been no hard feelings.

He looked up Crouch's mobile number and dialled it.

To his relief after two rings he heard his voice. 'Kipp! Long time no hear, how are you?'

'I'm – OK.'

'You're doing pretty well by all accounts – giving me a hard time!'

'I'm just a minnow compared to your empire.'

'So, to what do I owe the honour of this call?'

'I need help, Steve.'

'Are you OK? You sound – stressed?'

'I am, very.'

'What's the problem?'

'What do you know about Bitcoins?'

'Not much, but I'm starting to get asked by a few clients about these and other cryptocurrencies – there's a growing raft of them.'

'I've been asked to make a substantial transaction, Steve – a quarter of a million pounds in Bitcoins, to be followed by a further sum of over two million, and I need to know what I'm doing – and if I should do it at all.'

'I'd be bloody careful.'

'That's what I feel.'

'Do you know Clive Bennett?'

'No.'

'His daughter-in-law used to work for me – she's just left on maternity leave. He's your man. Would be worth speaking to him. How urgent is this?'

'I have to make a transaction today – like, immediately.'

'I've got his mobile number. I talked to him a couple of days ago, you'll find him helpful.'

Kipp wrote down the number, thanked him and immediately dialled. After six rings, it went to voicemail. He left a message.

'Hi, Mr Bennett, Steve Crouch gave me your number. My name is Kipp Brown and I need, very urgently, some help with a Bitcoin transaction I've been asked to make.

Any chance you could give me a call back as soon as you get this?'

He ended the call, stood up and paced around his office, fretting. What should he do? What *could* he do?

He stared at a large photograph of Stacey, Kayleigh and Mungo on mountain bikes, up on the South Downs, all wearing their helmets and smiling. Then he looked at the photograph of Mungo. It had been taken a few years ago, when he was about nine or ten, up on the Devil's Dyke – ironically, close to where he had driven to last night. Mungo was running towards the camera, in jeans and a striped T-shirt, and with his long hair floating like a mane, he looked impossibly cute.

Kipp's insides felt knotted.

Suddenly, his phone rang, momentarily startling him. The display showed the number was withheld. Great! Clive Bennett, he hoped. 'Kipp Brown,' he answered. But it wasn't Bennett, it was DI Branson.

'Kipp, where are you? I hope I've caught you in time – have you paid the ransom?'

'I had to go into the office, I'm in the process of trying to – this Bitcoin thing is quite elaborate.'

'Don't pay, hold. We have a development – we may have found the people who've taken your son.'

He felt a burst of elation. 'You have?'

'I can't tell you too much but we believe we've identified their vehicles – we've a good chance of an arrest soon.'

'OK – great – but what about Mungo? Will he be safe if you do?'

'We're pretty sure he's not with them, that he's still where they've hidden him. I strongly advise you not to pay the ransom until we've clarified the situation. At least give it another hour. Can you stall them?'

'I would if I could, but their comms are all one-way. I've had the payment instructions.'

'Can you send them to me?'

'OK.'

'Sir, I think you should come back to your home – we may have some very quick decisions to make.'

'I'm on my way,' he said.

Brown logged off, grabbed his keys, hurried back down into the empty reception area and out into the glorious early afternoon sunshine. And saw something pinned to the windscreen of his car by a wiper blade. Something white. A flyer of some kind, he presumed, a pizza delivery place or car-wash advert.

As he neared the car he saw it was an envelope.

He lifted the wiper and picked it up. There was something inside it, something soft and lumpy.

He ripped it open, then stood still. Staring in shock and horror.

'Oh God. No. No.'

81

It had been a long time since Sussex Police had been involved in a kidnap with a ransom demand at this level. Roy Grace hated the idea of the kidnappers getting away with a ransom, but if it meant the safe return of Mungo Brown, so be it – his primary goal was to protect the boy's life. The worst possible result would be the family paying the ransom and Mungo being found dead. From the evidence he had so far, the kidnap was professional and well thought-out, which made him optimistic. If they were after money, it was unlikely the kidnappers were going to let Mungo die, regardless of their threats to the father.

He thought about Mungo's original plan, hatched with his mate, Aleksander Dervishi. Was this boy's criminal father, well-known to Brighton police, the mastermind behind it all? Some kind of elaborate double-bluff going on? He didn't think so. He had grounds to arrest him, but what would that achieve at this moment? He had hoped the man would say something to Norman Potting and Velvet Wilde that would give them a lead. But so far, nothing.

He looked at his watch. It was 1 p.m. If the tide chart was to be believed, in less than five hours' time Mungo Brown would drown. However much he doubted the people behind this would let that happen, he wouldn't bet the ranch on it.

Giles Powell suddenly hurried over to Roy Grace. 'Sir,' he said, with excitement in his voice. 'We have a development.'

'Tell me?'

'Following the alert that was put out for the Audi and Golf, an NPT car crew spotted both vehicles on Dyke Road Avenue, twenty minutes ago. They turned and followed – at a safe distance – and observed both vehicles turn into the entrance of Boden Court.'

'Those blocks of flats at the top?' Grace asked, his adrenaline surging.

'Yes, sir.'

'Dyke Road Avenue is the same street Kipp Brown lives in – can't be more than about half a mile away from his house,' Grace said, then wondered. Was this deliberate? The kidnappers staking him out from there? Whatever. He balled his fists and banged them together. 'Brilliant, Giles! Do we know if the vehicles are still there?'

'They are, sir – Oscar-1 instructed the unmarked car to park up and keep watch.'

Grace thanked him, went over to his desk and hurriedly scribbled out the paperwork for a search warrant. He didn't strictly need one, but it was belt and braces; all officers had the power to force an immediate entry into premises where life was believed to be in danger. He dispatched DC Davies to the on-call magistrate to get it signed. Then he called the Force Gold and Critical Incident Manager, in turn, to inform them of the development. Next, he called Oscar-1, requesting the vehicles and personnel he needed.

As soon as he'd ended the last call, he told DC Hall to accompany him, and raced out to the car park.

82

Kipp Brown stood outside his office building, staring at the contents of the envelope. He was shaking, his eyes blurred with tears, his heart filled with anger. Staring at a severed human ear, partially covered in congealed blood, that looked fake, like something you'd buy in a joke shop. But this was palpably real. As was Mungo's terror in the Polaroid photograph that accompanied the ear. It showed the bloody bandage taped to the right side of his head. The ligature round his neck.

The palm of a hand was in shot, holding a wristwatch on which the time, clearly visible, was 11.55 a.m. Just over an hour ago.

God, you bastards.

His mind was spinning. The detective said they'd identified the kidnappers' cars. But they hadn't arrested them. They didn't know where Mungo was. Time was running out. They wanted two and a half million pounds but were willing to accept a deposit today, of a quarter of a million. That felt like one businessman talking to another. His language. If he paid the deposit, the kidnappers would know he was real, that he was going to pay the full ransom. They wouldn't be cruel or dumb enough to harm Mungo, would they?

One of them was clearly watching his office, from

somewhere nearby, and had put this on his car the moment he had gone inside. He spun round. Looking at the ASDA superstore across the road. At the parked cars alongside the pavement. No one in sight.

His phone rang. Number withheld. The kidnappers?

'Mr Brown?'

'Speaking.'

'It's Clive Bennett.'

'Oh – hey, Clive – right – thanks so much for calling back.'

'How can I help you?' He sounded friendly but direct.

'I need to make a Bitcoin transaction, but I've never done anything with cryptocurrencies before – and Steve Crouch said you might be the man who could help me.'

'Sure. What do you need to know? There's Bitcoins, but there's also a whole range of other altcoins, too – Ethereum, Ripple and Litecoin are some of the bigger ones – there's a pretty wide choice these days.'

'It has to be Bitcoins,' Kipp said.

'OK.'

'What I need is a helping hand to make the transaction.'

'Sure, I could meet you sometime this week?'

'I have to make the payment now,' he said. 'I mean – literally now.'

'How much money are we talking?'

'Two hundred and fifty thousand pounds. I need to buy Bitcoins to this value and then deposit them.'

For a moment, there was no response. Then Bennett said, 'That's a big lump for your first Bitcoin transaction.'

'I know, that's why I need help to make sure I don't screw up. And tomorrow I have to send a further £2,250,000.'

'Excuse me asking, Mr Brown, but are you under some kind of pressure? It's not my business, I know, but I'm just getting a sense of something not quite right here. But feel free to tell me to mind my own business.'

'No – I – I'm not in any trouble – I'm acting on behalf of a very big client who wants to get into this emerging market.'

'Emerging, but pretty volatile,' he warned. 'So urgently it can't wait until business hours tomorrow?'

Kipp's head felt on the verge of exploding. 'OK, look, I'll level with you, Clive, if you just keep this to yourself.'

'Sure.'

He told Bennett, in quick summary, what had happened. When he had finished, Bennett replied, sympathetically.

'God, I'm sorry. I don't really know what to say – what a nightmare for you and your wife. Of course I'll help you, but you do need to be aware that once you enter the ransomer's code on your Bitcoin wallet, that will be it, the money's gone, irretrievably. It's an uncrackable code even with today's technology. Are you confident this will get your son back?'

'No, I'm not, but I don't have any choice. They're threatening that my son will die this afternoon if I don't pay it.' He pictured in his mind the photograph of Mungo running towards him. 'Maybe I'm being a fool but I can't risk it. I've just got to do what they demand.'

'OK, so are you in front of your computer now?'

'Just give me thirty seconds.' Kipp went back up to his office, switched on to speakerphone and listened to Bennett's instructions as he guided him through logging back on to Coinbase. This time he clicked on INDIVIDUAL.

Bennett continued talking him through the process, with Kipp in turn sending him screenshots of each stage. Within five minutes he had purchased, with money from his clients' discretionary fund, Bitcoins to the value of £250,000 and placed them in his virtual wallet.

Next, he downloaded the QR reader app and scanned the square, black-and-white QR code.

After a short delay a window appeared on his computer screen. At the top, it said: DEPOSIT BITCOIN (BTC)

Below was the warning: I acknowledge the following information: By depositing tokens to this location you agree to our deposit recovery policy. Depositing tokens other than BTC to this address may result in your funds being lost.

It was followed by a code of letters and numbers written inside an address box.

GP1tr57a30ZxgF3di9nH7a904ft2hbV6x

Thirty-three digits, Kipp counted. From what he knew about security codes, six numbers were extremely hard to crack. Thirty-three, alternating upper- and lower-case letters and combined with numbers, was way beyond the capability of any computer system currently in existence.

His fingers hovered over the keys. Was he making a huge mistake? He thought of Detective Branson's cautioning words.

'What do you think, Clive?' he asked.

'I can't tell you what to do, Kipp. All I can tell you is that your Bitcoins will go to the address you've been given. Once you've sent them, they're gone, no getting them back. It's your call.'

Kipp looked back at the photo of Mungo on his desk.

Then he hit the keys.

Seconds later he received an acknowledgement.

Thank you. Your funds have been received. You may not reply to this message.

83

'Shit, man,' Fatjon Sava said, feeling more than a little drunk as he topped up his glass of the sharp rakia. He peered, having difficulty in focusing, at his two colleagues, Valbone and Kushtim. 'What is this?'

'You like it?' Valbone Kadare asked. 'It's made by my cousin back home. We have mulberry and cherry also. Good, eh?'

'We have to drive, Fatjon,' Kushtim said, reminding him and slurring his words. 'Only a few hours before we need to get the boy! No more drink!'

'So why the fuck is his father not coming back to us?' Valbone, still stone-cold sober, asked.

'You need a drink, Valbone!' Fatjon said, walking unsteadily towards him, brandishing the bottle.

The Albanian covered his glass of water with his hand. 'You want one of us to get arrested for drink-driving with the boy in the boot of the car? I don't think so, Fatjon.'

'Go fuck yourself,' Fatjon replied. He necked the bottle and staggered sideways, colliding with the table. Peering through unfocused eyes at Valbone, he rocked his head from side to side. 'Not bottling out, are you?' He roared with laughter at his joke as he held up the bottle. 'You have another?'

'You've had enough,' Valbone said.

Fatjon turned on him, aggressively. 'Oh? Valbone is telling me I've had enough to drink. Really? Poor sober Valbone!'

The ting of a bell suddenly silenced all three of them. The doorbell. It tinged again.

They nodded at each other.

Valbone walked out of the lounge, along the short hallway, and peered through the spy hole. The wide-angle lens showed a distorted image of his colleague, Dritan Nano, out in the corridor, wearing motorcycling leathers, holding a crash helmet in one hand and a carrier bag in the other.

He unhooked the safety chain and opened the door with a broad smile.

'Hey! Good to see you! Come in!'

'How's your day so far?' Dritan enquired.

84

Roy Grace sat in the passenger seat of the unmarked Mondeo, updating the Force Gold and the CIM, and giving fast-time instructions to the Oscar-1 Inspector as he marshalled his team into place. In silent concentration, Kevin Hall drove at high speed on blue lights, siren wailing, passing the Amex Stadium to their left and the leafy, red-brick Sussex University campus to their right. Cursing, he suddenly braked hard, throwing Grace forward against his seat belt, and momentarily changed the pitch of the siren to a deep honking blast at a driver who had pulled a small Fiat straight out into the overtaking lane in front of them, without apparently looking in his mirrors.

'Get out the way, you dozy git!'

The Fiat shot back into the gap it had vacated, and Hall sped on past. He headed up the long hill, down the far side, passing the Hollingbury Industrial Estate where their former CID HQ had been housed, drove down into the valley and swept up the far side. There was a windmill to their left, and to their right the open countryside of the South Downs National Park. Roy Grace was focused on his screen, using Google Earth to take an aerial view of the complex of separate four-storey buildings that comprised Boden Court, and the eighty or so flats they housed.

He was wondering how they could identify which flat the kidnappers were in. Speed was key in any raid. If they were wrong about where Mungo was being held and the kidnappers did have him in there, the big danger was alerting them to the police presence. They could just be vicious enough to kill Mungo out of spite in the moments before they were arrested. Grace could not take that chance, which was why he had ordered all units to stay well outside in the street, until further instructions.

Hall switched off the siren and blue lights half a mile before the approach to the roundabout at the top of the hill, not wanting to risk signposting their arrival to the kidnappers, and turned left into wide, residential Dyke Road Avenue. A couple of hundred yards ahead, on the right-hand side of the road, was the entrance to the cluster of brick buildings of Boden Court, marked with a bold, white sign. A number of police vehicles were pulled up a short distance further on, all parked along the cycle lane. Among them were two white vans, containing Local Support Team officers, with their Inspector, Ian Allchild, in the lead vehicle. The whole area looked like a military battalion had moved in. If any of the kidnappers drove out now they would panic for sure.

No doubt there would be some bolshy letter in the *Argus* later this week about the police blocking the cycle lane, Grace thought, but it was the very least of his problems at this moment.

Several plain-clothes officers, casually dressed and wearing earpieces, were milling around on the pavement, out of sight of any of the flats, trying unsuccessfully to look inconspicuous. To the left, almost opposite the entrance, was a small car park with a stall selling ice creams and soft drinks. Grace saw two dog-unit vans parked in there, along with another van, one of their own, today camouflaged with the name BRYAN BARKER BUILDERS. Inside was a mobile phone tracking team, scanning the complex across the road, trying to pick up a signal from the phone they had identified.

'Pull in here, Kevin.'

'Want an ice cream, do you, guv?'

'Haha.'

Roy Grace called Oscar-1 and told her he was at the scene. In earlier days, he would have had no hesitation in leading a raid from the front, heading straight to a suspect's dwelling and putting the door in with his shoulder or boot. But hide-bound by the current rules of Health and Safety, every action had to be risk assessed. It was only trained officers from the Local Support Team, the specialist public order unit, who were allowed to effect entry, under their Section 17 PACE powers.

As so often happened in the case of a raid, there was an air of uncertainty. Everyone was here, waiting, pumped up and ready to go. But exactly where? And the biggest uncertainty facing Roy at this moment was which of the flats his suspects were in. There was no way they could go charging around, banging on every door. They were either going to have to find them by stealth or wait for them to show themselves – though in his view it was too time critical to wait, that wasn't an option for him.

Instructing Hall to remain in the car and keep watch, he climbed out and hurried across the road. He strolled in through the entrance, trying to look nonchalant in case the kidnappers were keeping a lookout from a window. He carried on, down a ramp, passing a visitor's parking area containing two vehicles, an older-model Jaguar and a red van with the wording in white letters MATTHEW MURPHY

ELECTRICAL SERVICES, a man and a woman sitting in the front.

He walked alongside the van, curious to know what they were doing here on a Sunday, and decided to check them out. He went up to the driver's window, holding up his warrant card discreetly.

The window lowered. He rapidly satisfied himself they were bona fide, Matthew Murphy and his wife, Sam, who jointly owned the company. They'd only been here a few minutes, collecting payment on a job their firm had completed in one of the flats. Neither of them had seen any car come in or leave.

He thanked them and approached the entrance to the first building. The smell of cooking wafted from a window, roasting meat – Sunday lunch. It gave him a sudden pang of hunger, reminding him he hadn't eaten anything since a sandwich in the early hours and a muffin.

Staring at the entry panel, he found the nameplate he was hoping for: CARETAKER. He pressed the buzzer beside it. Would he or she be in?

There was a crackle and an Italian-sounding voice. 'Hello?'

'Police,' Grace said. 'Could I have a word, very urgently.'

'Police? OK.' There was a click of the door's latch and Grace pushed it open. There was a stronger smell of Sunday roast now, as well as stale cigarette smoke. He was mindful that it was possible the kidnappers could be using the caretaker's flat. But when he saw the door open at the end of the corridor and the very short man of around sixty, wearing white-flecked dungarees and a liberal amount of paint on his face and hands, shuffle towards him, he decided they were not.

'Hello, officer,' the caretaker said. 'I'm not usually in on

Sunday, but I'm decorating today – so how can I help you?' He sounded Italian.

Grace showed him his warrant card. 'What's your name?'

'Vince.'

'OK, Vince, I'm looking for the drivers of two cars,' he said. 'An Audi A4 and Volkswagen Golf.' He told him the registration numbers. 'Does either vehicle ring a bell?'

The man thought, screwing up his forehead, then shook his head. 'We have a lot of cars here. Quite a few Audis and Golfs, you know – very popular cars.'

'Where does everyone park – are the garages round the back?'

Vince shook his head again and pointed a stubby, nicotine-stained finger at the floor. 'Underground.'

Grace felt a sudden flash of excitement. 'Is there a separate car park for each of the buildings?'

'No, one big one, with separate lifts up to each building.' He looked at Grace with a kind of beady, mischievous excitement in his eyes. 'What's up, officer? We have terrorists here? Bank robbers?'

'I can't tell you at the moment, I'm afraid. Can you show me the car park?'

He shrugged. 'Sure.'

Grace followed him along the corridor, the man walking unhurriedly, almost painfully slowly, a big bunch of keys dangling from his belt. He pressed to open the lift doors, waited for Grace to enter, then stepped in.

They went down one floor. The door opened and they stepped out into a sparsely lit expanse of parking bays, about a third of them empty. It was dry and warm, with the same familiar smell of engine oil, spent exhaust fumes and rubber compounds as most underground car parks Grace observed, other than municipal ones which tended to smell of urine, as well. But they were in upmarket territory here.

'Are the bays allocated to specific flats, Vince?'

'Yes, numbered.'

'So, from the number of the bay, you can identify the building and the flat number?'

'Sure.'

Grace strode along towards the far end, with Vince keeping pace. There was a wide range of cars down here, mostly modern and across the price spectrum, as well as a 1970s Bentley coated in dust and with flat tyres, that didn't look like it had moved in years. A short distance along they passed what looked like the shape of a Porsche beneath a dust sheet. He reached a Golf, and checked the number plate against the one stored in his memory: TR57 GPN. It was different, but he still patted the bonnet, just to check. Stone cold, the car had not been driven today.

As they turned a corner, passing a wide concrete pillar, he saw an Audi and a Golf next to each other, some bays along. He broke into a run, and as he came closer looked at their number plates.

TR57 GPN; RW15 AVU.

It was them.

85

Kipp Brown remained at his desk in his office, staring at the words on the screen.

Thank you. Your funds have been received. You may not reply to this message.

He took a photograph with his iPhone, then sent DI Branson an image of the severed ear, the Polaroid and the receipt, by WhatsApp. At the end he added the words,

Please do not tell my wife about the ear.

It was only seconds before Branson phoned him. 'Are you on your own?'

'Yes, in my office.'

'Listen, Kipp,' Branson said, keeping his voice low – perhaps Stacey was nearby, he wondered. 'I need you to do something for me. Neither Jack nor I can leave here, obviously. I need this ear and the photograph to go very urgently to Surrey and Sussex Major Crime Branch forensics in Guildford, along with some items from Mungo that would contain his DNA – his toothbrush and hairbrush, perhaps? We've got to establish this is a DNA match to your son, and if there is anything we can get, forensically, from it.'

'A DNA match?' Kipp said. 'Does that matter? You can

319

see the bandage over his ear in the photograph pretty clearly.'

'We may be able to get a fingerprint off the ear,' Branson replied. 'We also have techniques now for reading finger-prints off a photograph. The way the man is holding the watch, palms out towards the camera, means there's a very good chance of the fingerprint team getting something.'

'What do you need?' Kipp Brown was relieved to have something positive to do.

'Would you normally take your dog out for a walk?'

'Yes, every day at some point.'

'In the car?'

'It depends. Sometimes.'

'OK, good. If you can, come back here quickly.'

86

Roy Grace patted the bonnets of both the Golf and Audi. Each was warm, only recently driven. 'Where are the bay numbers, Vince?'

'On the floor.'

As Grace knelt the caretaker said, 'No, it's OK, I know these three bays.'

In the next one along was a black Range Rover with tinted rear windows.

'Whose is that?' Grace asked.

'They rent – pay for three parking spaces.'

'Do you know their names?'

'No – is rented by a company.'

'But you've seen them?'

He shrugged. 'A few times. They come and go, you know.'

He went over to the Range Rover and patted the bonnet of that, too. It was also warm. 'Are they English, Vince?'

'No – Europeans, maybe.'

'Albanians?'

'Possibly. I hear them speak sometime, I don't know the language.'

'Do you have CCTV cover?'

'Yes, in the car park and outside, but it stopped working yesterday. I'm waiting for the engineers to come.'

Coincidence, Grace wondered? He doubted it. 'Right, Vince, I'm going to need your help. How many exits are there?'

'They're on the fourth floor. One exit is down here – the main entrance we came in and the fire exit for this car park.' The caretaker was starting to become animated. 'Then there is the front entrance and the rear to their building. So, this is a drugs raid?'

Ignoring the question, Grace said, 'Vince, I'm going to be moving vehicles in here. I want you to do three things for me. The first is to disable the car park entrance door, so no one can drive out. The second is to open the front door to this block, and the third is to show my team the fire escape exits. Can you do that?'

'Sure,' he said, with a knowing twinkle in his eyes. 'No problem. Like James Bond?'

Grace grinned and gave him a pat on the shoulder. 'When Daniel Craig quits, we'll put your name forward, eh?' Then he began giving instructions, calmly but urgently, into his radio, and ran back out, followed by the caretaker, to the front of the building, as the first of the two Local Support Team vans arrived. These contained more officers than he reckoned he would need for the raid, but he wasn't taking any chances.

Vince opened the glass front door of the building and shoved a wedge beneath it. Inspector Ian Allchild jumped down from the passenger seat in full blue riot gear with body armour, holding his vizored helmet; the driver climbed out also. A further six officers, all similarly clad, descended from the rear, while Grace briefed the Inspector. Allchild, a tough former army officer, with a no-nonsense voice, responded enthusiastically. This was the kind of job he and his team were trained for and the kind of job which they all loved. The second van pulled up behind them and another team of eight climbed out. Allchild briefed the skipper to have his team spread out around the building, in case anyone tried to leg it.

Grace's adrenaline was surging. He directed the two vans containing dog handlers to follow the caretaker, then said to Allchild, 'Ready?'

'Ready, sir.'

Grace radioed the Critical Incident Manager that they were going in, then instructed Kevin Hall to bring all vehicles in now and to block the entrance. No one was to enter or leave Boden Court until he gave the all-clear. He turned to the Inspector. 'OK, go!'

Allchild gave the signal to his team. One officer, holding the red bosher, led the way in through the front door and up the fire escape stairs. He was closely followed by a short but very strong sergeant, Lorna Dennison-Wilkins, holding a hydraulic ram, then Allchild and his remaining five officers. Grace ran up the four flights, just a short distance behind.

At the top, the team moved silently along the corridor, halting outside a door. It was too far away for Roy Grace, panting with the exertion, to see the number. All of them pulled their vizors down.

The officer with the big red key rang the doorbell, and waited.

There was no response.

Then he knocked on the door. The classic policeman's knock. Unsubtle and loud. *Rat-a-tap-tap-tap-tap*. Then, *BLAM-BLAM-BLAM*.

Again, nothing.

He turned to Lorna and nodded.

She stepped forward, wedged both arms of the ram

against the sides of the door frame, and powered it up. As the grinding howl of the machine splintered the wood, forcing the frame outwards on both sides, her colleague swung the ram against the door, sending it crashing open at the first attempt.

With a unified bellow of, 'POLICE! POLICE! POLICE!', boots pounding, they burst like a tornado into the interior.

Grace stood back, outside, with the other four blocking his view.

'Shit,' one of them said. 'Shit.'

'What is it?' Grace asked, easing his way through them to the doorway. And saw a body prostrate on the floor, and a lot of blood. Allchild, vizor pushed up over his face, came back out, carefully stepping past the body, followed by two of his team. He looked grim. 'Sir,' he said. 'I'm sorry, we've trampled all over it. You have a bit of a crime scene in there. No young boy anywhere. Two adult males dead, looks like gunshot wounds, one badly injured. I've radioed for paramedics.'

'Is the injured one conscious?'

'Barely, sir. I've left Lorna with him, in case. He looks in a bad way.'

Grace hurried in. A motionless, tattooed and shaven-headed man in his thirties, dressed in jeans, trainers and a grey hoodie, lay on his back on the floor. He had a startled expression; a trail of blood and gunk leaked from a hole in the centre of his forehead, staining the beige carpet, and there was what looked like another bullet wound and a large amount of blood spreading across the front of his T-shirt. The fact that the blood hadn't dried meant this was very recent. Was the shooter still inside the building, he wondered?

Mindful of not further contaminating the crime scene,

Grace stepped carefully past the evidently dead man, noticing the faint, familiar coppery smell of blood, and along
the corridor towards an open door at the far end.

He entered a kitchen that smelled of cigarette smoke,
and stopped in his tracks.

One casually dressed man, in his late forties, he estimated, was seated in a wooden chair at a pine table, on
which lay two globe-like bottles of alcohol and an ashtray
overflowing with cigarette butts. His head lolled back over
his shoulders, dark hair brushed back. There was what
looked like a gun-shot entry wound through his right eye,
from which a trail of dark fluid ran down his cheek and
neck, and another through his bloodstained chest. His
good remaining eye stared fixedly ahead.

The second man, younger and also casually dressed,
with short, wiry hair, lay on his back, close to an upturned
chair. He had a bullet graze along the top of his forehead
and the front of his light windcheater was blood-drenched
and heaving. He was looking up at Grace with large, sullen
eyes and wheezing, painfully, clearly breathing with difficulty.

Indicating to Lorna that she could go, Grace knelt
beside him. 'There's an ambulance coming,' he said.

The man's chest jerked. His breathing was becoming
fainter by the second.

'What happened?' Grace asked him. 'Do you know
where Mungo is? Mungo Brown?'

The man tried to speak, then gasped in pain. He started
juddering.

'Mungo Brown? The boy you took?' Grace pressed. 'Do
you know where he is?'

Fixing him eerily with his eyes, the man said something

in a guttural voice, in a language Roy Grace did not understand. It sounded like, '*Ick largo skow gee veten.*'

Then a rattle came from his throat. Grace recognized it. He had only seconds left. Hurriedly, he pulled out his private iPhone, opened the voice recorder app and activated it, then held it close to the man's mouth. 'Can you repeat that?' he asked, urgently.

The man stared ahead. Finally, struggling, he uttered the words again.

They were followed by another rattle. A hollow, rasping sound.

'Stay with us!' Grace said. 'The ambulance is coming.'

The man's chest became still. He stopped blinking, eyes open, fixed on Grace. But now sightless.

Gone.

The Detective Superintendent stood up, took photographs of each of the three dead men's faces to hopefully get a quick identity on them, then called Nikki Denero on his job phone.

She answered almost immediately.

'It's Roy Grace, Nikki. Can you help me translate something that may be critical to our enquiry – it might be Albanian? You speak the language, don't you?'

'Yes, I'm reasonably fluent.'

'Good. If I play it over the phone can you translate?'

'I'll give it a go.'

Roy Grace held his iPhone over the speaker of his job phone, turned the volume up to max and pressed the play button. The dead man's last words came out.

'*Ick largo skow gee veten.*'

When the playback was finished, Grace stopped the machine. 'Did you get that, Nikki?'

The PC sounded hesitant. 'Yes, I did, sir.'

'And?'

'I don't think you're going to like it.'

'Tell me?'

'Well, sir, you're right, it is Albanian. He's saying, *Go fuck yourself.*'

87

Mungo was struggling to keep his balance. He had been standing for some minutes now, scared of the rapidly rising tide. Each time he moved, the wire noose again cut into his neck. The water was over the top of the plinth on which he had been sitting, and was now approaching his knees. With each suck on his legs as it withdrew, he had to fight harder to resist being pulled forward and unbalanced.

He kept working on the bonds that held his wrists behind his back, the ligature rubbing more and more painfully with each attempt.

Please. Please help me, someone.

Someone would come soon, surely?

For a while, bright sunlight had shone in through the slit in the wall, but now it was moving away. He could still just see it if he tilted as far back as he dared.

Aleksander!

He was parched, starving.

There was a sudden deep, booming splash. He felt spots of water on his face. The water level had now gone over his knees for the first time.

When were they coming back?

He was shaking. Trying not to cry any more but, instead, to think. What could he do? He tugged again on the restraints round his wrists, trying to pick at the hard material again and again with his fingers, but it didn't feel as if he was getting anywhere.

What time was it?

Mum. Dad.

He hadn't seen the dead crab in a long while, now. Just dark, restless water. Rising.

Somewhere outside he suddenly heard a woman's voice. It sounded like she was calling her dog.

'HERE! HERE, BOY!'

He tried to call out to her.

'Mmmnnrrrmmmm.'

'Good boy! GOOD BOY!'

Then silence.

It seemed only minutes later that the water reached his thighs.

Help me.

Help me.

He shivered in terror.

Please someone help me.

88

Stacey looked at Kipp anxiously and expectantly as he came in through the front door. She was holding a small plastic bag in one hand and the dog lead in the other, quaking. The two detectives stood some distance behind her.

'What happened? How did it go? Did you—?'

He closed the door. 'I paid the deposit they asked for, two hundred and fifty thousand pounds' worth of Bitcoins.'

She closed her eyes in relief. 'Thank God.' Then she stared hard back at him. 'Why – why do – do they want Mungo's toothbrush and hairbrush?' She held up the bag. 'Have they found him? Is he dead? Are you not telling me?'

'They just need to have it on file, darling,' he said, relieved Branson had evidently not told her about the ear.

'There's only one reason they'd need it on file,' she said darkly. 'That's to identify his body. You see it all the time on television in cop shows.' She began crying. 'They've found him, haven't they? He's dead, isn't he, and they're not telling us?'

He put his arms round her and held her tight. 'Darling, Stace, I've paid the ransom, the deposit they asked. They're not going to harm him if they know they've got another two million coming.'

'So, did you get the proof he's alive and OK before you sent the deposit – like Detective Branson told you?'

'Yes.'

'What proof?'

'They texted me a photograph, showing the time,' he fibbed. He had left the envelope with the ear and photograph in the car.

'Let me see.'

He pulled out his phone and showed her.

As she looked at the image, she broke into a piercing scream. 'My God, he's bleeding, his head, look! Look! What have the bastards done to him?'

'Maybe he put up a fight to get away,' Kipp replied, fast.

Her legs suddenly collapsed beneath her. Kipp just caught her in time, dropping his phone in the process. 'Come and sit down,' he said, opening the drawing-room door and helping her in, then guiding her down onto a sofa.

'Let me see again.' She was gasping, as if struggling to breathe.

He retrieved his phone, relieved the screen wasn't cracked, brought it in and handed it to her.

She peered at it closely, wiping her tears with the backs of her hands.

'You can see the time on the watch, Stace.'

'What use is that? 11.55 when? Last night? How does this show he's OK? They should be holding a page of today's newspaper or something.'

'Yep, well I can't communicate with them, all I can do is get messages and instructions from them. I'm sure he's OK, I really believe it.' He sat beside her and squeezed her hand, feeling utterly helpless and impotent. He'd done what had been asked of him. Were they going to hurt Mungo further or, God forbid, kill him, despite his paying the money over?

Sensing their distress, Otto padded up to them suddenly, and sighed. He sat down and leaned against his master's legs. Kipp stroked him with one hand, absently, as Stacey sobbed uncontrollably.

A shadow loomed over them. It was Branson. The room was stifling, airless, all the windows shut despite the glorious summer's day. It was often the same, from the detective's past experience of bereaved households. It was as if no one wanted to let fresh air or the outside world in to intrude on their thoughts.

'Kipp,' he whispered. 'It would be good if you could get going, we're time critical.'

Kipp nodded, carefully disentangling himself from Stacey. 'Babes, I'll be back in half an hour.'

'I'm coming with you,' Stacey said. 'Where are you going?'

'Just to walk Otto.'

'It's better if you stay here, Stacey,' Branson said. 'In case Mungo suddenly turns up.'

'Please – please get my boy back. Please, I – I can't stand it.' She buried her face in her hands and shook with wracking sobs.

Glenn Branson looked at her, thoughts spinning through his head. He knew how he would feel if this had happened to his own son or daughter. He would want to tear the bastards' heads off with his bare hands.

But equally, he knew – although not wanting to say anything inappropriate – what had made the Browns' son a target: the family's conspicuous wealth. Not that it meant if you were rich that you should go into a life of hiding.

As they walked to the front door, followed by Otto, Kipp asked the detective, 'What do you guys know about Aleksander Dervishi's father?'

'Very little, sir, other than rumour,' Branson replied.

'Rumour?'

'I can't say too much.'

'Detective Branson – Glenn – our son's life is at stake and you can't say too much? What kind of bullshit is that?' Stacey said. 'Isn't Jorgji Dervishi reputed to be part of the Albanian mafia? Is he known to you – to you lot – to Sussex Police? Is he what you call a *Person of Interest*?'

'Stacey, I'm not able to discuss that.'

'Really? Come on, you're a father, right?'

He nodded.

'Imagine this was your son,' Kipp interjected. 'Just tell me the truth – I know someone who has power, who might be able to help.'

The truth. Glenn Branson wanted to be as honest as he could with the Browns, but equally he did not want to cause them needless distress or send them spiralling into worse panic than Stacey, in particular, was already suffering.

The truth?

How on earth could he tell them it was possible that the only three people who knew where Mungo was, and who might have been able to save him from drowning, were all dead?

89

There was a view south across the city and the English Channel, and the distant wind farm off the coast, from the fourth-floor kitchen window at Boden Court. Grace stared across at the single chimney stack rising high above Shoreham Power Station and the large residential colony of Shoreham, to the west. Somewhere there, close to the sea, close enough to be affected by the tide, Mungo Brown was imprisoned, a ligature round his neck and the water level rising.

Who had killed these three men and why? Greed? Was it perhaps a fourth partner who knew where Mungo was and stood to get all the money?

His phone rang – Glenn. 'How are you doing, boss?'

'Not great.'

'We have a development.'

'We do?'

Branson talked him through the latest texts, the Polaroid photograph and the severed ear, then sent him the images.

'Do you know for certain it's the boy's, Glenn?' Grace asked.

'It has to be, boss.'

'Has to be?'

334

'Mungo has a bloodstained bandage over his right ear. Now we have a right ear.'

'I hear you.'

'*Ear* you?'

'I'm not in any mood for humour. I'm standing in a flat with three dead bodies, OK?'

'Yeah, sorry.'

Grace ended the call and refocused. A young lad, frightened out of his wits, with one of his ears hacked off, probably without any painkillers. He'd like to get his hands on the other people who were behind this, alone, just him and them in a dark room. But that wasn't for now. At this moment, there was one desperate priority and that was to save Mungo's life.

He made the decision to ditch all pretence of a covert investigation, and after a quick chat with the Critical Incident Manager, he instructed Oscar-1 to put a full-scale manhunt into operation. Two helicopters, if available, would be scrambled, one from the Solent Coastguard, the other, NPAS-15. Mungo Brown's photograph was to be circulated to all officers and to the media, very urgently.

Next, he contacted DCI Sam Davies, from the Major Crime Team, informed her what had happened and asked her to attend at the flat to pick up the job as SIO. He then requested Oscar-1 to get a team from Digital Forensics blue-lighted here immediately by a Roads Policing Unit driver in a fast car, to see if there were any immediate clues from any phones or computers in the flat. He was tempted to try looking himself, but did not want to risk making a mistake that could lose or mask anything crucial. That team could be here in less than thirty minutes. He also asked the Inspector to summon a Coroner's Officer, a CSI team and a Crime Scene Manager.

Where the hell are you, Mungo?

He looked at the two bodies in the room with him. They were like a waxwork tableau. Dummies. Unreal. Carrying the secret of Mungo's whereabouts to the grave.

Go fuck yourself.

He looked at the man lying on his back, his blood-drenched chest, the bullet graze on the top of his forehead, his glassy, sightless stare.

Tell you what, mate, he thought, irreverently. *You look pretty fucked yourself.*

He had another thought. One of the bits of technology he did know about was from a lecture he'd attended at the Homicide conference in Las Vegas two years ago. If you left the software activated, and most people did, iPhones kept a record of all your movements. He took a pair of protective gloves from his pocket and pulled them on, then, for the second time in this investigation breaking all the rules of crime scene management, rummaged in the pockets of the man slumped at the table and pulled out a cheap-looking Nokia, a burner.

Kneeling beside his new best friend on the floor, he searched first in his windcheater pockets, pulling out another cheap-looking throwaway phone. Then, exerting himself to move the man a little, he reached round into the back pocket of his jeans and felt, with hope rising, a familiar, slim rectangular shape.

He pulled out a recent model iPhone. But when he pressed the power button, the numerical keypad appeared along with the words, *Enter Passcode or Touch ID.*

It had been too much, he knew, to expect it not to be password-protected. In desperation, he grabbed the dead man's hand and pressed his forefinger against the power button. Nothing happened. He tried again, but still nothing.

He knew the forensics team had been working on software to enable a dead person's fingers to activate a touchpad. Had whatever electrical impulses were needed already left this man? He tried with the dead man's thumb, middle fingers, then with the fingers and thumb of his left hand, but no success. He was wasting critical minutes, he realized, glancing at his watch.

Less than three hours left.

He thought about the tide chart he had memorized. How the hell were they going to find Mungo in time? He stared around the room. What could he do that he was overlooking?

His eyes alighted on a set of Range Rover keys on the kitchen table. *Yes!* He photographed them and pocketed them, knelt back down and went through the anorak, then jeans pockets, of the man on the floor and found a set of Audi car keys. He pocketed them, too. He found a third set of keys, the Golf's, in the zipped hoodie of the dead man in the hallway, grabbed them, and ran out of the flat, past Inspector Allchild, and down the steps, radioing Kevin Hall to meet him in the underground car park.

As he burst through the door, he saw Hall running down the ramp. He thrust the Audi keys at him. 'Kevin, check the Audi's satnav. See what the last destination was!'

He went to the Range Rover, clicked the door lock to let himself in, sat in the driver's seat, looked around for the key, then realized the ignition had been switched on by keyless-go.

He pushed the button on the vehicle's display for satnav. The system opened and he studied it, then tapped RECENT DESTINATIONS.

Shoreham Beach came up.

Underneath was *Boden Court*.

Bugger.

He went to the Golf and repeated the process.

Shoreham Beach.

Boden Court.

Shit, shit, shit. He was no closer. He went over to Hall. 'Anything?'

'Zilch,' Hall replied. 'Gatwick Airport is the last entry.'

'We need to get back to HQ,' Grace said. 'Fast.'

90

As Hall drove, Grace updated Sam Davies on what he had done at Boden Court. He then called Oscar-1 to check on the ETA of the Digital Forensics team at the flat, and was reassured they would be at the scene within ten minutes. Next, he asked Glenn Branson for an update from the Browns' house.

As soon as they arrived back at HQ, Roy Grace held an emergency briefing of his team. Behind him on a whiteboard was a blow-up of the latest photograph of Mungo, together with the tide chart, with 17.40 p.m. highlighted in red.

'Right,' he said. 'If we are to believe this chart and the latest photograph, then in about two and a half hours the water will have risen above Mungo's head, and it's game over. The persons we believe were our three prime suspects, who might have been able to tell us his location, are dead. At this moment, we don't know who killed them or the motive. Unfortunately, the Boden Court CCTV system has been down for the past twenty-four hours.'

'Unfortunate or coincidental, boss?' Norman Potting asked, suspiciously.

'I don't have any information on that yet, Norman,' Grace replied. 'We are reasonably certain Mungo is being held in a location somewhere in or close to Shoreham.' He turned to the whiteboard and pointed. 'Here.' Then looked at DS Exton. 'Jon, I want you to get on to Shoreham Port Authority immediately – speak to Keith Wadey, the Chief Engineer, if you can get hold of him, show him a copy of this photograph and see if he can identify any possible location.'

'Yes, boss, but we need to bear in mind that it's Sunday.'

'Are you planning to go to church?' Grace gave him a quizzical look.

Exton looked unsure, for a moment, if Roy was joking.

'The port runs twenty-four-seven, Jon,' Grace said. 'If you can't contact anyone by phone, get down there immediately and find someone – the lock gates are manned round the clock, there'll be people there. Go immediately and use the blues – take someone with you—' He looked around and his eye fell on DC Davies. 'Alec, go with DS Exton.'

As the pair left the room, Grace went on. 'Right, we have a boy kidnapped at the Amex. Our information leads us to believe a criminal gang within the local Albanian community may be responsible. If we are correct, we are dealing with a particularly brutal group of people who do not give a toss about committing their crimes openly in public – in fact they embrace that as a warning to others. Surely, someone must have seen something? In the past twenty-four hours, there's been a bomb threat at the Amex. Human remains discovered at a crusher site in Shoreham. The crusher operator dead hours later – in possibly suspicious circumstances. And now three people dead in a flat in the city. Oh, and an unfortunate young drugs mule, dead at Gatwick Airport, with links to one of Jorgji Dervishi's businesses.'

There was a reflective silence from his team. 'Someone has to be able to connect the dots. OK? Someone, some-where, must have seen something. A boy disappears in broad daylight from a football stadium that has one of the world's most sophisticated security systems – not a tiny infant, a big, bolshy teenager. Someone *has* seen him. This boy is being held somewhere below the high-water level, where the sea is going to cover him – drown him. Someone out there knows how to save his life.'

Potting raised his hand.

'Yes, Norman?'

'Have Digital Forensics not been able to enhance any of the photographs, chief?'

'Not enough to reveal anything helpful, Norman, no.'

'In case it's significant, chief,' Potting went on, 'while DC Wilde and I were at Dervishi's house during the night, I went for a pee.'

'Good for you, Norman!' EJ Boutwood said with a grin. 'Hope you put the seat back down afterwards.'

Ignoring the jibe, Potting continued. 'He's got one of those photo boards in the downstairs loo. You know the kind of thing – him and his wife and son on a yacht. Pic-tures of them all at a big party. Pictures at a barbecue. Another at their wedding anniversary. I took a photo of it on my phone, to check it out afterwards. I thought my findings might interest you. There's one character who pops up in many of them, repeatedly – Edi Konstandin.'

Grace frowned. 'That name continues to worry me.'

'It should,' Potting said. 'He's Mr Big. One of the kingpins of the Brighton Albanian mafia – and quite a big pillar of the community. Lots of legitimate businesses: property, storage depots, warehouses, industrial units, estate agencies, bet-ting shops, launderettes, cafés and a couple of car washes.'

'I know all that. Does he have any businesses down in the Shoreham area, Norman? Any that are on the water-front?'

'I can find out, boss.'

Sunday. Damned Sunday, Grace thought. So many business premises would be shut today. Warehouses, industrial units, storage depots – all classic places to hide someone, alive or dead. Mungo could be in any of them – or not. If the video and photograph were for real, he was at the water's edge somewhere, below sea level.

He was repeatedly trying to hypothesize what might have happened, and to put himself in the mindset of the kidnappers. Mungo and his pal, Aleksander, had originally set this up. Aleksander had used his own father's trusted bodyguards, Valbone Kadare and Dritan Nano, to help Mungo with the sting. Then at some point a double-cross had happened.

Question: Was Aleksander involved in that double-cross or not?

If he was, he would know where Mungo was. And with the little time they had, the only way to flush the truth out of him might be to frighten the hell out of him in front of his parents. Read him the riot act, warn him if Mungo died he would face a murder charge. He needed to send in a bully, and realized the suspended Detective Sergeant Guy Batchelor would have been the ideal hard man to interview him. He felt Guy's absence from his team acutely, more than ever at this moment. And he still found it hard to believe what he had done.

Scarlett Riley, who was a trained cognitive interviewer and, despite her appearance, could be fierce when needed, would be a good person to interview Aleksander, he decided. To accompany her, he delegated another tough detective, the diminutive American FBI officer Arnie Crown – better known to the team these days as Notmuch, after a witticism by Norman Potting that had stuck. Arnie Crown had been seconded to them for training purposes as part of an information-sharing programme, and with his counter-terrorism background, he was highly experienced in extracting information quickly.

Grace stared at the large-scale map on the wall. He ran his index finger along from the start of Shoreham Port to where it ended, some way along the River Adur. There could only be so many hiding places along the wharves. Might a local historian know them? But who? And where were they going to find a historian on a Sunday afternoon? With the clock ticking, they just did not have the luxury of that time.

One option was a ground search along the entire water-front. He knew there were places along the harbour, such as by the lock gates, with hidden sluices and tunnels. He'd need divers as part of a search team to cover the seven miles, but he'd have to bring them in from outside, and it would take hours just to get them into place. Hours they did not have. Sussex Police once had their own dive unit, but that had been a victim of budget cuts a few years back. He desperately wished, at this moment, they still had it.

He switched his train of thought back to Boden Court. The blood on the victims was still wet, indicating they had all been shot only a short time before he'd arrived. Perhaps with a silenced weapon – or weapons. How had the killer – or killers – arrived and left? What was the motive? Was it greed? Taking out these three colleagues in the kidnap plan? Or was it more cynical? Perhaps someone cut out of the deal simply taking revenge and to hell with the boy? He looked at his watch. Felt panic rising.

3.28 p.m.

Just over two hours.

His phone rang. It was Cassian Pewe. 'What's the update, Roy? I thought you were going to call me earlier.'

'I'm sorry, sir, I've been a bit busy.'

'I've just heard that there's more bodies, in a flat in Hove.'

'Seems I didn't need to update you, sir, you're ahead of the curve. I guess that's the advantage of integrating multiple initiatives into a systems-level approach.'

'I beg your pardon? You've lost me, I'm afraid.'

'Your words, sir,' Grace reminded him, smiling privately. 'May I call you back in a little while, we're very time critical at the moment.'

'Are you getting this young lad back? Mungo Brown? Give me a straight answer, Roy.'

'Well, sir, we're working on the aggregation of marginal gains.'

'What?'

As soon as he had got the ACC off the line, Roy took several deep breaths. He had to forget his anger at the man, stay focused, think this through, look at the positives. Two hours. They still had *just over two hours*. How could he use them to the very best? What could he do that he wasn't already doing?

What bases was he not covering?

At times like this, it felt like he had the loneliest job in the world. Sure, there were other detectives with kidnap experience he could call on, but he'd need to bring them up to speed and that would all eat into critical time. He had to accept that these next hours could be life or death for Mungo Brown. Very possibly depending on the decisions he now made and the actions he took.

One thought occurred to him as he hastily updated his Policy Book – making sure he had answers for the inevitable inquest Pewe would hold, regardless of the result. As he wrote, he turned to DI Dull. 'Donald, can you check all serials in the past twenty-four hours, look for anything that has been reported within the Shoreham Harbour and Beach area. OK?'

'Yes, sir, I'll get on it after the briefing.'

'No, start *now*.'

'Roy?' Forensic Podiatrist Haydn Kelly, looking like he'd done an all-nighter, his complexion pasty, his suit heavily creased and his tie slack, said, 'I've been working together with JJ from the Super Recognizer Unit looking for the lad. We haven't found images of him yet, but from the CCTV footage at the stadium we've viewed, we believe we've identified the individual in the red baseball cap who left the camera on the seat, then went through the doors and disappeared.'

Kelly pointed a laser at a new whiteboard, on which was a very clear blow-up of the man in the cap. Next to it was a photograph of a man of similar age and build, wearing a blue-and-white striped Seagulls shirt, a matching scarf and bobble hat, and blue jeans. Beside that was a large mug-shot.

'JJ and I both believe this is the same person,' Kelly said.

'And your reasons are?' Grace asked. 'Apart from it being odd to wear a bobble hat in August.'

The Super Recognizer, a tall DC in his early forties, with short, blond hair and the eager attitude of someone who clearly loved his job, responded first, pointing the red dot of the laser at the chin of the man in the first photograph, then again at the second. 'In my opinion,' Jonathan Jackson said, 'this is an identical match.' Next, he pointed the dot on the first man's nostril, then on the second. 'Another match.' He paused then went on. 'The odds against any two persons having an identical chin and nostrils run into millions to one,' he said, then gestured to Haydn Kelly, indicating it was his turn.

Kelly returned to the board. He pointed first at the man in the red cap. 'Roy, I've analysed this man's gait from the Amex CCTV footage, from the time he stood up, to reaching the exit door of the stand.' He then pointed at the second image of the man in the blue-and-white bobble hat and Albion strip. 'I managed to obtain footage from BTP – it helped speed things up that their ACC, Robin Smith, is a former Sussex ACC,' he said, with a smile. 'It showed this man walking along the station platform just a short while after leaving the stand. My software analysis shows, beyond any doubt, this is the same person. I also managed to get this photograph of our suspect's face.' He pointed at it. 'Does anyone know this charmer?'

Nikki Denero spoke up. 'I know him. He's a member of the Brighton Albanian community. He's got past form as a petty criminal – shoplifting and a drugs possession case. He's linked – again small-time – to the local big crime families, the Konstandins and Dervishis.'

'Edi Konstandin?' Grace quizzed.

She nodded.

He turned back to Kelly and Jackson. 'Now you've got this second image, check out the CCTV footage from car park A, Bennett's Field, to see if there's any link with the green BMW car which I believe was the kidnappers' vehicle. Make sure you keep DCI Fitzherbert up to date with progress.'

Grace turned to Denero. 'How much do you know about Edi Konstandin and Jorgji Dervishi?'

'How long do you have, sir?'

'As long as a car ride to Konstandin's house takes. Where does he live?'

'Somewhere near Fulking.'

Fulking was a village fifteen minutes away.

'Can you check if he's home, Norman?'

'He's eighty-two, confined to a wheelchair after someone put a bullet in his spine twenty years ago. I doubt he's out gallivanting around – he's probably home, guv.'

91

Kipp Brown, with Otto barking excitedly in the rear of the Range Rover behind the dog guard, drove up the A23 north from Brighton, then took the slip road left to Pyecombe and headed over Clayton Hill, as he had been instructed by DI Branson.

He passed the turn-off to the Pyecombe Golf Club, carried on and then slowed as he reached the crest, spotting the turn-off onto the single-track road coming up on the right.

To his relief, nothing followed him in. He drove along, as instructed, and then turned into the empty car park for the Jack and Jill windmills. He climbed out, pressed the clicker to open the tailgate, and as he did so heard a motorcycle approaching.

Apprehensively, he grabbed Otto's lead and held it as the dog barked. A BMW bike drove in and stopped beside him. Its leather-clad rider raised her vizor and said, 'Apple. Mr Brown?' She produced a police warrant card with the name PC Georgina Lestini.

Kipp handed her the plastic bag, inside which was the ear, now in an evidence bag, as well as Mungo's toothbrush and hairbrush. PC Lestini asked him to sign, date and time the transfer of the items on the evidence bag. Then she slipped them into a pannier, thanked him and accelerated away. The encounter had taken less than thirty seconds.

Otto tugged, excitedly, on his leash, barking again.

'OK, boy! OK!' Kipp walked the dog away for some distance, waited until he could no longer hear the bike's engine, then knelt and unclipped the lead. The dog raced off happily. Kipp followed, tugging his phone from his pocket. He pressed to bring up his *Contacts* list, then again to bring up his *Favourites*.

Near the top was one of his biggest clients, who had been with him at the Amex yesterday. He hit the man's name.

Edi Konstandin answered on the third ring. 'Kipp!' the eighty-two-year-old said. 'I'm so sorry I never got to say goodbye to you at the Amex yesterday. Shame about the result, eh?'

'Yep – but hopefully the team will settle down.'

Despite everything, Kipp could not help it, a nagging voice in his mind was telling him that he needed to start thinking about strategic bets on future Seagulls games.

'You're a betting man, like me, Kipp,' the old man said in his strong Albanian accent. 'You think they'll stay up?'

'They will.'

'I think so, too. But on a Sunday afternoon – I sense you're not calling me just to discuss football?'

'No, Edi. I need help.'

The crime kingpin responded, guardedly, 'What kind of help?'

Kipp knew he was treading a fine line here. Not only was Konstandin one of his biggest clients in his own right, but for the past decade he had been his gatekeeper to many of the wealthy – and less wealthy – members of the Albanian community in the city. Whatever Edi Konstandin recommended, the Albanian expat community followed.

'My son has been kidnapped, Edi. He disappeared at the Amex Stadium yesterday while we were there, and I've subsequently had a ransom demand. The police believe an Albanian gang is behind it. I'm calling you out of desperation to see if you can help me.'

There was a long silence. Kipp began to wonder if he had been cut off. Then he heard the old man's voice again.

'Kidnapped? Your son? The police are wrong, Kipp. I can assure you. My people are keen to integrate into your society. It has been a taboo for a long time for any Albanian here in Brighton to step outside our boundaries. None of our people commits crimes against the local community.'

'Does the name "Dervishi" mean anything to you, Edi?'

Another long silence. 'Jorgji Dervishi?'

'Yes, and his son, Aleksander.'

'You think Jorgji Dervishi is involved?'

'I think he and his son might be.'

After another long silence, the old man said, 'You'd better start from the beginning, and tell me everything you have.'

92

Cleo normally found it easy to chat to anyone she met. She had a friendly, caring countenance and people tended to warm to her instantly. Partly, that was because people interested her; Cleo had a theory that everyone had a story, that everyone had had something happen in their time, however pedestrian their lives might outwardly seem, if you could just get it out of them. It could be an adventure they'd been on, an extraordinary relative, a terrible tragedy, a serial killer they'd been to school with or an inexplicable mystical experience. It was there, if you could mine it, and she had always been good at doing that. But her one failure to date, the one person whose story she had not yet mined, despite many hours spent with him over the past few years, was Home Office Pathologist Dr Frazer Theobald.

All she knew about this quietly spoken figure, with his threadbare dome, hooter of a nose and Groucho Marx moustache, was that he was married to a lecturer in microbiology and liked solo dinghy sailing in his time off. She was also starting to realize that he might be either greedy or insecure – or perhaps both. There were only thirty-two similarly qualified pathologists in the country. Which meant that, with around six hundred homicides a year in the UK, as well as many more seemingly suspicious deaths, they all got a decent share of the lucrative payments for Home Office postmortems.

Usually, Brighton and Hove City Mortuary averaged around twelve to twenty Home Office postmortems a year, compared to around 950 regular ones, but today an unprecedented six, including Florentina Shima's which had taken place earlier, were lined up. The human remains from the crusher site, the crusher operator, Stephen Suckling, and the three gunshot victims from Boden Court.

The recently completed postmortem of Suckling revealed, in Theobald's initial opinion, that he had died from a massive overdose of barbiturates. The hospital report was that someone had switched his drip bag. The SIO, Detective Inspector Bill Warner, was continuing his investigation.

As each postmortem took around two to four hours, and sometimes longer, Cleo had suggested bringing in a second Home Office Pathologist to ease the workload – as well as freeing time for her, too – but Theobald would not hear of it. She was going to be stuck here with him, and the rest of the team needed for these postmortems, for the next two days without respite, she thought gloomily as she began removing each of the white plastic parcels containing body parts of the victim identified as Ryan Brent from the crusher site, and placing them on the stainless-steel postmortem table.

Aside from the two small nuggets about his wife and sailing, the only other conversation Cleo had ever managed to prise out of Theobald was an explanation of why, in his fourth year at London's Guy's Hospital, he had decided to specialize in pathology; she hadn't been able to tell whether he was joking or not when he'd told her that being a pathologist had two big plus points over being a doctor to the living. The first was that you didn't have to make house calls. The second was that you didn't have to bother with a good bedside manner.

And that latter, Cleo Morey often thought, really defined Theobald. Over the years she had been lumbered with this pedantic and totally humourless man on many of Roy's homicide investigations. But despite Roy's irritation at the man's snail-like speed, he told her he could trust Theobald implicitly to do two vital things. The first was to establish beyond doubt the cause of death. The second was to provide evidence that, when produced in court, would be bullet-proof to attacks from even the smartest defence briefs.

Theobald began positioning each of the parts very carefully, until finally all those recovered so far were laid out like a jigsaw puzzle, with bits missing, on the shiny steel. A right arm; a torso; a left leg. No head, left arm or right leg had so far been found. Each of the pieces, they could all see clearly, bore evidence of cuts with a sharp knife, possibly a box-cutter or a Stanley knife, Cleo thought.

There was a new SIO attending the examination, DCI Mark Hailwood. The HM Customs Officer had now left after signing off the sachets of cocaine discovered during Florentina Shima's postmortem, with a street value, he had estimated, of around £350,000, into temporary police custody. Other than that, the team remained unchanged.

With Roy full-on with his kidnap enquiry and the workload here looking like an all-nighter at the very least, Cleo stepped into her office and phoned Kaitlynn. She asked her if she could remain with Noah and Bruno until the morning, and probably throughout tomorrow, then returned to the postmortem room, in time to hear Theobald dictate his first observations.

'The presence of blood around the incisions on the body indicates to me these were made whilst the victim was still alive,' he announced into his machine, seemingly oblivious, as always, to his interested audience. 'Torture?'

That was Cleo's thought, too. Over the past couple of years there had been four partially intact bodies with similar cut patterns postmortemed here. She stepped out, back into her office, closed the door and dialled Roy.

93

Grace was regretting asking Potting to drive, which he had done to leave himself free to make calls. The DS drove at what seemed to him to be a ridiculously slow speed along the top of the Downs, almost making a mockery of the flashing blue lights and wailing siren.

The speedometer wavered between 45 mph and 50 mph.

'You could go a bit faster, Norman,' he encouraged.

Potting shook his head. 'You have to justify your actions, boss,' he said in a pedantic tone. 'I don't want them bastards in Professional Standards breathing down my neck because I crossed the limit.'

'This is an emergency, life at risk, just put your bloody foot down!'

Ten seconds later, Grace was regretting his instruction.

The car was flying. Now, at 70 mph, they were approaching a blind brow, with a golf club entrance to the right; a van was looking like it was about to pull out of it, in front of them.

Grace pressed his right foot hard against the floor.

Norman Potting was still accelerating, either oblivious to the danger or putting too much trust in the blues and twos. Fortunately, the van stayed put. They crested the hill.

'Sharp left-hander at the bottom, Norman,' Grace warned.

Potting grunted. At the last possible moment, he dabbed the brakes. Somehow, drifting wide into the oncoming lane, the car made the bend.

Sweat was popping on Grace's forehead. 'Maybe slow a little,' he suggested.

Potting gripped the wheel, his face set into a rictus of concentration. 'Don't worry, chief, I did the refresher course just recently – and DS Branson gave me some high speed roadcraft tips.'

'I can tell.'

Grace knew this road like the back of his hand, it was the route he often took home from Brighton. They were heading towards the brow of another hill, which had a nasty right-handed kink. As they crested it, the car dancing in Potting's hands, Grace saw the whites of the eyes of the driver of an oncoming lorry.

Somehow, they passed it, still alive.

He raised his voice. 'Turn-off coming up, left four hundred metres.'

To his relief, he felt the car slow, just a little. They passed a dangerous junction, shot down into a dip and up the far side, then Potting braked hard and made the left turn into a single-track lane.

A cyclist was struggling up the hill towards them, forcing Potting to pull hard over to the left into the semblance of a lay-by to let him pass. Grace checked his watch anxiously. At that moment, his private phone rang. It was Cleo. He always loved to hear her voice and he was determined not to make the mistakes he had with Sandy, of either ignoring her calls or cutting her short because he was busy.

'Hey, how are you doing?' she asked.

'Not great – you?'

The cyclist puffed past, glaring at them as if they had no right to be on the road instead of maybe thanking them, with their blue lights flashing, for courteously letting him pass.

'Look, I know you're under the cosh so I'll be quick,' she said. 'I have something that might be of help.'

'Yes?'

Potting drove on down the winding lane, siren wailing again.

'Theobald's started the PM on the body parts from the crusher site. They're covered in what looks like razor cuts – just like a few cases I've seen before, and one you dealt with a while back, that was linked to the local Albanian community.'

'Razor cuts as in torture?'

'Yes. Theobald says the cuts were made while the victim was still alive.'

Five minutes later, after winding through the villages of Poynings then Fulking, Potting turned right, pulled up in front of wrought-iron gates and switched off the blues and twos. Ahead, at the end of a long drive, was a handsome, imposing white Georgian mansion. He put down his window and pressed a button on the entry-phone panel.

'Thanks, darling, that might be really helpful. Call you in a bit.'

'Love you.'

'You too.'

'Police, we would like to speak to Mr Konstandin,' Potting said and held up his warrant card to the camera lens.

The gates opened and they drove up to the house. A bronze Bentley Bentayga was parked outside, along with twin, garish, black American SUVs. As they pulled up, the front door opened and two man-mountains emerged, similarly attired to the ones at Jorgji Dervishi's home that they had encountered last night.

As both detectives showed their warrant cards, a booming voice from somewhere inside, with a cultured, broken-English accent, said, 'Please, show our distinguished guests in!'

The two bodyguards stepped aside to allow the detectives through into an imposing hallway. The floor was black-and-white marble tiles, in a chessboard pattern, and the walls were hung with what looked, to Roy Grace's inexpert eye, like Old Master paintings. There were fine antique hall tables and chairs, as well as a number of busts on plinths.

A handsome, elderly, pot-bellied man propelled himself towards them in a wheelchair. He had bouffant silver hair and wore a checked sports jacket with a velvet collar, shirt and cravat, beige trousers and monogrammed velvet slippers.

'Good afternoon, gentlemen!' he said, oozing charm. 'Edi Konstandin, how may I be of assistance?'

Grace showed him his warrant card. 'We'd like to talk to you very urgently, sir, in case you can assist us.'

'Well, of course – any help I can give to Sussex Police, you only have to ask! This way, please. My wife is out riding at the moment, but she should be back soon, in case you would like to speak to her, too.'

He spun the wheelchair deftly round and shot back through the doorway from which he had emerged.

The two detectives followed him into a grand drawing room, furnished with antiques, the walls hung with more ornately framed paintings. The decor was muted pastels. Konstandin halted his wheelchair and beckoned them, with a hand sporting a flashy watch and several rings, to a sofa.

'Tea, gentlemen? Or perhaps something stronger?' he asked Grace and Potting as they sat down.

'We're fine, thank you, Mr Konstandin,' Grace said. 'We're actually in a very urgent and time-critical situation.'

The old man looked at them quizzically. 'Please let me know how I can be of help.'

'This is a very beautiful home you have,' Roy Grace said, watching his eyes carefully.

'Thank you.'

'How long have you lived here?'

'Fifteen years. I bought it from a Brighton antiques dealer – he restored it many years ago from a wreck, sparing no expense.'

'So I can see, sir.' Grace handed him the photograph of the man in the red baseball cap, continuing to watch his eyes carefully. 'Do you by any chance know this person?'

Konstandin studied it carefully. Grace saw just a glint of recognition. But he looked back at the detective and shook his head. 'No, I'm afraid I don't, I'm sorry, Detective – er?'

'Grace.'

'Detective Grace. I wish I could help you, but I can't.' He smiled. 'Truly, I wish I could. Is there anything else I can assist you with?'

'Actually,' he said, 'I think there is.'

'Oh?'

Grace looked pointedly at his watch. 'In precisely one hour and twenty-five minutes' time a teenage boy called Mungo Brown, who we believe has been kidnapped by Albanians, is going to die. He will drown, Mr Konstandin. We at Sussex Police know you are at the top of your tree, and good luck to you. We've been trying to forge relation-ships with you and your Albanian community for a long time and I thought we might be making progress. But events of the last twenty-four hours indicate otherwise.'

'Events?' the old man questioned.

'If I understand our intelligence correctly, the second-in-command in your empire is a gentleman called Jorgji Dervishi? Do you admit that? Do you admit to knowing him?'

'I'm not admitting to anything without my solicitor present,' he said, his genial demeanour turning to steely hardness.

'We don't have time for that, Mr Konstandin. Hear me out. Let's forget about your past, I'm not interested in that. In recent times, we are aware you have made creditable efforts at integrating the Brighton and Hove Albanian com-munity into the life of our city. But one of your underlings is undermining all that and you may not be aware of it. An innocent life is at risk, and we believe Dervishi is up to his neck in this kidnapping. We have an average of twelve sus-picious deaths a year in this county, but in the past twenty-four hours we have had six. An Albanian drugs mule linked to Mr Dervishi. Body parts bearing the hallmark of an Albanian revenge killing. A local heavy machinery oper-ator, suspected murdered last night, linked to the body parts. And, most recently, three men of suspected Albanian origin, linked to the kidnap, found shot dead in a Hove flat.' Grace watched him carefully.

Konstandin raised his arms in a gesture of innocence. 'What are you trying to say?'

All the man's body language told Grace he was not going to get anything from him by playing Mr Nice Guy. He changed tack. 'Allow me to continue. The photograph I just showed you has been identified as another of your country-men, who is linked to a bomb threat at the Amex Stadium, as part of an extortion plan. We know that your people don't talk to the police, but this has gone too far. I don't know how much of all this you are aware of, but let me tell you some-thing. You may be the local Mr Big, Mr Konstandin, but,' he said, tapping his own chest, 'I'm in charge of Major Crime in this city – and throughout Sussex and Surrey – and I won't put up with this kind of crap on my patch. If you don't cooperate with us, this instant, then for the rest of your life we'll be in your face, we'll be everywhere, crawling all over every one of your businesses, and every aspect of your life. Health and Safety will close your kebab houses down and your car washes, every single one of your employees will be interviewed by the Home Office Slavery Commission and the Inland Revenue will seize this house. I'm not having this behaviour in my city. Do you understand?'

'Very clearly, Detective Grace.'

'Do you have anything you would like to say, in light of that?' Grace glanced at his watch. 'Bearing in mind we're running out of time to save this boy.'

'I do,' Konstandin said. 'If you go back out of this room, turn left and walk down the hallway, you will find the front door. Good day, gentlemen.'

94

As Grace and Potting drove out of Konstandin's driveway, the DS said, 'He's a piece of work, boss.'

Roy Grace sat in silence, immersed in his thoughts as they wound back up the hill. Eventually, he said, 'His eye movements told me he was lying, Norman. Konstandin knows the man in the red cap. How much else does he know?' He glanced at the time as his phone rang.

'Roy, it's Dan Salter, Digital Forensics – we're at Boden Court and I've just found the burner phone that one of the ransom demands was sent from. Vodafone have come back to me on our request for information, and say it could be anywhere in the western part of Shoreham Harbour or Shoreham Beach.'

'There's no way they can pinpoint it any closer, Dan?'

'I'm afraid not, sir – because the mast is on the coast, they can't use triangulation.'

'Thanks, Dan,' Grace said, ending the call. 'Fuck.'

Potting looked at him.

'Anywhere in the western part of Shoreham Harbour or Shoreham Beach, Norman. Any thoughts? Any bright ideas about how we search about five miles of waterfront in the time we have left?'

Another call came in on his job phone.

'Roy Grace,' he answered.

It was DS Exton. 'Sir, I'm at Shoreham Port.'

'And?' Grace asked, expectantly.

'Not good news so far, I'm afraid. There's around twenty possibilities, maybe more.'

'Start working on them, Jon,' he instructed.

'I have, sir. Eliminated two already.'

'Keep me posted.'

'I will.'

Grace thought back to their encounter with Konstandin. The wily old bastard knew something and wasn't telling, wasn't responding to his threats. Why not?

He calculated the time.

Time they no longer had.

Seventy-five minutes.

He turned to Potting. 'Norman, head to Shoreham, as fast as you can.'

'Whereabouts in Shoreham, boss?'

'If I knew I'd sodding tell you.'

95

Mum! Dad!

The sea level was up to his groin now. Every few minutes the water would surge, breaking over his stomach and spraying across his face.

Aleksander. Someone. Please. Someone please help me.

The tape over his mouth stifled all his cries.

He was standing, struggling to stay upright, to maintain his balance. He knew he had to keep his feet on the ledge. Had to. It was getting increasingly difficult, but if he lost his foothold the wire round his neck would get him. Already it felt raw, even the smallest movement of his head was agony. And every retreating wave pulled at his legs, tugged at them harder all the time, as if the sea itself was trying to dislodge him. He had to fight back, hard. Concentrate every second.

Help me!

He thought about Steven Brathwaite at school. Big, tall, powerful Steven, who the whole of his class was afraid of. The class bully. School bully. Brathwaite picked on him because he was clever. The bully liked to sneak up behind him and kick him in the back of the knees, making his legs buckle, so he fell over. Mungo had learned to stand up to Brathwaite by bracing his legs hard, then flexing at just the right moment to absorb the kick. It annoyed the bully.

It served him well now.

As each wave tried to pull him over, to make him lose his balance, and the wire cut into his neck, he used the same technique as he used against the bully. Brace. Flex. Brace.

The water surged over his belt.

He looked around. Looked at the slime and weed on the walls – and ceiling. The weed, fresh and living, waiting for the water to come.

He had already checked his height against the high-water mark. That mark was a good six inches or more above the top of his head.

Water would fill this chamber completely.

He shook with terror.

96

Number 26, bearing a large name board, CABURN HEATING & PLUMBING SERVICES, was one of thirty-six similar units on the Ranscombe Farm Industrial Estate, two miles east of the county town of Lewes. All were constructed from galvanized steel, with both the office and the main up-and-over shuttered doors to the interior workspace painted in yellow.

Most of the businesses on the estate were closed for the weekend, their parking bays deserted, but there were two vehicles outside Number 26: a small, grey Hyundai saloon and a blue van bearing the name of the fictitious plumbing firm.

The front door opened into an office that was completely bare, apart from a few unopened circulars scattered on the floor beneath the letter box. A connecting door led into the 2,000-square-foot factory floor, where Ylli Prek and Luka Lebedev stood behind several sturdy metal tables that were linked together into an E-shape. The surfaces were cluttered with tools, opaque jars, reels of wire, the innards of mobile phones, a set of scales, a bottle of water, a gas cylinder and a Sony FS7 camera, similar to the one Prek had taken to the Amex yesterday.

The only other items of furniture in the cavernous space were two chairs, which looked as if they'd been retrieved from a skip, and a rack of Dexion shelving on which stood several jars of chemicals marked with danger symbols. There was also a small fridge, a kettle, a cluster of mugs and a catering-size tin of coffee. Beyond the end of the shelves was a kitchen sink and tap, and an open door to a toilet.

Lebedev, a shaven-headed, bull-necked man of forty, wearing a boiler suit, had a barbed-wire tattoo across his forehead, above a tiny skull, and a teardrop tattoo below his left eye. On his forearms were several dagger tattoos. At this moment, with a smouldering roll-up in his mouth, he was prising the back off a Samsung phone. When he had done that, he picked up a tiny ball, no bigger than a pea, of PE4 plastic explosive, and rolled it between his finger and thumb. 'You have to be careful with this stuff, Ylli. If I drop this—' He shrugged, gave a wan smile, then made a cut-throat gesture with his right hand.

'That's enough to kill us?' Prek responded, incredulous.

'You want to see what it can do – just this little amount?'

'OK,' Prek said, warily.

Lebedev placed the ball inside the phone and pressed the back on, fiddling with it until it clicked home. Then he walked over to the far end of the room and put it on the floor. 'Ready?'

Prek nodded.

Lebedev handed him a pair of ear defenders. 'Put them on.'

Prek did as he was instructed, and Lebedev donned a similar pair. Then he handed Prek a pair of protective goggles and also put on a pair himself.

'Ready?' he asked again.

Prek nodded, unsure what was about to happen.

Lebedev picked up a mobile phone from the table and

PETER JAMES

a torn-off sheet of notepaper on which was what looked like a phone number. 'Put these numbers into the phone.'

Frowning, Prek entered them.

'Good,' Lebedev said. 'Now send a message to this number.'

'What message?'

'Anything you like. *Do you want to have sex with me? How is your leg healing? Where do badgers live? Happy birthday!*' He shrugged. 'Anything.'

Prek typed *How is your day so far?*

'Now send it.'

He sent it.

Nothing happened.

'Send it again!' Lebedev commanded.

He resent it. Still nothing happened.

'Now again!'

He hit the send symbol.

Almost instantly there was a brilliant flash at the far end of the room, a fraction of a second ahead of a massive bang that he heard even through the defenders.

Smiling, Lebedev removed his headset and strode over to the end of the room, where there was now a pall of smoke curling upwards and a stench of burnt plastic. The phone was gone, leaving a sizeable indent, a metre across, in the concrete floor. He summoned his colleague.

Prek joined him and stared in shock at the small crater, and at the tiny fragment of phone casing that Lebedev held in his hand, no more than a quarter of an inch square. 'If you can find a bigger fragment of that phone than this, I buy you drink!'

Prek went down on his hands and knees for a short while, looking around. Lebedev was right, there was nothing left, just minute fragments.

'So, you are impressed?' Lebedev asked.

'That is powerful stuff,' the young Albanian said.

They returned to the tables, and Prek, in shock from what he had just seen, watched the bomb-maker resume his meticulous, intricate work.

Lebedev removed, bit by bit, the insides of the camera. When he was done, he began very carefully to pat into place, inside the camera casing, a kilo of the PE4 explosive, which he then methodically packed with nails and ball bearings, all the while talking Prek through the process.

'PE4, when triggered, will detonate at a speed of 8,000 metres a second. You must be careful, Ylli, you know – as you have seen, this is so volatile it can be triggered very easily. Its power, just like the dummy camera packed with explosives that you left at the Amex yesterday, would be enough to kill over two hundred people within the immediate area – and injure many hundreds more.'

Prek already had his instructions from Mr Dervishi. At the next home game he was to place the camera bomb in a concealed location, depart from the grounds and detonate it remotely by text. Within an hour, Dervishi assured him, he would be on board a private jet from Brighton City Airport that would take him back to Albania, with enough money to live comfortably for the next decade. At his young age of twenty-three, that felt to Prek like forever.

Not to mention a far preferable option than being fed to a crocodile.

'We use a new phone,' Luka Lebedev said. 'No one has the number, no risk of an accidental text.' He smiled, revealing a row of metal teeth, then placed the small Nokia inside the shell of the camera, pushing it hard against the sticky explosive until it was wedged in place. He pointed his finger at a yellow Post-it note stuck to the table surface.

'The phone number, Ylli. Try it, send a text from your phone!'

Prek looked at him dubiously.

'Go on, you are afraid?'

'The bomb is primed?'

The bomb-maker shook his head. He pointed at two separate wires inside the camera, just behind the lens, each of them sealed at the end with insulating tape. 'Just try, test it!'

Nervously, Prek took out his phone, looked down at the numbers, then tapped them in, slowly. When he was done, he looked again at Lebedev. 'You sure this is safe? We are not going to blow ourselves up?'

Lebedev tapped his chest. 'Do I look like a guy who wants to blow himself up? Send it. Send a message!'

Prek typed out, *How's your day so far?*

He hesitated again.

'What's your problem, Ylli? You don't trust me?'

'No, sure I trust you.'

'So, do it!'

97

The smell of cooking was tantalizing Jorgji Dervishi. Sunday lunch – today a very late one because of everything – was one of his favourite times of the week. When he sat down with Mirlinda and Aleksander and just talked, while they ate Mirlinda's wonderful food. She was a great cook. Whilst he had his mistress to satisfy his sexual lust, Mirlinda always satisfied his other hungers, which included beautifully cooked food and good conversation. And on a normal Sunday he liked to hear how Aleksander was getting on at school.

Of course, the Sunday meal was always to be accompanied by a fine wine, and then afterwards a nice sleep in front of the television. Perhaps later a walk. He had read an article in a newspaper by a famous food writer who had said that life was too short to drink bad wine. He agreed with this man. Standing at the kitchen sink, he carefully and lovingly removed the foil cap and inserted the corkscrew into one of the many treasures from his wine cellar, a 1989 Haut-Brion.

As the cork slid out with a satisfying *pop*, he held it to his nose and inhaled deeply. No hint of damp cardboard or mustiness. Perfume! Nectar!

He poured a little into his wide, deep glass. Swirled it around, smelled the aroma. Smiled.

'My darling Mirlinda, I think you are going to like this wine, very much – a quite sensational bouquet!'

'You know I always like your choices, my love.'

'Ah, but this one is special indeed.'

And it was. A single bottle, at auction, would sell for around £250.

Dritan had texted him the Bitcoin code from Valbone's computer at Boden Court, and a quarter of a million pounds in Bitcoins was in his account as of an hour ago. He could well afford wine of this quality.

He took another sip. It was improving, even more, by the second. 'Where is Aleksander?'

'In his room, crying.'

'Fetch him,' he commanded.

As Mirlinda left the room, his phone rang. The caller's number showed on the display. Edi Konstandin.

'Uncle Edi!' he answered, joyfully.

But there was no joy in the old man's voice.

'What do you think you are playing at, Jorgji?'

'What do you mean?'

'What do I mean? I've just had two detectives here giving me a hard time. Are you mad?'

'Mad? What do you mean, Uncle?' He stepped out of the dining room and walked along to his office.

'You've gone off-piste, very badly, Jorgji. We are family. And our family has only one boss, me. We have a code of honour, am I correct? We are on a mission to have Albanians in this city respected in the community. We harm the business contacts who cross us, but we do not harm innocent outsiders. You have family, you have a child – how would you feel if your boy, Aleksander, was blown up? Have you totally lost the plot? A bomb threat at the Amex? Kidnapping? What are you playing at?'

'I'm running the family's business now, Uncle. You gave me the authority, you said to me you are too old, you were letting me take over, is that not correct?'

'What I said was take it over, not put it down the toilet, you fool.'

'The world is changing, Uncle. You don't see that, do you? You put me in charge of the business and that's what I'm doing. Moving with the times.'

'Moving with the times? What kind of business involves bomb threats at the football stadium on the most important day in the local team's history? What kind of business is kidnapping the child of a high-profile local businessman?'

'A very lucrative business, Uncle Edi.'

'Lucrative? What are you talking about? *Lucrative* is a business that has a future. You are killing this future for yourself and for all of us. You are already a very rich man, why do you need to do this?'

'Uncle Edi, you are eighty-two years old. You aren't in touch with the modern world. You have to let me run this my way, now.'

'Your way?'

'Yes.'

Edi Konstandin was silent for some seconds, before speaking again. 'Since I came to this country, Jorgji, I've done all I could for my family. Sure, we've had some violence on the way, but now we have good, honest businesses. We don't need that any more. Why can't you just focus on what we have and stay under the radar? We're all making enough money to have a very good life here. Why do you want to risk destroying all of that?'

'Just retire, Uncle. Retire, OK? You've done it your way, now I'm doing it my way. If you have a problem with that, I'm sorry.'

'Jorgji, I want to see you now. Come to my house. We have to talk.'

'Uncle, I come later this afternoon, I'm about to eat – and lunch is late enough already.'

'No, you are not eating, you are coming to see me right away – NOW. Do you understand?'

'I understand very clearly my vision for the future. Did you never read the Bible, Uncle? The Acts of the Apostles? *Old men dream dreams, young men see visions*? No? Stick to your dreams, Uncle Edi, I'll stick to my visions. OK?'

'Since when were you a Christian? You come here immediately. No delay. Do you hear me? You don't come now, you are finished.'

'I've just opened a very nice wine, but I'm afraid it might not last as long as your dreams, Uncle Edi.' He hung up, just as Mirlinda came back into the room.

'Aleksander is coming down,' she said.

His phone rang again. On the display was **Edi Konstandin**. He killed the call and turned to his wife. 'I'm sorry, my love, an urgent matter has come up, I have to go.' He kissed her and walked across the room.

She looked worried. 'What is it?'

'Nothing, not important.'

'Not important? Not important but you have to go?'

He stopped in the doorway. 'I do. I need to deal with something.'

'Have your lunch first. I've cooked your favourite, roast rib of Scottish beef, and I've cooked it how you like it.'

'I'll have it later.'

'Later? The beef will be ruined.'

'If I don't go now, *everything* will be ruined.'

He hurried into his office, removed a spare pay-as-you-go phone from a drawer in his desk, picked up his wallet, cigar case and lighter. Then he went up to his dressing room, grabbed a lightweight sports jacket, and hurried out of the house into his garage, shaking with fury. That senile old fool was not going to dictate to him, no way.

In a short while, Edi Konstandin would be history.

But he did have a point about the kidnap – perhaps better to distance himself from that scenario. He'd scooped a quarter of a million for doing virtually nothing today. The balance of the £2,250,000 ransom payment would be very nice to have also, but he'd make much more than that amount with Konstandin out of the way. And there was nothing to link him to the kidnap. Unfortunately for Kipp Brown, the only people apart from himself and Dritan who knew where Mungo Brown was were now dead. He was very safely hidden. By the time his body was found, if it was ever found, it would be so eaten by crabs, lobsters, shrimps and other scavengers of the sea as to be virtually unidentifiable. A shame for a young boy to die. Collateral damage.

He climbed into his S-Class Mercedes and hit the clicker to open the garage door. As it clattered up, he phoned Dritan on the number his employee had used to text him the Bitcoin code, to inform him of his decision.

98

The water level was over his stomach.

When were they going to come back to get him out?

Were they coming back at all? Ever?

The water was lifting him, constantly now, and he rose and fell with the swell. Each time he fell, he tried increasingly desperately to regain his position on the ledge. Twice, in the past minutes, his feet had missed the ledge and he'd had a moment of panic about being garrotted by the wire noose, until the swell lifted him up again.

Help me! Help me! Help me!

He closed his eyes in prayer. *Please God, please, please, please, I'm sorry. Please help me.*

99

In a red mist, his nerves shredded, Dritan Nano had ridden recklessly out of Brighton on his Ducati motorcycle, his pride and joy, then randomly along the country roads of East Sussex, towards Kent, not even aware of where he was going, just riding, hard and furiously, as if trying to ride a demon out of his body. Eventually he circled back round towards the outskirts of Brighton. He was driving much too fast. Stupid, he realized, slowing right down to the speed limit as he joined the A27 dual carriageway, heading towards Lewes as he had been instructed. Maintaining the speed limit along the bypass, with the University of Sussex campus to his left and the Amex Stadium to his right, he was feeling increasingly shaken as the enormity of his actions was dawning on him.

I shot three people. Dead.

Because Jorgji Dervishi made me.

Made me.

Oh shit.

Now the boy is going to die.

He was close to tears.

This was not what he had signed up to when he had come to this country, when he had been honoured to take the job as bodyguard to the consiglieri. He had been there to protect Dervishi, not to kill for him. Now it was all falling apart. He'd killed his friend to protect his own family back home.

He and Valbone had done a deal with Aleksander. The plan was to help his friend, Mungo, screw some money out of his father. They would split it four ways. His share would have given him enough to afford to quit his job with Mr Dervishi and start his own coffee bar in the city. He had already identified one with a lease that was up for sale.

All that was gone now, since Dervishi had hijacked their plan. Dritan was a fugitive here in England. In a few hours, Mr Dervishi had promised him, he would be smuggled out of the country on the private plane which was kept at Brighton City Airport, with a pay-off big enough to start a new life back in his home country. The money Mr Dervishi had promised him, given him his word, his *besa*, would be enough for him to get an apartment in Tirana and buy a coffee bar there, instead. He just had to get safely to the rendezvous address he had been given, on an industrial estate that Mr Dervishi had built. And then he would be taken to the airport and flown out. Back close to where Lindita was.

He would find her. He would explain. She would listen to him, wouldn't she?

Please, Lindita, I can't live without you.

I am seeing someone else and I think he is better for me.

No, you can't. You are going to marry me. I will explain everything when I see you. I've changed. I'm not that person any more. I've changed. I love you, Lindita.

His eyes misted as he rode on past Lewes, down the long hill towards the Beddingham roundabout. A murderer. Could he trust Mr Dervishi to protect his back? Shield him? To do what he promised?

Of course he could. *Besa.* No Albanian, ever, failed to honour his *besa.*

The police would start a manhunt soon, if not already. A massive manhunt. For him.

The one person who could shield him was Mr Dervishi. With Dervishi's help he would be back in Albania tonight. But doubts filled his head.

Could he really trust his boss, despite his *besa*? The man had a hold on him. Multiple holds. He knew where his family lived and now he could quietly slip his name to the police.

Shit, what had he done?

Should he just leave now? Get out of here while he still could?

As he entered the roundabout he wondered should he turn right and down to Newhaven? Dump the motorbike and jump on a ferry and just get away? He could hitch-hike back to his home country to avoid being detected at railway stations or airports.

Good plan, apart from one big problem. His passport was in his room in the apartment he had shared with Valbone, above Mr Dervishi's garages.

He went round the roundabout for a second time.

Mr Dervishi had connections. Long tentacles. People would be capable of finding him, wherever he hid, however deep in Albania, if he further angered the man. And as Dervishi was well aware, they didn't even need to bother trying to find him – they knew where his family lived.

He had to follow his instructions. Hope for the best. And in a moment of clarity, he was comforted by the knowledge that it wasn't just Mr Dervishi who had a hold on him. He had a hold on Mr Dervishi, too. Stuff on his boss. Stuff he could tell the police.

Fortified by that thought, he continued round the roundabout, then back up the hill, faster now. He circled at the top, headed back down the hill and after a short distance turned left at the sign which read RANSCOMBE FARM INDUSTRIAL ESTATE.

He rode past a development of chalet-style holiday homes and entered the industrial estate, passing a noticeboard and a unit with two large skips in front, and then along past rows of identical steel units with yellow doors, all with deserted parking bays. One advertised itself as a pump specialist, another was pet food supplies and another recycled electrical waste. He threaded his way through the network of roads and units until he found the address he had been given. He cruised along, past a unit with an elderly model Jaguar estate car parked in a bay, then reached Number 26, CABURN HEATING & PLUMBING SERVICES.

Two vehicles were parked outside, a small Hyundai and a van bearing the business name.

Freewheeling onto the forecourt, he kicked down the stand and dismounted, carefully balancing the machine, before walking up to the office door and rapping on it, hard. There was a frosted-glass window to the right of the door, behind which the distorted shadow of a figure moved.

He heard the door being unlocked – two locks, then a third – and finally it was opened by a short, thin, bespectacled man in his twenties, with a shapeless mop of thinning dark hair. He was dressed in an anorak, badly fitting jeans and cheap trainers, and looked nervous. 'Ylli Prek?'

'Yes – Dritan?'

He nodded.

'Come in, quick.'

Prek peered past him, anxiously, then shut and relocked the door immediately after he had entered. Dritan followed him into the main workshop area of the unit and received a hostile glare from a shaven-headed man who was bent over the casing of a camera, a roll-up dangling from his lips.

The bomb-maker looked at the new arrival with suspicion. 'You are here why?'

'I work for Mr Dervishi. He told me to come here – to wait for him after a job I have done for him. What do you do here?'

'I make bombs for Mr Dervishi.' He removed his crinkled cigarette and smiled, flashing his metal teeth.

'You are making a bomb from a camera?'

'Yes.'

'You like some tea – we have Albanian Balcony Tea or coffee?' Prek asked the visitor.

'Tea, please.' He looked around, curious and wary. 'What kind of a bomb, exactly?'

'One that explodes!' Lebedev grinned. 'That's what bombs do, don't they?' Again, he grinned, put the cigarette back in his mouth and held the flame of a plastic lighter to the end.

While Prek filled the kettle, Dritan addressed Lebedev. 'You are happy for your handiwork to kill and maim innocent people?'

'It's not my skill that does this – that is the choice of the people who pay me.'

'I know what your tattoos mean,' Dritan replied.

'So?'

'They are Russian. You are Russian?'

Lebedev shrugged.

'Do they make you feel brave?' Dritan asked, coldly.

The bomb-maker stared at him. A long, silent, penetrating stare, full of loathing. 'Why don't you fuck off and mind your own business?'

'Each spike of barbed wire is a year spent in prison. The skull means you have killed someone. As does the dagger. You have four daggers on your arms.'

'Would you like me to make it five? It wouldn't be a problem, it would be a pleasure.' He tugged at each of his sleeves, provocatively, pulling them up as if readying for a fight.

The kettle began to whistle. At the same moment, there was a sharp *ratta-tap-tap-tap* from the direction of the office.

All three of them looked round.

The knocking repeated.

Ylli Prek hurried through, crouching low out of sight of the window.

Lebedev and Dritan stood still as he disappeared into the office. Dritan heard Jorgji Dervishi's voice, and moments later his boss strutted into the room, wearing a fancy checked jacket and holding a smouldering cigar in his hand. He looked straight at Dritan.

'So?'

'I did what you instructed, Mr Dervishi. You have the money?'

Dervishi nodded, drew on his cigar and strode over to Lebedev. As he reached him, he pulled a mobile phone from his inside jacket pocket. 'I want you to fill this with explosive, now, Luka.'

The bomb-maker frowned. 'Explosive? How much?'

'Enough to take a big house down – and everyone inside it. Enough to make sure no one survives. How quickly can you do this?'

'There's not enough room in the phone to make a bomb that effective.'

'Make the room.'

'Sure, I can make the room for the explosive, but not if you want the phone to work.'

'Think of something.' Dervishi puffed again and blew out a perfect smoke ring. 'That's why I pay you.'

'OK, come back tomorrow.'

'Tomorrow?'

'Yes.'

'I'm not having a pissing contest with you, Luka. I don't want it tomorrow, I want it in thirty minutes.'

100

Mungo's ears were filled with the echoing roar of the sea as it surged in, then sucked back out, pulling his legs harder and harder each time.

When it surged, the water level slopped up to his shoulders.

Oh God, help me please.

He looked up at the walls. At the vaulted brick roof covered in slime and weed, at another tiny crab that had suddenly appeared and was running up the wall a short distance from him, as if taunting him, as if saying, *I can do this, so can you!*

A takeaway carton floated past him. One way, then the other.

Mummy!

Daddy!

A massive surge of water came in, rising right up to his chin.

No. No. No.

101

Norman Potting shot down the oncoming traffic lane, lights flashing and siren wailing, as they approached the roundabout by the large modern structure of the Ropetackle Arts Centre. 'Which way, chief?'

Left would take them into Shoreham Village, along the north side of the harbour front. Straight over would take them across the bridge, with Brighton City Airport to the right and the residential maze of Shoreham Beach to the left.

Grace did not know. Now they were actually here, the sheer enormity of the area was dawning on him even more. 'Go round,' he instructed the DS.

Potting drove, siren screaming, a full 360 degrees.

'Over the bridge and pull in,' Grace instructed him again, his brain racing.

His phone rang.

'Yes?' he answered.

'Sir?'

He recognized the voice of Inspector Keith Ellis, who was back on duty as the Oscar-1.

'Keith?'

'I don't know if it's significant, but a forward-facing ANPR camera on Dyke Road Avenue picked up the index of

385

a motorbike heading away from Boden Court at high speed on the wrong side of the road, overtaking a vehicle. It coincides with the time shortly before you were on the scene of the triple homicide. It's on false, stolen or copied plates. Then an unmarked RPU car spotted it on the A27 near Lewes – they were alerted because it went twice round the roundabout, and they followed at a safe distance, mindful of your original instructions. They observed it retrace its steps, then head back down Ranscombe Hill and turn into a new development at Ranscombe Farm, where there is an industrial estate.'

'This could be significant, Keith. Where are they now?'

'Standing by, at the entrance.'

'Nice work! Send them in, discreetly, to do a cruise around. If they spot the motorbike, tell them to stand off at a distance and observe – and let me know immediately.'

'Roger that, sir.'

The moment the call ended, Grace's phone rang again. It was Detective Inspector Dull.

'Yes, Donald?'

'I may have something, sir, from the serials from Shoreham Beach.'

'Tell me.'

As they crossed the River Adur, Grace looked at the houseboats, then glanced down. The river was approaching high tide. How long did they have? Thirty minutes, maybe?

'It may be nothing, boss,' Dull said. 'Apparently the lady who rang this in, a Mrs Sampson, is a regular caller and a bit of a nuisance, but I thought it might be worth running by you.'

'What do you have?'

'Shall I read you the transcript?'

'Go ahead.'

'*I'm sorry, madam, we are very busy. What is your emergency, please?*'

'*I would like to report new vandalism at Shoreham Fort, please, and something suspicious.*'

'*Suspicious?*'

'*A new padlock, and I don't know why it's there. It might be pikeys, stealing metal from the cannon – they steal it from everywhere, don't they?*'

Grace felt a tiny spark of hope. He said to Norman, 'Shoreham Beach – take that turn-off!' Then he replied to Dull. 'What else?'

'I've got the lady's phone number.'

'Give it to me,' Grace said as Potting started the car, switched the blues and twos back on and drove the short distance towards the turn-off.

He memorized the number, thanked Dull, then immediately dialled it.

After three rings, it was answered by a very hoity-toity-sounding woman. 'Hellllloooo?'

'Mrs Sampson?'

'Yes, may I help you?'

'Where to?' Potting interrupted.

Grace pointed at a lay-by.

'This is Detective Superintendent Grace, Surrey and Sussex Major Crime Team,' he said, as Potting pulled over.

'Well,' she said indignantly. 'No wonder you people are short of resources if you have to have a Detective Superintendent deal with simple graffiti vandalism.'

'It's actually more serious than that, madam,' he said. 'I'm interested in your report about a new padlock.'

'Ah,' she said. 'You're after the pikeys, eh? Stealing the metal from the cannon?'

'Madam,' he said, 'I'm looking for someone whose life is in immediate danger.'

There was a long silence.

'Madam, are you still there?'

'Yes.'

'Where exactly did you see this padlock?'

'On the door to one of the gun emplacements – at Shoreham Fort.'

Grace's excitement rose. 'How far from Shoreham Fort do you live, Mrs Sampson?'

'Ten minutes' walk. I take our dogs there every day.'

'If you give me your address I'll pick you up and drive you there.'

'No need to do that, it's a pedestrian area, no cars. I'll meet you there.'

'Shoreham Fort?' he double-checked. As he spoke, he was opening Google Maps on his private phone.

'Yes.'

He thanked her and began keying it into the app.

'It's all right, chief,' said Potting, 'I know it – somewhere around here – the young lad of one of my exes was a volunteer there, helping on the restoration.'

An instant later it popped up. The map told Grace it was eight minutes by car from his current position.

'Go!' he shouted at Potting, holding up his phone in front of him, the arrow pointing a short distance ahead and then sharp left. 'Straight ahead then first left – go, go, go! Spank it, drive like you've stolen it!'

Norman Potting obeyed him.

102

For PCs Richard Trundle and Pip Edwards, in the unmarked BMW, Hotel Tango Two-Eight-One, it had been a Q Sunday up until now. *Q* stood for *Quiet*, the word no police officer dared to say because it was a jinx. They all knew the moment you mentioned it was a *quiet* day, everything would kick off.

Traffic officers had various games they played on such days, or nights, to relieve the monotony. One, on dual carriageways or motorways, in a marked car, was to gradually decrease their speed below the legal limit and watch vehicles behind them slowing down, not daring to pass. There was a method in this, because anyone driving a legal vehicle would have no hesitation passing them. But someone in an untaxed or uninsured vehicle would always hang back, nervous of being pinged by the in-car ANPR system, which would instantly alert the officers.

Two colleagues of Trundle and Edwards currently held the record for the Polegate Roads Policing Unit, of 35 mph in a 70 mph limit. When they'd finally pulled over the car behind them, it turned out to be a major bust. Untaxed, uninsured and twenty thousand pounds' worth of cocaine, at street value, in the boot.

Other games that traffic officers played regularly, often

in the small hours of a Q night, were either to invent a fatal collision that turned out to be, on investigation, an almost perfect murder, or to create the perfect bank heist.

Until they had spotted the red Ducati motorbike going twice round the Beddingham roundabout, it had been a boring shift for Trundle and Edwards. They were glad to have something to do other than driving around aimlessly, looking for cars passing too close to cyclists, speeding motorists and waiting for the all-too-inevitable Sunday shout to attend a fatal RTC. More often than not, the latter involved a 'born-again' biker – the moniker the RPU gave to middle-aged guys who had owned a motorcycle in their late teens, and had now, from their bonuses, bought a much more powerful machine than had been around in their youth, on which too many, tragically, would run out of road – or talent – at a vital point.

'Been to that new industrial estate before?' Trundle asked his colleague.

Edwards shook his head. 'No, it's only been finished very recently – you?'

Trundle shook his head. 'Me neither.'

On Oscar-1's instructions they drove past a small development of holiday-let chalets and in through the entrance of the Ranscombe Farm Industrial Estate, which was heralded by a small sign. Cruising slowly, they looked at the company names displayed and the empty parking bays: Yelland Flooring; Caburn Office Furnishings; Tuckwell Auto Spares.

At the end of the road they turned left, then left again, and drove along the second row of almost-identical units. And saw, parked on a forecourt, ahead to their right, a blue van bearing the name of a plumbing firm, a small Hyundai dwarfed by a large, black Mercedes, and a motorbike, a red Ducati.

Index K5 DGG.

Bingo!

They cruised on, as instructed, noting the name on the premises, Caburn Heating & Plumbing Services.

'Spin her round at the end and we'll park up,' Edwards suggested.

A couple of minutes later they pulled up beside a blue Jaguar estate car on the forecourt of a company called Cornelia James Ltd, which displayed a Royal Warrant crest beside its name. From this vantage point they were concealed behind the Jaguar but had a clear view through its windows of the vehicles outside the plumbing firm.

Pip Edwards radioed Oscar-1. 'This is Hotel Tango Two-Eight-One, we have visual on the target bike.'

Keith Ellis replied, 'Acknowledged, Hotel Tango Two-Eight-One. Stay out of sight but maintain obs on the bike. If the rider leaves, inform me, follow at a discreet distance but do not enter into pursuit. Stand by for further instructions.'

'Yes, yes.'

They settled down to watch.

'How's Beckie?' Pip Edwards asked. 'Still working at Tesco?'

'Seventeen years she's just clocked up, and still loves every day there. So how's the caravan?'

Edwards had just splashed out £20,000 on a caravan.

'Love it, the kids love it! Going to the New Forest next weekend.'

Trundle shook his head. 'Caravans, yech. My idea of luxury is a nice hotel, a spa, a pool.'

'And an RTC that's a murder?' Pip Edwards asked him.

'Yep. One that involves some poor sod of a motorist stuck behind a bastard in a caravan, on a hill,' Trundle retorted.

103

'Very clever,' Dervishi said.

It had taken the bomb-maker less than twenty minutes, so far.

'See, I knew you could!'

Luka Lebedev, watched by Dritan Nano, Ylli Prek and Jorgji Dervishi, carefully squeezed superglue along the back of the Samsung phone, then pressed the fake battery pack, which he had fashioned from black plastic, against it. He laid it on the work surface. 'Needs two minutes to bond.'

'You're sure there's enough explosive to do the job?' Dervishi quizzed, lighting a fresh cigar.

Lebedev began to roll a new cigarette with one hand.

'No smoking, please.'

He frowned. 'But, Mr Dervishi, you are smoking!' Lebedev carried on rolling.

Dervishi stepped forward, grabbed the partially finished cigarette from his palm and trod it into the floor. 'I don't want that cheap shit polluting my Havana, understand?'

There was a moment of awkward silence. Lebedev glared at his employer and, for a moment, Dritan thought the Russian was going to deck him.

Dervishi tapped his own chest, self-importantly. 'So long as I pay you, you do what I tell you, understand?'

Lebedev continued glaring at him.

'Are you going to answer my question, Luka? You are sure there's enough explosive in that battery pack? To blow up a house?'

'Let's try it.' Lebedev's lips parted in his malevolent grin. 'Maybe I'll stick it up your ass and try it.'

Dritan looked at the others, attempting not to show his utter contempt for them. Contempt for Ylli Prek, for even daring to think he might deliver a bomb to the football stadium. For Luka Lebedev for making these evil things. And way, way above these two, Mr Dervishi, the arrogant, murderous monster.

Dervishi caught his eye and smiled. 'My trusted Dritan, who has today killed three people who crossed me.'

'You told me, Mr Dervishi, that if I did this, you would give me the money you promised and arrange your private aeroplane to fly me home.'

'I did indeed, Dritan. Just one more task for you and then I will fly you home.'

'That wasn't our deal. You gave me *besa*.'

'I said I would fly you home in my private plane. I'm doing that.'

'You did not say there was *one more thing*.'

'You want to argue with me? You don't like it? Go – just leave, I won't stop you.'

Dritan hesitated. He was tempted to do just that. But, he realized, he was in Mr Dervishi's hands. His name and details might be all over the border controls imminently, if they weren't already. The only safe escape was by Mr Dervishi's plane from the local airport where there would be no questions asked.

Mr Dervishi had given him *besa*. He could trust that. 'I do it,' he said, reluctantly.

'Of course you will!' Dervishi smiled and pointed at the primed phone. 'I want you to go and see my uncle, Edi Konstandin. Take this phone to him and tell him it is a secure phone on which I will call him with a peace offering.' He handed him a slip of paper on which he had written Konstandin's address.

Dritan frowned. 'What do you mean?'

'You leave it with him and tell him I will be calling him on it. When you ride away, you then send him a text.' He smiled and blew out another perfect smoke ring.

'And what about if someone sends me a text, by accident, on my way?' Dritan asked.

Despite simmering visibly with anger, Lebedev said, 'It is secure. To prevent against random or accidental texts to a wrong number being sent, you have to send the same text three times within a sixty-second window. Miss the window and you have to start over. Simples!' Again, his metal teeth flashed. 'Enter the number on your own phone.'

Copying it from the sheet of paper, Dritan tapped it in. When he had done that, he asked, 'What should I do if your uncle is out, Mr Dervishi?'

'My uncle rarely goes out, except to the football. He is confined to his wheelchair and he is too afraid of enemies. I wonder why!'

They stood in silence, whilst Dervishi blew more smoke rings. Finally, Lebedev said, 'OK,' picked up the phone and handed it to Dritan, who took it very nervously and placed it in the top pocket of his leathers.

'One word of warning, Dritan,' Lebedev said. 'Don't drop your bike – or the phone. Or there might be no more Dritan and a very big hole in the road.'

Dervishi and the bomb-maker grinned.

'Text me when you have completed your mission,'

Dervishi said. 'My plane will be waiting. I will give you instructions where to find the pilot.'

Dritan, watching him closely, saw Dervishi shoot a glance at Lebedev. And he clocked the smile Lebedev flashed back.

It made him feel very uncomfortable.

Dritan put on his helmet, went outside and stood in the afternoon sunshine beside the van, Hyundai and large black Mercedes, looking around, carefully, warily. And thinking.

Could he possibly trust Mr Dervishi? He had moved the goalposts. Would he move them again?

He did not like that glance he had seen between Mr Dervishi and the Russian.

Mr Dervishi would kill anyone who crossed him or who got in the way of any profit he might make.

He entered the address he had been given into the maps app on his phone, started the engine and rode off, slowly. A few hundred yards from the unit he stopped his bike, the engine running at tick over, and stood still, his feet on the ground, thinking.

He had a primed bomb in his pocket. If he carried out this mission, what incentive did his boss have to fly him out of the country?

None.

Looking around, he clocked the blue Jaguar estate that had been here when he arrived. But there was something parked beyond it, a dark-grey vehicle that had not been there before. It made him nervous. Maybe it was innocent. Maybe not.

Should he cruise round the block and see if it moved?

But if it was the cops, how could they be on to him so soon?

Shit.

He started the bike and rode off, back the way he had come.

The BMW that had been parked on the other side of the Jaguar estate was still there.

104

The incoming tide had risen up to his chin. Mungo desperately trod water to avoid the wire cutting into his neck. His ears were filled with the roar of the sea. A sudden surge sent water breaking over his head and he took some in, accidentally, through his nostrils, sending a searing pain through his head.

He whimpered. *Help. Help. Help me.*

It had been a long while since his feet had touched the ledge. He was kicking with his legs, desperately trying to keep his head above the water. He was tiring. Close to exhaustion. Kicking, kicking, kicking.

The water was rising.

Rising towards the vaulted, slime-covered ceiling.

Before it reached it, he would be totally submerged.

'Owwwwwwwwwww!' His cry, as the wire suddenly bit into his neck, was muffled by the duct tape over his mouth.

I'm going to die.

105

Inside Unit 26, Jorgji Dervishi listened, smiling, to the sound of the motorbike roaring away into the distance. He puffed hard on his cigar and blew out two perfect smoke rings in succession. Then he turned to Ylli Prek and handed him the number of the phone Dritan Nano had in his breast pocket.

'Wait until he is well away. Ten – better fifteen minutes. I tell you when to send the three texts.'

'He is not coming back here?' Prek asked. 'Not texting you when he has done what you told him?'

'That's right, you got it in one,' Dervishi said. He blew another perfect smoke ring.

106

'Target's on the move,' Pip Edwards informed Oscar-1. 'He's leaving the industrial estate via the exit road – he has no alternative route.'

Keith Ellis well knew from his earlier days as a traffic officer the difficulties involved in following a target without being observed – especially motorbikes – and the dangers if it later turned into a pursuit. A couple of years ago an RPU officer had entered into pursuit with a motorcyclist who was weaving recklessly through traffic on a motorway. A short while later it had ended in tragedy when the biker turned off at an exit, lost control a few minutes later and hit a petrol tanker head-on.

Since then, and after a number of other motorcycle fatalities during pursuits, policy dictated that motorcycle pursuits should only be authorized in exceptional circumstances. As part of a kidnap in progress, this qualified.

'Hotel Tango Two-Eight-One, do you have visual contact?' Ellis asked.

'Not at this moment – we will shortly.'

'Follow at a discreet distance when you do.'

'Yes, yes.'

107

Norman Potting clipped a kerb, taking the racing line as he slid the car at speed through a left turn, onto a road that ran parallel to the pebble beach and the sea beyond. Roy Grace clung to the grab handle, glancing repeatedly at his watch. Less than ten minutes to rescue Mungo, if his calculations were correct.

They drove into a fenced parking area, with just a couple of vehicles in it, and both detectives jumped out almost before the car had stopped moving. A distinguished-looking blonde woman in her early fifties hurried towards them through the blustery wind. She was followed by a man in his forties, with a crew cut, wearing a grey top, jeans and trainers.

Grace flashed his warrant card. 'Mrs Sampson?'

'Yes – and this is Gary Baines – he's in charge of the restoration of the fort.'

Grace shook his hand and shot a fleeting glance around him, getting his bearings. They were on the west side of the harbour, in a huge, flat area of wild, unkempt grass, in a complex of old brick structures. Straight ahead to the east, visible beyond the low roof of a green corrugated-iron Nissen hut, was the superstructure of a white building bearing the large words, in black, NATIONAL COASTWATCH,

401

SHOREHAM. Past that, across the rippling water of the harbour mouth, were two arms; on the end of one he could see several anglers. Across the River Adur were the houses of Shoreham Village. To his right was a steep grass embankment topped by crumbling, buttressed flint and brick walls, with a pebble beach to the south and the sea beyond. Sunk into the embankment, every twenty feet or so, were brick steps down to solid-looking steel doors.

'That one there, officers!' Sharon Sampson said, excitedly, pointing at one pair of doors secured by a shiny brass padlock.

'What's down there?' Grace asked.

'The old gun emplacements,' Gary Baines said. 'These contained the cannon facing out to sea and across the harbour entrance, to repel any invasion by the French – which never happened, luckily. Some of the cannon were taken and smelted down, unfortunately, but we still have some here.'

'Are these emplacements above or below sea-level?' Potting asked.

'Well, these were constructed in the early 1850s, before anyone knew about global warming, sir. They're all submerged now at high tide – we're trying to salvage the remaining cannon and restore them.'

Sharon Sampson hurried over, down the brick steps, and pointed at the large padlock. 'This, see? You didn't put it on, did you, Gary?'

Baines shook his head. 'No, that's not mine.'

108

As he left the estate, and accelerated down the hill, Dritan
Nano was still thinking about that glance between Mr Dervishi and the hostile Russian. If he had learned one thing
about Mr Dervishi in the years he had worked for him, it
was that his boss never did anything that was not to his
advantage.

What, he wondered, was to Mr Dervishi's advantage in
paying him over £60,000 and flying him home to Albania?
Sure, it would distance his boss from any possible connection to the UK police investigation into the triple homicide.
But there were, surely, other much cheaper options for Mr
Dervishi. Dritan wondered what guarantee he would have
that, if he carried out these instructions and murdered yet
another person, Mr Dervishi would honour his word.

Despite his *besa*.

Lindita was right about Dervishi's morality. Somewhere
in the past decade, Dritan realized, he'd been intimidated
by his boss into losing all concept of what was right and
decent. At first, he'd been grateful just to be in the UK, and
to have a well-paid job here. That was why he'd carried out
terrible things for Mr Dervishi, the last of which was what
he had done just a short while ago. Valbone had deserved
it, but not the other two, who were strangers to him. Now

he was being sent to kill another man, again about whom he knew little, except that he was very powerful.

He turned as soon as he could and raced back to the industrial estate. As he rode in, he saw the BMW was no longer there. He pulled over a few hundred yards away from the bomb factory, and sat, both feet on the ground, the engine again idling. Then he made a snap decision.

He switched off the engine, kicked down the stand and dismounted. After ensuring the bike was safely propped up, he sprinted towards the unit he had just left. All three vehicles were still outside.

As he drew close he slowed to a walk, treading as quietly as he could in his rubber-soled motorcycling boots. Tugging the phone from his breast pocket, he laid it on the ground behind a wheelie bin between the office door and the workshop entrance, and sprinted back to his bike.

Mounting the machine, he looked over his shoulder, anxiously, but to his relief there was no sign of any movement. His heart in his mouth, he started the engine, again checking the unit in his mirrors before heading towards the entrance of the estate, using the throttle as lightly as he could. He picked up speed a little past the holiday units, then halted at the junction with the dual carriageway, where he would have to turn left.

And froze.

During his time working for Mr Dervishi, he had learned to spot unmarked police cars. The police mainly used German models, in dark colours, with four doors and blacked-out rear windows.

The BMW, in a lay-by a short distance down the dual carriageway, ticked those boxes. It was identical to the one he had seen earlier on the industrial estate. Was it the same car?

He would have to pass it. Then see if it followed.

Oh shit.

He removed one glove, pulled his own mobile phone from his inside pocket, unlocked it with a trembling finger and looked at the number he had entered. He tapped *send*. Waited, then tapped *send* again. His hand was shaking so much he had to take a breath before tapping *send* a third time.

And listened.

He heard nothing. No explosion.

He looked down at the display, puzzled. Had he entered the number incorrectly? Surely not, he had checked it carefully. Maybe he had let too much time elapse between the three. More than sixty seconds?

He tried again. Sent the same text three times in rapid succession.

No. No. He looked behind him, feeling very scared. What was wrong?

He put the phone back in his pocket and tugged his glove back on. He revved the engine, pulled straight out into the path of an oncoming lorry and accelerated, full tilt, past the BMW.

109

'Go, go, go!' Pip Edwards said, resisting the temptation to put the blue lights on, as Trundle waited for the lorry to pass, then floored the accelerator, pulling into the outside lane.

Edwards radioed Oscar-1. 'Hotel Tango Two-Eight-One, subject vehicle has just gone past at high speed, heading towards the Beddingham roundabout. We are following. For Oscar-1's info, driver is a green permit holder in a suitable vehicle.'

'Try to keep him in sight but don't let him see you are following. Do not attempt a stop.'

'Yes, yes.'

As they approached the roundabout at over 100 mph, they saw the bike circle it skilfully, then head back up the hill, passing them on the far side of the dual carriageway. Braking sharply, Trundle entered ahead of a car which just slowed in time, held the BMW in a power slide, then accelerated back up the hill. The motorbike was already out of sight. The BMW's speedometer read 110 mph. 120 mph. As they approached the next roundabout, where there was a build-up of traffic, they could not see which way the Ducati had gone.

Braking hard, Trundle said, 'What do you think?'

'Straight on. We'd have seen him if he'd gone round and right.'

Trundle raced in front of a van and carried on, accelerating again hard.

Edwards kept a commentary to Oscar-1. 'We are now heading westbound on the A27. Our speed is 105 mph. We no longer have visual on subject.'

He heard Oscar-1 put out a call for any units near the A27 to look out for the bike and report back.

A short while later, as they approached yet another roundabout, an instruction came in from Oscar-1.

'Hotel Tango Two-Eight-One, we have a report of a large explosion on the Ranscombe Industrial Estate. Abort area search and proceed back to the estate.'

A tad disappointed, Pip Edwards replied, 'Proceed back to Ranscombe Industrial Estate, yes, yes.'

110

Riding his machine flat out, Dritan passed the Amex Stadium and the Sussex University campus, leaning over for the uphill right-hander. He crested the hill, continued at 150 mph down the far side into the valley, then up again. There was no cop car in his mirrors. As he neared the top, he slowed, took the slip left, braked hard and turned right at the roundabout, past the top of Dyke Road Avenue. He raced along the spine of the Downs, then the fast, twisting road down into the valley, finally braking hard again and turning sharp left into the narrow lane leading down into the village of Poynings.

A few minutes later, holding his feet out to prevent the machine from slipping from under him on the gravel drive, Dritan pulled up beside a bronze Bentley Bentayga and two black Cadillac Escalades, outside a grand, white mansion. He kicked down the stand and dismounted, removed his helmet and placed it on the saddle.

Perspiring heavily, he walked up the steps to the entrance porch. The door was opened before he reached it by an unsmiling, shaven-headed minder in dark glasses. 'ID?'

Dritan produced his driving licence. A second minder appeared and frisked him. Then he was escorted along a black-and-white-tiled hallway, into a large, opulent draw-ing room. An elderly man in a wheelchair, talking on a mobile phone, sat on one side of a marble fireplace with unlit logs in the grate. Sunday newspapers were stacked on the coffee table in front of him, along with several mobile phones and a delicate china teacup on a saucer.

When he clocked his visitor he said, curtly, 'I will call you back in a while,' and ended the call, placing the phone down among the others.

One of the minders announced him.

Edi Konstandin greeted his visitor with an inquisitive smile and firm handshake. 'Please sit down, Mr Nano.' He beckoned him to the sofa opposite.

Dritan mopped his face with his handkerchief and sat, feeling uneasy and a little intimidated. His motorcycling leathers felt wrong in these grand surroundings. The oil paintings on the walls. The beautiful furniture. The sculp-tures on plinths. A different world, grander even than Mr Dervishi's home.

'Can I offer you some refreshment, perhaps? Tea, coffee, water?'

'No, thank you, I – I am good.'

Konstandin peered hard at him. 'Really, young man? You don't look too good to me, not good at all. You look a little agitated. Are you sure you are good?'

Dritan nodded, feverishly, still wondering why his three texts had not worked.

'To what do I owe the pleasure of your visit? You told my security that Mr Dervishi has sent you – for what purpose?'

Dritan's mouth felt dry. 'Yes – I—' He looked at Konstan-din's steel-grey eyes, fixed intently on him. He was shaking. 'I just need to talk to you, in private.'

Konstandin raised his hands. 'So, we are private here, talk!'

Dritan hesitated, then blurted it out. 'Mr Dervishi sent me to kill you.'

Konstandin looked amused. 'Well, you do not seem to be doing too good a job of it so far.'

Dritan smiled nervously back. 'You see – I didn't want to do that. I don't know you. So, I decided I wouldn't do it.'

'You've presumably killed other people you don't know, have you not?'

'I have changed.'

'That's what you came to tell me? That you were going to kill me but decided not to?'

'I came to see if—' He shrugged. 'If you could help me.'

'So how exactly were you supposed to kill me?' he asked.

Dritan told him.

When he had finished, Edi Konstandin was no longer looking amused. 'OK, so what is it you want from me? You want me to shake your hand and say thank you for not killing me?'

'I want to go home to my girlfriend, my fiancée, who is angry at me because of what I do. I need to find her and get her back.'

Konstandin smiled again, but there was no warmth in his face. 'Ah, a romantic. How lucky you are! A love story. You were willing to kill me for your love?'

'No, never. I never wanted to kill anyone, Mr Konstandin.'

'Yet in ten years of working for my nephew, you did kill people. You helped feed body parts to my nephew's crocodile, Thatcher, right?'

Dritan nodded, feeling deeply ashamed. 'Yes.'

'And now you have been offered money to come and kill me, and instead, being disloyal to the man who has employed you for the past ten years, you are warning me instead of killing me – why?' There was menace in his voice.

'Because—' Dritan said, scared suddenly. Had he made a mistake in coming? He had thought this man would be pleased.

'Because?'

'Because I am not a killer. I don't want to be a killer. I want to be a good person.'

'You don't think you have left that a bit late?'

'Can a person not change?'

'You believe you have changed?'

'Yes. That's why I am here.'

'And now you want to go home.'

'Yes.'

'So, go to Gatwick Airport and get on a plane!'

'I think that might not be possible for me. I wanted to ask if you could help me – I know you have influence and connections.'

'Perhaps you should let me have the whole story. If you want help from me, I need to know everything about you, everything you have done – right from the beginning.'

Dritan told him everything. Right from the start and up until the moment he had ridden up to the entrance gates, less than ten minutes ago.

Konstandin listened, only interrupting occasionally to clarify a point. When Dritan had finished, the old man sat in silence, staring at him with an unreadable expression. 'So much violence you have committed, and always at the request of my nephew, Jorgji?'

'Yes, yes always. And now a child has died.'

Konstandin fell silent, reflecting, then he said, 'You

411

know, young man, as I've grown older, I've found violence increasingly repugnant. I am proud of being born an Albanian but I am not proud of some of the things my people here in this country, in this city of Brighton and Hove, have done.' He studied Dritan. 'I would like you to know that if I am to help you to disappear from this country, it would not be out of gratitude for sparing my life – it's because I want to get rid of vermin like you who tarnish the names of all good Albanians, do you understand?'

Dritan felt his face burning. He wanted to say something back in his defence, to tell Mr Konstandin that he misunderstood him. But the old man didn't misunderstand him at all, he was right. That's how he must look to a man living in this grand style.

Vermin.

'Tell me about this former medical student, Gentian Llupa, who also kills people for Mr Dervishi. Do you know where he is?'

'Yes.'

'You are able to contact him?'

'Yes, he is my friend.'

'Of course he would be,' Konstandin said. He steepled his fingers. 'You may use my phones or if you need to go and see him, my driver will take you. I want you to give him a message. It is a very simple one, a choice. He leaves the country with you, today, or I will see to it, personally, that the police have enough to arrest and convict him.'

He paused to peer down at one of his phones, the display of which had lit up. Then he looked back up at Dritan. 'Breaking news: a big explosion on an industrial estate some miles north-east of Brighton. You wouldn't know anything about this?'

'Explosion? Where?'

The old man peered at the screen again. 'It says on the Ranscombe Farm Industrial Estate.' He looked at Dritan quizzically.

Trying not to show his excitement, Dritan thought, *It did work!*

'You know about this explosion?'

'No,' Dritan retorted, a bit too quickly.

'You just disarmed the phone to make it safe, and dropped it down two different drains, correct?'

'Correct.'

There was a long, uncomfortable silence between them. It was finally broken by Konstandin.

'So, Dritan Nano, how do you feel I should repay you for sparing my life?'

'Can you have someone fly me out of this country and back home?'

'How soon?'

'Today, if possible? One problem is I don't have my passport – it is at Mr Dervishi's house.'

Konstandin shrugged. 'I can arrange to get you home without your passport. But airports can be dangerous, Dritan, even our little local one. A boat might be a better choice – do you get seasick?'

'I don't know.'

The old man smiled. 'Let's hope not.'

111

Roy Grace sprinted over to his car, while Potting briefed Gary Baines, showing him the photograph of Mungo in the darkness, hoping he might find a clue in it. Baines peered hard at it, then shook his head. 'It could be anywhere, really, couldn't it? But it might be here, yes, of course.' He squinted at it. 'Just can't see any detail of the surroundings at all.'

Grace opened the tailgate, unzipped his go-bag and rummaged inside. He pulled out a pair of bolt-cutters, pliers and a short length of rope, then ran back over to the three of them standing by the door. He sheared the padlock clasp with the bolt-cutters and pulled the doors open, then went through, followed by Potting, Baines and the woman. Ahead of them were steps down, all but the top two submerged by seawater. 'Shit,' he said, despondently, his heart sinking. 'We're too late.'

'Well,' Baines said, shooting a glance at his watch. 'Not necessarily – it's not high tide for another fifteen minutes.'

'But it's underwater!' Grace said.

'Depends where the lad is in the chamber if he's here, which I think he might be,' Baines replied. 'He could be on the gun emplacement, and if he's standing up, like it shows in this photograph, he might still have air for another ten or twenty minutes.'

'How come?'

The curator pointed at the water. 'These steps go down about four more feet, into the gun emplacement room. The chamber itself has an arched ceiling, ten feet at its highest point – but it's some way into the chamber before it starts. At the far end is a small slit in the wall for the gun to fire through. That's what lets the water in, but it's not big enough for a human to pass through.'

Grace removed his jacket, knelt and unlaced his shoes.

'Boss, what are you doing?' Norman Potting cautioned.

He kicked his shoes off and removed his socks, trousers, tie and shirt until he was down to his underpants.

'Boss, you can't go in!'

Grace tugged his belt free of the trouser loops, then put it on around his midriff, buckling it tightly, and jammed the pliers inside it. Then he wound the rope round his waist. 'Fine, Norman, call out a dive team, they'll be here some-time tomorrow to recover a corpse.'

'I'm not letting you!'

'Call Oscar-1 for an ambulance and paramedics, Norman, and shut it!'

Ignoring the cold of the water, Grace waded in and down, up to his chest, then his neck. He paused, took a deep breath, hearing Potting shout again and taking no notice, and went down a further step, taking another two deep breaths in rapid succession before immersing his head and hoping to hell that Baines was right.

It was pitch-dark.

He launched himself forward and down, eyes open, swimming breaststroke hard for all he was worth, kicking with his feet, trying to put out of his mind the thought that if Baines was wrong, he had no way back. His head and back scraped along the hard, slimy surface above him.

Further. Further. Shit, his lungs were tightening. Further. Further.

Thoughts of Cleo flashed through his mind. Noah. Bruno. Never seeing them again. His body, along with Mungo's, recovered tomorrow.

His lungs were bursting.

He kicked, kicked, kicked with his feet, pushing through the water with his arms and hands, frantically, sliding along against the ceiling. Into eternal, never-ending darkness, his eyes stinging. Was this how it was going to end for him?

Keep going. Keep going. Keep going.

He was shaking. Shaking. Convulsing. His lungs were going to burst.

He was going to have to breathe. *Can't!*

He struggled on. His insides were being stretched on a rack. Every sinew was a string being wound tighter, tighter, tighter.

Have to take a breath.

Can't.

Water.

He would be inhaling water.

He would die if he did that.

Can't go on any more.

Have to breathe.

His lungs were going to implode, splitting his chest open.

Keep going. Keep going. Keep going.

No more. He could not keep going. He was going to have to let go. Breathe in. Breathe in and die, it would be a relief.

Let go, let go, let go! a voice screamed.

Breathe. Deep. All be over. Relief!

Suddenly, through the water, he saw very faint daylight.

An instant later, in an explosion of relief, he broke the surface. Tearing at the air with his mouth and nostrils, sucking it down, his whole body shaking, heaving, his head spinning giddily, like he had been momentarily concussed. He gulped it down, gratefully, ravenously. Filling his lungs through his nose and mouth, his heart pumping, filling with oxygen, breathing precious air in, out, in, out, as if he had never in his life breathed before.

I'm alive.

He felt dizzy and disorientated.

But he was breathing!

Sweet air.

He had made it through to the inner gun emplacement chamber.

His head bashed against something hard that was pressing down on him. The ceiling.

Faint streaks of light through cracks in the ceiling showed him dark water stretching out ahead, the arched brick roof above him coated in slime and weed.

'Mungo!' he yelled. 'Mungo?'

Silence.

Just the swell of the sea.

'Mungo?'

His voice echoed back at him.

'MUNGO!'

He choked, swallowing salty water. For some moments he panicked, struggling for air again, until he regained his composure.

'MUNGO!'

The water rose, bashing him up against the roof.

'MUNGO!'

Then he spotted a shape. A few yards ahead. A barely

visible silhouette through his eyes stinging from the salty water.

The swell rose up, momentarily covering Grace's head, and he swallowed more water, some of it shooting painfully up his nose, choking him.

Keep calm. Have to keep calm.

It was panic that killed people, he knew.

Keep calm. Breathe. Breathe!

When the water subsided, he could still see the youth, closer now. Much closer. Wire noose round his neck, duct tape over his mouth. Water up to his nose. Eyes wide with terror, fixed on his.

He swam as fast as he could towards him, before the swell rose again, once more submerging his head.

How long did they have?

Four more strokes and he reached him, just as the swell rose yet again, covering both their heads. As it subsided, he said, 'Police, I'm going to get you out, OK?'

Numb with fear, the teenager could hardly nod.

Grace lowered his feet through the water and found something hard to stand on. He stood, stretching himself as tall as he could, just above Mungo, pulled the pliers from his belt and cut the top of the wire noose, leaving for now the part of it round the boy's neck. Next, as quickly as he could, he tore the duct tape away from his mouth, hearing a yelp of pain.

'Sorry. Are you OK?'

'Please help me.'

'Mungo?'

A petrified nod. 'My hands. Can you free my hands?'

The thought flashed through his mind that he had both his ears intact. Whatever had been sent to the father must have come from elsewhere. 'Mungo, I'm going to get you out of here, but you have to do exactly what I tell you, understand?'

Another nod.

Grace ducked under water and looked behind the boy. But it was too dark to see. His wrists were bound by what felt like cable ties, with a chain looped through them and tied in a clumsy knot. He managed to free them from the chain, but did not dare try to cut the ties for fear of cutting Mungo's wrists.

Surfacing again, Grace took a moment to check any possible escape from here. All he could see was water, which seemed to be rising by the second, and the arched ceiling above, coming closer. With his arms behind his back, how the hell was he going to get him out?

'Mungo, are you good at holding your breath?'

'Yes,' he said in a tiny, trembling voice.

'Underwater?'

The boy stared at him with an unreadable expression.

'Underwater, Mungo? Can you? Can you hold your breath?'

'Yes,' he mouthed, nodding wildly.

Grace pointed back. 'We have to go that way, and quickly, we don't have long. I'm going to tie this rope round you. Follow me, OK, and use your feet to kick as hard as you can in the water.'

Mungo just stared at him.

He tied one end of the rope securely round the boy's chest under his armpits, and held the other in his hand. 'OK?'

'Yes.'

At that moment, a surge of water filled the cavern and started to suck them backwards, towards the sea. Fighting it with all his strength, Grace launched himself through the water, back the way he had come, pulling Mungo, who felt like a dead weight. As he rose to the surface, his head, then his body, hit the slimy ceiling. Shit, the gap was decreasing rapidly as the tide kept on rising. The swell carried him up, once more submerging his head. As it subsided again, he turned to see Mungo close behind him.

Just a few more strokes and he reached the entrance to the tunnel. The way into it was some feet below the top of the brick arch in front of him. His head broke the surface and he turned round, to see Mungo's head appear also. 'How are you doing?'

He nodded, looking scared as hell.

'Now, you are going to have to do something really hard. How long can you hold your breath?'

'I don't know,' Mungo replied.

'Take several deep breaths, first, then a really big one, OK?'

'OK.'

'Start now.'

As he watched the boy taking his breaths, Grace did the same. There was no going back from what they were about to do. If either of them ran out of air before they reached the steps at the entrance, they would die down here. There was no one to rescue them.

Grace took four breaths. Five.

Now!

He launched himself forward and down beneath the tunnel entrance, pulling the rope, feeling his head again scraping against the roof. He swam down, deeper, going as fast as he could, his eyes open and stinging in the ink-black water.

On.

On.

For several strokes he felt fine, powering along. Something kept touching one of his feet. Then his lungs began tightening.

Keep going.

He was running out of air. *Keep going!*

His chest was hurting. His lungs bursting. He didn't know if he could go on much more than a few seconds. His throat was tightening, he was shaking. Shaking. Convulsing. He was going to have to—

To let go.

No.

Going to have to—

He wasn't going to make it.

His hands bashed hard against something solid.

The steps.

From somewhere he got a second wind.

Felt Mungo strike his feet.

He stumbled upwards, waited, feeling the teenager's weight on the rope.

Only seconds more. Please, only one more step!

Then one more!

He was going to have to breathe. Was going to have to. Could not go on. This was the end.

One more step.

Got to breathe.

Then, suddenly, air!

Air.

He gulped it down, reached back, found an arm and pulled, as hard as he could. An instant later Mungo's head broke the surface alongside his, gasping and spluttering, coughing up water.

Alive.

Grace looked up and saw an anxious face. Never, in all his life, had he felt more pleased to see the Detective Sergeant.

'Nice swim, chief?' Norman Potting enquired.

112

Invisible to the outside world, Dritan Nano sat uncomfortably on the bare metal floor of the van. It was travelling at speed and, with nothing to hold on to, he was thrown around every time the van braked hard or negotiated a bend. The exterior of the vehicle bore the name NEWHAVEN WET FISH SALES – WHOLESALE AND RETAIL, which had been stencilled on both sides and across the rear doors in Mr Konstandin's garage an hour ago.

Opposite him, looking increasingly nauseous from the motion, was the young medical student, Gentian Llupa. All the personal belongings the pair could carry were crammed into two rucksacks in the rear with them. The exhaust resonated as if they were in an echo chamber and the gaseous fumes, leaking in from somewhere, were making Dritan feel queasy.

Neither of them spoke much. Dritan's mind was preoccupied with Lindita. He kept looking at her photograph, his heart hurting each time. He could not wait to be back and go in search of her. He rehearsed, over and over in his mind, what he would say when he found her, to convince her he *had* changed. He *would* convince her. She *would* believe him.

Wouldn't she?

He would take her flowers. She liked red flowers. He would take her the biggest bunch of red flowers she had ever seen in her life.

He peered, anxiously, past the driver and out of the windscreen, at the falling dusk. Somewhere out there a massive manhunt would be underway for him. He had to trust Mr Konstandin. He had no option.

As the van slowed, approaching the Newhaven swing bridge across the River Ouse, Dritan said to the quiet young man, 'How are you feeling about going home?'

'England – Brighton – is my home,' Gentian Llupa replied, curtly.

'You can continue your medical studies back home.'

'Maybe.'

'It is better than the alternative,' Dritan said.

'I was a refugee from Kosovo. Now I am a refugee from England. How do you think I feel?'

'Perhaps you should feel fortunate to be alive.'

'I find it hard to believe Mr Dervishi is dead,' Llupa said.

'So do I.' Dritan attempted to sound sincere. 'While he was alive we were safe. Now, no longer. Once the police begin investigating him, they will soon be looking for both of us. We don't have an option.'

'No,' Llupa agreed, reluctantly.

'We will be safe away from here,' Dritan said.

'I hope so.'

Dritan looked out through the windscreen as they drove along a wharf past warehouses. The van pulled up.

Edi Konstandin's driver said, curtly, 'Here.' He climbed out and pulled open the rear doors for Nano and Llupa.

They stood with their bags in the failing light and a strong breeze that smelled of salt and rope and seaweed. Below them a cluster of different-sized fishing boats was moored. A vessel with its navigation lights on cruised past them, on the inky water, out towards the open sea and a distant, flashing green light. On the far side of the harbour, Dritan saw an orange-hulled boat with a white superstructure alongside the quay. Two large containers, marked EWALS CARGO CARE, sat above it.

'I really, really do not want to go,' Llupa said.

'Fine, stay. I come to visit you in prison in ten years' time. Bring you some cake. Is that what you want?'

The medical student said nothing.

'Gentian, I think that you, like me, never came here to this country with the intention of doing bad things. We got influenced, right? Bad influence, Mr Dervishi?'

'Maybe.'

'He was able to protect us. Now he is gone, we no longer have that protection. It doesn't mean we cannot return one day. But for now, we should be grateful to Mr Konstandin, I think.'

'Maybe,' he said again.

A surly-looking bearded man in a beanie, dressed in baggy oilskins and rubber boots, suddenly appeared from below the edge of the quay and hauled himself up. 'Nano and Llupa?' he asked in a coarse voice.

'Yes,' they both said.

'Come with me. I'm Nick, your skipper. I'm taking you out to Mr Konstandin's yacht that's waiting for you. Be careful, the ladder is steep.'

Nano and Llupa tugged on their heavy backpacks, then followed the man down a vertical ladder fixed to the weed-covered harbour wall and stepped onto a floating pontoon that formed part of a network.

Taking a moment to adjust to the motion, they followed him past moored yachts of varying sizes, rigging clacking in the wind, to the far end of one pontoon, where a fishing launch was berthed, stern-in. It had a wide deck at the rear and a tall superstructure, with twin satellite dishes mounted high up on the cross-beam of a radio mast. Its name was *Sweet Suzie*.

Their skipper ran, deftly, across the narrow gangway, waited at the rear of the boat and took each of their rucksacks, placing them down on the deck. Then he held out a hand to help both of them on board, all the time looking around, edgily.

Dritan jumped down onto the deck, breathing in a strong stench of rotting fish, varnish and diesel.

'If you need the heads, they're down below. But you're less likely to puke if you stay up here in the open. It's going to be choppy out there. I suggest you sit out on the deck, where you are, and focus on the horizon.' He clambered up some steps to the bridge, perched on the one chair and started the engine, which began ticking over with a loud, metallic knocking sound. He clambered back down, again looking up and around warily, then ran back along the gangway onto the pontoon. He knelt and unhooked one hawser from a bollard, tossing it onto the deck, then another. As the boat began to drift, he leaped back aboard and pulled up the gangway, then clambered up onto the bridge again.

The vessel began picking up speed, Dritan felt the breeze much stronger now. He stared at the white, thrashing wake. At the sky, seemingly teeming with seagulls. At the silhouettes of cliffs sliding by and the slanted wooden pilings of the harbour mole. And at the lights of Newhaven town beyond. As they neared the harbour mouth and the open sea, the boat began to pitch and roll increasingly. He worried he might feel sick. He had been sick the last time he went on a boat, on a fishing trip with Valbone and a friend of his, out of Brighton Marina.

Valbone.

He felt guilt.

They passed a huge auto-graveyard on the quay. A hill of metal, crushed almost beyond recognition, with a green grabber crane at the edge. Where the cliffs ended he saw the long, stone, west mole. Several blocks of flats, with many lights on. Then, on either side of the harbour mouth, a red and a green light.

He listened to the pitch of the engines as they picked up speed out of the harbour speed restrictions. Felt the motion of the boat as they ploughed on into increasing darkness. The only illumination here on the deck, faint and shadowy, was thrown down from the boat's masthead light. Soon, all he could see behind were twinkling white lights and the flashing of a lighthouse and a red aircraft warning beacon high on the top of the cliffs. All of them were fading steadily. England was fading steadily. Somewhere over to his left were the Seven Sisters and Beachy Head. That must be the lighthouse he could see.

He was hungry, trying to remember when he had last eaten anything. Wondering how long before he could get something. Perhaps there were chocolate bars or biscuits or something on board.

He shouted at the skipper on the bridge. 'Nick, do you have anything to eat?'

'Yeah, sure, I'll give you a menu.'

'Menu?'

'What do you want? Caviar? Steak and chips? Lobster Thermidor?' the skipper shouted back. 'We have a signal booster for mobile phones on board. You should have a good strong signal – why don't you phone ashore for a take-away? A curry? Thai? Kebab?'

Dritan took a moment to realize the man was joking. 'Any biscuits?'

'I'm sure when we RV with Mr Konstandin's yacht, you'll have a nice dinner waiting.'

'How long will that be?'

'Twenty minutes.'

'OK, thank you!' he shouted back against the rising wind.

Gentian Llupa, who had not uttered a word in some while, suddenly stood up, stumbled to the side of the boat and puked over it.

'You OK?' Dritan rose to his feet, but the boat rolled suddenly, sending him hurtling back down onto his hard seat and bashing his elbow painfully.

Llupa puked again.

The smell was making Dritan feel queasy, too. He shivered, wishing he had put warmer clothes on. He had a lightweight anorak in his rucksack, but it had slid some distance away from him, towards the steps down into the cabin. Looking for something to grip, he stood up, carefully holding the side of the boat, planting his feet and waiting, steadying himself. He was very definitely feeling a little giddy and sick himself now. And really shivering.

He reached his rucksack. Holding on to the top of a locker with his left hand, he knelt and unzipped the centre section of the bag with the other, looking for a pullover. Just as he did so, a familiar voice behind him startled him, making his skin crawl. It came from inside the unlit cabin.

'How's your day so far?'

113

Dritan, crouched on the heaving deck, was gripped with fear. He must be dreaming. It could not be him.

Could not. He was dead, wasn't he?

As he turned, he found himself staring straight into the muzzle of a shiny automatic. Mr Dervishi, in yellow oilskins and a heavy sweater, stood securely wedged between the two sides of the cabin entrance, holding the gun in his good hand.

'Much nicer for me to see you, Dritan, than for you to see me, I imagine, eh – and a little surprise?'

Dritan's mouth had dried up.

Dervishi kept the gun trained on him. Out of the corner of his eye he could see that for the moment, at least, Gentian Llupa was out of it, slumped over the deck rail, still retching. 'Clever trick of yours, to circle back on your Ducati and put the phone behind that wheelie bin. Next time you try a stunt like that, permit me to offer you some advice. Stop further away, OK? Your Ducati has a very distinctive rattle when it is idling – because of its dry clutch, I believe.'

In the darkness across the water, some distance beyond his boss, Dritan could make out, from his kneeling position, a tiny, static light. Just below it was an intermittent flashing one.

'I'd like to give you some more advice, Dritan – not that you will need it where you are going. Never try to mess with a family as tight as mine. Blood means everything to us. Did you really think my uncle Edi would take you seriously? That he would believe a pathetic loser, a nobody, over me, his nephew and successor?'

'It's not what your uncle said to me.'

'No? In a few minutes, I will show you something. But at this moment, let me *tell you* something. I'm the man with the gun in his hand and you're the shitbag who is about to die. When we stick weights on you and dump your body overboard, unlike me, you are not coming back. You'll be gone. No one will ever know what happened – ever know the truth. *Oh, that low-life, Dritan Nano. He vanished one night. I suspect he went home to Albania, to search for the girl who dumped him.*' He smiled. 'That's what everyone will think, Dritan. That you went home to find little Lindita. Well, you're going to have a new home now. Inside the stomachs of crabs, prawns and lobsters.'

'Go fuck yourself.'

The static light Dritan had seen was getting larger and brighter. And he was starting to make out more lights now. The apparition was shaping up like a liner. Was it a ferry? A cruise ship? Could he somehow signal to it?

He felt growing hope. As they churned steadily forward through the swell, it was clear their paths were almost going to intersect.

Would they pass close enough for him to shout out, Dritan wondered?

Dervishi turned his head, as if to see what Dritan was peering at, then looked back at him. 'My uncle's yacht, Dritan. It is a lovely boat. Only Roman Abramovich and a handful of other billionaires have bigger ones. Today he has given it to me as a gift. Gentian and I will be enjoying a luxury cruise aboard, all the way to the Port of Durrës. Each time we dine on lobster, we will raise a glass of fine wine to the ones that are feasting on you!' He grinned.

The hull of the massive craft was looming rapidly closer, the lights in the portholes getting brighter. Dritan's brain was racing in blind panic. Could he rush the man? Dive at him and grab the gun?

The boat rolled again, sharply, unbalancing him. He fell sideways, onto the wet deck, and lay for a moment, heart thudding in panic, looking back at Dervishi's laughing face, feeling utterly humiliated.

An instant later a powerful lamp shone down from the yacht onto his face, dazzling him. The beam swept backwards and forwards across their little fishing boat. Dritan could see three men in white tunics standing on the deck of the yacht. One of them hurled a rope ladder, which tumbled down, uncoiling, all the way to the water. He heard the change of pitch of the fishing boat's engine, felt the craft accelerate briefly, swinging round, coming alongside.

He waited for the right moment. For Mr Dervishi to be distracted.

But his boss kept the gun, and his gaze, steadily on him.

He saw a row of fenders lowered down the side of the yacht, seconds before the two vessels nudged against each other. At that moment he saw Nick, their skipper, leap from the bridge and grab the rope ladder. Seconds later, as he clung to it, there was a deep, sonorous roar of powerful engines, and thrashing water, the smell of exhaust fumes, and Edi Konstandin's yacht moved away.

In less than a second, a gap of several metres had opened up between the two boats. The fishing boat rocked wildly in the wake, almost unbalancing Dervishi.

To Dritan's astonishment, the yacht was powering away into the distance.

And evidently, from his expression, to his boss's astonishment, too.

'Hey!' Dervishi turned his head and shouted at the yacht, but still kept the gun trained on Dritan. 'Hey! Hey!'

The yacht was clearly not coming back.

'HEY!' Dervishi yelled, venting his lungs, his fury, his astonishment. 'HEY!' he yelled again and again, until he was spent. Although he was still pointing the gun, he no longer looked venomous. Instead he looked lost, bewildered.

'Maybe they didn't like your face?' Dritan said.

The lights of the yacht and the drone of its engines were fading away.

Dervishi used his free hand to pull a phone from his pocket. Without moving the gun, he peered at the display, then tapped the phone with his mechanical digit, and held it to his ear.

Dritan, unable to suppress a grin, waited. Waited for the right moment to make his move.

Gentian Llupa retched again.

Dritan kept his concentration on Dervishi, who still held the phone to his ear, looking increasingly bewildered and angry.

He lowered the phone, peered at the display once more, then stabbed the buttons with his thumb and raised it to his ear again.

'Seems like whoever you are calling must be out, Mr Dervishi. Are you sure you are so very important?'

Then he heard the ping of an incoming text. It came from behind his boss, somewhere inside the cabin.

Dervishi turned his head, frowning.

Seconds later, there was another ping.

Dritan shook his head in disbelief. This could not be happening.

'Phone!' Dervishi screamed, suddenly, in blind terror. 'Whose? Where is it? Throw it overboard for God's sake – where the fuck is—?'

114

Mungo was released from the Royal Sussex County Hospital shortly after 10 p.m. He had been thoroughly checked over, and the cut on his ear and the wound on his neck from the wire noose had been dressed.

As Kipp Brown drove the Volvo SUV out of the grounds, Stacey sat in the rear, in the darkness, cuddling their very distressed son.

'I'm sorry,' the teenager said. 'Are you mad at me, Dad? Mum?'

'No, my love,' she said. 'We are not angry at you. We are just happy to have you back and safe. Aren't we, darling?'

'Sure,' Kipp said, flatly. He would be having a stern conversation with Mungo later about all the trouble and the potential grief he had caused, but for now he was just relieved to have him back safely.

'I thought – you know – like – you would want to kill me.'

'Look, you've been through a horrendous thing, your mother and I love you very much, all we care about is you're safe.'

'Is Aleksander's dad angry with him?'

'I don't know – I haven't spoken to him. I think the police have been with him much of the time.'

'Will Aleksander and I go to prison?'

'No, darling, you won't!' his mother assured him.

'I've ordered you a new iPhone,' his father said. 'It should arrive tomorrow.'

'You have?' Mungo sounded brighter. 'Wow!'

Kipp drove along Eastern Road, travelling slowly behind a bus. His relief that his son was back with them and safe was clouded by one very big thing. The knowledge that he had against all the regulations taken a quarter of a million pounds from his client account, and that the money was gone – irretrievably, the police had confirmed. What the hell was he going to do?

He was already thinking about the bets he would place tomorrow. His luck had to change.

Had to.

Maybe getting Mungo back safely was the sign?

All his staff would be back at work in the morning. His Chief Operating Officer would discover what he had done and would grill him. The financial services industry was very strictly regulated. There was no way any of his team could risk jail sentences by covering for him. Somehow, he had to replace that money and fast. Very fast.

He glanced in the mirror. In the glare of the street-lighting he saw Stacey's smiling face. His son looking as if nothing had happened, now that he knew he was getting another iPhone.

Crisis over.

Crisis beginning.

The bus stopped and he slammed on the brakes, very nearly running into the back of it.

'Kipp!' Stacey reprimanded.

115

Roy Grace arrived home at 10.30 p.m. As he climbed out of his car, nearly on his knees with exhaustion, a text appeared on his job phone.

It was from Cassian Pewe.

I want you in my office at 9am without fail, Roy.

He stood, staring at it, thinking about something he had read in a management training course he had been on, some years back. *Too often in organizations, sooner or later incompetent people fail upwards.*

He was so tempted to text that to the ACC. Instead he sent a terse, one-word reply.

Fine.

It might have been nice if his boss had said a thank-you for what he had done today – even just a tiny one. But it seemed Cassian Pewe had been born with the ability to give praise missing from his DNA.

Humphrey barked as Roy walked in the pitch-darkness from the car towards the house. The security light came on. He unlocked the front door and patted the excited dog, then went through to the living room. Cleo, looking as drained as he felt, was on the sofa, a glass of white wine on the coffee table in front of her, watching the news. Her face lit up as she saw him. 'You're back! What happened? I just saw on the news that the boy – Mungo Brown – is safe.'

He kissed her. 'Yep, he is. He was an idiot and it could have had a very different outcome. How was your day?'

'About as good as a day spent doing postmortems with Frazer Theobald is ever going to get. And we start again at 8 a.m.'

'How's your back been today?'

Cleo's back had not been right since her pregnancy with Noah, made worse by the lifting injury a few months ago. The mortuary had invested a substantial sum of money with a Sussex firm, Posturite, for an ergonomic chair and workstation area to help her, as well as a specially support- ive chair for her at home.

'It's been OK, thanks, I'm seeing the chiropractor again on Tuesday. Next time we get a forty-stone whopper to lay out, I'm hiring a fork-lift truck.'

He grinned.

'How about you – how are you feeling?'

'I've a meeting with my good buddy Cassian at 9 a.m. Followed by a briefing from DS Sally Medlock on a gang of particularly nasty romance fraudsters – she needs Major Crime to help catch them.'

'I thought you might be occupied. I've got Kaitlynn here all day tomorrow from 7 a.m.'

'Thanks.'

'You look like you need a drink. There's some in the bottle in the fridge.'

'I need something stronger.' He walked over to the drinks cabinet and poured himself a large whisky. 'How are the boys?'

'I've hardly seen them. Kaitlynn said Noah's been good

as gold. I looked in on Bruno a short while ago and he's playing some war game again. Oh, by the way, before I forget, I need some dates from you for our appointment with Alan Larkin.'

'Alan Larkin?'

'The solicitor at the Family Law Partners, to see what he suggests we do about finalizing all the paperwork with Bruno's move here from Munich.'

Sandy's parents, always difficult people at the best of times, were being a nightmare recently, and he was glad to have Larkin on board as a collaboratively trained lawyer to help with their differences over both access to Bruno and the provisions for him made in Sandy's will.

'Great, thanks.' He popped a couple of ice cubes in his whisky and joined her on the sofa.

'So?' she quizzed. 'I haven't seen you since yesterday. What's been happening, Mr Mystery?'

'Well – it's been a good day and a bad day.'

'You want to start with the good or the bad?'

He filled her in, with as much detail as he could. When he had finished he asked, 'Tell me, the body parts that you've recovered from the crusher site. Did the head turn up yet?'

She frowned. 'Yes, it was brought in earlier this evening – but oddly missing an ear.'

'Which one – left or right?'

'The right.'

He smiled. 'That makes sense.'

'I'm glad it does to someone.'

He stood up. 'Maybe I should look in on Bruno?'

'Sure, but don't be long, I have plans.'

'Plans?'

She gave him a very sexy smile. 'If my darling super-hero, swimmer extraordinaire, is not tooooo tired, that is.'

He grinned back, hurried upstairs and stood outside Bruno's door, listening. He heard a staccato burst of gunfire, followed by another, then the sound of his son cursing loudly in German. He tapped on the door and entered.

Bruno, dressed in a hoodie, jeans and white socks, was lying on his bed, holding his Xbox controller, concentrating hard as figures darted across the television screen. As each appeared, he stabbed buttons on the controller, and the character was blown away. Then the screen froze and a score appeared.

'*Jah!* You bastard, I got you! *Du bist der verlierer!*' Without turning his head, Bruno said, 'I won!'

'See, Bruno, the lessons in shooting I gave you have paid off!'

'Maybe.'

'So, how've you been? Mr Allen brought you home from the Amex OK, yesterday?'

'*Jah.* He has an Audi A6.'

'How did you get on with his boys – he has two sons, right?'

'Boys? They were babies. Like, I don't know, nine or seven or something. Logan and something like *Jensen*.' He kept his focus on the screen, tapping his Xbox, starting another game. 'So, what happened to the boy who was kidnapped?'

'He's safe, back with his family.'

'The kidnappers did not get any ransom?'

'They got some – part of it.'

Bruno nodded, approvingly. 'That is good.'

'Good? Good that they only got part of it?'

'No, Dad, good that they got some money. Won't they be disappointed they did not get the rest?'

Grace frowned. 'Why do you say that, Bruno?'

Two names appeared on the screen, *Erik* and *Bruno*.

'Why do you say that, Bruno?' he repeated.

'I have to concentrate now.'

Grace looked at the screen. It looked like a medieval fort, from the point-of-view of the camera. A man dashed across a gap at the end. Bruno hit a button and yelled out, in frustration, 'No! I missed!'

Grace pulled the control box from his son's hands, in fury. 'Listen to me. I just asked you a question and I expect you to answer. Right?'

'You are going to let Erik win this game?' Bruno retorted.

'No, Bruno, let's get something straight. It is *you* who is going to let Erik win by not answering me. I'm asking you a question. Why did you say it's good that the kidnappers got some money – and would be disappointed by not getting the rest?'

His son gave him a sullen look. 'They took a risk, don't they deserve some reward, surely?'

Some minutes later, Grace went back downstairs. It was the second time this weekend that Bruno had made a very odd remark. Just what kind of upbringing had Sandy given him? One with a very strange, skewed moral compass, it seemed. Or maybe it was a rebellious phase he was going through, still unhappy about being displaced, taken away from what he had always considered home?

But he was too tired to think about it any more.

116

The first floor of the handsome Queen Anne mansion was where the top brass had their offices. Pewe's assistant, who had escorted Roy Grace up here, knocked on the door and opened it. From the tone of the ACC's text last night, Roy Grace figured the man wasn't about to greet him with a bunch of flowers.

He was right.

'Roy,' he said, 'so good of you to be able to spare your time to see me. Do come in, take a seat, have a quick read of this.'

As Grace perched on one of a pair of L-shaped sofas around a mahogany coffee table, the ACC literally threw down a copy of the morning's *Argus* newspaper. The headline was stark and clear.

BRIGHTON NEW MURDER CAPITAL OF EUROPE?

'I have to step out for five minutes to see someone in Corporate Comms. Have a good read through, see what a great job you're doing as Head of Major Crime.'

Pewe walked out, slamming the door behind him.

Since a few months ago, due to further budget cuts reducing the number of police buildings, the senior officers at Sussex Police HQ were required to make do with much smaller work spaces. They had to accommodate, as well as

441

other police officers, the recent arrival of the East Sussex Fire Brigade command team. The Chief Constable had led the way by having her once-imposing office reduced in size by over a half. Yet, somehow, Pewe had so far retained his own large office in its entirety. Word around the force was that his ego wouldn't fit into anything smaller.

Grace speed-read the alarmist front page of the newspaper, and coverage of the grim events of the weekend on subsequent pages, with photographs of some of the victims as well as of police cars, crime scene tape and CSIs in their oversuits. There was speculation regarding the three dead men found at Boden Court, that this was an internal Albanian settlement of scores.

He was relieved by one thing, that in all the seeming mayhem, the coverage of the bomb hoax at the Amex amounted to only a few column inches towards the centre of the paper. After a quieter weekend he'd have probably been the front-page splash, with an embarrassing photograph of him running with the camera.

He looked up the paper's online pages on his phone to see if there were any updates reported.

Among the new headlines there was one that caught his eye.

NEWHAVEN LIFEBOAT INVESTIGATING EXPLOSION REPORT

He read the short article. The crew of a private sailing yacht crossing the Channel had radioed the Coastguard shortly after 9.30 p.m. yesterday, reporting a large explosion a few nautical miles south of Newhaven. The paper reported that a search of the area had been carried out by the lifeboat and the Coastguard helicopter into the night, after debris had been sighted in the approximate area. Early this morning, the Newhaven lifeboat had recovered a life-belt stencilled with the name *Sweet Suzie.* It belonged to a deep-sea fishing boat permanently berthed at Newhaven Harbour that had last been seen heading out to sea earlier the previous evening.

Was there any connection, he wondered, noting down the boat's name. He would get a check on the owner. As he did so, Pewe came back into the office, closing the door firmly, and stood over him.

Grace looked up. 'A quick update on the kidnap, sir. The original kidnap turned out to be a plan by two teenage boys – the victim himself and his friend, the son of Jorgji Dervishi, a major Albanian crime boss in Brighton – to extort money from the victim's father. Our enquiries revealed that the plans changed, and other Albanian gang members hijacked the original kidnap plot, because they became greedy. Finally, it appears, Dervishi himself saw an opportunity to get in on the act.'

Pewe stared at him, glassily. Grace went on. 'Although we believe that Dervishi was also behind the bomb threat and extortion attempt at the Amex, we are confident that these were not linked, but coincidental.'

Pewe continued staring at him, his face tense. 'Roy, taking a helicopter view of this past weekend, we seem to have moved the Major Crime needle somewhat. I'd say we've been pretty much thrown under the bus. What is your elevator pitch on events?'

Grace stared back at the ACC, trying to interpret his latest corporate-speak.

'It's been a bit shit, sir.'

'A *bit shit*? Really? Perhaps we need to dive deeper on this issue? Open the kimono?'

'You've lost me, sir,' Grace said, politely.

'I've lost you? I'm so sorry. Let me jog your mind by winding the clock back over the last forty-eight hours. We've had a bomb threat at the Amex. A teenage boy kidnapped. A female drugs mule dead at Gatwick Airport. Body parts showing evidence of torture found at a crusher site at Shoreham Harbour. The crusher operator dead under suspicious circumstances in the Sussex County. Three people shot dead in a flat in Hove, yesterday. An explosion on an industrial estate outside Lewes, at what might have been a bomb factory, with two separate sets of body parts identified so far. Not bad for one weekend, wouldn't you say?'

'We recovered the kidnap victim, which was my case and my priority, sir.'

'Really? Jolly well done. From 40,000 feet that looks good. But once you get into the weeds, it all looks a little different. Would you like to explain everything else to me? Sussex has an average of twelve murders a year. In just this past weekend we have had eight – and counting.'

Grace, feeling in need of a strong coffee, was about to respond when the Chief Constable, Lesley Manning, entered.

'Roy!' she said. 'I heard you were in. I just want to congratulate you on your bravery this weekend.'

He jumped to his feet. 'Thank you, ma'am!'

'Excuse me, ma'am,' Pewe interrupted. 'Detective Superintendent Grace broke every rule in the book yesterday. He behaved in a reckless manner over a bomb threat at the Amex. And he subsequently ignored all Health and Safety guidelines in the way he recovered a kidnap victim.'

She looked at her ACC with a puzzled expression. 'Is that correct?'

'Yes. I want to suspend him from all duties, pending a full investigation of both events.'

'ACC Pewe,' she said in a very formal voice, 'as I understand, the bomb – a fake as we now know – had a timer activated on it. At the time Detective Superintendent Grace picked it up and ran with it, not knowing whether it was real or not, he made a calculated decision, at great personal risk to himself. Is this not upholding one of the sacrosanct traditions of the police? To serve and protect?'

Pewe looked like he was chewing a wasp.

She went on. 'I have been told that Roy was correct when he recognized the device had a timer mechanism which informed his decision. Roy not only saved a potentially highly-damaging situation at the Amex, which would have had a serious impact on the future of the stadium and the economy of our city, he went on to risk his life saving a teenage boy. I am going to put forward a recommendation for Roy, with my strongest possible endorsement, for a Queen's Gallantry medal. I very sincerely trust you will support this?'

'Yes, well, of course, when you put it like that, ma'am,' Pewe simpered. 'I completely concur. Of course, I'll support it fully.'

'That's very generous of you, ma'am,' Grace said, then turned to the ACC. 'And of you, sir. Thank you both, thank you very much. I'm honoured.'

'We are honoured to have you on our force, Roy,' Lesley said. 'Wouldn't you agree, Cassian?'

The ACC nodded, his face twitching.

It looked to Roy Grace like the wasp was putting up a pretty good fight. And winning.

117

Monday 14 August

Kipp Brown sat at his office desk, his mind in turmoil. It was just past 10.40 a.m. He stared at the photographs of his family. And especially at Mungo.

God, he loved this kid so much. And yet he was causing him so much grief.

Two hundred and fifty thousand pounds' worth of grief, to be precise.

Bob Carter, his Chief Operating Officer, had already sent him an email querying the transaction from the client account, checking to see if Kipp was aware of it, and that they weren't victims of an online fraud over the weekend.

He was trying to think of what to reply, wary that emails were dangerous because of the trail they left that could never be erased. Sometime very soon he would have to go along to Carter's office and give him an explanation.

But what?

What could he spin him that would extricate him from the very deep shit he was in?

There was no way he would even try to persuade Carter to help him cover up this loss. That could lead to a prison sentence for Carter and the end of his career. Kipp was going to have to take the blame, and the consequences, himself. The price he had paid to try to save his son's life.

If it came to a prosecution, he could only hope for sympathy from the judge. But his own career would be finished.

Shit.

His mobile phone rang.

'Kipp Brown,' he answered, trying to sound brighter than he felt.

'Kipp, it's Edi.'

Edi Konstandin, his biggest client. They spoke around this time most mornings, with the Albanian wanting updates on the overnight stock market movements, or on Mondays, those influenced by any weekend events.

'Hi, Edi, how are you?'

'More to the point, how are you? You have your son, Mungo, back safely?'

'I do.'

There was a brief silence before Konstandin spoke again. 'I owe you an apology, Kipp.'

'An apology?'

'I need you to believe me, please, Kipp. I had no knowledge of your son's kidnap, which was done by my crazy, reckless nephew, Jorgji Dervishi. Please believe me.'

'Of course I believe you, Edi. You are a trusted friend.'

'I think I have some nice news for you. Jorgji has gone away and will not be a problem ever again. But before he went, I made him pay the quarter of a million pounds he extorted from you, to me. I've arranged for it to be transferred to you this morning. My bank tells me it will arrive in your account before midday.'

Kipp could scarcely believe his ears. 'That's amazing, Edi. I – I don't know what to say.'

'You don't need to say anything, Kipp. My mission in my declining years is to show that my countrymen – those over whom I have influence, at any rate – are decent people. I won't tolerate anyone stepping out of line. Jorgji crossed that line. Now he has made restitution. I hope we are square?'

'We are square!' Kipp said, trying to play down the elation he felt. 'Thank you. I don't know how I can ever really thank you properly.'

'I'll tell you how,' the old man said. 'By just keeping doing what you are doing. Keep making me money, OK? Deal?'

Kipp grinned. 'Deal,' he said.

118

Moments after Kipp ended the call with Edi Konstandin, a text came in from his horse-racing tipster.

> **Good morning Mr Brown, we have two bets today. The first horse is MUNGO and take the 4/1 with Betfred. Also back KAYLEIGH'S MOTHER and take the 5/1 with Paddy. Both horses should be backed this morning taking the early price and both are WIN bets. Good luck – TONY FORBES.**

He stared at the text in disbelief. A horse called *Mungo*. A horse called *Kayleigh's Mother*.

He rang Forbes.

'Tony, is this some kind of a joke?'

'Joke, Kipp, what do you mean?'

'These horses are real?'

'Absolutely. Both horses are working really well at home and they are strongly fancied. I would be very keen on both of them today.'

Thanking the tipster, he ended the call. Unreal. It had to be a racing cert. His luck, finally, was on the turn. He had a guardian angel!

He dialled his private bookmaker who placed all his bigger bets for him. 'Justin, there's two horses today and I want one hundred thousand on each of them.'

'Are you sure? Two hundred grand, Kipp?'

'Yes, I'm sure. Can you take it?'

'That's some way above your normal range – I'd have to have collateral – and I'd need to lay some off.'

'I can give you collateral.'

'How much?'

'The full amount if you need it. I should be able to get it to you by around 1 p.m.'

'OK.'

Ending the call, Kipp Brown sat very still. Those two horses had to be a sign, didn't they?

He emailed his COO back.

> Bob, the money will be back in our account later today with massive interest. Used it for an investment opportunity too good to turn down.

Then he sat, very still, deep in thought. Had he just been dug out of one hole only to fall into another?

Shouldn't he just count his blessings?

Every half-hour throughout the rest of the morning he checked his account. But no money came in. At 12.30 he called Edi Konstandin who apologized profusely, but his computer system was down and he was unable to make any transactions. His geek was on it.

Konstandin's geek was still on it, two and a half hours later.

Kipp was shaking with frustration. His bookie was unable to place the bets without a major portion of the cash being deposited.

It wasn't until close to 5 p.m. that the money finally hit his account.

Despondently, he checked the racing results online. In the 3 p.m. at Brighton, Mungo had come under starters orders, but then refused to leave the gate. The moment a horse came under starters orders, the bet on it was valid. He would have lost the entire amount. In the 4.15 at Doncaster, Kayleigh's Mother had been three lengths clear when a nutter had sprinted, naked, across its path, freaking out the horse, which threw its jockey.

Relief surged through him. Maybe, he thought, some days you should count your blessings – however few and far between they were.

GLOSSARY

ANPR – Automatic Number Plate Recognition. Roadside or mobile cameras that automatically capture the registration number of all cars that pass. It can be used to historically track which cars went past a certain camera, and can also trigger alerts for cars which are stolen, have no insurance or have an alert attached to them.

CAD – Computer Aided Dispatch. The system where all calls from the public are logged and, if they require police attendance, the live time record of who is attending, how it is developing and what the outcome is.

CID – Criminal Investigation Department. Usually refers to the divisional detectives rather than the specialist squads.

CIM – Critical Incident Manager. A chief inspector who has responsibility for the response and management of all critical incidents within the force area during their tour of duty.

CSI – Was SOCO. Crime Scene Investigators (Scenes of Crime Officers). They are the people who attend crime scenes to search for fingerprints, DNA samples, etc.

EOD – Explosives Ordinance Disposal. Specialist Military bomb disposal teams.

FLUM – Flash Unsolicited Message. A direct short message sent between computer screens, mainly in the control room, to alert other controllers or supervisors to either a significant incident or an important update on an ongoing incident. It flashes up, alerting the recipient to its content immediately.

HOLMES – Home Office Large Major Enquiry System. The national computer database used on all murders. It provides a repository of all messages, actions, decisions and statements, allowing the analysis of intelligence and the tracking and auditing of the whole enquiry. Can enable enquiries to be linked across force areas where necessary.

HTCU – High Tech Crime Unit. Now renamed Digital Forensics. The body which examines and investigates computers and other digital advisors. Part of SCC.

IFA – Independent Financial Advisor.

IMEI code – A fifteen-digit number used by a mobile network to identify valid devices and therefore can be used for stopping a stolen phone from accessing that network or to trace phones used with any SIM card.

LST – Local Support Team. The standing unit of officers who provide public order, search and low-level surveillance tactics on a division.

Match Commander – The senior officer at the football stadium who has operational command of the police working within and in the vicinity of the stadium.

MO – Modus Operandi (method of operation). The manner by which the offender has committed the offence. Often this can reveal unique features which allow crimes to be linked or suspects to be identified.

NaCTSO – National Counter Terrorism Security Office. A national police unit that leads on the fight against terrorism.

Glossary

NASA – National Aeronautics and Space Administration. The US Space Agency.

NPAS 15 – The call sign for the helicopter that provides air support to Sussex Police.

NPT – Neighbourhood Policing Team. A team of officers and Police Community Support Officers (PCSOs) who are dedicated to a particular geographical area, primarily to reduce crime and improve people's feelings of safety.

OSCAR-1 – The call sign of the Force Control Duty Inspector, who has oversight and command of all critical incidents in the initial stages.

PM – Postmortem.

QR Code – A form of barcode which, when scanned, diverts the reading device being used to a website.

RPU – Roads Policing Unit. The name for the Traffic Division.

RTC – Road Traffic Collision (commonly known as an 'accident' by the public, but this term is not used as it implies no one is at fault when usually someone is).

RV Point – Rendezvous Point. The designated location where emergency services meet prior to deploying to the scene of a crime or major incident. Used when it would be too dangerous or unwieldy for everyone to arrive at the scene at the same time in an uncoordinated way.

SECAMB – South East Coast Ambulance Service.

Section 17 PACE Powers – A power of entry under the Police and Criminal Evidence Act 1984 which allows officers to enter premises without a warrant to make an arrest, to save life or limb, or to prevent serious damage to property.

SIO – Senior Investigating Officer. Usually a Detective Chief Inspector who is in overall charge of the investigation of a major crime such as murder, kidnap or rape.

SLANG AND PHRASES

All-ports alert – A nationwide alert for all air and seaports to be on the lookout for a particular person, vehicle, etc.

Bosher – The heavy metal hand-held ram used to force open doors and allow officers to enter a locked premises or room swiftly and with the advantage of surprise.

Burner phone – Slang for a pay-as-you-go mobile phone, which is used once then disposed of to avoid the user being traced.

Golden hour – The first hour after a crime has been committed or reported, when the best chances of seizing evidence and/or identifying witnesses exist.

HOT Principle – An acronym to assist in assessing whether a suspect package is likely to be an explosive device:

> **Hidden**: Is it obviously hidden? Has someone deliberately tried to conceal it?
>
> **Obvious**: Is it obviously out of place and out of context for its environment? Are there any wires, switches, batteries or components visible?
>
> **Typical**: Is it typical of an item usually seen in the environment?

Q word/Q day – Short for 'quiet'. Emergency services personnel never say the word 'quiet', as it invariably is a bad omen, causing chaos to reign!

CHART OF POLICE RANKS

Police ranks are consistent across all disciplines and the addition of prefixes such as 'detective' (e.g. detective constable) does not affect seniority relative to others of the same rank (e.g. police constable).

Police Constable   Police Sergeant   Inspector   Chief Inspector

Superintendent   Chief Superintendent   Assistant Chief Constable   Deputy Chief Constable   Chief Constable

ACKNOWLEDGEMENTS

As ever I owe an enormous debt to so many people who have generously helped me with the authenticity of what I have written, by checking facts and often making brilliant suggestions which have enhanced this story in so many ways.

My first thanks are to many officers and support staff of Surrey and Sussex Police, the Metropolitan Police and the City of London Police: Sussex Police and Crime Commissioner Katy Bourne; Chief Constable Giles York QPM; Assistant Chief Constable, BTP, Robin Smith; Detective Chief Superintendent Nick Sloan; Detective Chief Superintendent Jason Tingley; Chief Superintendent Lisa Bell; Detective Superintendent Jason Taylor; Detective Chief Inspector Mike Ashcroft; Chief Inspector Steve Boniface; DCI Stuart Hale; DI Richard Haycock; DI Bill Warner; Inspector James Biggs; Inspector Jason Cummings; Inspector Chris Smith; DS Phil Taylor; DS Grant Webberley; PC Jon Bennion-Jones; PC Darren Balkham; PC Pip Edwards; PC Jonathan Jackson; PC Richard Trundle; Dog Handler PC Sian Weston-Smith.

One police officer I need to single out for the introductions she made and the help she gave me in understanding the world of the Albanian communities in the UK, is PC Nikki Denero.

Maria O'Brien, James Stather, Chris Gee, James Gartrell from Forensic Services. Annabel Galsworthy, Comms. Aiden Gilbert, Joseph Langford, Graham Lewendon, Shaun Robbins and Daniel Salter from the Digital Forensics Unit.

Also to the following retired officers: Chief Superintendent

Acknowledgements

Graham Bartlett, Detective Chief Inspector Trevor Bowles, Inspector Keith Ellis, Inspector Andy Kille, PC David Rowlands.

Katie Perkin, Jill Pedersen, Oliver Lacey and Suzanne Heard from Sussex Police Corporate Communications.

Further key research help came from: Gary Baines of Shoreham Fort; Paul Barber; Ben Bennett; William Blanch; Alan Bowles; Ashley Carr; Chris Cohen; Chris Diplock; Dr Peter Dean; Sean Didcott; Ross Duncton; Enver Godanc; Gillian Griffin; Claire Horne; Haydn Kelly; Rachel Kenchington; Iain and Georgie Maclean; Adrian Morris; Miriman and Svetlana Nela; Phil Nunn; Nick and Emma Oliver-Taylor; Ray Packham; Mike Sansom of BrightFire Pyrotechnics; Denis Sazonov; Richard Skerritt; Michelle Websdale; Sam Windridge; CEO Brighton Racecourse; Amy Woodard.

There are numerous people in the background working on the editing, sales and marketing of the book, each playing a vital role: My wonderful agents, Isobel Dixon, Julian Friedmann, Conrad Williams, James Pusey, Emanuela Anechoum, Hattie Grunewald and all the team at Blake Friedmann. My incredibly patient and supportive editor Wayne Brookes, my wonderful mentor and mate, Geoff Duffield, and all at Pan Macmillan, in particular: Sarah Arratoon, Jonathan Atkins, Anna Bond, Jeremy Trevathan, Stuart Dwyer, Claire Evans, Lucy Hines, Daniel Jenkins, Neil Lang, Sara Lloyd, Natalie McCourt, Alex Saunders, Jade Tolley, and Charlotte Williams. My editor Susan Opie. My publicists, Tony Mulliken, Sophie Ransom and Alice Geary. Brooke O'Donnell and all at Trafalgar House in the USA. Elena Stokes, Tanya Farrell and Taylan Salvati of Wunderkind and all the rest of Team James Stateside.

I'm fortunate to have an incredible support team who help me to hone the manuscript into shape long before it reaches my agent and publishers. My brilliant PA, Linda Buckley, who manages calmly to keep my head above water!

Acknowledgements

My book-keeper Sarah Middle, Danielle Brown who helps us around the clock on social media, and my crucial first-look editorial team who give me so much guidance: Anna Hancock, Susan Ansell, Helen Shenston, Martin and Jane Diplock.

Much of the shape of the book and the fact that I delivered it almost on time (!) is due to the constant vigilance, hard slog and input of my taskmaster, former Detective Chief Superintendent David Gaylor, my inspiration for Roy Grace. I'm immensely grateful to him in so many ways.

My penultimate and biggest thanks are to my wife, Lara. For her endless patience, wisdom, energy and enthusiasm – and always keeping my spirits up.

And my final thanks to our adorable dogs, Oscar, Spooky and Wally. Walking them, in any weather, always clears my mind and puts a smile on my face.

A huge thank-you to my readers! Your emails, Tweets, Facebook, Instagram, blog posts and YouTube comments give me such constant joy. Keep them coming, I love to hear from you!

Peter James

contact@peterjames.com
www.peterjames.com
www.peterjames.com/youtube
www.facebook.com/peterjames.roygrace
www.twitter.com/peterjamesuk
www.instagram.com/peterjamesuk
www.instagram.com/peterjamesukpets

AVAILABLE NOW

ABSOLUTE PROOF

KILL TO GET IT. DIE TO KEEP IT.

A breathless race against time to solve the greatest mystery of all.

Turn the page to read an extract from this international thriller by Peter James . . .

8 Years Later
Wednesday, 1 February 2017

The old man was trembling as he made his way slowly up the steep Somerset hillside in the darkness, weighed down by the burden he carried in his heart. The weight of all human history. The eternal struggle of good versus evil. The love and wrath of God. The mockery of Satan.

Unaware of the night-vision binoculars trained on him, he trod carefully on the slippery grass, guided only by the weak beam of his small torch, the GPS coordinates on his phone and the sense of mission in his heart.

Destiny.

His feet were wet inside his sodden brogues and a bitter wind blew through his thin overcoat; a chill clung to his back like a compress of cold leaves. He carried a heavy spade and a metal detector.

It was 3 a.m.

A skein of clouds raced across the sky above him, pierced for fleeting moments by shafts of stone-cold light from the full moon. Whenever that happened he could see the dark shadow of the ruined tower on the hilltop, a short distance to his right. There was a preternatural feeling to the night. The clouds felt like the travelling matte in one of those old Hollywood films. Like a scene he remembered where Cary Grant and Grace Kelly were driving along in a convertible, apparently at high speed, with the scenery passing behind them, but their hair remained immaculately in place.

But tonight, old movies should be a long way from his mind, and his thoughts on just one thing.

Destiny.

Tonight, here, was the start of the journey. He was frail and he did not know how much time he had left on this earth. He had been waiting for the Call for so long he had begun to doubt it would ever come. And when it finally did, it was in His mysterious way.

There was someone whom he had been told could help him, but he was not able to find this person, not yet. And because time was running out on him, he had decided to go it alone.

The air was alive, electric; he could feel the prickle on his skin, like goosebumps. The wind was full of whispers he could not decipher.

He smelled the sweet grass. Somewhere close by he heard a terrible squealing. A fox taking a rabbit, he thought. The squealing became increasingly pitiful and finally stopped.

He checked the constantly changing coordinates on his phone against the ones on the slip of paper he had in his breast pocket. Closer. Closer.

Nearly there.

He stopped, drawing breath, perspiring heavily despite the bitter cold. It had been a tiring two-and-a-half-hour drive to get here, followed by a long walk round the perimeter, in search of a place where he could scale the fence. He'd forgotten his gloves, but it was too long a walk back to the car to fetch them.

Pulling out the scrap of paper, he studied the coordinates in his meticulous handwriting once more.

51°08'40"N 2°41'55"W

He was close.

He felt a burst of energy. Took several paces to the left, then a few more, further up the hill.

Closer!

An instant later, the digits on his phone's compass app matched.

51°08'40"N 2°41'55"W

He was here. On the spot. And at that moment the clouds above him moved away from the moon and a beam of light shone down from above. Someone up there was showing him. This was the sign.

His destiny!

Feverishly he began to dig, gripping the spade as hard as he could with his frozen, arthritic fingers. He dashed it into the ground, stood on it and pushed it down, then levered up the first clump of earth. Several worms squirmed. He moved the spade back a short distance, and dashed it in again.

As he did so, a bright light from out of nowhere danced all around him. Not the moon, now, but the beam of a powerful torch. Two torches. And he heard a voice. An angry male voice.

'Hey! You!'

He turned round. For a moment he was dazzled by the beams directly in his face. Blinking hard, he directed his own more feeble torch beam back. The light fell first on a young, uniformed police officer and next on the middle-aged man, in a parka, standing beside him.

'It's here,' he replied. 'Right where I'm digging. It's right under my feet!'

'What do you think you're doing? Are you crazy?'

'I'm saving the world.'

'You're defacing private property.'

'Listen, please listen.'

'No, you listen,' the man in the parka said. 'You are trespassing. Who the hell gave you permission to start digging up sacred ground in the middle of the night?'

The old man replied, simply, 'God.'

Thursday, 16 February 2017

Ross Hunter nearly didn't answer the call. The display on his landline read NUMBER WITHHELD. Probably yet another of the automated nuisance calls that were one of the banes of everyone's lives these days. He was on a deadline with his editor, Natalie McCourt, at the *Sunday Times* Insight section, who needed his piece exposing six Premier League footballers involved in a film production tax evasion scheme by 4 p.m. – exactly twenty minutes away.

Montmorency, their dark grey labradoodle, lying on the floor close to his desk, seemed focused on two deadlines at this moment. Would he finish that bone, which he was crunching noisily and irritatingly, before his master took him out for a walk? And would they go out for a walk before it was dark?

In the days that followed Ross often wondered just what it was exactly that *had* made him pick up the phone. But he figured even if he hadn't, the caller would have almost certainly rung back. And then rung back again. Ross was pretty high profile these days, and knew better than to ever dismiss any call he received. His first big break, twelve years ago as a fledgling reporter on Brighton's *Argus* newspaper, was just such a call out of the blue. That had led him to the story of a sex scandal, which had ended with a local MP having to resign his seat.

'Ross Hunter,' he said, staring down at the darkening Patcham street from his den in the former loft of the house he and his wife, Imogen, had moved into, trying to start over, soon after that terrible afternoon when he had arrived home from Afghanistan to find her in bed with another man.

She'd begged forgiveness. Told him she'd been dreading being informed by the Foreign Office that he was missing presumed killed, and that she'd sought comfort with an old friend. Desperate to regain normality back then, he'd accepted her explanation and forgiven her. Subsequently he discovered she had not told him the truth and the affair had been going on for far longer. Their relationship had never been quite the same again. It was like gluing together the pieces of a broken glass. It was intact but the joins were ever present. They'd tried to paper over the cracks by moving home. Now she was pregnant, but he still felt doubt.

He just could not trust her. Not totally. There were days when she arrived home late from work with excuses he wasn't sure he believed. Occasions when she awkwardly ended a phone call when he walked into the kitchen. Always then the memory returned. Her naked body on top of the bearded man in their bed.

A delivery van, its lights on, was driving slowly past. He saw one of his neighbours arriving home from the school run in her people carrier. She opened the rear door and from the glow of the vehicle's interior light he could see her helping her small son, an irritating brat who always seemed to be screaming, out of his seat belt.

The voice at the other end of the line was that of a cultured-sounding elderly man. 'Is that Mr Hunter, the journalist?'

'Speaking – who is this?'

'Thank goodness I've got the right person. It's taken me a while to get your phone number – I've phoned every R. Hunter in the phone book in Sussex.'

'You could have contacted me on social media – I'm fairly active on Twitter and Facebook – or you could have just emailed me – my email is on all my bylines.' Ross sipped some tea from the mug on his desk.

'This is not a social media or an email matter, Mr Hunter. Email is not secure, I could not take that risk. I've read many of your pieces. I was very impressed with the article you wrote some years ago for the *Sunday Times* about the government failing our troops in Afghanistan.'

'You read that?'

'My son died in Helmand Province. Killed by *friendly fire.* Or *blue on blue* as they call it, I believe. If he'd been issued with a battlefield beacon, he might still be with us today.'

'I'm sorry.'

'It's not the reason I'm calling, but thank you. My late wife and I tried not to be bitter about it.'

Ross was starting to think this was going to be a waste of some of the very few precious minutes that he had left to finish and then proofread his article.

'I'd just like to assure you I'm not a nutcase, Mr Hunter.'

'Good to hear that,' he replied.

'My name is Dr Harry F. Cook. I'm a former RAF officer and a retired history of art professor at Birmingham University and I know this is going to sound strange, but I've recently been given absolute proof of God's existence – and I've been advised there is a writer, a respected journalist called Ross Hunter, who could help me to get taken seriously.'

'What?'

'I know it must sound strange. I appreciate that.'

'Well, yes, actually, it does.' Ross thought for an instant. 'Exactly which God is it you have proof of?'

'There is only one God, Mr Hunter. There are many prophets and many different faiths, but there is only one *God*. He is God of all faiths.'

'May I ask who told you I'm the person who could help you?' Ross asked, watching his neighbour shepherd her son up to the front door of their bungalow.

'God Himself,' Harry F. Cook replied, simply. 'Could you indulge me for a couple of minutes?'

Ross glanced at his watch, at the precious minutes ticking away. 'I'm afraid you'll have to make it very quick, Dr Cook, I'm up against a deadline.'

'Well, I'll be as brief as I can – or would you prefer me to call you back in a while?'

'No, go ahead.' He picked up a pen and scribbled down the name, *Dr Harry F. Cook*, and *Birmingham University – Art History – retd*. Then he took another sip of his tea, which was turning increasingly tepid.

'Well, the thing is, Mr Hunter, I need to come and see you, and explain everything more fully. I can assure you that I won't be wasting your time. I don't doubt you get oddballs contacting you every day. Would you meet me for just half an hour? I'll travel to anywhere that's convenient for you. And I have something I really believe you might want to hear. I have a message for you.'

'You do? From whom?'

'From your brother, Ricky.'

For some moments Ross sat, numb. Wondering if he had heard right.

'You have a message from Ricky?'

'I do.'

'Can you tell me it?'

'Not over the telephone, Mr Hunter.'

Ross felt a cold wind blow through the room. The lights out in the darkening street seemed to flicker, like a thousand candles guttering in a blast of wind. He shivered, and scribbled down some more with a shaking hand. 'You really have a message from my brother?'

He saw the blue flashing lights of an emergency vehicle heading up the street, and heard the wail of a siren. For a moment, he wondered if he was dreaming this conversation. 'Who exactly are you, Dr Cook?'

An ambulance raced past.

'Please believe me, I'm just an ordinary man, doing what I've been told. Please, Mr Hunter, I urge you, can we meet?'

Ross had dealt with and dismissed many nutters over the years, claiming to have world-shattering stories for him. But something in this man's voice sounded sincere – and intrigued him.

'I'll give you half an hour, OK? I can meet for a cup of tea. If you're able to convince me when we meet that we need longer than that, we'll take it from there. All right?'

'That's very fair. Very good of you. As I said, I'm happy to travel to meet you anywhere convenient to you. If you just let me know when and where?'

Monday, 20 February 2017

At 3.50 p.m., ten minutes before Dr Harry F. Cook was due to arrive, Ross was staring out of the window of his second-floor den, thinking about a news story he was writing for the *Sunday Times*, which was going to make a certain National Health Trust executive squirm. He watched an immaculate white Nissan Micra pull up against the kerb in front of his house.

A text pinged.

Looking down at the phone, he saw it was from Imogen.

> **Will be home late, around 7pm. Want me to pick up**
> **a takeaway? Fancy Thai? Beware of your nutter**
> **– don't want to find you in little bits in the fridge!**
> **Love you. XXXX**

He texted back.

> **Sure! Chicken satay & a green curry with fish, pls.**
> **Am armed to the teeth! Love you. XXX**

He returned to his work and tried to focus, but he could not. Late home again, he fretted. Why? What was she up to? He stared, distractedly, out of the window at the man in the little Nissan.

Moments later as he walked downstairs into the hall,

the doorbell rang. On the nanosecond of 4 p.m. He opened the front door.

A tall, elderly man stood there, holding an enormous attaché case. He was in his mid seventies, Ross guessed, neatly dressed in a pin-striped suit with matching tie and pocket handkerchief.

'Mr Hunter?' He held out a hand.

'Dr Cook? You found us OK?'

'Oh I did, indeed, thanks to the wonders of satellite navigation.'

As they shook hands, Cook leaned forward and said, staring at him imploringly, with sad, rheumy eyes, 'It is very good of you to see me, Mr Hunter. You do understand that you and I have to save the world?'

Ross gave him a hesitant smile. 'Well, I'll do my best!' Seeing the man so smartly dressed, he wished for a moment he had on more than an old pair of jeans, a baggy jumper and broken-down slippers.

'Mr Hunter, I can't tell you how much this means to me – and to the human race.'

Ross smiled. 'Yep, well, let's see. Come in, can I get you something to drink?'

'A cup of tea would be most welcome.'

A loud barking came from the kitchen.

'Monty, quiet!' Ross called out.

The labradoodle ambled across the black-and-white chequered tiles of the hallway, his tail wagging clumsily.

Ross patted the dog, then turned to the man, who was peering apprehensively at the curly creature. 'He's a total softie – the loveliest nature. Are you OK with dogs?'

'Oh yes, absolutely fine. *Monty*, did you say?'

'Yes. Short for Montmorency.'

'I seem to remember Montmorency was the name of the dog in that wonderful book, *Three Men in a Boat.*'

'That's where we got it from – well, it was my wife's idea, she always loved that book.'

It was one of the books that he and Imogen had taken to Italy on honeymoon, and both read – he for the first time and Imogen for at least the third – and laughed at a lot, particularly at the first chapter, when the character was bemoaning feeling too seasick to eat anything on a cruise. Ross and Imogen had been on a free cruise, for the travel section of the previous magazine she worked for, and they'd been flat on their backs, feeling like death, for the first two days crossing the Bay of Biscay in a storm.

'My wife and I were always more cat people,' Cook said.

'We had a cat, too – a rescue one. Cosmo. But he was very odd, used to disappear for days on end sometimes.'

'Very hard to know the mind of a cat.'

'Yep. One day he disappeared for good. Maybe he got a better offer.'

The old man chuckled. 'Maybe indeed.'

Ross guided him to the sofa in their modern, airy lounge, then went through to the high-tech kitchen, which Imogen had chosen, and which had cost more than the national debt of a small nation – far more than they could sensibly afford – and put the kettle on. He made the tea then delved into a cupboard and found a pack of chocolate digestive biscuits, which he ripped open and tipped out onto a plate. Then he placed everything on a tray and carried it through.

A few moments later, seated in an armchair opposite Cook, and with Monty at his side, beadily watching the stranger stirring his tea, Ross said, 'So, you said you had a message from my brother, Ricky?'

'Let me come on to that.' Cook took a sip of his tea, then nodded pensively, lost in his own world for some moments. 'Allow me to begin at the beginning.'

Ross nodded.

'Well, you see, my wife, Doreen, was also an academic, lecturing at the same university, in physics. Six months ago she passed away from cancer.'

'I'm sorry to hear that.'

'Thank you. The thing is, Mr Hunter, during her last days in a hospice she asked me to promise I would go to a medium after she died, to try to make contact with her. She was really insistent about this. Frankly, as a committed Christian, I've never been a subscriber to that kind of stuff, but she became increasingly anxious, so of course I promised I would. And naturally after she passed I had to fulfil my promise.'

'Of course.' Ross was wondering where this was going.

'I managed to find a very nice lady, who came well recommended, and I had a sitting with her about three weeks after my wife's funeral. But instead of any communication from Doreen, a man came through who claimed he had a direct message from God. He said that God was extremely concerned about the current state of the world, and felt that if mankind could have its faith in him restored, it would help to bring us all back from the brink. As proof of his bona fides, he said God had told him to give me three pieces of information that no one on this planet knows, in the form of compass coordinates. And he said there was a respected journalist, called Ross Hunter, who could help me to get taken seriously.'

'Really? I had no idea I was so highly regarded.'

'This man said he had someone with him who had a message for you. He said he had your brother, Ricky. He asked me to tell you that Ricky knew you did not like him, although he never understood why. But he forgives you.'

Ross stared at him, mesmerized. 'Did he say anything else?'

'He said he wanted you to trust me. He said two names – I think it was Bubble and Squeak. He said remember Bubble and Squeak. Remember when Squeak bit you?'

Ross stared back at him, feeling numb. Bubble and Squeak were two gerbils their parents had given them on their ninth birthday. Squeak had bitten him on his index finger, really hard. How on earth could this man, Dr Cook, possibly know this?

The old man looked down at the attaché case on the floor beside him, and nodded at it. 'It's all in there, Mr Hunter.'

'Right.'

Cook opened the case and pulled out a massive bundle of A5 paper, held together by elastic bands. 'I think we should start with you reading this. This was channelled to me directly from God, over several days following my visit to this medium.' He handed it to Ross. 'I have of course inked those compass coordinates out, Mr Hunter, in case this fell into the wrong hands.'

It was heavy. The top page was creased and blank, with a dog-eared corner. The journalist took a quick look through. There were no chapters, it was just continuous writing on lined paper – slanted, tiny, scrupulously neat, in black ink, with little patches of Tippex here and there, and peppered with annotations of arrows and boxes. The pages were numbered at the bottom. The last page was 1,247. 'Right,' he said. 'Well – if you leave it with me, I'll take a look.'

The old man shook his head, regretfully. 'I'm afraid

that's not possible. You see, this is the only copy in existence.'

'You haven't made a copy?'

Cook looked almost affronted. 'I couldn't possibly take the risk of a copy falling into the wrong hands. I need to be here while you read it.'

Inwardly, Ross groaned. As he feared, this man was beginning to sound like a nutter. Yet he couldn't dismiss what he had said about Ricky. How could he possibly have known about the two gerbils? He'd never written about them and, so far as he could remember, he'd never talked about them. So how did Dr Cook know? How? He held the manuscript up, weighed it in his hands, then flicked through it. 'This would take me about four days to read!'

The old man raised a finger. 'That's about right.'

Ross shook his head and smiled, humouring him. 'You're going to sit there, on my sofa, for *four* days, while I sit here reading this?'

'I cannot let it out of my sight.'

Ross shook his head again. 'Dr Cook, it's not going to happen. I'm sorry, but quite apart from anything else, I don't have four days free. You're going to have to take a massive leap of faith – either you leave this with me and I'll read it when I can, in my own time, or you take it away with you. And before I even start, I need to know a lot more about what's in it. And about this *proof of God* you claim to have. What are these three pieces of information you say you have?'

'I have been given three sets of compass coordinates – the first is for the location of the Holy Grail.'

'The Holy Grail?'

'Correct.'

'That's a pretty big ticket,' Ross said, noting it down.

'Not as big as the next, Mr Hunter. The coordinates for the location of a significant object relating to our Lord, Jesus Christ.'

'Does it come with a certificate of origin?'

'Please, Mr Hunter, as I said to you, I'm not some kind of a crackpot. Please hear me out. The third set of coordinates is for something so important it will, I assure you, have a tumultuous impact – in a truly positive way – on the world.'

'Are you going to tell me what this is?'

'In due course but not now, not until I can be sure you are the right man for this. But let's say the third set relates to the Second Coming.'

'The Second Coming?'

'That is correct.'

Ross thought for a moment and doodled a halo. 'OK. Have you checked any or all of these out, Dr Cook?'

Cook took a sip of his tea, then nodded pensively, lost in his own world. 'Indeed, I have. I've checked out the coordinates for the Holy Grail. They give the location as Chalice Well in Glastonbury.'

'Really?'

'As you know, this has long been reputed to be the place where Joseph of Arimathea is buried. Chalice Well is one of Britain's most ancient wells, in the Vale of Avalon, between Glastonbury Tor and Chalice Hill.'

'I do happen to know quite a lot about that, actually. I wrote a large piece on the Glastonbury Festival and the myths surrounding Glastonbury Tor for the *Guardian* a few years ago. All the Arthurian legends about the Holy Grail stem from around there.'

'Good, then you will know what I am talking about. Of course, there is disinformation put out by enemies of Our

Lord. I suspect you are man enough, Mr Hunter, to see beyond that. It's probably one of the many reasons why your name was given to me as the man who could help me.'

'So, have you investigated this claim?'

'I've been there with dowsing rods and with a metal detector, in a wide arc around where the compass coordinates pinpoint, and there is something down there.' Cook's eyes lit up with an almost messianic zeal. 'Chalice Well is run by a group of trustees, whom I then approached, asking for permission to carry out an archaeological dig, but despite explaining why I wanted to do this, they refused.'

'Did they give you a reason?'

'I've done all I can to persuade them, but I just don't think they take me seriously. I believe it would be very different with you – with your reputation for integrity, they'd have to take you seriously.'

'That's very flattering.'

'True, Mr Hunter.'

'There is a very big problem,' Ross said. 'From what I remember from my own research, yes, it is possible that Joseph of Arimathea came to England after the crucifixion.'

'Absolutely,' Cook said. 'Quite likely sailing across the flood plains of the Somerset Levels, bringing with him the Chalice that contained some of Jesus's blood from his crucifixion, and arriving at the legendary island of King Arthur's Avalon, a hill now known as Glastonbury Tor. For safekeeping he buried the Chalice in a secret place. Seven centuries after the death of Jesus, Glastonbury Abbey was built. In 1191, monks at the abbey claimed to have found the graves of King Arthur and Queen Guinevere. I believe all records were lost during Henry VIII's Reformation – when the Protestant Church broke away from the rule of Rome, and most monasteries were razed to the ground with their relics and records destroyed or lost forever.'

Ross sipped some of his tea. 'Yes, but during research for my article I discovered that many of the medieval monks were pretty commercial animals, and income from tourists was as important for the monasteries as it is for many seaside resorts today. Quite a number of scholars have said the discovery of these graves was made up, aimed at getting religious tourism. How much do you know about this, Dr Cook?'

'I know all about it. As a shrine, the place would have been visited by thousands of pilgrims. There would have been all kinds of holy souvenirs, and charlatans selling supposedly magical relics. But that was the norm for many monasteries. You are quite right to question this, Mr Hunter. And with so much destroyed in the Reformation, it is impossible to establish the truth all these centuries later.'

'Quite. So, have you checked either of the other two coordinates yet?' Ross asked him.

'I have. But I'm afraid that until I have your absolute commitment to helping me, I cannot reveal them.'

Whatever his scepticism at this moment, Ross could not dismiss what Cook had told him about Ricky. And there was a sincerity about Cook that he found touching. Clearly, beyond any doubt, Cook believed in what he had been given.

And yet.

'Dr Cook, you said God felt that by having faith in Him re-affirmed, it would help steer the world back from the brink, right?'

'Absolutely, Mr Hunter.'

'But the world never has been on an even keel, has it? Go back over the past thousands of years, and for much of

this time almost everyone in the world believed in a god –
or gods – of some denomination, and worshipped them.
Throughout time people have done the same horrible
things they still do around the world today. Even though
they believed ardently in their deity.' He paused for a
moment and looked at the old man, who was staring at him
attentively.

'Surely, Dr Cook, if he truly is God, and wants to see us
all back on an even keel – whatever he means by that – why
can't he just do it?'

'Because God gave us all free will. He sent his son to
save us, and we ridiculed and murdered him. We've been
suffering the consequences since. Now we are being given
a unique second chance.'

All Ross's instincts were telling him this was a hiding to
nothing. A simple Google search would have told Cook all
he needed to know about him having a twin who died in an
accident.

But Bubble and Squeak?

He decided to play a bluff. He glanced at his watch.
'Well, I'm afraid that's all I have time for – so I don't really
know where we go from here. I suggest you take your manuscript away, make a copy and send it to me, if you'd like any
further input from me. Otherwise –' he stood up – 'it's been
very nice to meet you.'

Cook did not move. 'All right,' he said, pursing his lips
and nodding pensively. 'I trust you, Mr Hunter. I'll leave the
manuscript with you if you give me your reassurance you
will not make a copy of it.'

Ross nodded.

'If you could read it as quickly as you can, then we can
meet again and develop our strategy for saving mankind.'

'It's a plan,' Ross said. 'On one condition.'

'Which is?'

'You give me all three sets of compass coordinates you have.'

Cook hesitated, his eyes narrowing with suspicion. 'Why do you need them?'

'You're asking me to take on a big commitment of time. I'd like to check them out for myself.'

'I'll give you the precise coordinates I have for Chalice Well as a token of good faith, Mr Hunter. It's not, of course, that I don't trust you, but I cannot risk them falling into the wrong hands.' He stared intently at Ross again. 'You do understand there are a lot of people who would want them? In the wrong hands they could be extremely dangerous.'

'What kind of danger?'

'Need I spell it out?'

Ross could now see the teacher in the man. The impatient lecturer trying not to talk down to an imbecilic student.

'Lucifer, Mr Hunter.' Cook gave him a reproachful look. 'Satan. Kicked out of Heaven, he vowed to return and is biding his time.'

'OK,' Ross said, trying not to look as though he was humouring the man.

'When I feel it is safe, I will let you have the remaining coordinates. And I will also need your word that you will not attempt to excavate at Chalice Well – or at any of the other locations – without my being present.'

'You have my word.'

With some reluctance, Cook opened his wallet, took out a tiny square of paper, no bigger than two inches by two inches, and handed it to Ross.

He could barely see the tiny handwritten numbers and letters. Squinting, he read the coordinates out aloud:

'51°08'40"N 2°41'55"W –'

Then he read the numbers that followed:

'14 9 14 5 13 5 20 18 5 19 19 20 12.'

He looked at Cook. 'What are those numbers? They're not compass coordinates.'

'No, indeed not.'

'Is it some code?'

'I honestly don't know. I had a good look around Chalice Well whilst I was there, seeing if I could spot any numbers corresponding, but no dice. But they are clearly there for a reason.'

A few minutes later they shook hands at the front door.

'You will be careful with the manuscript, won't you, Mr Hunter?'

'I'll guard it with my life.'

Ross stood there, watching Cook climb back into his car, switch on the lights and drive off. It was a few minutes to 6 p.m.

Then he closed the door, went upstairs to his den and began to read.

The man in the dark-grey Vauxhall saloon, parked a short distance along the road, lowered his night-vision binoculars, switched off the video record mode and made a few notes on his tablet, before starting the car and pulling away.

Tuesday, 28 February 2017

At 5 p.m., an hour before Imogen was due to arrive home from work, Ross loaded up the boot of his car with all the equipment he reckoned he would need, much of which had been delivered yesterday and stored in the garage. He was glad of the pelting rain and dark skies to give him extra cover – and hoped the weather would remain bad, as forecast.

He left her a note on the kitchen table.

Gone out on a work assignment, might be late.
Monty fed. Have a fun book club nite! X

Then he headed off on the long, crawling drive through the afternoon rush hour, with Glastonbury programmed into his satnav. He was so focused on his task ahead that for some while he did not notice, in the fading light, the dark saloon, staying a steady two or three cars behind him all the way along the A23, the M25 and then the M3 motorways passing Basingstoke, then Salisbury, then almost three hours into his journey, passing Stonehenge on the A303.

That was when he first became aware that someone might be following him. Just after the car right behind him had turned left, off the road, and the lights of the vehicle behind seemed familiar. Most lights, apart from those of recent model Audis and some other high-end cars, which had distinctive LEDs, were the same. Moments later, in a blare of blue-tinted light, something came up close in his mirrors then shot past him with a roar. The tail of a Porsche 911.

There were no longer any lights behind him.

Whoever it was must have turned off, he thought to his relief. But he remained wary and vigilant. And his nerves were jangling about the task ahead of him.

It was shortly after 8.30 p.m. when he finally arrived in Glastonbury. The weather was on his side – it was still pelting with rain.

Perfect. He could not have hoped for better cover.

Then, with a twinge of unease, he thought he saw something in his mirror. He slowed right down, repeatedly checking as he passed beneath street lights. Nothing.

Just his imagination. He was being jumpy.

Jumpy as hell.

He pulled into the deserted car park, in the forecourt of the factory outlet, turned off the lights and sat, looking around, but there was still no sign of another vehicle. It was raining too hard for anyone, except the most diehard of dog walkers, to be out on this foul night.

Then his phone pinged, startling him.

It was a text from Imogen.

> **Hope you're OK. Big argument about this book going on! X**

They had been reading *Shantaram*. He texted back.

> **Tell them you think it's the new Fifty Shades Of Grey!**

He started the engine and drove back out of the car park, looking for any parked vehicle that hadn't been there when he had driven past a few minutes earlier, but still could see nothing.

He turned left, into the lane between Chalice Well and Glastonbury Tor, which he had walked up on his visit here last week, and drove on, then swung into the lay-by where the footpath to the tor began. There was ample room for his car. It was perfect. No one around at all.

He opened the boot and lifted out the three waterproof holdalls into which he had packed all the kit he thought he would need. Then he lugged them the short distance back down the lane, ready to dive into the shadows and freeze if any car came by. He pulled on a head torch with a red filter – a low-level light, he had researched, could not be seen from any distance – and hoisted each bag over the fence, letting them drop down the other side, then clumsily scrambled over.

He stared around at the darkness, trying to accustom his eyes.

Could he really go through with this?

His phone pinged loudly again.

He tugged it out and glanced at the display. It was another text from Imogen.

Ha! XX

He smiled, uncomfortably, feeling bad that he'd had to avoid telling her the truth about what he was doing tonight. But he hadn't wanted to scare her. He turned the phone to silent.

A tiny speck of light flared in the darkness, then died, on the far side of the fence. He switched off his head torch, his heart thudding, breaking into a cold sweat, and stood still, staring.

Nothing.

After waiting for a couple of minutes, with the rain continuing to pelt relentlessly down, he turned away, switched the torch back on, picked up the bags and trudged towards the well. Carefully descending the treacherously slippery steps, he stopped in front of the wellhead, with its raised circular lid.

This is crazy.

Go home.

He was soaking wet, cold, apprehensive and feeling increasingly scared about just what he was getting into.

You idiot, he thought to himself. *Forget it.* Images of Harry Cook's horrific death flooded through his mind. Were the old man's torturers and killers waiting out in the darkness, here for him?

He shivered.

Forget it, his brain screamed at him. *Go home, find another way to save the world.*

But he had come this far.

He put down the bags, walked to the edge of the narrow well and peered through the metal grid down at the inky water below. A smell of moss and weed rose from it. He was thinking about that crumpled page he had recovered from Cook's waste bin. The compass coordinates and the email Boxx had sent him deciphering the numbers.

Nine Metres S (south?) T (turn?) L (left?) Helpful?

If you paced *nine metres south and turned left*, from the exact spot those coordinates indicated, you were at the wellhead.

He bent down, unzipped one bag and pulled out an adjustable spanner. For several minutes, he struggled to undo each of the nuts and bolts that held the grid secure. None of them, probably, had been moved in years – or even decades. By the time he had undone the last one, he was sweating from the exertion. Then just as he kneeled down to try to lift the grid, hoping it wasn't going to be impossibly heavy, he heard the sound of a car.

It was driving slowly up the lane, on the other side of the fence. He held his breath. If it was local police would they wonder what his car was doing there – or just assume he was a night walker gone for a stroll around the sacred hill?

He could see the glow of the headlights on the over-hanging branches. Moving past. The sound of the engine faded and he resumed his task. Gripping his hands around two of the black metal cross-bars of the cover, he pulled sharply upwards.

Nothing happened.

Shit.

He tried again. Then again.

Until he saw the problem. He'd only removed five bolts. There were six holding the grid in place, and the sixth one was by his left hand. He had missed one.

His nerves, he realized. He wasn't thinking clearly.

He removed the final nut and bolt, bent down and gripped the bars again. The grid came away easily; it was lighter than he had expected.

Breathing deeply with relief, he laid it down carefully to the side of the well, then delved into another bag and pulled out the improvised piece of kit he had rigged earlier today. It was his GoPro camera in the waterproof casing he used on scuba diving holidays, attached to a metal wrench for weight, and with a waterproof LED torch secured to it, along with a polypropylene rope.

He switched on the torch and the camera, set it to video, then lowered the contraption into the water, paying out the cord as it went down, keeping a rough count. Ten feet. Twenty feet. Thirty. Forty. Fifty.

The guidebook said it was eighty foot deep.

Sixty. Seventy. Eighty.

The cord went slack.

He pulled it taut, then slowly twisted it round for several revolutions, before, slowly and steadily, hauling it back up. Every few moments he paused to look around him in the darkness, his torch casting a red glow along the circular stone wall beyond the wellhead.

Then he heard a footstep.

He stopped. Turned his torch off. Sat very still, listening. The rain pattered down. He hauled the camera up further, then stopped and listened again.

The only sound was the rain.

Shivering from the cold, he switched the torch back on. The camera surfaced with a tiny plop.

He lifted it up, popped open the casing and removed the camera itself, then sheltering it as best he could from the rain, inside his parka, he pressed the replay button for the video.

For a minute, maybe longer, he watched as the video played, the grainy image showing bare wall, some with moss and tendrils of weed, as the camera descended. Then the image jigged, unsteadily. The camera must have reached the bottom.

It began to rotate. He could see what looked like a number of coins. The camera completed what seemed like a full rotation, stirring up silt. Nothing.

Shit, shit, shit.

But at least now he knew. Harry Cook had been—

Then he froze as the camera rotated again, and he noticed something in the murk.

He stabbed the pause button.

There was something that was not part of the bottom of the well, nor the wall. A dark shape. It lay on the bottom. He replayed it. And he could see it slightly more clearly now as his eyes were adjusting to the gloom down there.

It felt like a bolt of electricity had shot through him.

What was it?

He replayed the image a third time. There it was, nestling in the silt. Impossible to figure exactly what it was. Maybe it was just a large stone.

Next, he pulled out the sections of flexible wire caving ladder he had bought on the internet, along with Maillon Rapide section joins, and began assembling it with shaking hands.

When he had finished creating it, he used a tow strap to anchor the rope-like ladder to a tree at the edge of the fence, then lowered it into the well, paying it out until he reached the end.

From the third, and very heavy bag, he removed his scuba equipment. Then he stood still. Staring at the darkness all around him. Shivering. This was madness. Forget it. Go home. The well was barely wide enough for him to fit into.

He asked me to tell you that Ricky said you should trust me. He said to mention Bubble and Squeak.

Harry Cook's voice was echoing all around him.

He'd come this far. He would bloody well see it through.

He stripped off his clothing and, shivering from the cold, wormed into the wetsuit. He tugged on rubber shoes and gloves, secured the air tank to his buoyancy jacket and then fixed the regulator in place. He turned on his air and checked the tank capacity. He only had half a tank left. He cursed himself for not having checked it, but was sure it would be more than enough for the depth he was likely to be descending to, especially as he would not be contending with any current – unlike his last and rather hairy dive last summer, with Imogen, on the Elphinstone reef in the Red Sea. He fastened his weight belt, strapped his diving knife holster and powerful underwater torch to his legs, donned his jacket, head torch and dive computer, grabbed his mask and then scooped up the first bag. He climbed over the rim of the wellhead and, gripping the sides of the ladder, handles of the smallest holdall over his arm, began to descend.

The man who had followed him all the way down here from Patcham, concealed nearby, watched him through night-vision binoculars with a built-in video. A hazy green image. Shortly after Ross had disappeared from view, he zoomed in.

Tuesday, 28 February 2017

Ross climbed down the swaying, unsteady ladder, increasingly nervous with every step, until after only a short distance from the wellhead he reached the surface of the water. He hesitated. All his instincts were screaming at him to pack up, forget all about this, go home. But after some moments he finally plucked up courage, grabbed the mouthpiece of his regulator, adjusted his mask and gently let himself down.

Instantly, as his head went below the surface, he felt its icy chill.

Tendrils of weed touched his face and he shuddered. A short distance down he stopped and attached the holdall he was carrying, with its contents, to a rung.

Then he continued his descent into the eerie darkness that was only faintly illuminated by his head torch. He could hear the steady roar of his breathing, the popping of bubbles and the *thud-thud-thud* of his heartbeat. He was shivering with cold despite the protection of his diving kit.

It seemed he was going down for an eternity.

And he felt very scared.

He stopped, wondering whether to abort. The cold was getting worse and he wasn't even halfway to the bottom.

Probably just a damned bit of rubbish down there.

The sound of his breathing was getting louder, echoing.

More weed growing off the wall brushed his face like a cobweb. His feet found the next rung. And the next. That was the final rung. Twenty feet down from the top now. He released his grip and sank, steadily and rapidly.

It felt like he was gaining speed.

Thirty feet. Forty. Fifty.

He'd dived inside sunken wrecks off Barbados, in caves in the Red Sea, down deep shelves off the Maldives, and he'd never been scared before. But now he was terrified. Sinking deeper and deeper down this narrow, inky shaft.

Sixty feet.

He thought about their unborn baby. Then Imogen. Diving solo, anywhere, was a no-no. Diving solo into a confined space – an unknown one at that – was insane. If he got into trouble of any kind, no one was going to be coming to rescue him. He'd never see his child born.

Seventy feet.

In his nervous and fearful state, he made the cardinal mistake of not checking his buoyancy and, like a rank novice, squelched down heavily on the soft, muddy floor at the bottom of the well shaft.

Furious at his own incompetence, there was nothing he could do as the mud rose like fog around him, and he could only wait for it to settle. Checking the pressure gauge on his regulator, he saw that his air supply would only allow him another fifteen minutes or so. His panic had caused him to use far more air than he would do normally.

Stupid to panic, he knew. That was what killed divers. He had to calm down. Somehow. But his thoughts were ragged with anxiety.

It had taken him seven minutes to descend and he needed to allow all of that and more to ascend. But the water was still too cloudy to see anything.

Slowly it began to clear.

Eleven minutes left.

Ten.

He could see a few coins, what looked like a KitKat wrapper, a partially disintegrated takeaway carton, then a large, old-fashioned Nokia mobile phone. *Can't have been the object that the camera saw? It was bigger. Much bigger.*

He turned, and more mud rose, obscuring everything. He knelt and groped around in the deep mud and slime with his gloved hands, stirring it up even more, and feeling repulsed. What was down here? What disgusting things? What dead animals – or live bottom feeders? He touched something that felt like a dead frog and shuddered. Then a solid object. Covered in slime.

The shape he had viewed on his GoPro?

He lifted it up, bringing it close to his face, and could just see, in the faint glow of his head torch, strands of slime and weed hanging from it.

He wiped them away, and finally saw, to his disappointment, that it was a child's red wellington boot, filled with silt.

After making sure there was nothing else he was missing down here, he at last began his ascent.

Eight minutes left.

He rose as fast as his bleeper would allow, pausing briefly at the rung, some way below the surface, where he had attached the holdall on his way down. He unzipped the bag a little, to let water in, and zipped it again. He carried on up and broke the surface, pulled out his mouthpiece and with relief gulped down the fresh night air. He slung the bag over the top of the wellhead onto the ground.

And froze.

A shadowy figure was standing in front of him.

Something hard slammed into his face, knocking him off the ladder. He began plunging feet-first back down the well, dazed, scrabbling feebly with his hands for the ladder and swallowing water.

Finally getting a purchase on the ladder, and holding his breath, he scrambled as fast as he could back up. As his head broke the surface he coughed, spitting out water and looking up, and pulled his diving knife out of its sheath, gripping it tightly with his right hand. He continued climbing. In the darkness, it was hard to see how far he was from the top, so he slowed now, ascending one rung at a time, stopping after each and waiting.

Suddenly, he heard the roar of an engine firing up, the squeal of tyres, then the sound of a car heading away, fast.

Bastard.

He scrambled up the remaining rungs to the top, then stopped, in shock.

The metal grid had been put back into place above him.

His nose hurt, but he barely noticed as he peered, tentatively, through the grille. His plan had worked.

The two large holdalls were still visible, but whoever his assailant was had taken with him the smaller bag and its contents that he had put up there moments earlier. The contents which he had bought yesterday in the flea market. A rusty 1930s biscuit tin and a silver-plated christening mug which he had wrapped in cloth and placed inside it.

He waited, listening carefully for any sound of movement, but could hear nothing.

Finally, he pushed hard against the grille, but it would not budge.

He was entombed.

THEY SAID THE DEAD CAN'T HURT YOU...
THEY WERE WRONG
THE CHILLING NEW STAGE PLAY FROM THE NO.1 BESTSELLING AUTHOR
JOSHUA ANDREWS and PETER JAMES
present
PETER JAMES'
THE HOUSE
ON COLD HILL
Adapted by SHAUN McKENNA Directed by IAN TALBOT
WORLD PREMIERE THEATRE TOUR 2019
For venues and tickets go to www.PeterJames.com
/peterjamesstage
@peterjamesstage

extracts reading groups
competitions books new
discounts extracts extracts
competitions reading groups
books new extracts discounts
events books
extracts new
new reading groups
interviews
events extracts
discounts
new books events
events new
discounts extracts discounts

www.panmacmillan.com

extracts events reading groups
competitions books extracts new